D0014123

The assassin turned hi[s head] to [check] the television picture. The presi[dent moved] slightly to the left-hand side of the lectern, and Al-Akir adjusted his rifle accordingly. When he fired, he would actually be watching the screen to guide his next shots, if they were necessary. If not, he would be gone from Crystal City before the Towers were even sealed off.

Al-Akir pawed the trigger. There was no reason to wait any longer. He slowed his breathing by taking several large breaths, then exhaled slowly and deeply, his right eye cocked toward the television set.

The president was smiling. He had just made a joke.

Al-Akir pulled the trigger.

THE
VENGEANCE
OF THE TAU

Jon Land

FAWCETT GOLD MEDAL • NEW YORK

A Fawcett Gold Medal Book
Published by Ballantine Books
Copyright © 1993 by Jon Land

All rights reserved under International and Pan-American Copyright Conventions. Published in the United States of America by Ballantine Books, a division of Random House, Inc., New York, and simultaneously in Canada by Random House of Canada Limited, Toronto.

Library of Congress Catalog Card Number: 93-90198

ISBN 0-449-14776-2

Manufactured in the United States of America

First Edition: September 1993

For Derringer and Ruby—
my true collaborators

ACKNOWLEDGMENTS

With each book the desire to sustain continued improvement makes my reliance on the help of others greater. With this one I start as always at the top with a wondrous agent, Toni Mendez, who has been there since the first beginning and all the ones that have followed. Ann Maurer continues to amaze me with her detailed eye that misses nothing. And Daniel Zitin deserves special commendation for never tolerating anything but my best work possible.

Because of Emery Pineo, of course, I can make anything happen, and because of Walt Mattison (the real Blaine Mc-Cracken) it happens with the proper equipment. Mort Korn and Tony Sheppard lent their customary expertise with the early drafts, a feat for which they deserve medals. Nancy Aroche, meanwhile, provided priceless input toward making credible all things archaeological. A special appreciation to the Saltuks for translation of the Turkish passages, and to Dr. Dennis Karambelas for unlocking the mysteries of the eye.

For geographical assistance along the way, I am indebted to Tom Holleb for his help with Chicago, especially his father's house; Michael Sherman for New Orleans; Skip Trahan for Crystal City and Washington; John Balletto and Kent Thaler for San Francisco. And an extra special acknowledgment to the brilliant translator of my German editions, Uwe Anton, for his help with Germany.

A final thanks go to Art and Martha Joukowsky for suggesting a while back that someday I do "something" with archaeology. That was where the idea for this book was born.

PROLOGUE

Occupied France, 1942

THEY rumbled through the school gates in trucks the same gray color as the sky. A *Kübelwagen* led the motorcade, its passenger standing up on the floorboard and gripping the windshield frame for support. His black uniform was darkened by the storm that had soaked it. A jagged scar ran the length of the left side of his face beneath the cheekbone.

"Abgesessen und sich in einer Reihe aufstellen!" he ordered after stepping down into the muck.

Instantly troops in heavy wool uniforms poured from the back of the three trucks. Their rifles leveled before them, most swept across the schoolyard to cut off any possible escape. The rest came to attention two yards behind the man in the black uniform.

"What is the meaning of this?"

The speaker was a priest, who strode defiantly across the yard past the guards who had taken up their positions. He stopped a rifle's distance away from the dark figure, the rain pounding both of them.

"Are you the one in charge?" the German demanded.

"God is in charge."

A thin smile bent the scar running the length of the Ger-

1

man's face. "Not anymore. I am Colonel Erich Stimmel of the Gestapo, priest—"

"Father Desmarais," the priest interrupted.

"—and you will hand over to me the Jews you are harboring."

Father Desmarais held his ground. "I am afraid you have made a mistake."

Stimmel circled him, beads of water running off the slope of his black cap. "Then you will not mind assembling all of your students and faculty in this yard to satisfy my curiosity."

The priest seemed to notice the rain for the first time. "The cafeteria would do just as well."

"Out here will do fine."

"We have nothing to hide."

Stimmel waved a hand at the troops behind him. "My men will make sure of that."

The assembly began forming seconds later. The first of the boys emerged tentatively, prodded by the soldiers who had burst into their classrooms. After a few further moments of confusion, the school personnel and student body poured from the building in a flood rivaling that of the water tumbling down from above. Teachers struggled to organize their young charges in neat lines. Some of the boys wrapped their arms tightly around their shoulders. Most continued to shiver. The day was unforgiving. Stimmel made them wait there until the troops he had assigned to the building had completed their sweep.

"Now, priest," he said to Father Desmarais loudly enough for all to hear, "you will give me what I have come for, and my men and I will be gone."

"I cannot turn over what I do not have."

"I give you one last chance to be reasonable."

"You need not bother."

"As you wish," Stimmel said more softly, in a voice colder than the rain.

He spun rigidly on his heels and strode to the center of the drenched, shivering group of boys. Silence followed his steps, the only sound that of the rain beating against the muddied ground.

"The following three boys will step forward without delay," the colonel announced suddenly, his eyes back on Father Desmarais. "Edelstein, Sherman, and Grouche."

The priest's knees buckled slightly. The fear he had successfully suppressed swam freely in his eyes now.

"No," he mouthed.

"I have my sources, priest," Stimmel told him, and then repeated, "Edelstein, Sherman, and Grouche."

Before him the boys remained frozen in place.

Stimmel moved back to the front of the assembly and paced along the front row. "I give you one last chance to make this easy on yourselves. Edelstein, Sherman, and Grouche, come forward."

No one moved.

"Very well," Stimmel said, and pulled a quartered set of papers from his inside pocket. "Because you have chosen to be difficult, I must do the same. I am going to read the names of three other boys from the master list. These three will come forward and be shot."

"Stop!" Desmarais protested. He started toward Stimmel and was restrained by a soldier at either arm.

Stimmel had just gotten his pages unfolded when a boy advanced from the middle of the pack. His shoes sloshed through the mud and kicked it up against the lower part of his school trousers. His brown, curly hair was matted to his skull. Wisps of it stuck to his forehead. His face was blank and pale. He had barely advanced ahead of the front row when two other boys slid forward, flanking the first on either side. All three were shivering horribly. Masks of confused shock coated their faces.

"Edelstein, Sherman, and Grouche." Stimmel nodded. "Regrettable that this priest put you and myself in such a difficult position." He turned to the troopers behind him.

"Place them against the front wall. No blindfolds. Let the rest be given a warning."

"No!" Father Desmarais screamed, trying to pull free of the men holding him. "You can't! There's no *reason*!"

"A lesson must be taught the others, priest. You defied me. Punishment for that must be dispensed."

"Then kill me!"

"I plan to," Stimmel assured him. "But not before you watch."

The three boys had been backed up against the stone wall. One was sobbing desperately now. A second had sunk to his knees. The third stood transfixed, disbelieving.

"Gewehr anlegen!"

Six troopers standing thirty feet before the boys raised their rifles into the ready position.

"Animals!" the priest screamed.

"Ziel nehmen!"

The troopers aimed their rifles.

"Butchers!"

"Feuer!"

"Please!"

The bullets thumped out in staccato bursts, like minor claps of thunder. The boys' bodies jolted backward. Two keeled over. A third slumped down the wall still facing forward. Legs and hands twitched. Eyes were locked open and sightless. The storm swept the blood away.

Those who had borne witness sobbed in shock. A few fainted and were left there in the mud. The ones who tried to turn away were twisted harshly back around by the troopers patrolling the rows.

Father Desmarais crossed himself. "This is the devil's doing," he spat at Stimmel.

"No, priest, it is your doing." Stimmel swung to face the population of the school. "This is the final lesson you will ever receive here. Let it be one you remember always." He turned back toward Desmarais. "This school is being closed."

The priest's eyes never left Stimmel as he was led to a position just in front of the three dead Jewish boys. He stood rigid, face twisted in a hate that made his misting breath seem like steam.

"Any final prayers, priest?"

Father Desmarais was trembling with rage. "You will pay for this."

"Will I?"

Desmarais turned his gaze to the sky. The rain pounded his eyes, and his palms opened upward as if to catch it. He looked to the ground and then straight at Stimmel. "In the name of justice, I place a curse on you. May the evil that begat you bring the pain that you have suffered on others upon you a hundred times over. May your life be snatched away as you have snatched it from these innocent boys to-day." Desmarais cast his stare beyond Stimmel now, into the storm toward eternity. "I give up my soul to the power that can visit such a wrath on this man and others like him in the years to come. Take me in return! *Take me!*"

"I will," Stimmel said, and he nodded toward the firing squad.

The rifles thundered again, and Father Desmarais stood upright for what seemed like a very long time before crumpling.

Erich Stimmel would recall that day fondly for years to come. It was never far from his mind, especially during sex, when to achieve pleasure he needed to conjure up memories of the atrocities he had been party to. The pain of others had come to mean ecstasy for him.

After the war he had escaped punishment at Nuremberg and slipped into a new identity, thanks to the organization known as ODESSA. He had become a gunsmith in Vienna and earned enough money to buy his prostitutes without having to tap into the accounts provided by those who had settled him here.

It was the winter of 1947, a week into the new year, and his memories of the boys and the priest were especially sharp.

"Stop," the whore beneath him pleaded. "Please."

"Shut up!" Stimmel shouted, and slammed deeper into her anus. The gunbelt he wore over his naked waist dug into her. His holster slapped against her flesh. The whore cowered beneath him, shivering, an animal and nothing more. Let it hurt, *make* it hurt. Yes . . . *Yes!*

With one final thrust, it was over. Stimmel pulled out and left the whore to her whimpers.

"The bathroom," she muttered.

"Use it, bitch," Stimmel said, as he rolled onto his back and sank into the down-filled quilt covering part of the bed. "Then leave."

It hurt to walk even that short distance, and the woman closed the door behind her, feeling for a lock and trembling anew when she saw none there. She sat on the toilet seat and held herself, not wanting to die, hoping he would let her leave. She suddenly felt sick and turned herself round to face the bowl. The vomit rushed up her throat and left her breathless and gasping. Dry heaves racked her repeatedly.

Oh, God, please let me live. Please don't let him kill me. . . .

It was then that she heard the sound of a thump followed by the madman's voice:

"What . . . *Wh—*"

A gunshot sounded, and then another.

"Noooooooooo!" he bellowed.

The prostitute sank to her knees. A horrible smell that made her retch anew filled her nostrils.

"Ahhhhhhhhhhh!"

The drawn-out wail curdled her ears, fading to a rasp and then a wet gurgle. Something sloshed about in the room beyond. Soft thuds pounded the wall, and the woman held her breath against the chance that she might be discovered.

She remained motionless until all sounds in the adjoining room ceased. When she eased open the door, a wall of utter coldness slammed into her, a fierce dead chill pouring in from the bedroom accompanied by waves of the god-awful, nauseating stink. The woman emerged from the bathroom holding the doorframe tight and dropped to her knees at first sight of what lay before her.

Blood. Everywhere. Covering everything. The madman's blood.

He had been torn apart. Pieces of him lay strewn about beneath scarlet patterns embroidered upon the walls. His pistol lay on the bed, grasped in a severed hand. The prostitute leaned over and gagged, unable to breathe. She crawled across the floor through the grotesque remains, the stink and the cold all but unbearable.

She emerged into the street below naked and screaming, screaming of monsters loose in Vienna, screaming that no one was safe. The few people on the street gave her a wide berth as she ran past them. But none of them listened, and the woman rushed on through the night toward the false promise of morning.

PART ONE

The Dig

Alexandria, Virginia: Monday, two P.M.

CHAPTER 1

THE president's limousine swung off Eighteenth Street and turned toward the entrance of the Crystal Gateway Marriott. Abu Al-Akir turned away from the television broadcasting the limousine's arrival over CNN and brought the rifle back to his eye. Getting used to the heft of the Weatherby, the way it felt against his shoulder, was crucial. Since there had been no opportunity to test-fire the weapon, he would have to rely on feel and instinct to provide the mandated minute adjustments. He had killed many men in his time, but the kill he was going to attempt today was by far the most challenging. He would be firing a blind shot through a mezzanine window ten stories below at a target speaking in a room off the lobby yet another floor down.

Well, not quite blind . . .

The president would be addressing a crowd of chamber of commerce representatives from all over the country in the Marriott's Lee Room. The only question now was whether the door to the room would be open or closed; his choice of bullets depended on what CNN showed him.

The sole bit of furniture in this twelfth-floor apartment that had been rented for him weeks before within Crystal Towers was a television perched upon a stand. It was set against the wall in a way that required him to turn his head only slightly to watch the screen. In a few minutes CNN would be carrying the president's speech live. Al-Akir cringed at the memory of how the preliminary team had forgotten to have the apartment's cable switched on, not realizing that the all-news network couldn't be picked up otherwise. Al-Akir himself had uncovered the oversight and the activation had been completed only yesterday.

The remainder of the logistics had proven brilliant in every respect. The preliminary team had cut a hole in the bedroom window just large enough to accommodate the very tip of his sniper's rifle. With the president's guards concentrating their efforts inside and around the Marriott, there was no way they could possibly notice such a slight anomaly. Beyond that, it was extremely unlikely that anyone could have foreseen the type of shot Al-Akir was going to attempt.

He had practiced it a thousand times on a replica of these conditions with a twin of this Weatherby .460 Magnum, chosen for its legendary flat trajectory, which was a prime requisite today. Of course, precise weather could not be factored in, but today's air was cool; low humidity and very little wind. In other words, perfect. He would be firing the bullet through the glass of a Marriott mezzanine window on a downward trajectory for the Lee Room and the president's head, timed off with the help of the CNN broadcast five feet to his right. The logistics were stored in his memory. Minor alterations would be programmed into his computerlike mind. Both varieties of his custom-made bullets accounted for a pair of twelve-shot clips. Guided by the CNN picture, Al-Akir guessed he could squeeze off a minimum of seven and still avoid capture.

On the screen, the president was shown being ushered through the Marriott lobby for a speech that he was now fifteen minutes late for.

Al-Akir lowered his Weatherby back to the floor. He had picked up the rifle only that morning, the final safeguard of the plan. Al-Akir knew the Americans were looking for him, and one man in particular. The trick was never to wander into their, or especially *his*, grasp. Never surface to make a drop or a pickup. Everything was conducted through intermediaries, a long chain that, if broken, would mean the cessation of his mission. Al-Akir took chances, but very few risks.

Along with Abu Abbas and Abu Nidal, he was one of the world's most wanted terrorists. While these others had grown fat living off their reputations, Al-Akir had stayed sharp, never straying from his deadly trade. The order to kill the American president came from high up in the movement, but it was only part of the reason why he was in the country. From here he would travel to San Francisco on the most crucial mission of his life. The Arab people were about to seize their own destiny. The means were at last at hand. The death of the president would mark Day One in a new and fateful calendar.

Al-Akir turned his attention back to the television. He had already turned the volume off so that it would not distract him. Seconds later he watched the president enter the Lee Room and shake an army of hands en route to the lectern. He took his place behind it and waited for the applause to die down. Al-Akir waited for CNN to cut to a camera angle that included the door.

Initially he had been worried that the bullet's path would be distorted by the thick glass of the mezzanine's window, not to mention the inch and a half of wood forming the Lee Room door. As difficult as it appeared, though, Al-Akir had managed it in practice on a replica ninety-two of his last hundred attempts *on the first try.*

On the television screen, CNN had cut to a side angle of the president that pictured a pair of Secret Service agents standing in the *open* doorway of the Lee Room.

Al-Akir reached into his pocket for the proper clip: it contained long-grain platinum tips, instead of the full metal jackets he would have needed for better penetration. He snapped the magazine home, returned the rifle to his shoulder, and pushed his eye against the sight. The night before, another of the team members had marked the precise spot he was shooting for on the Marriott's mezzanine glass with a marker visible only to the kind of infrared sight he was using. It resembled the variety devised for night shooting.

The assassin turned his head ever so slightly toward the television picture. The president was standing directly behind the lectern, and Al-Akir adjusted his rifle accordingly. Once he fired, he would turn instantly back to the television to guide his next shots if they were necessary. If not, he would be gone from the area before the Crystal Towers were even sealed off. His primary escape route actually would take him through the huge underground shopping mall that began beneath the Marriott. He had learned long ago that escape was best managed by fleeing *toward* the point of attack where the chaos was greatest. "Follow the bullet" was the common way of putting it.

Al-Akir pawed the trigger. There was no reason to wait any longer. He slowed his breathing by taking several large breaths, then exhaled slowly and deeply, his right eye cocked toward the television set.

The president was smiling. He had just made a joke.

Al-Akir returned to the sight and pulled the trigger between heartbeats.

His last thought was that the recoil was greater than it should have been—far greater indeed, since the entire weapon had exploded with the pulling of the trigger. The blast shattered the weapon's stock and turned the splinters into deadly projectiles rocketing backward. Al-Akir's head was sliced jaggedly off at the neck and, thanks to the angle it had been cocked at, it slammed into the television screen that he had been watching just an instant before. The glass shattered in a spiderweb pattern. Al-Akir's head bounced once on the floor and came to a halt still staring at the remnants of the screen.

Fazil was right on schedule. The escape route Al-Akir had worked out was intricate, and his was the first and most important step. The car was hidden in the garage halfway down this alley in the Anacostia section of Washington, and Fazil arrived at the exact time Al-Akir had specified.

He checked his watch. By now the president of the United States would be dead. The greatest holy war of all time would have begun.

Of course, if all Al-Akir needed was a vehicle, Fazil's presence would be superfluous; he had a much more important role to play at this point. Fearing capture, Al-Akir had given him an envelope, with specific instructions where to take it if he did not arrive as planned. Fazil had no idea what the envelope contained; he knew only that the means to continue the holy war were inside.

Fazil entered the alley with the envelope tucked in his pocket. The alley at first glance looked deserted.

"A hundred bottles of beer on the wall, a hundred bottles of beer . . ."

At the sound of the slurred voice, Fazil's spine tensed. His hand dipped for the pistol wedged in his belt. The homeless were everywhere in this part of Washington, which accounted for Al-Akir's choosing it.

"You take one down, pass it around, ninety-nine bottles of beer on the wall . . ."

The bearded bum sat on the stoop of a long-abandoned building the garage had once been a part of.

"Ninety-nine bottles of beer on the wall, ninety-nine bottles of—" The bum suddenly noticed Fazil. "Hey, 'the fuck you doing in my alley?"

Fazil was reassured by the man's beery voice. He reached for his knife. No need for the gun with this one.

"Hey," the bum said, the knife out and swooping down. *"Hey!"*

Fazil drove the blade forward. But the bum was gone, just air in the spot where he had been. Fazil saw the blur of a shape whirl before him, and suddenly his wrist wasn't his own anymore. His frame followed it sideways and then over, as the bones snapped with a grinding *whap*! Fazil gasped and tried to cry out, but a steellike hand slammed into his throat and choked off his breath.

"Been a long time, Fazil," Blaine McCracken said.

Twelve years before, McCracken had been working with the British Special Air Service when a plane was commandeered at Heathrow Airport. The bureaucracy had taken hold, and a hundred and fifty passengers had ended up losing their lives. To show his displeasure, Blaine had gone promptly to Parliament Square and machine-gunned the groin area of Churchill's statue there. The incident had earned him the now infamous nickname "McCrackenballs" and a banishment from the intelligence community. Subsequent investigations conducted over the years, though, had revealed that the perpetrator of the Heathrow hijacking was none other than Abu Al-Akir, whom McCracken had been pursuing off and on ever since. So when word reached him that the terrorist assassin was in-country, Blaine went right to work.

The calling in of countless favors and grilling of a number of Arab informants revealed the monstrous scope of Al-Akir's mission. Ultimately, Blaine was able to tap into the killer's network. But this meant little, since Al-Akir was never anywhere long enough to be caught. No one ever saw him. If they waited around, he wouldn't show up. He always worked alone.

From his inside sources, McCracken learned the drop point for Al-Akir's rifle and ammunition. If he had merely intercepted and retrieved them, however, the terrorist would have disappeared once again. Blaine calculated that, all things considered, this would be the best chance he would ever get to dispose of Al-Akir once and for all. And once he devised the technological specifics of the plan, McCracken was certain that the president would never be at risk. Pretty simple stuff actually. Inlay some plastic explosives through the rifle's butt and stock and then rig all of the bullets in both clips, on the chance Al-Akir reordered them, to backfire.

Word of Al-Akir's demise had reached him only minutes

before Fazil's arrival in the alley. It was time to finish this chapter of his life once and for all. Johnny Wareagle was always saying life was a circle. Well, maybe this proved it.

"McCracken!" the terrorist uttered, struggling feebly. His eyes darted toward the head of the alley.

"Al-Akir's not coming," McCracken said. He had tousled his close-trimmed beard and oiled his wavy hair to better look the part of a wino. The scar through his left eyebrow caused by a bullet's graze twenty years before further added to the disguise. "You helped him with Heathrow, Fazil. It's only fair you join him now. In hell."

The terrorist gasped again as Blaine readied the quick twist that would snap his neck.

"Wait," Fazil managed to utter.

"Sorry. No can do." But he had let up the pressure.

"I want to deal!"

"You have nothing to deal with."

"No! Please! *Listen!*"

Fazil grabbed as much breath as he could. McCracken's hold had slackened enough for him to peer backward. He looked into Blaine's eyes and nothing but black looked back; the whites of them appeared to have been swallowed. McCracken's complexion was ruddy. His beard showed some gray, but Fazil didn't know if this was part of his disguise or not.

"In my jacket pocket, there's an envelope," he continued.

"So?"

"Inside it is something to do with the most crucial element of the holy war."

"Which has been going on futilely for two thousand years."

"It is different this time: we have found it."

"Found what?" Blaine asked, curiosity getting the better of him.

"A gift from Allah—that is what Al-Akir called it. A force that will allow us to destroy our enemies at last. A force that makes whoever holds it invincible."

Force . . .

The word stuck in Blaine's head. Not a weapon.

A force . . .

He spun Fazil around and slammed him against the building. The terrorist's one-hundred-and-eighty-pound frame was like a playtoy in McCracken's hands. He was still pleading when Blaine yanked the envelope from his pocket.

"Take it. Just let me live."

"I could take it and still kill you."

"But you won't. I know how you work."

"You were to give this to Al-Akir."

"I was holding it for him. It tells where he was to go next."

"Better place than where he is now, I'd wager."

"Let me go. I'll run. I'll disappear."

McCracken was still holding him. "Good idea, because I'm going to put word of our little meeting out. Only I think I'll make it known that you were the one who gave Al-Akir up. His friends will want you dead, Fazil. Matter of fact, I'd say the next time you lay eyes on any of them, it'll be the last thing you'll see."

Blaine hoisted him from the wall and tossed him effortlessly to the pavement.

"Get out of my sight, Fazil."

The terrorist scampered down the alley, looking back until he was halfway to the street. McCracken checked the envelope for explosives and then opened it cautiously. Inside was what appeared to be a jagged piece of ancient parchment, the Arabic symbols too faded to be read. Along with this was a business card for an antique store in San Francisco's Ghirardelli Square.

A force that makes whoever holds it invincible.

Whatever that might mean, it was what Al-Akir had been pursuing, and thus what McCracken would now pursue in his place.

Starting in San Francisco.

CHAPTER 2

"It might help, *Sayin* Winchester, if you told me exactly what we are looking for."

Alan Winchester redoubled his handkerchief and dabbed the sweat from his forehead. "We'll know if we find it," he told Kamir, the Turkish work foreman who had been with him through the entire four-month duration of this dig.

Winchester's was one of seven teams that Professor Benson Hazelhurst had dispatched throughout the Middle East. Each had one of seven different maps that all reportedly led to the same destination. Besides his team, two were operating in Israel, two in Egypt, and one each in Iraq and Syria. Only one map, of course, could lead to the find, if in fact the find existed. More likely, in Winchester's mind, this entire business was a hoax that the brilliant Hazelhurst had fallen for in his old age.

Winchester's map had brought him to Ephesus, one of the world's richest sites for unearthing archaeological treasures. Located on the Aegean coast in southwestern Turkey, the rolling, fertile plains and hills of Ephesus had previously yielded such finds as the Citadel and Basilica of St. John, the Library of Celsus, and the purported final resting place of the Virgin Mary. It had always been rich in the tradition of religious mysticism.

But the site Winchester's map had directed him to was located in the middle of the area's arid bushy lowlands, miles from any other reported find. Upon arriving, he had arranged, through the foreman Kamir, for aerial photography of the general area to pin down the specific find. The plane flew over the area several times at both dawn and dusk, when the shadows were longest, searching for indications of disturbed earth that would reveal signs of an earlier excavation. The results, though not conclusive, had proven indicative enough to give Winchester at least a starting point.

If he himself had believed in what they were seeking, Winchester might have confided in Kamir, whom he had come to trust during their four months of fruitless searching. Benson Hazelhurst might be the foremost archaeologist alive today, but this time the old man seemed way off base. Winchester's team had now dug down twenty feet in a roughly thirty-foot-square area without unearthing a single thing. Each time Hazelhurst visited the site, his only instructions were to keep going. These instructions belied the fact that twenty feet meant upward of three thousand years of layered history. With no firm indications of earlier civilizations and nothing discovered down to this depth, there seemed little point in continuing. But Hazelhurst insisted that this was exactly what he had expected.

Not that it mattered to Winchester. The mere thought that this find *could* exist was extremely unnerving to him. Better off if—

"Bir sey bulduk! Bir sey bulduk!"

The excited shout came from down in the rectangular pit that had so far yielded nothing. Winchester got up from beneath his shaded lean-to and met Kamir at the rim.

"Iste! Cabuk!" one of the workmen shouted up at them. *"Sanlrlm, aradiglmlzl bulduk! Cabuk!"*

"He says that—"

"He found something that meets the description," Winchester completed for his foreman, who was already lowering himself into the excavation. Keeping his excitement and uneasiness down, he began to descend the rope ladder after Kamir.

"Cabuk! Cabuk!" the workman was shouting excitedly from the center of the excavation, urging him to hurry up.

When he dropped off the rope ladder, Winchester could see that the man's face was encrusted with chalk-white dust and yellowed dirt. But his eyes were alive with excitement as he tapped his shovel against the object of his enthusiasm. *ping . . . ping . . . ping . . .*

Whatever lay beneath it was hard and thick—at least eight feet in length, Winchester calculated. He moved quickly in Kamir's wake and joined the foreman on his knees over what had been unearthed. Winchester withdrew what looked like a whisk broom from his pocket and began clearing away debris from the object's top. Barely a minute's labor revealed an eight-by-six-foot slab of stone, its surface like none Winchester had ever felt before. Neat impressions and carvings were chiseled into it, slowly gaining shape as the archaeologist brushed the dust and debris clear of them. He could make out drawings now as well, but the language was utterly unfamiliar to him.

One of the workmen was gazing over his shoulder, trying to read along. As Winchester swept away the last of the dirt, exposing the outlines of the largest recessed figures, the man gasped and shrank back.

"O ne?" Winchester asked him in Turkish. *"Ne goruyorsun? . . .* "What do you see?"

"Hayir! Olamaz!"

"What can't be?" Winchester demanded. He swung toward Kamir. "Ask him what's wrong! Ask him what he saw!"

Kamir translated the questions. The workman shook his head determinedly, needed more prodding before he spoke quickly in a panicked tone.

"He says it is a warning, *Sayin* Winchester. He says we should go no farther."

The workman was talking again, Kamir preparing to translate.

"He says—"

"I know what he said. He wants me to bury this find so no one will ever come upon it again."

Kamir nodded his acknowledgment, but Winchester had already gone back to work clearing the message chiseled into the stone tablet. The rest of the dig team was hovering behind him, trying to see the results of his labor for themselves. When his work with the whisk broom was completed, Winchester went through the arduous process of laying strips of onionskin parchment over the figures and tracing out the message revealed. He numbered and dated each sheet and stowed them in an environment-proof plastic pack. To supplement these efforts, he snapped off a full two rolls of film with two different cameras to record the markings on the tablet. In archaeology, redundancy was a fact of life.

"Have we found what you are after, *Sayin* Winchester?" Kamir asked when Winchester was at last finished.

"I won't know that until we open it." Winchester stopped and held his foreman's stare. "Order the men to remove the tablet."

Kamir, a veteran of dozens of digs, gazed at him incredulously. "Did you say *remove* it?"

"I did."

"Please, *Sayin*, you know better than I that proper procedure dictates—"

"Now."

It took an additional four hours to fully unearth the stone slab. It was twelve inches thick, an unheard-of bulk, meaning that its total weight was likely in excess of a ton. Whoever had sealed what lay beneath it almost three thousand years before certainly had meant for the contents never to be uncovered again. In the sky the sun had turned red, with the last of the afternoon fleeing like the loser from a dogfight.

"We should wait until morning to proceed," Kamir cautioned.

"I want it lifted off," Winchester insisted.

"The light, *Sayin* . . ."

"Will do just fine."

It was another forty minutes before the dig team managed to free the slab, then twenty more before they could budge it. At last the workmen found the proper leverage, and it slid a foot back from its perch.

The smell flooded out in a violent gush of air, a rancid stench worse than death itself. But even Winchester would have conceded it was more than just a smell that escaped. Something seemed to brush him aside, something like talons formed of hot steel slicing him in the chest on their way by. Winchester looked down at his shirt, expecting to see a neat gash with blood streaming from it.

He shook himself alert as the Turkish workmen staggered backward, falling to a position of prayer. Trembling himself, Winchester was conscious of some of the workmen's pleas and prayers.

"They say it is an entrance," Kamir translated fearfully, "an entrance to—"

"We go no farther tonight," Winchester interrupted, composing himself. "We go no farther until Hazelhurst arrives."

Hazelhurst was at one of the dig sites in Israel. He could be here as early as tomorrow afternoon, depending on when the message reached him.

"Find me a man to take a message into Izmir," Winchester ordered Kamir.

Then he yanked his notepad from his pocket and began writing as fast as he could:

Professor Hazelhurst:
I've found the doorway. . . .

CHAPTER 3

"**C**AR Fifteen, do you copy?"

Detective Sergeant Joseph Rainwater pulled the headset off his ears and lifted the microphone up to his lips. "Copy, Twelve."

"How's it hanging, Injun Joe?"

"Not bad for a fucking stakeout. You got a reason for calling, Hal?"

"Figured I'd cheer you up, pal. 'Sides, me and the boys are ordering out and I wanted to see if you wanted anything. We're going with your native stuff tonight. You know, that new Indian place? Bearded maître d' walks around with a turban on his head?"

"You're a fucking riot, Hal. Hope you get the runs."

"Love you too, Sarge."

Joe Rainwater smiled in spite of himself as he returned the microphone to its clasp. The companionship, distant and garbled as it was, was greatly appreciated. He'd been pulling twelve-hour shifts on this stakeout for weeks now. Putting the headset back into place, he let himself wonder if Captain Eberling hadn't been right when he'd pulled the plug on this part of the machine. Trying to nail Ruben Oliveras, the big fucking cheese of the whole Chicago drug business, had become an obsession for Injun Joe. Too often he'd seen the

24

results of Oliveras's work, and so he was only too glad to accept the special assignment. Then, when the bugs they'd managed to plant through the drug lord's mansion turned up zilch, Rainwater found he couldn't let go. It was just him and one other cop pulling shifts now, and before much longer they'd be yanked, too.

Injun Joe changed the channels on his receiver to check out the sounds in the wired rooms of Oliveras's mansion. In the automatic mode, it would lock on the room with the most auditory activity. Not that they ever could have wired *all* the rooms, not in the former Japanese consulate building that Oliveras had snatched up as soon as it came on the market. Son of a bitch just couldn't resist that three-story red-brick mansion on Forest Avenue in Evanston, with Lake Michigan in its backyard. Bought and paid for with drug money.

Injun Joe was parked just over a block away on a circular drive between a small neighborhood park and the beach. Best entertainment on these spring nights was watching the Northwestern kids strolling along. He'd made a game out of trying to guess when the couples were going to kiss, but it didn't help much. The nights were getting longer, and the black coffee was beginning to chew a hole in his gut. What Injun Joe should do, he should go up to the door and just blow Oliveras's brains out.

Fat chance, since Oliveras had bodyguards coming out his keister. A dozen guys with Uzis and .44 Magnums around him twenty-four hours a day to protect against attacks from his enemies. Enemies? What a crock. The only attack Oliveras had to worry about was one from his conscience, since he controlled every major dealer in the whole city. A fucking monopoly to rival the old AT&T and no one was taking him to court on it.

Joe Rainwater started flipping through the channels of his receiver like it was a cable TV control. Eight bugs had been placed throughout the mansion and at night all of them would be silent for long periods. It was starting to get to him, every bit of it. Two months ago his wife walked out, and now he's spending his nights parked in view of one of suburban Chicago's most glamorous neighborhoods. Check out the houses in it and maybe dream a little when there wasn't something buzzing in his ear.

It was a far cry from the Comanche reservation where Rainwater had grown up. He had come back from Vietnam the most heavily decorated Indian vet of the war and a hero to his people. He still spent holidays and some weekends in his boyhood home, would probably spend more there now that Sarah had left him. In any case, the council of elders wouldn't be able to warn him anymore about bringing mixed children into the world. No problem there, since he and Sarah never even tried, never even—

A garbled rasp like feedback filled his ears. A bolt of pain seared his eardrums behind it. He was about to yank the headset off when he heard the first scream, a wail of agony that froze his blood. Suddenly gunshots rang out, and the *rat-tat-tat* of automatic submachine-gun fire became a constant din over shouts of men that gave way quickly to more anguished shrieks.

"What the fuck . . ."

Injun Joe had the microphone back at his lips in the next instant, not bothering to remove his headset this time as he spoke.

"Central, this is Fifteen."

"Go ahead, Fifteen."

"I have shots fired—repeat, shots fired—at the Oliveras residence! 1112 Forest Avenue. Request backup!" More screams filled his ears. "Jesus Christ, *lots* of backup!"

"Roger, Fifteen. Backup is rolling."

"So am I."

The big car lurched forward as Rainwater jammed the pedal and shifted into drive at the same time. The tires spun madly before finding the road surface, startling several of the college couples strolling nearby.

The screams were still reverberating in Injun Joe's ears

when the big car bore down on one of those couples as they crossed the street with twin Walkmans donned.

"Shit!" Rainwater bellowed, as he turned the wheel to avoid them.

The car wavered out of control and sideswiped a tree. Injun Joe braked and composed himself, giving the big car gas slower the last stretch to Forest Avenue. Once on Forest, though, he floored the pedal. The engine's roar almost drowned out the torturous sounds still raging in his ears.

Then suddenly, just like that, the sounds ceased. A few stray gunshots lingered before silence took over. Where chaos and death had run rampant less than two minutes before, there was, simply, nothing.

Joe Rainwater drove straight up to the main gate of the estate and lunged out of his car. The gate was locked, but the brick fence was only five feet high. He scaled it and dropped to the mansion's sprawling front lawn. His 9mm Glock pistol palmed, Injun Joe advanced warily toward the house.

He came upon the first body ten feet in, at least what was left of it. Cooling blood and entrails steamed upward into the night. The smell made him gag. The guard's midsection had been shredded. He had been virtually disemboweled. His face was frozen in agony.

Rainwater came upon the remains of two additional men before he reached the mansion's entrance. There might have been more, but for the last stretch his attention was focused on the empty hole where the front door used to be. Wooden shards of it lay all over the porch. Injun Joe had to step over larger fragments as he crossed the threshold. Inside, the air was thick with the smell of gunpowder. Its telltale smoke still hung in the air. Around him bullets had shattered virtually every visible window—bullets fired from the inside by Oliveras's guards toward whatever was killing them.

Another trio of bodies lay at absurd angles at various levels of the curving staircase. The blood of the lowermost one oozed to the marble foyer and formed a pool. Injun Joe did his best to avoid it as he mounted the spiraling steps toward the mansion's second floor.

Jesus Christ . . .

Like the guards outside and on the stairs, the men on the second floor had been torn apart. Two lay facedown at the head of the hallway in widening pools of their own blood. Rainwater could hear the wail of approaching sirens now and debated whether to go on alone. The chance that whoever had done all this was still within the mansion was quite real, and the thought of facing them with only the Glock did not strike Rainwater's fancy. Then again, he was a cop who was looking at the upshot of eight months' work that might have cost him a marriage. The cop in him made a mental note that the walls on this floor, like those of the first, had been peppered by bullets. Oliveras's guards hadn't gone without a fight, then, but there was no evidence that they had scored a single hit on whatever had killed them.

The sirens were really screaming now, and Rainwater proceeded on down the second-floor hallway. He took a long step across one body lying crosswise in the hall and leapt over a second that had been turned into little more than butcher meat. A third corpse's eyes were cocked right on him as he skirted it and headed toward Oliveras's bedroom.

The drug lord's door resembled the front one downstairs except that there was even less remaining. Part of it still stood attached by the hinges, but the result was almost comic. The inside of Oliveras's bedchamber was anything but.

Joe Rainwater tried to tell himself it was for the best, that justice had been served perversely, though appropriately. But there was nothing even remotely pleasing about the coppery, musty smell or the sight of red splashed across the floor and walls. Only a single reading lamp was on, and the lack of light spared Rainwater the full brunt of the sight. In three tours in 'Nam and fifteen years on the force, Injun Joe had never seen anything like this.

The remains of Ruben Oliveras were . . . *everywhere!*

He could hear the police cars rolling onto the property

now, more sirens already blazing in their wake, as he backed out of Oliveras's bedroom. Outside in the hallway Injun Joe leaned over and inspected the guns of the nearest corpses. The clips of two automatic weapons had been nearly drained. A pump-action shotgun had been emptied of all six shells. Again, though, there was no evidence to suggest that they had hit a damn thing. A dozen heavily armed men, professional men, plus Oliveras, cut down in two minutes tops without taking one of the attackers with them.

Joe Rainwater gazed one more time at the impossible and then headed for the stairs to greet the arriving officers.

CHAPTER 4

"**M**AY I help you, sir?"

"Yes, I think you can," Blaine McCracken said to the proprietor of Collectibles, who was standing near a display of smoked glass.

Collectibles was located in Ghirardelli Square, San Francisco's answer to Boston's Faneuil Hall or New York City's South Street Seaport. Ghirardelli took its name from the chocolate factory that had once occupied the red-brick structure now housing dozens of stores ranging from trendy knickknack shops to upscale boutiques. There were actually six separate buildings with as few as two and as many as five levels. The buildings enclosed an outdoor courtyard, lined

with benches and small tables that provided the square with
a parklike atmosphere.

McCracken had strolled purposefully about this courtyard
for nearly a half hour before making his way to the first of
the Clock Tower Building's two floors where Collectibles
was located. He wanted to make sure he had not picked up
any unwelcome escorts on his way to the antiques store that
the business card in the envelope had directed him to. It was
warm for April, with only a slight breeze. So the lunchtime
rush had seen the courtyard grow more crowded by the minute and McCracken became more edgy. He took no comfort
in a crowd that would allow a potential enemy to easily
become lost.

Cursing his own timing, Blaine had moved on to Collectibles and let the jingling door bells announce his arrival to
the proprietor.

"I believe you have something for me," McCracken continued, handing over his jagged piece of parchment.

The proprietor took it and stepped behind the counter,
eyes reluctant to leave McCracken. He was a tall, lean man,
floral shirt worn over baggy pants dominated by pleats. His
skin and eyes were dark. He might have been Arab, but not
necessarily. Blaine tensed as the proprietor's hand dropped
beneath the counter and then came up fast. He relaxed when
he saw it was holding a second piece of torn parchment. The
man fit the two fragments together. The jagged edges filled
in against each other. The match was perfect. The proprietor
gazed again at McCracken.

"I have what you have come for in the back. If you'll give
me just a minute . . ."

Without waiting for a reply, the proprietor disappeared
through a bead curtain behind his counter. No further discussion was either required or expected. The fact that an
elaborate signaling procedure had been set in place indicated
to McCracken that the proprietor had no idea who would be
coming to make the pickup. He was simply a go-between.

The man reemerged wordlessly through the curtain, leaving the beads to clack against each other in his wake. Without comment, he handed Blaine a simple manila envelope that had packing tape wrapped around its top so that the metal clasp was obscured. McCracken folded the envelope in two, pocketed it, and turned back for the door. Simple as that. Playing a role, about to find out what Al-Akir had so desperately sought.

"A gift from Allah—that is what Al-Akir called it. A force that will allow us to destroy our enemies at last. A force that makes whoever holds it invincible."

Blaine found that the Arab Fazil's words were far less unnerving now that the envelope was in his possession.

He stepped out of the shop and headed back for the courtyard. Around him Ghirardelli Square was even more crowded with lunchtime shoppers and strollers, many wishing to partake of the various eateries and stands. Any one of the dozens of people could have been watching him, and McCracken was sensitive to the feeling of eyes cast his way. He took his time making his exit, emerging finally on Beach Street, the same route by which he had entered.

Beach Street runs parallel to the bay, and is flat as a result. It is the only street adjacent to Ghirardelli, and having its own red-brick storefronts built into the square's side resulted in an outdoor mall-like strip made up of the same type of shops as those found within. Beach was open to traffic, but cars had to inch their way forward against the frequent clutter of shoppers spilling out into the street before them.

The beautiful spring afternoon did nothing to make McCracken relax. Around him San Francisco breathed like no other American city. Young men buzzed the streets on Rollerblades. Couples of both the mixed and single-sex varieties strolled arm-in-arm without hesitation or reservation. McCracken fell in behind a youngish pair of men sporting identical ponytails.

"I told him no way I'd pay that kind of rent," McCracken heard a high-pitched voice saying, directly to his rear. "I mean, can you believe it? I mean, have you ever?"

McCracken kept walking. Before him, a pair of balding men in dark suits slid in behind the young ponytailed couple. Something about the motion disturbed Blaine. He started to slow, considered veering off, and moved his hand ever so slightly for the SIG-Sauer 9mm pistol holstered on his hip.

''Keep walking, sweetie,'' the already-familiar high-pitched voice ordered from a yard back. ''And please, please, don't reach for the gun.''

Blaine let his hand dangle back by his side.

''That's better, sweetie. Keep walking now.''

McCracken's eyes cheated about him. He'd been boxed in; that much was clear. What remained to be determined was exactly how many were enclosing him. There were four at least, two in front of him and two behind, and four could be handled.

''My,'' the high voice started, ''you're a big one, aren't you? Know what I'd like you to do now? Just whip out that oh-so-big weapon of yours and hold it by the barrel. Play any games and I'll have to shoot you, and wouldn't that be a waste?''

McCracken's hand slid up the nylon of his holster. He could take out the pair of balding men before him without bothering to draw the SIG, but that would still leave the two behind him, including the speaker. Obnoxiously high voice or not, the leader had played this game before and knew what he was doing. At the very least Blaine needed the gun free before he acted. He slid it from the holster, holding it along the top halfway down the barrel. Then he started to ease it out from beneath his jacket. A simple matter now to have it palmed and ready to fire.

McCracken heard the grinding of wheels an instant before one of the young men on Rollerblades sped close. Before he could respond, the SIG was torn from his hand and the young man was gone.

A high, piercing laugh invaded his ears. ''Weren't expecting that, were you, sweetie?''

''Can't say that I was.''

"He speaks! Oh my, I'm in heaven. I always did want to meet you, Blaine McCracken. We were expecting someone else entirely. An Arab, and I do detest them so." The laugh again, slightly embarrassed. "I have your picture."

"Don't tell me, you want my autograph."

"No, sweetie, what I want is for you to keep walking to that van parked up there on our right with its rear doors open."

McCracken had picked out the van in question several seconds before. Chancing a move now unarmed, with no clear picture on the enemy's strength, was suicide. He had no choice other than to cooperate until he could make a more defined assessment.

Rollerbladers . . . What was next?

"I like your beard, so scruffy and ruffled-looking. Makes you look strong. Tell me, do you lift weights?"

McCracken twisted his head backward in order to glimpse the high-voiced speaker. The man was short and frail looking with close-cropped hair over a balding dome and baby-perfect skin. His teeth looked like something ordered out of a catalog.

"Do I please you? Think hard now. Your fate rests in my hands."

"My fate . . . Could be worse, I guess."

The little man's expression stiffened. "The van's just up ahead, sweetie. No tricks or you'll have to be hurt."

"You'd like that, wouldn't you?"

"Yes. I would."

McCracken returned all of his attention to the van, now only twenty feet away. Heavyset men in workmen's overalls stood on either side of the open rear doors. The Rollerbladers were coasting about the front. The little man had been waiting for Al-Akir, obviously to keep him from retaining the manila envelope and to ensure that he would never pursue it again. So somebody else knew about the prize the Arabs were seeking, somebody whom the little man was working for.

"Slide to your left now, sweetie."

Blaine knew that once he was inside the van, it was over. If he was going to make a move, it had to be outside. It had to be now.

"Looks like you've finally met your match, sweetie. This is one for the record books. I can't *wait* to tell my friends."

Almost to the van now, Blaine knew he would have to try something desperate and hope for the best.

"Be a good boy, sweetie."

McCracken had tensed his fingers for action when he saw the group of seven Chinese teenagers swaggering down the sidewalk in the van's direction twirling nunchaku and clubs about in their hands. He figured they were the little man's final bit of insurance, until he sensed behind him that the dandy had tensed slightly. The boys were wearing matching black vinyl jackets with red Chinese writing stitched across both sides of the chest. The lead ones slid close, and Blaine saw the fire-breathing dragons embroidered on their jackets' rears.

McCracken halted a mere six feet from the van.

"Hey—" the little man started, reaching to push him on.

But Blaine had other ideas. "Fuck the Dragons," he said loudly to the group just passing.

The boys swung on their heels and turned his way in unison, showing their weapons.

"What'd you say, man?" said the one in the front menacingly.

"Wasn't me," McCracken told the kid. "It was *him*!"

As he spoke the final word, Blaine grabbed one of the pair of balding men and flung him toward the gang members. A club swished through the air and cracked the man's skull. The gang members stormed forward with weapons swinging. Blaine stepped into the confusion, grabbed a boy who was wielding a set of nunchaku, and tossed him into the little man, who had just managed to free his gun. The little man's face exploded in rage, the soft flesh seeming to tighten and tear.

"*Ahhhhhhhhhhhhh!*" he screamed, and fired off a trio of

shots into the Chinese boy's belly and then shoved him aside. *"Get him!"*

But McCracken was already sprinting down Beach Street through the crowd of stunned bystanders, many of whom were ducking for cover. He had glanced back at the sound of gunfire and was revolted by the little man's excessive response, blaming himself for involving the gang in the first place. But he'd have to save the lamenting for later. The little man had steadied his pistol Blaine's way when another of the gang members slammed into him. A club smacked against his wrist, and the dandy's gun went flying. McCracken had gazed back over his shoulder just in time to see the little man twist from the next blow and launch a deft flurry of fists and kicks. With the rest of the boys converging on him, he became a whirling dervish wielding a vicious round of blows from the center, no longer the feathery dandy taunting Blaine from the rear.

McCracken moved faster, catching only glimpses of the rest of the gang members falling or fleeing.

"Get him!" the little man's still-high voice repeated.

A series of gunshots thundered Blaine's way and chewed red brick from the storefronts around him. Another now-familiar sound reached him from behind.

The pair of Rollerbladers in their fluorescent spandex rolled down the sidewalk in his wake, scattering pedestrians in all directions. Cars braked and swerved to avoid them as they darted into the street in frenzied pursuit. Blaine heard metal crunching, glass breaking.

And bullets slamming all around.

A quick glance to his rear was all Blaine needed to show him the submachine guns in both the riders' hands. They were gaining steadily and were already drawing a bead on him. He came to the intersection where a left off Beach led to a steep climb up Polk Street. Blaine saw a cabbie just coming back to his car with a grinder in one hand and a Pepsi in the other. The man squeezed the soda can to his chest and

had his hand on the door when Blaine tossed him backward
and ripped the keys from his grasp.

"Sorry," McCracken said.

He gunned the engine and tore off up Polk's steep grade.

Blaine was able to breathe easy only until he caught a
glimpse of a bus turning up Polk behind him. Holding on to
either side of its rear were the Rollerbladers, machine guns
dangling from shoulder-slung straps. When McCracken
avoided a traffic snarl by swinging right onto the level North
Point Street, another quick gaze into the rearview mirror
showed the young men disengaging themselves from the bus.
They kept up with the traffic, weaving their way between and
around cars when the flow allowed.

Closing the gap.

Before him the traffic light turned yellow and then red.
McCracken jammed the cab's brakes abruptly. Three cars
lay between him and the intersection with Van Ness, which
provided another steep grade for his pursuers to manage. He
drew his eyes to the rearview mirror and saw the Rollerbladers only a dozen cars back now. Well behind them, the familiar blue van had just turned onto North Point.

The Rollerbladers were bringing their submachine guns
up once more.

McCracken twisted the taxi's wheel to the left and lurched
onto North Point's left-hand side against the flow of traffic.
A car that had just swung onto the street clipped his fender,
but Blaine kept right on going. He swung left onto Van Ness
and gunned the engine to speed his climb. Order had barely
been restored when the van smashed its way through a narrow opening toward the Rollerbladers.

To McCracken, escape seemed as close as Lombard Street
and the curvy one-and-a-half-mile jaunt to the Golden Gate
Bridge that it offered. He turned onto it with the rearview
mirror clear.

The first stretch of Lombard is formed of nonstop tight
curves and tough corners. Blaine took them at dangerously
high speeds. The taxi's suspension system squealed in pro-

test. The road began to level off after a steep decline, the Golden Gate coming into clear view. The rearview mirror remained clear, but once over the bridge he'd be able to lose his pursuit for good. He had just caught sight of the bridge toll plaza a hundred yards ahead when a sudden snarl of traffic forced him to a screeching stop. At first he thought it was the routine delay caused by the collections process. Then he saw that construction had shut down one lane of the Golden Gate in both directions, accounting for a backlog of traffic that would linger through the entire day.

McCracken's eyes locked on the rearview mirror. He caught first sight of the Rollerbladers when they emerged between a pair of tractor-trailers fifty yards behind him. He could no longer see the van they must have ridden up Van Ness holding on to, but they posed enough of a threat all by themselves. Watching them weave their way forward through the stuck traffic, Blaine resolved that he had no choice but to abandon the cab and continue on foot.

He threw open the door and stuck his hand under the seat. Cabbies often stowed weapons there, and the operator of this taxi was no exception. McCracken's fingers closed on a tire iron. He slammed the door behind him and rushed down the last stretch of Lombard Street, Route 101 now, leading onto the bridge.

The Rollerbladers continued to close on him, not rushing to use their machine guns since they believed they had him trapped. McCracken kept his body low as he ran to utilize the frames of the stalled cars for cover. He moved in an erratic zigzagging motion, anything to confuse the aim of the spandex-clad young men.

Just fifty feet away, the Rollerbladers sped toward Blaine in single file down a narrow channel between the stopped cars. He turned to face them, the tire iron gripped low by his side. The lead skater brought his submachine gun up. McCracken tossed the tire iron, not high for the obvious head strike, but low at ankle level.

The tire iron crashed into the wheels on the lead Rollerblader's skates. He was tossed airborne instantly, landing hard on the hood of a car. He bounced once and then crashed to the road directly in the path of the other skater, who spun out of control trying to avoid him. But the second Rollerblader recovered his balance quickly after bouncing off a trio of cars and surged forward, machine gun leveled once again.

McCracken seized the momentary advantage he'd gained by continuing with his original plan, albeit on foot instead of behind the wheel. There was no other option at this point.

The Golden Gate Bridge offered his only chance for escape.

CHAPTER 5

BLAINE reached the start of the bridge and rushed down the wide right-hand sidewalk toward the sounds of a jackhammer chewing up asphalt. As he closed on the roped-off construction area, he saw that a man in an orange vest was waving his flag frantically in an effort to make him veer away.

"Get down!" Blaine screamed as he dove past the man.

Too late. The fresh barrage from the final Rollerblader's submachine gun slammed into the man's midsection and blew him backward. McCracken was reaching for him when he saw that just beyond the spot where the flagger had dropped, the entire roadbed was missing—eaten partially away by the elements and then jackhammered into oblivion to make way for new asphalt. This hole that dropped straight to the waters of the bay below lay between a circle of sawhorses.

Bullets clanged off the steel support rails of the bridge. Construction workers scattered in all directions. Frustrated drivers ducked low beneath their dashboards. Blaine heard screaming coming from every direction. Daring the spray of automatic fire, he darted outward and tossed the sawhorses enclosing the missing chunk of roadway aside so he could feign taking cover behind them. Before him the Rollerblader snapped home a fresh clip and picked up speed before opening fire anew.

McCracken felt the heat of the rounds surge by him. From any distance beyond thirty feet, the Uzi was a weapon of chance for all but the most experienced in handling it, especially when on the move. That provided his hope

The Rollerblader's single-minded vision provided the rest. Gun aimed high and straight from chest level, he didn't see the hole in the roadbed until it was too late. He managed to twist his blades sideways, but couldn't slow himself fast enough. His hands flailed out for something to grab and then disappeared along with the rest of him through the gap.

His drop might have allowed McCracken to relax, if it hadn't been for the sight of the blue van streaking down the sidewalk in the Rollerblader's wake. The sidewalk was barely wide enough to accommodate its width, forcing it to hug the steel guardrail for much of the ride. Sparks leapt into the air. The bridge had erupted into total chaos. Drivers and passengers alike abandoned vehicles and fled to escape the battle.

The van's driver was tilting a machine gun Blaine's way now. Fresh bullets split the air, and McCracken saw his luck running out in a pained instant. A previous glimpse over the side rail had shown him the scaffolding that bridge workers had used to access the roadbed's underside. It was suspended halfway between the asphalt surface of the bridge and the steel superstructure beneath it. Blaine vaulted over the side rail and pitched down onto the scaffolding.

A sitting duck if he remained in this position, he located

the control panel and lowered the scaffolding platform enough
to gain access to the superstructure. He climbed halfway out
and then smiled. With his weight shifted almost entirely onto
the superstructure, Blaine pulled the cotter pin from the platform's right-side cable lock.

He reached the heavy steel superstructure just as the van
screeched to a halt above him, directly in front of the hole
the second Rollerblader had plunged through. Around him,
McCracken could see evidence of the workers who had been
here until just minutes ago. Their abandoned equipment included thick hoses coiled like snakes about the superstructure.

Blast hoses. Used for stripping old paint and rust from the
steel components of the bridge, the hoses pushed coarse black
sand made from iron-mill slag called Black Beauty out at
incredible pressure. McCracken figured this black sand
would be the number forty-five size. With the air pressure
set at 175 pounds and pushing 365 cubic feet of sand per
minute, the hose could slice through granite blocks, never
mind flesh and bone.

"Get him! *Get him!*" shouted the high-pitched nasal voice
of the dandy.

Two 9mm pistols poked through the opening, followed by
a pair of balding heads Blaine recognized from back in Ghirardelli Square. McCracken grabbed one of the blast hoses
and aimed it their way. He squeezed the deadman switch,
and a dark blanket roared out in direct line with the faces of
the balding members of the assault team.

McCracken could not recall ever hearing screams worse
than the ones that followed. He abandoned the hose and
swung to the left at the sound of a *thump*. One of the big men
in overalls he had glimpsed standing at the van's rear back
on Beach Street had dropped down onto the scaffolding platform from the rail above.

"Kill him!" the dandy screamed.

Before the big man could carry out the order, the cable
with the missing cotter pin let go, dropping the platform and

sending the man tumbling. He managed to grasp a rail at the last and hung there with legs dangling desperately four hundred feet above San Francisco Bay.

"Fuck!" the high, nasal voice wailed.

McCracken had already rushed off toward the labyrinth of catwalks and beams that formed the superstructure. If the roadway above was the Golden Gate's heart, then this was its soul: ten million square feet of steel layered in all directions, spanning the entire scope of the bridge.

Blaine eased himself from the yard-wide catwalk onto a narrow steel rail to quicken his escape. He walked down the rail gingerly, holding fast to thick support beams whenever possible. In the near distance, he heard sirens screaming.

A pitter-pattery sound behind him made Blaine swing round.

"Aye-yahhhhh!"

The martial arts kiai preceded the dandy's kick by an instant, long enough for Blaine to move his head out of its direct path, but not enough to avoid the strike entirely. The kick smacked his temple and drove him backward against a support beam. The dandy stalked forward with light, graceful steps, never even looking down. He moved from one rail to the next with a hop step and came straight at McCracken.

"What's the matter, sweetie, don't want to take your medicine?"

Blaine lunged forward with a kick of his own. But the dandy blocked it effortlessly. At the same instant, he slammed his other hand into the inside of McCracken's thigh, narrowly missing his scrotum. Again Blaine reeled backward, just managing to catch his balance before the edge came up.

"Yeah, you're strong all right, sweetie, but it's not gonna help you. Not against me. Come on, show me what you've got!"

McCracken jumped up and grabbed hold of a steel crossbeam. He swung forward and dropped down on an adjacent catwalk to buy space and time. Four feet separated him from his toying adversary now, the dandy not looking too concerned.

"You can do better than that, sweetie."

Blaine again leapt for hold on a neighboring crossbeam. Only this time he threw his whole body forward with legs lashing outward. The move seemed to fail when the dandy grabbed his outstretched ankles and held them in place.

"I had expected so much more from a man who calls himself McCrackenballs," the dandy taunted, in total control.

"Really?"

His position solidified, Blaine snaked his legs up across the too-soft face before him and trapped the man's thin neck between his knees. The dandy's face reddened. He fought to break the hold, but leverage was against him now. McCracken jerked him forward and the dandy pitched forward off the rail. His legs kicked at the air, as he grabbed on tight to Blaine's knees. With the little man's features purpling, McCracken knew he could either let him drop to his death or strangle the life out of him. Considering the dandy's death grip on his legs, Blaine opted for the latter.

He thought it was over when the little man let go with one of his hands. But then he noticed the life rope dangling thirty feet down from the girder directly overhead. The dandy caught it with his free hand and twisted abruptly out of Blaine's leg hold. Swinging on the rope, he propelled himself up to the catwalk McCracken was standing on.

The dandy's face was still purple, though with rage now. He stormed forward, launching a blinding flurry of blows Blaine's way. McCracken managed to block or deflect all of them, his defensive posture precluding any opportunity to launch any decent strikes of his own in response. His back pressed up against the outermost support beam on the bridge's superstructure. Then the momentum of a furious kick from the dandy drove both of them backward onto another motorized scaffolding platform.

Blaine nearly tripped on the high-pressure painting equipment that had been left upon it. He drove himself upward, pushing off a control panel that sent the platform climbing high for the Golden Gate's center span. He managed to right himself, but the little man drove a knee square into his groin. McCracken pounded the man's face with a trio of hard blows. The dandy deflected the fourth, then came up and under Blaine's outstretched arms.

Before McCracken could respond, the dandy was behind him, grabbing his head and neck in a death hold. Blaine heard him scream triumphantly before he felt his air seize up en route to the brain. His limbs became feathery and numb. He could feel his legs starting to give way.

As the platform continued rising, Blaine cast his eyes about for a weapon of some kind. The only thing he could see was one of the high-powered bridge-painting devices lying just beyond his grasp. McCracken willed the feeling back into his left hand. Breath bottlenecked in his throat, and his oxygen-starved brain denied him focus. He grappled desperately for the nozzle, but it remained barely out of reach.

With loss of consciousness only moments away, and the dandy's grip forcing his head downward, Blaine now saw that the control box for the ascending platform was just beside his left foot. He kicked out toward it, aiming as best he could. The OFF button depressed beneath the pressure of his shoe, and the platform jolted to a halt, left to the whims of the wind.

The abrupt stop loosened the dandy's grip enough to allow McCracken to sweep down and out with his hand. He located the paint hose and closed his hand on the control nozzle.

The dandy screamed again and wrenched Blaine's neck to secure the last of his lock.

"What do you see, sweetie? Look at death and tell me what you see. . . ."

All in the same motion, McCracken got the nozzle up behind him and activated it. Orange paint flew out and swallowed the little man's eyes, particles of it splashing back against Blaine's shirt. The dandy released his grip and wailed horribly, hands flailing about his face.

"Why don't you tell *me* what it looks like?" Blaine asked. Then, as oxygen flowed back into his lungs, he smashed his adversary twice in the stomach and once in the face.

The little man launched a wild blow in response. When Blaine ducked under it, the blow's momentum carried the dandy's upper body over the safety rail that rimmed the platform. McCracken threw himself at the little man with all his force and power, angling his thrust upward. The impact pitched the dandy headlong over the rail, still flailing for something to grasp when McCracken tossed him forward with a final burst of strength.

"Have a nice flight," Blaine said as the little man's snarling face disappeared toward the blue waters below.

McCracken saw him hit with a spraying splash and nothing more. Still, he stayed on the platform for a brief time, as if expecting the dandy to rise. When he didn't, McCracken moved off, anxious to open the manila envelope that was still in his pocket and learn what inside it could have caused all this.

McCracken waited until he reached San Francisco International Airport before calling Sal Belamo from a private room in the American Airlines Admiral's Club.

"Why do I always hate hearing from you?" the pug-nosed ex-boxer greeted him.

They had worked together on several occasions, although not so much recently since Sal had been appointed chief troubleshooter of the Gap, the organization Blaine had recently helped throw into a shambles. Belamo looked more like a cheap thug than the sharp operative he was, courtesy of an undistinguished boxing career that had left his face looking the worse for wear.

"Because you're jealous of my charm and good looks."

"You ask me, we spent too much time at the same salon, the both of us. What's up?"

"Need you to check on someone for me. Hired hand. Little guy with lots of martial arts in his background. . . ." McCracken provided as complete a description of the dandy as he could manage.

"Don't have to go to the computer for that one, McBalls. Guy's name is Billy Griggs, alias Billy Boy. One deadly son of a bitch. Hand specialist in more ways than one."

"So I gathered."

"Yeah, Billy Boy's 'bout as queer as a three-dollar bill plus change. You whack him?"

"Sent him for a swim."

"Your sake, I hope he doesn't come up for air."

"Five-hundred-foot dive off the Golden Gate."

"You ask me, don't count him out until the fish eat his eyeballs. Like to hear what he did in 'Nam?"

"Not really."

"Dressed himself up as a gook, little shit that he was, and took Charlie out from the inside that way. Got himself transferred to Special Forces and even they couldn't deal with him. What I hear, he went home and accepted his medal in gook makeup and black pajamas . . . you make of that."

"Sorry I iced a war hero."

"Don't cry yourself to sleep. Griggs's nickname over there was 'Charlie Cat' on account of he had so many lives. Plenty have tried to put him down before. None been very successful." Belamo paused. "So what's next?"

"You have someone meet me at Kennedy Airport with a passport complete with entry visa for Turkey."

"Turkey?"

"Night flight to Istanbul, Sal."

McCracken had inspected the contents of the manila envelope in the backseat of the cab that had taken him to the airport. Just a single sheet of paper, obviously a photocopy of something larger that had been reduced to a more manageable size.

It was a map, of all things!

Judging by the poor print quality, the original must have been old and tattered. The photocopy included handwritten instructions in German scrawled in the blank space near the bottom to further supplement the map's directions. The site was Turkey, specifically the southwestern part near the Aegean Sea known to be rich in archaeological treasures:

Ephesus.

CHAPTER 6

Benson Hazelhurst's jeep had threatened to give out on at least three occasions and had finally quit two miles from the find.

"Try it now, Daddy," his daughter urged, pinching something with a pliers underneath the raised hood.

Hazelhurst turned the key, and the jeep's engine grumbled, then shook to life.

"That's got it," Melissa said. She pulled out from under the hood and slammed it back into place.

"What would I do without you, Daughter?"

"Die of heat exposure, for starters. Want me to drive?"

"No need. We're almost there. Driving will occupy my mind. I don't think I could endure this last stretch without something else to concentrate on."

Melissa Hazelhurst closed the passenger door behind her and frowned.

"Speak your mind, Melly," her father urged.

Benson Hazelhurst was almost seventy years old now, but he still had most of his hair and much of the muscle of his youth. Hazelhurst had married a much younger woman thirty years back, and they had wasted no time conceiving their only child. Melissa had inherited her father's greenish-blue eyes, and her auburn hair was the same shade his had once been. She was tall enough to have been taken for a model on numerous occasions and in good enough shape to have been mistaken for a professional swimmer and runner. Melissa's mother had died when she was four and she had been paired with her father ever since.

"I think you're getting your hopes up," she warned. "That's all."

Hazelhurst pulled back onto the road. "I've seen that frown before. You don't believe it exists, do you?"

"No," Melissa admitted.

"I see," her father returned, obviously hurt.

"I want to," she tried to explain. "I mean, I've tried. But every time I start to believe, something pulls me back."

"Reason, perhaps?"

"Yes, reason."

"Then what about the claims of the Phoenicians, the ancient Egyptians, the Persians, and the old priests? Different cultures that all described virtually the same thing, all searching for it at different times through history."

"And never finding it."

"Not to our knowledge, anyway."

Melissa slid her arm to her father's shoulder. He stiffened slightly at the touch. "Father, I've never questioned or doubted you before. I'm not sure I am now. It's just that, well, I know how much this means to you and I don't want to see you disappointed."

"Winchester's message left little reason to expect I will be."

"He's not an expert."

Hazelhurst chuckled humorlessly. "He was the best student I ever had. Doesn't say much for me as a teacher, does it?''

''That's not what I meant and you know it!''

His hand touched the one of hers still resting on his shoulder. ''Of course. I'm sorry. You've been good to have humored me for so long. Lord knows you had no reason to before I located those maps.''

Melissa eased her hand away. ''You never told me where they came from.''

''Yes, I did. The museum.''

She hesitated. ''No. I checked.''

''*Through* the museum, then. At least that was how the contact was made.''

''What contact?''

''The possessor of recently discovered archives in Germany that the museum knew I would have interest in.''

''Germany?''

''The archives contained materials from World War II, my dear. They belonged to the Nazis.''

Melissa was shocked.

''Makes perfect sense,'' Hazelhurst continued. ''Think of your history, Melissa. Hitler was obsessed with the mystical: astrology, the power of ancient artifacts, the occult. He had scores of archaeological teams scouring areas all over the Mideast in search of any object even remotely thought to possess some sort of spiritual or supernatural power.''

''Which led them here.''

''But the war ended before they had a chance to determine whether their findings were correct. The maps were stowed away and hidden, in all probability by parties already planning for the Fourth Reich.''

Melissa stared at her father for a long moment. ''And now we're picking up right where they left off.''

Benson Hazelhurst kept driving.

The drive took another ten minutes, their jeep bouncing and tilting along the uneven terrain. Winchester's dig site was located in a secluded valley protected by small hills playing the role of time's centurions. The area near Ephesus was for the most part composed of lush, fertile plains. But here there was barely any trace of green, as if all the flora had browned and died. Dirt and chalk dust blew about in the afternoon sun.

As the jeep drew closer, Winchester's dig took shape in the form of layered piles of neatly excavated stone and dirt. The only vehicle present was a four-wheel-drive parked just beyond the heaps. The dust thickened against the windshield of the Hazelhursts' jeep and, as if in a final act of protest, the engine sputtered and died a good hundred yards from the other vehicle. Melissa climbed out with canteens in hand and waited for her father.

"I don't see anyone," she said, stiffening.

"They could be, should be, down inside the excavation."

"Winchester knew we were coming. He would have had someone waiting. And, besides, someone would've heard us coming."

Hazelhurst rewrapped his bandanna over his brow to add protection for his eyes. "This wind can steal the voice of the man next to you, never mind a raspy engine. And I never advised Winchester of our plans."

To reinforce his assertion, Hazelhurst plodded forward toward the site. Melissa lingered slightly behind him. She squinted her eyes against the flying dust, the leather of her well-worn boots chipped by the onslaught of the unforgiving ground.

"Damn," she muttered.

"Shield your eyes," her father called back to her.

She had been on digs before, but had never experienced anything quite like this. It was almost as if there was some sort of force intent on keeping them beyond the piles of excavated rubble. Hazelhurst reached the stationary four-wheel-drive vehicle and leaned against it for protection from the wind. Melissa nestled near him. One of her hands slid onto the hood.

"It's still warm, Father. Winchester or someone in his party must have returned within the last hour."

Hazelhurst turned away from the vehicle and headed for the excavation.

"Dad!" Melissa called after him, trying to keep pace.

Hazelhurst reached the rim and peered down.

"Good lord," he rasped.

Melissa saw the body an instant after her father did. It lay facedown not far from a yard-square rectangular opening in the ground, created when what looked like a massive stone tablet had been slid backward. The dust and dirt had already showered the body, soon to render it invisible.

"Is that—"

Melissa interrupted her question when she saw her father locate the rope ladder and begin to climb down. It wobbled, and the old man clutched a rung for dear life, his bones brittle from decades of exposure to the calcium of lime-stone.

"Hold it steady, child."

"Let me go first."

"Do as I say!"

She obliged and then followed her father down, joining him near the body he had just flipped over.

"Winchester," Benson Hazelhurst muttered, kneeling over his ex-student, who stared up at him now with eyes glazed over by death.

In the center of Winchester's forehead was a small black hole. It was jagged, as if someone had jammed in a thick Phillips-head screwdriver and twisted it around a bit. Beside the bullet hole's dried edges, there was no blood.

Hazelhurst's eyes wandered about. "There should be workers here. Winchester hired over a dozen, perhaps more by the look of things."

His gaze fell on the rectangular opening that accepted the blowing dust and dirt like a vacuum. The thick stone tablet had obviously been parted from the slot it must have occupied for centuries.

A shuffling from above made Hazelhurst break off his thinking. He grasped Melissa and drew her behind him as he gazed upward into the sun and blowing dirt. A figure was standing at the rim above, directly over the rope ladder.

"Who are you?" Hazelhurst screamed up, while behind him Melissa cursed herself for not bringing a rifle with them from the jeep. "What do you want?"

"Professor Hazelhurst?" the confused reply followed in English.

"Yes," he yelled, his own echo blown back at him. "Who are you?"

"I am the foreman—Kamir. What has happened?"

Hazelhurst felt himself relax. "You'd better come down here."

"*Sayin* Winchester sent me to Izmir for more men and—"

"Come down here," Hazelhurst repeated, "but leave the men up there."

Kamir said a brief prayer over the body.

"Who did this to him?" he asked, looking up at Hazelhurst and Melissa.

"I thought it might have been you."

Kamir's eyes bulged indignantly. "No, *Sayin* Hazelhurst. I left *Sayin* Winchester here and went to hire new workmen after the others fled this morning."

"Fled? Why?"

Kamir gestured toward the massive tablet. "The work frightened them. The warning . . ."

Hazelhurst exchanged glances with Melissa and then moved toward the tablet. With his hand he brushed away the dust and dirt that had collected atop it and traced the carvings with his fingers as well as his eyes.

"I've seen this before—only a few times, but I recognize it. Dates back to an ancient religion that predates Christianity by over a thousand years."

"One of the men who fled insisted the words were a warning, that we had already gone too far and must turn back before it was too late.''

''And then they fled.''

Kamir's eyes darted briefly to the rectangular opening. ''But not before *Sayin* Winchester ordered us to move the tablet. They were gone in the morning.'' His eyes grew fearful. ''I do not blame them.''

''Why, Kamir?''

''It, it is difficult to explain, *Sayin*.''

''Just out with it, then.''

Kamir's lips trembled. ''When the tablet was moved, I . . . felt something.''

''Felt what?''

He shrugged. ''I . . . do not know. It brushed by me, icy and hot at the same time.''

Hazelhurst looked at the guide very closely. ''Did you share this with Winchester?''

Kamir shrugged. ''I did not have to, *Sayin* Hazelhurst—he felt it, too.''

''And then?''

''This morning *Sayin* Winchester sent me to get new workers.'' Kamir's voice lowered. ''I left him here alone. If I had stayed . . .''

''You drove off in one of the vehicles.''

Kamir looked confused. ''We've only had the one truck, since the other broke down last week.''

A chill swept through Hazelhurst. ''That jeep not far from the rim . . .''

''I thought it was yours, *Sayin*.''

Hazelhurst turned to Melissa, his eyes speaking for him.

''*Sayin* Hazelhurst, what is it? You must tell me.''

''Winchester's killers must have come here in it,'' Hazelhurst said to his daughter.

Kamir felt for the sheathed knife wedged through his belt. ''Then where are they, *Sayin* Hazelhurst?''

The old man's eyes moved to the opening in the earth that Winchester seemed to have been clutching for as he died.

"Let's get the equipment," he said to Melissa.

"Dad, you're not going to—"

"Yes, Daughter," he interrupted, still peering downward. "I am."

CHAPTER 7

"**N**ow, Daughter," Benson Hazelhurst said two hours later, "you're quite sure you don't want me to strap a ray gun onto my side?"

"What I want," Melissa Hazelhurst told her father, "is for you not to go down there at all. If you're right about what this place is, you can't go down until you've had time to take precautions, obtain the proper equipment."

Hazelhurst couldn't believe his ears. "More equipment than we have already? What more could we need?"

"Please, not another speech about finding the treasures of Tunis with a pickax and a chisel."

"As I recall, it was a hammer."

"You know what I mean."

"What I know is that a dozen workmen ran away from here this morning, which means that the truth of this find will be all over Turkey by tomorrow at the latest. This place will be swarming with curiosity seekers and tourists mucking about. I can't have that. I've worked too long to take that risk."

"The biggest risk lies in going down there."

The old man's face softened. "My last dig, Melly. Let me retire to the drudgery of academia with memories of my own choosing. Now, are you ready yet or not?"

Melissa was too busy checking the volume meters on her recording equipment to pay his remark any heed. She slid the headphones briefly off her ears.

"Would you mind repeating that, Father?"

Benson Hazelhurst merely raised his eyebrows in response. He knew he must look as absurd as he felt, far more like an astronaut than a sixty-nine-year-old professor of archaeology. The white suit covering him from neck to foot was thermally warmed and cooled, adjusted automatically by body temperature. An oxygen tank with a twenty-minute supply was strapped to his back. The hose running from it snaked up over his shoulder and finished in a mask attached to his equipment vest at lapel level. The vest was equipped with special pockets that held two flashlights angled downward to provide as good a view of his descent as possible without tying up his hands. He would need them to steady himself and feel his way in the darkness for walls and corners, Melissa knew.

Her father's helmet, meanwhile, looked at first glance like a motorcyclist's. Actually, though, it was equipped with an infrared visor to maximize vision. And built into its crown was a miniature video camera that, over a limited range, would beam pictures of everything he saw up to a recorder at ground level. This would allow her to monitor his progress, as well as preserve the step-by-step process of whatever he uncovered.

His gloves were reinforced with Kevlar to prevent scrapes to his hands. His shoes were fitted with special rubberized soles that prevented slipping when the total weight of the wearer was brought to bear. A microphone and receiver were built into his helmet.

"I feel like a fool." Hazelhurst sighed.

"A safe fool."

"Yes."

"Don't forget, I'm bringing you up at the first sign of trouble."

"Then you're still expecting some."

"Whoever killed Winchester must have run into it."

Her father seemed maddeningly unmoved. "Perhaps."

"Knowledge won't protect you, Father."

"Ignorance couldn't have helped those who descended before me."

"Turn around," Melissa ordered.

As he crouched at the edge of the chasm, she fastened the winch holds into the two slots in her father's vest, which was tailored for them. The winch apparatus would serve as Hazelhurst's express elevator up when it came time for his return, or in the event of trouble. It would also lower him at a slow, careful pace that he could control with a remote transistor box. Additionally, the mechanism was fitted with mercury switches that snapped the line taut in the event of a sudden drop, responding much faster than the reflexes of any standard line bearers could ever hope to.

"I think I'm ready, then," Hazelhurst said, and pushed the helmet tight over his head.

With his visor still raised, he swung round and eased his legs into the chasm ahead of him. Melissa touched him on the cheek and lowered his visor.

"Keep in touch," she said.

"I suspect you'll be sick and tired of my voice before this day is over," Hazelhurst answered, and then lowered himself into the darkness.

Melissa returned to her machines instantly, searching out the comfort and security they provided. Throughout the two hours of setup and preparation, she had been haunted by memories of childhood nightmares of monsters with spade-claw hands. She was only three, almost four, when they started. Night after night she would wake up screaming. Her mother would come into the room and still her trembling. In between the tears, Melissa would tell her about the monsters. They weren't real, her mother would say. They were just the product of dreams.

Dream Dragons.

And one night when the nightmares came, she didn't cry out to her mother. Another night, she woke up without screaming. Then, finally, the nightmares stopped altogether.

But today, strangely, the memory of them had returned.

"Can you hear me, Daddy?"

"Not so loud, Daughter, please. And don't call me 'Daddy' on a tape with historic implications."

"Sorry."

"I'm kidding. How's the picture coming through?"

"Darker than expected. I can hardly see."

"Can't you do something?"

"To view a finished tape, yes, but not while monitoring."

"Oh," Benson Hazelhurst said.

Before her, the red level indicator on her sound meter dipped and darted with the sounds of her father chuckling. All her machines, in fact, were working, but Melissa nonetheless sat amidst them feeling helpless. The workmen continued to stand guard on the ground above, all too happy to remain as far away from the find as possible. Only the two Kamir trusted the most and Kamir himself were down here with her, on the chance that the winch needed to be operated manually.

"How far down am I?" her father wanted to know.

A counter with an LED readout rigged to the winch was there to tell her. "Fifteen feet. My screen is just about black. What do you see?"

"Dead space. Wide open. Nothing to the sides or below I can make anything out of, except for the fact . . ."

Melissa's heart skipped a beat. "What was that? You broke up."

"No, I just stopped talking." Her father's rapid breathing filled her ears. This was taking far too great a strain on him. "Wanted to make sure of myself before I spoke. I'm sure now. This cavern is perfectly rectangular, as I suspected. Twenty feet by fifteen would be a fair estimation. The wall I'm up against has a hewn feel to it. Aren't you getting any of this?''

Melissa slid closer to the screen and squinted. "Not enough," she replied. "Did you say hewn?"

Again his rapid breathing preceded his sharp retort. "Where's your textbook knowledge, Daughter? This must be some sort of overchamber carved out by those who years ago sought the same thing we do. We're not the first ones who have been here."

"Your theories . . ."

"Fits right into them. The actual doorway was discovered and barricaded thousands of years ago."

There was a brief thud over the monitoring equipment as he at last struck bottom. Melissa caught a brief glimpse of the floor as her father gazed down at it, before his helmet-mounted camera came up again.

"Strange," he said.

"What?" Melissa followed into her headpiece.

"I'm inspecting the walls. God, I wish you could see this more clearly. Everything's been filed too clean, too neat. The walls are perfectly symmetrical, right down to the grooves."

"Impossible!"

"Unless we've got our dating wrong."

Melissa swallowed hard. "Any sign of Winchester's killers?"

"Nothing. Wonderful, isn't it?"

"Why?"

"Think, Daughter. We know they didn't leave the site in their vehicle, which means they could only have ventured down here. But since there's no trace of them . . ."

"They must have found the passage to the next level down," Melissa completed.

"No wonder you were the finest student I ever had."

"I thought Winchester was."

Benson Hazelhurst's reply was to begin a careful, system-

atic check of the walls and floors in search of the entrance to
the next level. Melissa followed his progress as best she
could, finding herself increasingly anxious over the lack of a
decent picture. Next time, she would have to come up with
a way to create a wider beam of focused light. . . .

"Wait a minute," Melissa heard her father say, "I found
something."

"What?"

"Piece of clothing. From a jacket, I think. Or a vest like
mine."

"One of Winchester's killers?"

"I'm in the far southwest corner. Walls feel the same as
they did on the other side."

"Yes. That much I can see. If you could just—"

The picture blurred, faded, sharpened briefly again.

"I'm going at them with my file. The finish isn't as gritty
or chalky, and it feels damper. I'm going to try something."

"What, Father? What are you going to try?"

"Hush, Daughter. I'm not so old that I can't exert a little
pressure."

The sound of his labored breathing filled her ears, followed by soft, shallow grunts. Then there was a rumbling,
like the sound of heavy furniture being dragged over a floor.
On the screen before her, Melissa could make out a segment
of the wall shifting inward.

"That's got it!" Hazelhurst's tired voice beamed.

Melissa squinted again, fighting to see what he saw. "The
passageway to the next level," she realized.

"There are stairs," her father said. "I'll keep my eyes
steady for a time so you can see for yourself. The staircase
is very narrow. I can't see the bottom. I'm going to take the
first step down."

"No!" The urgency in Melissa's voice made Kamir swing
toward her.

"Easy, Daughter. I've waited my whole life to find what
may be at the bottom of this stairway."

"Then you can wait a little longer. Please. Just until we can get better equipment."

The screen before her showed the blurred shape of the stairs as her father took them.

"Three steps down now. The steps feel . . ."

"Damn!" Melissa muttered, as the picture wobbled and started to break up.

". . . like they were chiseled at the same time as the walls and floor above. You know what that means, of course."

"No! No, I don't. . . ."

The sounds of Hazelhurst's breath intermixed with the rustling noises of his descent. "Think, Daughter! Whoever built this chamber over the actual doorway wasn't trying to entomb it; they only wanted to conceal it. Everything in the construction points to the fact that regular forays were made down here by the overchamber's builders." More rustling noises. "Difficult to date the work. Early Phoenician or even— That's it! This reminds me of the way the Egyptian pyramids were constructed. That might give us more of a clue as to the dating. The steps are narrowly spaced. Don't you understand what this means?"

"Any sign of Winchester's killers?" Melissa could see virtually nothing now, the dim light giving little back to the camera.

Hazelhurst answered his own question when she failed to. "The builders of the overchamber didn't construct these steps; they merely discovered the entrance to them, then sought to conceal and guard them. The steps were waiting when they came, waiting for who knows how long." The old man's voice turned reflective. "I wonder how far down they got. I wonder how far . . ."

Melissa estimated that her father had covered forty to forty-five steps now.

"There's something down here," he said suddenly.

"What?"

"Just a glimpse. I caught a glimpse. I think I'm almost to the bottom. It must lead into another chamber."

"Stay where you are. Let me try and get a look. . . . ."

"I'm starting to make sense of this construction now. If I'm right— Oh my God. . . ."

"Father, what is it? What do you see?"

"No! *No!*"

Melissa squeezed close enough to the screen to draw static. "What's going on? I can't see *anything!*"

The camera wobbled, as her father took three rapid steps down.

"Daddy, get out of there!"

"Yes, I'm sure now," Benson Hazelhurst's slightly panicked voice returned. "At the bottom of the stairs, I can see . . . bodies. Aren't you getting this?"

"Daddy, just get out of there."

They must be the men who killed Winchester. But what hap—"

There was a sudden flash, and then the picture scrambled into oblivion.

"Daddy!"

"Ahhhhhhhhhhhhhhhhhhhhhh! . . . ."

Her father's high-pitched screech froze Melissa's insides. Her breath left her in a rush, barely enough retained for another desperate cry.

"Daddy! . . ."

His scream gave way to a wet, slurping sound. What might have been grinding and tearing, or . . . chewing followed. The screen continued to show nothing. Melissa pounded its top in frustration.

"Get him up!" she yelled at Kamir.

Instantly he moved to the winch and reversed its pull. The steel lifeline grew taut, wouldn't give. Kamir looked over at Melissa helplessly.

"By hand, then! By hand!"

The two other workers joined Kamir reluctantly and began to hoist on the line. It resisted at first and then started to rise. Melissa watched them from the midst of a nightmare.

"Daddy, can you hear me?" she said into her headpiece.

Nothing.

"Daddy, can you hear me?"

Not even static.

"Oh, God . . ."

Lips trembling and breath heaving, Melissa tore her headphones off and rose to her feet. Kamir and the two workmen had the cable coming up very fast now; too fast, as if her father had grown somehow weightless. No, he had fallen and somehow snapped the cable line in the process. His communication equipment had shattered and that was why he had not been able to reply to her calls. That was it; that *had* to be it. And as soon as Kamir retrieved all of the cable, she would suit up herself and rescue her father. She would—

"Tanrl yardimcimiz olsun!"

One of the workmen had plunged to his knees in a position of prayer. The other ran screaming for the rope ladder that would lift him free of the excavation. Only Kamir remained to pull the rest of the cable up. He backpedaled, staggering, then leaned over and retched. Melissa came forward on feet that seemed made of steel. Kamir's position blocked her from sight of whatever had been lifted from the chasm.

"No, miss, don't."

It was too late. Melissa had drawn up even with him. She looked down. Her world wavered. She threw her head back for a scream that never came. It seemed to her that her breath had been torn away. She sank to her knees, gasping.

Before her, the remains of her father lay on the rim of the rectangular entryway. She recognized his shredded safety vest, now drenched in blood. The upper part of his torso was still tucked within the vest, though it, too, had been badly torn. The right half of his stomach was there as well, along with his neck and a portion of one of his arms.

The rest was . . . gone.

No legs, no head. Sinewy entrails and intestines hung down from the torso, dripping blood and gore.

The Dream Dragons, Melissa thought as she sank to her knees.

Dream Dragons . . .

But this time they hadn't come from nightmares at all. This time they were real.

And they were still down there.

Dream Dragons

PART TWO

Dream Dragons

Germany: Tuesday, eight P.M.

CHAPTER 8

FRIEDRICH Von Tike stared fixedly at his favorite Impressionist painting as he listened to the voice of the man sitting opposite him.

"*Herr* Von Tike, my company and I have been loyal to you ever since the merger," Lars Heidelberg said earnestly. "We've gone along with the layoffs and cost-cutting procedures. But this we cannot overlook."

"Is that a threat, *Herr* Heidelberg?"

"Not at all, sir. What is being threatened here is the very survival of the many villages on the shores of the Rhine that will be destroyed if this flow of pollutants from our company is not halted."

Von Tike fingered the report Heidelberg had brought with him. "I find your data unconvincing."

"How many cases of cancer will it take, *Herr* Von Tike? How many abnormal births? This company could never survive the backlash. No company could."

"And do you suppose, Heidelberg, we could more easily survive the kind of retooling your report calls for? Listen to me, I purchased your company and all the others so I could expand production, not slow it. If those victims of our progress elect to sue, we will settle their cases as generously as we are able."

"These are simple people. Even if they made the connection, they are hardly likely to . . ." Heidelberg cut his own words off, realizing.

Across from him, Von Tike smiled. "Precisely, *Herr* Heidelberg, precisely. I think you have grasped my point at last."

Heidelberg rose and leaned across Von Tike's desk. "*Herr* Von Tike, I beg you, sir, not to do this. I beg you to close these plants until the proper modifications can be implemented."

"Your suggestions have been duly noted and will be taken under advisement," Von Tike snapped off curtly, and rose to face him. "Now, if you will be kind enough to excuse me . . ."

Shoulders slumping, Heidelberg was halfway to the door when Von Tike spoke again.

"Oh, and *Herr* Heidelberg, I trust this conversation will be kept between ourselves."

Heidelberg stiffened and turned.

"After all, my friend," Von Tike continued, staring him straight in the eye, "there are your wife and children to consider. Three boys, ages eight, ten, and thirteen. The youngest has brown hair and blue—"

"Enough! You've made your point."

"Good," Von Tike said. "Now get out."

After Heidelberg had closed the door behind him, Von Tike sat down again and reached for his pocket-sized tape recorder. He composed his thoughts before beginning to speak. Von Tike owned the controlling portion of Levenhasse, a thriving giant in the German military-industrial complex. He had made his first fortune selling major components for advanced weaponry to any country that could afford them. Oh, nothing that could be traced back in any amount great enough to do Levenhasse significant harm. Recent disclosures, though, had become a nuisance, and, worse, the fall of the Soviet Union had led to a drastic reduction in military orders. Von Tike saw his empire crumbling and was scrambling to reroute his priorities.

As a result, companies like Heidelberg's had been swallowed in a series of monstrous gulps to expand Levenhasse's industrial base. Many possessed inadequate and antiquated equipment. Von Tike's engineers had updated them and increased their efficiency at the expense of dumping huge volumes of pollutants into the Rhine and its tributaries. It was a cost Von Tike found easy to accept. As far as he was concerned, all of the backward villages bordering the river could be wiped out, so long as his company's revenues continued to rise.

Von Tike switched on his tape recorder and spoke into it. "Meeting with Heidelberg, April seventeenth. Commissioned his own report on pollutants flowing out of his plant and several others. Probably intends to approach the government with his findings now, which we cannot allow to—"

Thump . . .

Von Tike eased the machine away from his mouth. He looked toward the door to the conference room.

Thump . . .

Coming from inside it. Who was there? There was no entrance to the conference room other than through his office, and no one had passed that way.

Thump . . .

Von Tike rested the still-running tape recorder atop his desk and stood up. He moved out from behind his desk and started toward the conference room.

He was almost there when the door crashed inward. The force blew Von Tike backward, nearly spilling him over.

"What?" he managed. "Who the devil is—"

The scream that followed was the last discernible sound on the tape the security guards would later find. They arrived barely a minute after Von Tike uttered the scream, but it took them several more to locate the recorder, because it was hidden beneath their employer's severed arm. The blood had rendered the recorder inoperable, and it was some time later before another was found, and the guards could listen to the last agonizing moments in the life of Friedrich Von Tike.

* * *

Javier Kelbonna stood on his balcony watching the night waves break over the shoreline. He was the master of all that he saw, all that he could see. The island belonged to him. It had been granted along with asylum after he had fled his own country in the wake of a disastrous civil war.

The world had judged him wrongly, harshly, and in the end had turned his own people against him. They had risen up in the streets, and Kelbonna had ordered his militia to use all means at their disposal to quell the violence. Then crowds had gathered to oppose him, and the militia had fired on them, regardless of whether or not the crowds were armed. Preemptive strikes were launched against the insurgent leaders' villages. The fact that many of these raids had claimed only women and children as victims meant nothing to Kelbonna. After all, the young who did not grow up could not threaten him—the ultimate preempt.

When the Americans had interfered, with air strikes and a massive amphibious landing, Kelbonna had had no choice but to flee. A thousand of his elite guards and closest associates had accompanied him, and all now called the island their home as well. Kelbonna knew that the Americans would try for him here if given the chance, so he had turned the island into a fortress. Even a vastly superior invading force could be repelled by the defenses laid about and manned twenty-four hours a day. Sophisticated radar and sonar equipment had been installed to provide early warning of an approach by sea or air.

Kelbonna stood on his balcony with no concern for his safety at all. Even if by chance a small elite troop managed to slip through his elaborate defenses, they would still have to contend with his heavily fortified mansion. Armed guards patrolled the hallways all day long. At night, when he was within his chambers, no less than four were posted outside his door. Kelbonna was untouchable, so long as he remained on the island.

Of course, he didn't know exactly how long that would

be. Someday he would return to the Central American island country he had built from nothing and claim it for his own again. The Americans had had their chance at him and missed. How they would be sorry for what they had done. . . . Indeed, Kelbonna was ecstatic to learn that many thousands of them had taken up permanent residence in his former country, lured by the low prices and lush surroundings. They would become his hostages when he made his triumphant return. He would execute them one by one until the American government had made good on the wrongs they had done unto him.

Leaving the balcony doors open, Kelbonna stepped back inside the master bedroom and started to take off his bathrobe.

Rat-tat-tat . . .

The sound of machine-gun fire echoed in the night. Screams followed and then more fire. Orders were shouted.

Kelbonna felt a numbness in his gut.

They were on the grounds of his residence!

Since his bedroom overlooked the sea and not the front of the walled complex, he could not view whatever was going on. He rushed toward the entrance to his bedroom just as a hard knocking rapped upon it. Kelbonna threw it open to find the captain of his private guards before him.

"We are under attack, Your Excellence."

"By whom?"

"Unclear at this time, Your Excellence. I have called for more troops. The house is secure. Please stay within your rooms until you hear different from me."

Kelbonna nodded and closed the door, locking it. He strode to his desk and removed his own pistol from the holster resting atop it.

Poof!

The sound came as he checked the clip. He was trying to identify it when the screams of his men in the corridor beyond began to ring out. Cold fear had already flooded him when the shooting started, bursts of gunfire vying with the sounds of his men's screams. Kelbonna discarded his pistol and instead grasped the machine gun perched by the head of his bed. He took up a combat-ready stance directly before the door.

The Americans! The damn Americans! . . . It had to be them, had to be!

The screaming stopped, and what sounded like a guttural, back-throat growl reached Kelbonna.

"Come on," he urged whatever lay beyond the door softly. "Come on!"

Losing his bravado much faster than he had found it, Kelbonna had started for the balcony to climb for safety when the double-doored entrance to his bedroom exploded inward. He swung his rifle toward it and opened fire, screaming. The clip exhausted quickly, and he discarded the rifle and lunged back toward the balcony's rail.

He was halfway over it, eyeing the sea, when he felt the scratch down his spine. Strangely, that was all it felt like, but the warm gush he sensed spilling from him and the numbness that quickly ascended told him he had been ripped open. The feeling in his legs deserted him and then his hands seemed to seize up. He tried to hold on to the railing, but there was nothing left to hold on with, and Javier Kelbonna dropped down into the night toward the rocky shoreline below.

"What am I going to do with you?" Heydan Larroux asked the man seated in the chair before her. "You know the rules, Jersey Jack, and you broke them."

"Yes, ma'am."

Heydan Larroux pulled an old fashioned cat-o'-nine-tails from her desk and walked toward the chair. She had men outside the office, but none of them inside with her. The day she couldn't control her people by herself would be the day she found a different line of work.

The cat was made of tawny leather, almost the same color as the elegant brown dress she was wearing. Heydan Larroux always dressed in colors that highlighted the power and sultriness of her natural features. She had long jet-black hair, which she wore stylishly permed. Her eyes were big and black, too large for the rest of her demure face. Her cheekbones were set high, and she wore little makeup and only enough perfume to let visitors know it was there. Though she was not especially tall, her firm posture and strong build gave her the illusion of height. No matter. Her people looked up to her in any case.

"I've got reason to punish you, don't I, Jersey Jack?"

"Yes, ma'am."

"I want none of my stuff ending up in the hands of kids. *Never!* You been selling to schools."

"No money in the streets, ma'am."

"Haven't I always taken care of you no matter what?"

"Yes, ma'am."

"I ever let bad times affect the way I treat my people?"

"No, ma'am."

"But then you go and sell in the schools."

Jersey Jack's black face was dripping with sweat. He had a gold tooth right in the front which seemed to have lost its shine.

"I—I wanted to impress you with my receivables."

Heydan Larroux slapped the cat-o'-nine-tails against the back of his chair. "And look where it's got you." She came back around the front. "Who am I, Jersey Jack?"

He looked up at her. "Ma'am?"

"Describe me in a word."

It took him a long couple of seconds to come up with it. "Important."

"People respect me."

"Hell, yeah."

"The police leave me alone, even though they know what I do."

"Yes, ma'am."

"Know why, Jersey Jack? 'Cause I make sure my people stay clear of the work that really pisses the cops off. Kind of like an unwritten agreement. They don't want a war, and they know so long as I'm in charge of this end of things, they won't have to wage one. You hearing me, Jersey Jack?''

''Yes, ma'am.''

''Look around you. Tell me what you see.''

Jersey Jack described her office as best he could. The vast book collection, the wood-paneled walls and matching mahogany desk. The Oriental rug that cost more than most men made in a year. The hardwood floors she'd had taken up from a house she'd lived in for the better part of her life and laid down here to remind her of her roots.

That house was a bordello that Heydan Larroux had entered at the age of fifteen, a far cry from this Southern mansion on Chappatula Street in the Uptown section of New Orleans. She had made a name for herself, and by the age of nineteen she had been getting top dollar and booking by appointment only. By the age of twenty-five she had been running the place and three others like it. And when the RICO commission had decimated Louisiana's crime lords, she had stepped in and filled the void. She'd consolidated power and now ran it all: prostitution, gambling, drugs. Never sold to kids, though. That was the golden rule. From the lowest dealer on the ladder to the high-echelon suppliers, everyone knew the rule. Break it and you paid the price.

''I got all this by toeing the line,'' she said when Jersey Jack was finished. ''Ever since I started out, that's the way I've done business. You've done a good job for me, Jersey Jack.''

''Thank you, ma'am.''

''You came in on that bus out of Newark two years back and told me you wanted to make something of yourself.''

''I did, ma'am. I *do*.''

Heydan Larroux made sure he could see the cat as she spoke. ''I think we're gonna let it go this time, but I can't let you go out of here unmarked. I've got a business to run and I can't let anyone think I was hesitant or weak.''

Jersey Jack swallowed hard. ''I un-ner-stand.''

"Lift up your shirt. Turn around and hold on to the chair's arms. Hold tight."

He was so tense that he was shaking as he bent slightly and grasped the arms of the chair, his eyes squeezed closed. Heydan Larroux brought the cat up and snapped its tails down against Jersey Jack's back. He gasped in pain. His upper body spasmed and went rigid. She hit him again, and blood sprayed into the air.

"I think that'll be sufficient."

Jersey Jack struggled to his feet, biting his lip. His shirt slid back down. His eyes were still bleeding tears.

"Thank you, ma'am."

"You won't let me down again, will you, Jersey Jack?"

"No, ma'am."

"Leave me."

He turned and walked gingerly to the door, each step driving shards of pain through his back. He closed the door behind him.

Beyond this office was a private sitting room. None of Heydan's employees, not even the highest in her chain of command, had ever been inside it. Heydan moved through the door and locked it behind her.

"Well?"

Her question was aimed at a shape sitting cross-legged in the center of a bare wood floor that had also been lifted from the first cathouse where the Larroux legend had been born. The shape belonged to an ancient woman with thin, long wisps of white hair and skin the consistency of dried parchment. The pupils of her eyes were virtually indistinguishable from the whites, looking as though they had been painted over. She had been blind since the time Heydan Larroux had met her and long, long before that.

Some said the Old One had seen enough of the Civil War to be able to write chapter and verse on the individual battles. Legend had it that she had come over on a slave ship from Africa, bringing with her the black arts from her native country. She'd had eyes then, and the legend said that she had

traded them for immortality. But the dark forces she had
bargained with had fooled her: while she would indeed live
forever, she would continue to age and waste away until little
more than her bones remained.

The Old One wore dark rags for clothes. They swam
over her frail frame, as if they had outlasted the generations as she had. It seemed to Heydan Larroux that this
was the very same outfit the Old One had been wearing
the day they had first met. Heydan had taken her in off the
street where she had been begging, offered her food and
shelter. The Old One paid her debt with the only thing of
worth she had. That was three years ago, and they had
been seldom far apart since.

The Old One was her most trusted adviser. Never did Heydan make a major decision until she had consulted with the
Old One. This ragged bag of bones was able to look with
blind eyes into a pool of water and direct Heydan's actions
based on what it showed. The Old One had been proven right
more times than even Heydan wished to admit. It had been
the Old One who had told Larroux of Jersey Jack's indiscre-
tion.

How could she have known?

Heydan Larroux had stopped asking such questions long
ago.

"Well?" Heydan Larroux repeated.

"What do you seek, child?"

"You know what I seek, Old One. Don't tease me."

"I cannot see what is not yet before me."

Heydan tucked the folds of her Giorgio Armani dress beneath her and sat on the floor in front of the Old One. A
large bowl of water rested between them.

"Take the stones," the Old One instructed, and eased her
crinkled hand outward.

In it were a half-dozen ordinary stones. Heydan took them.

"Begin, child."

"Have I rid myself of the evil?"

Heydan Larroux punctuated her question by dropping one of the stones into the bowl.

Plop . . .

The Old One angled her eyes at the rippling water as if she could see. Her right ear was her good one, and she cocked it toward the water as well.

"It still comes," the Old One told her. "Not from within. From without."

"What do you mean?"

"Another stone, child . . ."

Heydan let the second one fall.

Plop . . .

"You have been marked. It comes for you."

"Who?"

Plop . . .

"Not who."

"Righting my wrongs didn't help. . . ."

"It does not approve."

"What can I do?"

The Old One just looked at her. Heydan let the fourth of her stones drop into the water.

"Nothing. Wherever you go it will find you. Whatever you do it will seek you."

"When?"

"For each question . . ."

"Yes. All right."

Heydan closed her hand on the two remaining rocks. When they were gone, no more answers could be had before the next session. An hour from now perhaps. Or tomorrow. Or next week. With the Old One she never knew.

Plop . . .

The old woman listened and turned her blank gaze up at Heydan. "Soon, child. Very soon."

Heydan heard a scream ring out from somewhere on her property. A brief burst of machine-gun fire came next, followed by an even worse wail.

"Now," the Old One said.

Heydan lunged to her feet and rushed to a small writing desk. She pulled a pearl-handled 9mm pistol from its bottom drawer and charged for the door.

"You can't fight this with guns," the Old One advised.

"What am I fighting?"

The last stone splashed water from the bowl on both of them. The Old One flinched.

"What am I fighting!" Heydan demanded.

The Old One's head raised slowly. "No answer comes to me."

Heydan rushed through the door back into her office. The invaders were clearly inside the house now. And if the screams were any indication, the guards she had posted based on the Old One's warnings were falling quickly despite their weapons. The sounds she heard from beyond the heavy door made her shudder. The 9mm pistol felt pitifully worthless in her hand.

The invaders were almost to the office now.

Heydan Larroux charged back into her private chamber and bolted the door behind her.

"Old One, I must—"

She stopped. The Old One was gone, only the bowl of water left in her place.

You can't fight this. . . .

The lavish Oriental rug that adorned the center of the floor had been pulled back enough to reveal the entrance to the secret tunnel, part of the old Underground Railroad, that ran beneath her property.

Heydan pulled the hatch up to reveal a ladder. A smell of dirt and mustiness flooded her nostrils. Gathering her skirt around her, she held it with one hand while she used the other to grasp the ladder and begin descending. She managed to get the hatch closed again behind her and was almost to the ladder's bottom when she heard the sound of the door crashing inward in the room above.

Heydan Larroux grabbed the flashlight at the foot of the ladder and used it to illuminate the pathway. Then she charged down the narrow, sloping corridor, fearing it would not be long before whatever had entered the house would be coming down after her.

CHAPTER 9

"You really think this guy can help us?'' Detective Hal Repozo asked Joe Rainwater.

"If anyone can, it's him.''

"What'd you call him, a charmin?''

"That's the toilet paper, *wajin*. This guy's a shaman.''

"What's that mean?''

"Indian for 'medicine man,' sort of.''

"And what's *wa-jeen* mean?''

" 'White fuck.' ''

It was early Wednesday morning. Almost thirty-six hours had passed since Injun Joe's stakeout had resulted in his being first on the scene of the massacre at the Oliveras estate Monday night. A dozen heavily armed men had been carved up in a two-minute span.

"How were they killed?'' Rainwater had asked Estes, the department's chief pathologist, outside the drug lord's mansion the previous morning.

Estes had worked through the night and looked it. His thinning grayish-brown hair was ruffled. The top buttons of his shirt were undone, and his tie was only half-knotted. He smelled of alcohol and formaldehyde. Rainwater had watched

Estes sit down on the mansion's front steps only after checking to make sure they were clear of blood. The medical ex-
aminer stuck a cigarette in his mouth but didn't light it.

"They were torn apart."

"I saw that much for myself."

Estes lit his cigarette and held it away from his face. "Then
you know as much as I do."

Rainwater didn't see Estes again until he stepped outside
the precinct building just after four Tuesday afternoon.

"You spare an hour?"

Injun Joe sighed. "I'm due back at ten and I got to chair
a meeting of the Informed Indians' Council right now."

"Cut the shit, red man. I'm being serious. Something out
at the Oliveras house I want to show you." He paused. "I
wasn't all the way straight with you this morning. Guy like
you deserves to know, 'spite of the orders."

"Orders?"

"You'll see."

Thirty minutes later, Estes slid his car through the main
entrance, past the police guards posted before the mansion.
He got out and led Injun Joe across the front lawn. Almost
at the mansion's entrance, Estes knelt down and ruffled a
patch of grass.

"Take a look at this."

"At what?"

"Found it right about here after you left this morning. Sun
musta dried it out."

"Dried what out?"

Estes looked up at him. "Made a plaster impression of it.
You don't believe me, I'll give you a look. You and nobody
else. I'm staying clear of this one."

"You talking about a footprint? That qualifies as evidence
even on the reservation, *Kemo Sabe*."

"This wasn't like any footprint I ever saw. Took it to a
friend of mine at the zoo over lunch hour. He thought I was
playing a fucking joke on him. Said nothing owns that print

ever walked on this earth. Said it looked like a combination of a bird and a lizard.''

"You find only the one?''

Estes stood back up. "I look like a douche bag to you or what? Found two more between here and the gate. This was the clearest.''

"Nothing about footprints in your report.''

"Brass thought it'd be a good idea if I kept it out. Look, two years from now I pick up my pension and do consulting work on the side. Bad time to make waves.''

"Yet you brought me back here.''

"Yeah,'' Estes said softly. "Thing is, red man, you get all the weird cases, and most of the time you solve them. Serial killers, kid busters, whackos . . . Way I see it, whatever did this last night is still out there. I figured you had a right to know that.''

Rainwater nodded. "Any way you can give me a better idea of what this print looks like?''

Back at his car, Estes pulled a plaster impression of the footprint from his trunk. Injun Joe took it from his grasp and ran his hands over the clawed extremity.

"This was a man's foot, how tall would he be?''

"It's not a man's foot.''

"Educated guess.''

"Okay. You wanna hear it, I'll tell you: based on the angle of the bone structure and the way these, well, *talons* I guess you'd call them, curve inward, whatever calls this its foot would be between eight and nine feet tall. Weigh maybe two-fifty, three hundred pounds.''

Injun Joe handed the plaster impression back to him.

It was too late to bother with sleep before beginning his ten o'clock shift, not that he could have managed to even close his eyes. He stayed at his desk throughout the night, uneventfully save for a pair of phone calls. At midnight he called a number and left a message. At six a call came in that had brought him to the airport where the United Airlines

ten A.M. flight out of Boston into O'Hare had just locked
home against the jetway.

"What'd you say this shaman's name was?" Injun Joe's
sometime partner Hal Repozo was asking now.

"I didn't."

"You grow up with him or something?"

Joe Rainwater's face grew reflective. "Yeah. I guess you
could say that."

"I hate when you get like this. Talking mumbo-jumbo
and—"

Detective Hal Repozo stopped when Joe Rainwater stiffened at the sight of a figure that had just emerged through
Gate 15. Repozo followed his eyes and did a double take.

"Are you fuckin' kidding me? . . ."

The figure was that of an Indian who was seven feet tall if
he was an inch. His coal-black hair showed a tint of gray and
was tied behind his head in a ponytail. He wore a leather vest
over a blue denim work shirt and thick khaki pants with badly
scuffed brown boots tucked inside them. His face was as
leathery as his vest, and his eyes were black ice on a winter
night.

"Hello, Joe Rainwater," the big Indian greeted him when
he was a yard away from Injun Joe.

"Hello, John Wareagle."

The two Indians looked at each other, motionless for what
seemed like a very long time. At last Joe Rainwater extended
a hand. Wareagle's grasp swallowed it.

"Thank you for coming, John Wareagle."

"Old times' sake, Joe Rainwater."

After being introduced to the big Indian, Detective Hal
Repozo couldn't resist asking what was on his mind. "Hey,
how you guys know each other? Same tribe or something?"

The two Indians again exchanged stares, as if each was
waiting for the other to speak. It was Rainwater who broke
the silence.

"I'm Comanche. He's Sioux."

"Is that important?"

Wareagle looked down at Repozo. "If you're a Comanche or a Sioux."

"Okay, what then?"

"The hellfire," Wareagle said.

"Say what?"

"Let's go for a walk, John Wareagle," Injun Joe said.

Wareagle's luggage consisted of a single shoulder bag, almost hidden by his great bulk. He shifted it from his right shoulder to the left one as he and Rainwater moved slowly through the terminal, Repozo hanging well back.

"I really meant it when I thanked you for coming," Injun Joe started. "I know you didn't have to. I know seeing me brings up memories you'd rather leave buried."

"Memories are never buried, Joe Rainwater. They are pushed aside by one plow into the path of another, but always they remain."

"I was out of line with you way back when. You were more patient than you should have been. I didn't know, didn't realize. If I had . . ."

"Past, Joe Rainwater."

In Vietnam, Captain Joe Rainwater had commanded a company composed entirely of native Americans. Tribal distinctions were meaningless. Rainwater had been possessed by a fierce nationalism for both his country and his heritage. His would be the greatest company in the war. He would recruit the finest native Americans available.

He had crossed paths with Johnny Wareagle on several occasions when Wareagle was training with the Special Forces. Rainwater had offered him a chance to pull out and sign on with his unit, which by then was already known as Shadow One. But Wareagle had elected to stay with SF and, much to Rainwater's dismay, ended up with the cutthroats of the Phoenix Project.

The war had ended for Rainwater and Shadow One when the company was virtually wiped out at the Tet Offensive. Rainwater came home with a limp he sweated to lose and a legacy he fought to preserve. Shadow One had been on the point of every major assault it had participated in. A record number of Silver Stars and Purple Hearts were given out, too many of them posthumously. Burning with the pride of his people, Rainwater wanted the whole country to know. He organized the American Indians Veterans Association and tracked down Wareagle in the backwoods of Maine to sign him up.

Wareagle had refused. Short and simple. Rainwater had berated him, taunted him, insisted he was letting his people down. Wareagle had listened to it all without response, obviously hurt.

"I cannot join," was all he had said.

"Why?"

"I cannot join."

Rainwater had left enraged. It was not until over a year later that he uncovered precisely why Wareagle had so steadfastly refused. According to all official records, Johnny had never gone to Vietnam. The unit he had served with had never existed. Johnny Wareagle, apparently, had *never* existed. He couldn't speak, couldn't march, because if someone dug around, a little too much of the Phoenix Project's dirt might be shifted in the wrong directions.

Joe Rainwater had apologized. Johnny Wareagle didn't seem to think it was required. Injun Joe had kept in touch with him sporadically over the years and had learned what questions not to ask.

"I'm glad I was able to come," Wareagle said suddenly, stopping just past the security station before the entrance to the United gates. "I believed in your work back then. I believe in it now. Forsaking you made me feel as if I was forsaking my people."

"You were under orders, John Wareagle. That takes precedence."

"*I* determine precedence in my life now, Joe Rainwater. I would help you in your work still, if it were possible for me to."

"It's possible for you to help here. That's more important."

"Why did you call me?"

"Because the spirits still speak with you, John Wareagle. And I think we need them now."

They drove out to the Oliveras mansion on Forest Avenue in Evanston, the ride agonizingly silent with Repozo behind the wheel. He remained there when Rainwater led Wareagle onto the grounds through the front gate, skirting the yellow POLICE! DO NOT CROSS! strips.

Wareagle had read Estes's report in the car on the way over, so he knew exactly what had happened. Then, as Rainwater looked on in amazement, Johnny stopped at each spot on the grounds where Injun Joe recalled a body having been discovered.

"Four out here. Nine within," Wareagle said suddenly.

"Right. Thirteen in all, including Oliveras."

"Where were the footprints found?"

Rainwater brought him to the spot where Estes had lifted the clearest one, then pointed out the other two. "Leading to the house, if the indications are right."

"What about leading back out?"

Injun Joe shook his head. "Nothing."

"Strange."

More uncomfortable silence passed between them.

"You couldn't feel where the prints were," Rainwater raised in a half question.

"No."

"The bodies, but not the prints . . ."

"Show me the inside, Joe Rainwater."

Injun Joe led Johnny Wareagle inside, talking the whole time.

"I been a cop, shit, fifteen years now. Seemed like the best thing to go into after the war. I've seen things in those years, awful things. And I saw worse things with Shadow One. But this, this is different."

Rainwater stopped in the center of the mansion's main foyer. He seemed to be grasping for words.

"I've heard tales of the old-time shaman summoning evil spirits to punish those who wronged the tribe."

Wareagle smiled slightly. "As I recall, Joe Rainwater, the true old ways never held any interest for you."

"Because I passed them off as legend, folklore—the way the tribal chiefs could keep their people, as well as their enemies, in check."

"But you feel differently now."

Rainwater's expression tightened. "Nothing on this earth could have done what I found here. Nothing on this earth stands eight feet tall and leaves a print like the ones left here Monday night."

"Perhaps you do not know the earth as well as you think you do, Joe Rainwater."

Johnny Wareagle walked about the foyer in a wide circle. Then he started up the spiral staircase. At the top, Injun Joe moved in front of him and pointed to a spot on the Oriental runner that curved up off the stairs down the hallway.

"One body here, another four feet from it." He kept walking. "Ten feet on, two almost right next to each other. . . ."

"I need to see the pictures," Wareagle said, right next to Rainwater without Injun Joe having heard his approach.

"They're in the car."

"Get them."

It appeared to Injun Joe that Johnny Wareagle acted more like a cop than a shaman. He moved about the scene in methodical fashion, studying each picture within the context of the hallway. Rainwater could tell he was trying to see the scene as it had been two nights ago, just prior to the massacre. Wareagle came to the shattered door leading to Oliveras's bedroom and stopped.

He was still standing there when Injun Joe drew up even. "I felt something when I stepped inside this house, John

Wareagle. It may have been gone by then, but not its residue.''

''Not it.''

''What?''

''Not it, Joe Rainwater—they.''

''More than one?''

''At least three. Potentially more.''

''Oh, shit . . .''

''Two entered through the shattered front door downstairs first. The other or others launched their attack after them from the opposite end of this corridor.''

''No guards down there. . . .''

''Right.''

''The spirits told you that,'' Rainwater concluded.

''They only helped me see. The way the bodies fell, Joe Rainwater, it is clear they were under attack from both directions.''

''They got off two hundred rounds and didn't hit a single thing except air and walls.''

Wareagle came closer to him. ''But you don't believe that, do you?''

''No.''

''You believe the bullets struck their targets but did not fell them.''

''I believe what killed Oliveras and his guards wasn't human. Say what you will, John Wareagle, but you and I are both full-bloods. We have the old ways running through our veins, even though they run slower through mine. We know the tales of our ancestors who were able to conjure up beings from other worlds to do their bidding. And we can be sure our ancestors were not alone in this ability.''

''Times long forgotten.''

''And now, perhaps, skills recalled. We must track these things down before they can kill again.''

''Perhaps they already have, Joe Rainwater.''

''What do you mean?''

''I'll show you.''

* * *

"You made my day, big fella, let me tell you," Sal Belamo said on the other end of the line at Gap headquarters in Virginia.

"Thank you, Sal Belamo."

"Hey, just Sal, okay?"

"Yes. Sal . . ."

"This gotta be the first time you and me ever talked, McCrackenballs wasn't around. They got me manning a desk now, you know. Watchdog, overseer—some bullshit job like that. Not my style at all. I like it better out there with you boys. Hey, if you're calling for McCracken, he left for—"

"No. I'm calling because I need you."

"Wow, this must be something! What can I do for ya, big fella?"

Wareagle told him about the murder of drug lord Ruben Oliveras in Chicago.

"Yeah," Belamo said, "I read about that. You ask me, it's first-class fucking-A weird."

"I need to know if there have been any other killings like it, Sal Belamo. Anything familiar that's been reported any time in the recent past."

"Check it for you pronto. And hey, big fella, just Sal, all right?"

Billy Griggs pulled his car up to the corner and looked at the pay phone he had been instructed to go to. A handwritten out-of-order card was taped across its front, covering the touch-tone buttons. Billy turned to the boy sitting in the passenger seat, reached over, and smoothed his hair.

"I won't be long," he said in the gentlest voice he could manage.

Then he grabbed the thick blond locks and jerked the boy's head backward.

"Make sure you don't go anywhere. Okay, sweetie?"

Billy let the boy nod.

"Very good," he said, and stepped out of the car.

Normally he might have used a gentler approach, but he hadn't been in a very good mood since plunging four hundred and fifty feet off the Golden Gate Bridge. He still ached everywhere. It was the first time, 'Nam included, Billy Boy had ever considered he might die. He had hit the water with legs in a half spread to slow his plunge, but it had still taken forever to claw back to the surface. He'd taught himself how to hold his breath for maybe four minutes in 'Nam; had to, or the gooks would have sliced his balls off and fed them to him. Down in the black of those tunnels they could hear you if you breathed, so you held it. Simple as that. It all came back to him when he hit the water, the tunnels all over again. Don't panic, *never* panic. Billy was starting to lose it just before the surface, but he held on, thought of the scores he had to settle. Never mind that McCracken was the best. Billy had had everything in his favor and the big bearded fuck had still bested him. Billy wanted revenge.

He moved to the pay phone and stood by it patiently. It rang within seconds.

"Yes," he said, receiver pressed against his ear.

"Your failure was regrettable."

The voice didn't sound human, because it wasn't. It was channeled through a digitalized transfer device which totally obliterated all voiceprints. What Billy was hearing was a machine's interpretation of human speech, only the words remaining the same.

"Hey, I explained all that."

"Your explanations are meaningless to us."

"I didn't know it was going to be McCracken. No one told me it was going to be McCracken."

"You fear this man?"

"Billy Griggs doesn't fear nobody."

"Too bad. Fear can be a worthwhile ally. It prevents over-confidence. It promotes reason. Perhaps if you had been scared of this man, he would not remain at large."

"I'll get him. You just find him for me and leave everything else to—"

"No."

"What?"

"Do not mock me, Mr. Griggs. I have read about this man since your report reached me. He is exceptionally dangerous. He could bring us down."

"One guy, okay?"

"Mr. Griggs, you are trying my patience. Your work for us has been most acceptable up till now. Please do not spoil it."

Billy Boy Griggs squeezed the receiver tighter. "Hey, all I'm saying—"

"If you know as much about McCracken as you claim to, then you know what I speak is the truth. We cannot afford to have him on our trail with the attainment of our ultimate goal so close to being realized now."

"So what do you need me for? You already said I wasn't up to the job."

"You are going to coordinate the assignment with some outside contractors who we feel may be the only ones who can get the job done."

"Who?"

"The Twins."

"Oh, Christ . . ."

"You've heard of them, I see."

"I've heard they're not human."

"Most proficient, yes. That proficiency is needed now."

"I won't be responsible for their actions." Billy wondered how obvious the reluctance was in his voice.

"You are merely their guide and our conduit. We will direct you to them and then point you toward McCracken."

"You know where he is?"

"His options are limited."

"Just make sure the Twins understand the score, okay?"

"Your tone disturbs me. I expected as much. Look at this as a second chance. You won't get another. I could have made your punishment far more severe."

"What punishment?"

"Do not underestimate the scope of our power, Mr. Griggs."

"What punish—"

Click.

The line was dead.

Billy Griggs glided from the phone back toward his car.

The Twins. The goddamn fucking Twins. . . .

For just an instant, Billy considered ditching this whole business. Get behind the wheel and take his boy-toy somewhere they'd never find him. Kid was a winner. Last him a few months, anyway, and then he'd find himself another.

Billy climbed into the driver's seat and locked the door behind him. The boy-toy had slumped against the passenger door, passed out with his head low against the window. Billy had been too generous with the dope.

"Hey," Billy said. "Hey, I'm talking to you. . . ."

He jostled the boy-toy's shoulder. Kid slumped like a loose sack of rags. Billy gasped. The only thing propped against the car's door was the boy-toy's trunk.

His head was gone, sliced clean off while Billy had been on the phone right here in public. There was blood everywhere. Billy could see it now, splotchy in the darkness.

My punishment, Billy realized, as he lost his breath and stepped from the car. *My punishment. . . .*

CHAPTER 10

THE guards began swinging open the gate at first sight of the car heading down the dirt road late Wednesday afternoon.

"You're late," one said to the driver, as the car inched through the entrance.

"She's waiting, then."

"For hours. You've thrown off her routine."

"Couldn't be avoided. The messenger was running behind."

The woman drove the car into the kibbutz and parked it next to the memorial to the war that had seen Israel take the Golan Heights. The memorial was an old tank, still functional and well-maintained, but covered with roses, violets, and daffodils. The planters enveloped the entire bulk of its frame. The turret alone gave away what it had once been, and the contrast was intentional. On top of this battle-scarred land, an entire people had built a beautiful nation. Israel would live with the dichotomy of beauty and force forever. The symbol of the tank was enduring.

The woman climbed out of the car and took with her a hefty stack of newspapers from all over the world: major dailies from the United States, Germany, France, and England through that very day; Austria, Switzerland, and Italy through three days before. Holding the stack in both arms, she moved in a fast walk toward a cottage isolated in the commune's rear. The pair watching over the old woman today motioned the visitor toward the wrought-iron table where the figure in the wheelchair was seated, turned away toward the trees. She plopped the stack down atop the table and straightened it.

"I'm sorry for being late."

The figure in the wheelchair did not turn. "Leave me."

All too glad to do just that, the woman turned and was on her way.

This kibbutz looked much like the other self-sufficient communes that were scattered all across Israel. Large fields of crops dominated the setting. Farm animals were corraled in a number of areas. The squawk of chickens could be heard for a considerable distance. Cows looked up from their grazing to utter an occasional sound. Dogs sauntered lazily about or lay in the shade of large cedar trees and the kibbutz's numerous buildings. Many of these were small, cottagelike structures that mostly held families. A number of larger structures were actually dormitories that housed the children. Still more buildings contained offices and classrooms for the children's daily lessons. The largest was the cafeteria where the kibbutz members took all their meals. The synagogue could be found in the second largest.

This kibbutz would also have seemed at first glance to be like all the others in terms of the residents going about their daily chores and duties. Routine provided security, not tedium. For the residents, discipline was everything.

But a closer look revealed something odd about this kibbutz's residents: each and every adult was female. Men were nowhere to be seen. In addition to that, this particular kibbutz enjoyed no formal registration, nothing whatsoever that provided proof of its existence. All mail was delivered to a single post office box twenty miles away to be picked up every day, or sometimes every other. To those in the government aware of the commune's existence, it was referred to simply as "Nineteen."

The women of Nineteen could call it home for as long as they desired. Many of the residents were war widows who came to escape the violent world that was the Israeli way of life. There was ample time to get on with their lives later. For now, their spirits needed to mend, and they stayed as long at Nineteen as necessary to see this come to pass.

It was similar for female soldiers who came to Nineteen with nerve strings frayed to the very edge. Though it had been twenty years since Israel had been attacked, and a decade since she had invaded Lebanon, limited engagements and skirmishes were a fact of life. These, too, exacted a price from those who fought in them repeatedly.

Still more of the kibbutz's residents were widows as well, but of a different sort. Spanning the scope of ages, they had lost husband or children to terrorist attacks or the Intifada. They came to Nineteen with a rage that could be calmed but never vanquished. These would spend portions of each day on the commune's gunnery ranges firing at black cardboard silhouettes they imagined to be the ravagers of their lives, trained by the very female soldiers who had come here to put their guns down. Contradictions at Nineteen, as in life, were everywhere. There were no easy explanations. The staccato bursts of gunfire here were no different than the clucking of chickens or laughter of children. They were accepted. Part of the routine.

And the founder of all this, of Nineteen and everything it encompassed, was the old woman who lived apart from everyone else and spent much of her days scanning newspapers from all over the world. Her cottage was the only one featuring a screened-in porch. Instead of stairs leading up to the entrance, it had a ramp for her wheelchair. A pair of neat grooves were worn into either side. The wrought-iron table had been set beneath a tree in front of the cottage, and it was here that the wheelchair rested most of the day.

"Can we get you anything?" one of the guards asked after approaching tentatively when the old woman had remained still for too long.

The old woman, half-blind in one eye, her head crowned by a cloud of silver hair, adjusted the blanket over her useless legs and spun her wheelchair so it faced the table. Her hand shakily grasped her glass of mint iced tea and drew it to her lips.

"No," she answered, placing her other liver-spotted hand atop the pile of newspapers just brought her. "Leave me."

The guard reslung her Galil machine gun over her shoulder and backed off. It was hers and another's day to watch over the old woman, and this was not a task any on the kibbutz took lightly. Some knew her name, but not many. Her daily chores consisted of nothing more than going over her newspapers, in search of what, nobody knew.

The old woman set her unfinished glass of tea down and began paging through her papers in the same deliberate fashion as always, while her two guards continued their silent vigil. Had the guards been watching the old woman more closely, they would have seen her lean forward when she came upon an article on page one of the Wednesday *New York Times* headlined "Exiled Island Leader Javier Kelbonna Slain in Bizarre Execution."

Her hand trembled as she rapidly turned through the front section of the paper to where the article was continued. She flipped quickly through another two newspapers before an article on the fourth page of the German daily froze her. An industrialist named Friedrich Von Tike had been found murdered last night in his office.

Bizarre circumstances again.

When she moved on to the Tuesday edition of *The Times*, there was no need to turn the pages at all. What she sought was right there at the top of page one: a picture of Ruben Oliveras placed just beneath the headlines on the bottom half of the page: "Reputed Drug Lord, Guards, Slain in Chicago Stronghold."

"No," she muttered, too softly for her guards to hear. "No! . . ." Louder this time, loud enough to make them turn.

The old woman brushed the entire contents of the wrought-iron table to the ground in a single swipe. Her glass of mint iced tea smashed on impact, dousing the discarded papers and making her guards go rigid.

"It can't be," she moaned. "They've come back. God help us all, *they've come back!*"

CHAPTER 11

"*Sayin* Hazelhurst!"

Kamir's call stirred Melissa Hazelhurst from her stuporous vigil before the video monitor.

"There is a jeep approaching, *Sayin* Hazelhurst!"

Melissa rose stiffly and emerged from the cover of the canopy down in the excavation. "How many men?" she called up to Kamir.

"Just a driver," Kamir returned, hands cupped before his mouth to make sure he could be heard.

She swallowed hard. "Make sure all the men are at their posts. I'm coming up."

Two of the men, though, had run off following the death of her father, leaving only seven in Kamir's replacement team.

Melissa had spent much of last night and all of Wednesday perched on a stool set behind the nine-inch video monitor. The recording made by the camera in her father's headpiece would have been considered brilliant under ordinary circumstances given the available light. But these were hardly ordinary circumstances, and Melissa found it little better than useless.

Running it over and over again. Different speeds, different filters . . . Always the same.

So often throughout the day she had wanted to give up and break down. Have the equipment packed up by the workers and flee this place. But she couldn't, not yet.

Because something down there had killed her father. And Melissa could not leave, could not run, until she knew what it was. But maybe she already did.

The Dream Dragons . . .

They had been waiting for him down there. They had been waiting for the men who had killed Winchester, as well. Perhaps they were always waiting, left there by the true builders of what lay beneath the surface to deny entry to those who did not belong. *We are, after all, trespassing on the past,* Melissa recalled from another lesson of archaeology. But no one else would ever be trespassing here again, because tomorrow she was going to seal the chamber her father had uncovered. What might be the greatest find in the history of mankind would be buried once more, hidden before more damage was done.

Melissa reached the ladder and stretched before beginning her climb. Her legs were asleep from her being seated for too long. Her neck and shoulders ached with stiffness. She tried to rub the blood back into them and then began to pull herself upward.

Kamir reached down to help her over the rim, just as the jeep drew to within a hundred yards of the site. Her father had been clear about the possibility that rumors of the dig would draw hordes to it. And there was also the possibility that the jeep's driver was connected to Winchester's killers. Melissa looked on neither option favorably and made sure that the jeep's driver would be able to see she had rifle in hand when he approached.

The man parked his jeep behind Kamir's truck and stepped out with his hands in the air.

"Say, anybody know where I can find a cash machine around here?"

The long flight from Kennedy Airport to Istanbul had left McCracken little time to catch the next fifty-five-minute commuter flight to Izmir. He had landed barely an hour ago, rented the jeep, and pieced together the most direct route here possible, following the map obtained in San Francisco as best he could.

The armed woman standing before him was obviously not impressed or soothed by his sense of humor. She stood her ground silently.

"Okay, let's try it this way," he said to her, eyes trained on her rifle. "I'm Blaine McCracken and you're fucking up royally."

"Excuse me?"

"Every man and every gun you've got is in sight. You can't do that. You can never do that. Never let the enemy see everything you've got."

"Then you're the enemy."

"Lady, if I was the enemy, you and your boys here would already be waiting to become some future archaeologist's find."

Melissa felt uncertainty sweep through her. The man before her who called himself McCracken was tall and very broad. Even through his baggy, sweat-soaked white shirt she could see his upper body was sculpted into a muscular V exaggerated all the more by the stance of having his hands clasped over his head. He had a close-trimmed beard and a pair of dark eyes that never seemed to blink.

"If you're a fortune hunter, you've come to the wrong place," Melissa said, the words sounding incredibly lame even to her.

"You're British."

"Very observant."

"Spent some time there myself. Didn't make a lot of friends."

"Somehow I'm not surprised. Who *are* you?"

"We've moved beyond the name stage. Excellent. The truth is, I'm not even sure I'm in the right place; at least, I wasn't until I encountered your hospitality."

"Where did you come from? How did you find out about this place?"

"There's a map in my right-hand pants pocket. I'll take it out and—"

"Stay as you are! Kamir will relieve you of this map." She looked toward the foreman. "Kamir."

"Yes, *Sayin* Hazelhurst."

Kamir had started forward when McCracken spoke again.

"No, no, no! You don't send an armed man to retrieve something from an unarmed man, especially when the armed man is carrying one of the best weapons in your arsenal," Blaine said, his eyes gesturing toward Kamir's M-16 rifle. "Quickest way to have the tables turned on you in a hurry. But you told him to do it, because he's the only other one here who speaks English. 'Nother bad move on your part."

"What should I do, then?"

"Have me pull the map from my pocket with two fingers and toss it away from my feet. Then send an *unarmed* man over to pick it up."

"Are you that good, Mr. McCracken?"

"You don't have to be that good, given this opposition."

Melissa smirked. "Then let's handle it just the way you suggested. . . ."

Blaine followed his own advice precisely and watched a workman who had temporarily discarded his rifle approach to retrieve the map. The workman delivered it in tentative fashion to the British woman. She unfolded it and McCracken watched her eyes bulge.

Melissa realized instantly that it was a copy of the same map her father had entrusted to Winchester, one of the seven different ones that had sent his dig teams scouring the Mideast; maps that had once belonged to the Nazis.

She stormed forward toward McCracken, thrusting the map outward, rifle slung from her shoulder and totally forgotten.

"How did you get this?" she demanded.

"You're breaking the rules again, miss. Approaching with a loaded gun. . . ."

"Shut up or I'll empty it into you! Now tell me how you got possession of this map!"

"I gather I've come to the right place."

"Talk!"

"Long story. Better told in the shade over a glass of mineral water."

Melissa backed away from him, shaking her head. "You really don't know what this is, do you?"

Blaine gazed over her shoulder to the crater that had been dug in the ground. "I assume whatever it might be is over there, Ms. Hazelhurst."

"Don't call me that! Don't call me *anything*! I don't know you! I don't want to know you!"

Again Blaine aimed his gaze over her shoulder. "What's down there?"

"Leave! Get out of here!"

"Maybe I can help."

"I doubt it."

"Let me try."

Melissa felt herself weakening, although she never could have said why. "Why should I?"

"Because it's what I do."

"Archaeology?"

Blaine shook his head. "Helping."

"I don't need your help."

"I think you do. You're no match for whatever it is you're up against."

"How could you know that?"

"Because I left a trail of bodies between the shop where I

picked up this map and the Pacific Ocean, before I headed to Turkey.''

McCracken watched her stiffen.

"Judging by your reaction, Ms. Hazelhurst, I'd say that trail has extended all the way here.''

"There's nothing you can do,'' she told him.

"Won't know that till I try.''

"You don't understand. You could never understand.''

Blaine slid a little closer to her. "Won't know that till you tell me.''

Melissa Hazelhurst was sitting before the tiny video screen beneath the canopy when Blaine climbed down the rope ladder into the excavation. He got his first look at the raised rectangular opening and knew that he was face-to-face with what the map obtained in Ghirardelli Square had directed him to—what Al-Akir had sought and what Billy Griggs was determined to keep from being uncovered. Back on the surface he had inspected the remains of both Winchester and Benson Hazelhurst. Hazelhurst's corpse caught him totally off guard. He had been expecting anything, but not this.

There was barely enough left of Hazelhurst to identify him as a human being. . . .

What could have done this to him?

"If you're not an archaeologist, Mr. McCracken,'' Melissa said without turning from the screen as he approached, "just what is it that has brought you out here?''

"It's a little difficult to explain.''

She swung toward him. "It seems everything about you is a little difficult to explain. Let me hazard a guess, though. The way you're built, the way you move, you must be some sort of soldier or mercenary.''

"Was. Not anymore.''

"But I'm close. Your hands are callused and that climb down the ladder didn't even get you red in the face.''

"I guess I'm still a soldier, just not in anyone's army except my own. I choose my own wars or—''

"Like this one?"

"You didn't let me finish. Or sometimes they choose me. Like this one."

Melissa Hazelhurst looked up into the big man's black eyes and noticed the scar running through his left eyebrow for the first time. Though she couldn't have said why, he frightened her at the same time as she found his presence comforting.

"Let me give this to you in a nutshell, Ms. Hazelhurst—"

"Call me Melissa, please."

"Melissa. I took the place of a certain Arab agent at a shop in San Francisco. That's where I came into possession of the map. After fending off a rather concerted attempt to remove it from my person, I flew over here and followed it to this dig."

"A concerted attempt . . . That's what you call that trail of bodies you said you left behind?"

"Everything's relative."

"What about this Arab agent? What's his role in all this?"

"He thought the map would lead him to the ultimate weapon, something that would help his people settle their scores once and for all."

Melissa's face instantly paled. "Oh my God . . ."

Blaine fixed his stare briefly on the opening in the ground ten feet away.

"Was he right, Melissa?"

She swung back toward the screen, fleeing from the answer. Blaine watched her back arch as he continued to speak.

"Keep something in mind. There's another party extremely interested in that map: the ones represented by those who tried to kill me as soon as I came into possession of it. Makes me think they've already got one of their own. Makes me think they don't want anyone else joining the party."

Melissa looked at him again. "Do you think they were the ones who killed Winchester?"

"Could be." He hesitated. "What is this place, Melissa?"

"I . . . can't tell you."

His eyes went to the monitor screen. "Show me, then. Let me see for myself."

"What's it like spending your life helping people, Mr. McCracken?"

"Blaine."

"Blaine."

McCracken had sat down on the stool with the monitor's remote control in his hand. He shrugged noncommittally.

"I think sometimes I do them more harm by trying."

Melissa tried for a smile. "Not possible this time." She eased the headphones over his ears. "We'll run the whole thing in regular motion. It's not very long."

Blaine pressed PLAY and glued his eyes to the small screen. With dusk approaching, the contrast was better, but there still wasn't much that could be made out clearly. A few times he stopped the tape and watched the portions again in slow motion. The last stretch, though, he watched frozen without expression, turning the machine off as soon as the screams were finished.

Behind him, Melissa was cringing as she lived the sights and sounds yet again.

"You saw this as it happened?" he posed.

"Yes."

"He went on even after he saw the remains of Winchester's killers at the bottom of those stairs."

"My father thought he was beyond such a thing happening to him, especially inside a dig. It was like, well, it was like his home down there."

"In the U.S. more people die at home than are murdered every year."

Melissa swallowed hard. "My father was always cautious, almost plodding. As soon as he saw the bodies, he should have come back up. I told him to, but he wouldn't listen."

"I heard."

Melissa stood at his side rigidly, staring straight ahead. McCracken angled his head to watch her.

"I'm going down there tomorrow morning," she insisted flatly. "I'm going to seal the chamber where he was killed."

"Before you know what lies beyond it?"

"That's the thing, Blaine. I *do* know what lies behind it. I didn't believe it before, but now I—"

"*Sayin* Hazelhurst!" Kamir's shout from the rim above threw a shudder through both of them. "*Sayin* Hazelhurst!"

She moved out from the canopy and looked up at him. "Yes, Kamir."

"You must come up here. Come quickly. Please!"

"Why? What is it?"

"Hurry, *Sayin* Hazelhurst. You must see for yourself."

CHAPTER 12

THE tires on all three vehicles, including McCracken's jeep, had been slashed.

"Two more of the men are missing, *Sayin* Hazelhurst," Kamir reported. "It must have been them."

Melissa looked at Blaine. "Somebody wants to keep us from leaving."

"Because they think you've seen too much," he confirmed, "and they don't want you spreading the word."

"Me? What about you?" Melissa gazed down at the shredded tires. "They could have done this because of you, then. They could have followed you here and—"

"Nope," Blaine interrupted. "Whoever did this was planted in the replacement work team your foreman hired in Izmir long before I showed up. Your father's death and my appearance on the scene just speeded things along a bit. But relax, Melissa. The plant doesn't necessarily know who I am."

"And that's supposed to help?"

"Oh yeah."

Blaine knew the enemy would come at night, when the mounded dirt and debris pulled from the nearby excavation would make for decent camouflage, and he spent the last hour until dusk preparing for it. They had seven rifles left for six men, not including himself and Melissa. McCracken let Kamir keep the only fully automatic one and watched Melissa grab the semiautomatic A-2 for herself, handling it nimbly.

"You take a firearms course back at archaeology school?"

"These days it's a required part of the curriculum," she told him. "Word spreads of an especially good find and the vultures circle. More than one team recently has been ravaged by greed."

"Wish our problems were that simple."

The rest of their arsenal was composed of M-2 carbines dating back nearly forty years. He redistributed them among the five remaining workmen and gave Kamir instructions on exactly where the men should be placed. For his own part, Blaine was more than happy with his SIG-Sauer 9mm pistol. Sixteen shots plus one in the chamber and four spare clips.

As night fell their camp stood ready. Melissa crouched next to McCracken behind a mound of earth.

"How long?" she asked him.

"Oh, not long now."

"How can you be so damn calm?"

"I was about to ask you the same question."

Her eyes sought his out. Even in the night he could see they were vacant.

"Because," Melissa started, "I don't care what happens to me tonight. I don't care about anything."

"Bad idea."

"Why?"

"Because when you don't care, you make mistakes. Other people get killed because of your indiscretions."

"And what do you care about?"

As Blaine looked her way again, both of them heard a faint rustling sound nearby.

"They're inside the camp!" Melissa rasped.

McCracken touched a finger to his lips signaling her to be quiet.

"But—"

The rustling came again. Melissa swung about trying to pinpoint the source of the noise.

"Do something!" she implored.

"I am," Blaine said, holding his gun by his side.

There was a thumping sound from very close by.

One of the workmen advanced forward with Kamir's M-16 leveled before him. Just behind him Kamir and two more figures appeared with their hands clasped over their heads, prodded forward by a pair of rifle barrels wielded by the final two workmen.

"Silahlarinizi birakin!" the workman in the front commanded.

"He says to drop your weapons," Kamir translated out of turn, and one of the workmen at his rear slammed him in the knee with his rifle in response.

"Shit," Melissa muttered, and tossed her A-2 aside.

McCracken held fast to his SIG.

The man in the middle repeated his command and the workman on his right shoved his two prisoners to the ground.

"Are you crazy?" Melissa whispered Blaine's way.

McCracken looked at Kamir. "Tell them if they drop their guns now I won't kill them."

"But—"

"Do it!"

Kamir obeyed reluctantly. The three gunmen laughed.

Blaine laughed with them, SIG held a little higher. The leader in the center came forward and aimed his carbine straight for McCracken's head. He smiled and pulled the trigger.

Nothing happened. The leader kept pressing. McCracken slid forward, and the two other gunmen tried to fire—with the same results. Blaine leveled his gun a foot away from the leader's face.

"Kamir," he said with neither his eyes nor aim wavering, "tell them to drop their guns."

Still on the ground, Kamir gave the appropriate order. The three men's weapons clacked to the earth. Blaine felt Melissa drawing up close on his right side.

"I removed the firing pins," he told her. He turned his head slightly toward Kamir. "Yours, too. Sorry about that."

"I understand, *Sayin*," the foreman said.

"You knew the ones who ran off weren't the only infiltrators," Melissa concluded.

"And the thing I had to do was flush out the rest."

"I'm impressed."

McCracken moved more forward and pressed his pistol against the leader's forehead. The man's eyes bulged in terror.

"Tell him my gun still works," Blaine instructed Kamir, who was back on his feet. "Tell him I will kill him unless he tells me how many more are out there and where."

The leader spat out his pleading reply rapidly before Kamir had even completed his translation. His hands assumed the position of prayer.

"He says death at their hands will be much worse if he talks. He says he has made his peace with Allah and is prepared to join his ancestors."

"Really? Then I guess I'll have to come up with something more creative. . . ."

He grabbed the man by the scruff of the neck and dragged him ten yards to the edge of the excavation the find was located within. Following his lead, the two workmen who had been taken prisoner did the same with the pair of remaining infiltrators. Melissa and a limping Kamir brought up the rear.

"We're going to throw you all down there and then drop you through the doorway."

Kamir translated McCracken's words, but he didn't have to. The trio of infiltrators sank to their knees, bowing to Blaine as if he were Allah.

Kamir was smiling. "I think they are ready to talk now."

"Ask them how many?"

"They say they do not know," the guide translated when the reply came. "But they think many men, easily more than a dozen."

"Where are these men?"

"Everywhere around us," Kamir translated gravely.

"How did they know when to make their move?"

Again Kamir listened, then spoke. "A brief flash of light was their signal." His voice lowered. "I did not see it."

"And how were they supposed to signal they had us?" McCracken asked in more of a rushed tone.

Kamir was halfway through the translation when the burst of bullets blazed in. Two of the infiltrators were the first to be hit by the spray, along with one of the still-loyal workmen. McCracken dove on top of Melissa and took her to the ground.

"Stay here!" he ordered her.

The third infiltrator scampered away. He stumbled and Blaine watched his spine arch when twin fusillades of bullets stitched up front and back.

They were surrounded!

Kamir had taken cover behind a stack of equipment, gun tilted around it. He aimed it into the night and pulled the trigger. It wouldn't give.

"My rifle!" he shrieked.

"The firing pin!" Blaine said, and tossed Kamir the proper one for his gun.

He had pulled Melissa behind a mound of earth and debris before grabbing the discarded rifles. In less than thirty seconds, he managed to get three of their firing pins back into place.

Nearby, the loyal workman who had not been hit had crawled to the body of the one who had. Much to Blaine's surprise, the man stirred, grimacing. He pointed to his shoulder as the origin of his wound. Weakened and incapacitated, he could still fight, at least shoot. Good. McCracken slid the trio of salvaged carbines their way and signaled them to take cover.

Blaine turned to speak to Melissa only to find her gone. He spotted her crawling in the direction of her jeep, tempting enemy bullets.

"Damn!"

He tried to go after her, but another cascade of gunfire pinned him down.

"Cover me!" he ordered Kamir.

"What?"

McCracken pointed to the front of their camp. "Most of the gunmen are approaching from there. Fire brief bursts in line with where I'm pointing. Order your men to watch either side. Tell them to fire at anything that moves that isn't us."

"Yes, *Sayin.*"

Blaine rose into a crouch.

"Now!"

He was away an instant before Kamir had fired his first burst, Melissa then in the process of reaching into her jeep's cargo compartment. He got to her just as bullets shattered the window inches over her head and sprayed both of them with glass. Again he took her forcibly to the ground. They ended up on their sides staring at each other.

"Not too bright, Melissa."

"Not as stupid as you," she shot at him, showing a pair

of neatly wrapped square packages. "You could have blown us both up."

"Plastic explosives?"

"They couldn't do us any good in the jeep."

"I'm not sure they can do us any good now."

The gunfire had reached a crescendo. It seemed to be pouring into the camp from everywhere at once. The workmen's fire with the carbines was proving ineffectual. Kamir was holding the enemy reasonably at bay from the front, but he had already changed clips once and would have to do so again before the next minute was up, leaving him with only one in reserve.

A trio of black-clad men rushed into the camp from the left. McCracken rolled out and fired five shots from the SIG their way. Their bodies had not even gone still on the ground when another two burst in behind the wounded workman and tore him apart with automatic fire. Blaine rose into a crouch to shoot them, a pair of bullets for each.

"Jesus," Melissa moaned, "how many of them *are* there?"

"Too many for us to get, and they don't seem to be in a negotiating mood."

A fresh burst ricocheted just over their heads.

"If it's the find they want, they can have it!"

"Sorry, Melissa. It's us. They want to make sure no one ever learns what you uncovered here."

"How can you know that?"

"Logic. Just like I know since we can't outfight them, we've got to get out."

"They've got us surrounded!"

McCracken looked her square in the eyes. "Then we get out without leaving."

"There?" Melissa posed fearfully with her gaze moving to the excavation just ahead of McCracken's.

"It's the only chance we've got right now."

"No! You don't under—"

A scream sounded from the center of the camp, and they

ooked through the night to see the second workman writhing
on the ground, holding his midsection. His hands locked
over the gaping wounds, and he shuddered one last time
before death took him.

"Come on!" Blaine ordered.

Before Melissa could protest, he grabbed her arm and
yanked her forward. A gunman charged them from the side,
firing, and McCracken shot him in the head. Another rushed
from the opposite angle and Blaine pumped a trio of rounds
his way. They reached Kamir as he was jamming a fresh clip
home into his M-16.

"Let's go!" McCracken screamed over his return fire,
grasping him.

"Go *where*, *Sayin*?"

"The excavation!"

"But—"

McCracken grabbed the M-16 from his hand. "Hurry!
They're hesitating!"

Blaine shoved Kamir behind him and let Melissa lead the
way toward the excavation. M-16 in one hand and SIG in the
other, he fired nonstop in an arc before him. He estimated
that more than half of the attacking team had already perished for their efforts. The remainder of the opposition were
choosing their way cautiously now. They could afford to do
so, since they believed that they had their targets hopelessly
pinned down, leaving them with no reason to rush.

Melissa clutched the two tightly wrapped packets of plastic
explosives to her, as she nimbly descended the rope ladder
with Kamir just above her. She unshouldered her semiautomatic rifle and handed it to him when they reached the bottom.

"Hurry!" she yelled up to McCracken, who had just
clambered over the rim of the pit.

Blaine took the rungs so fast that he seemed to be sliding
down rather than climbing. At the bottom he emptied the last
of the M-16's second clip into the top of the dangling rope
ladder. All twenty feet of it dropped downward. Any pursuit

that came now would have to come in a straight twenty-foot drop. He grabbed the severed ladder and brought it with him to the opening of the find. Melissa dropped the bulk of it down inside and wedged the topmost part beneath the unearthed stone tablet to hold it in place.

"You can't go down there!" Kamir pleaded.

"No other choice I can see, and you're coming with us."

As Kamir started to protest, a bullet thumped into his thigh and he pitched sideways with a grunt. Another slammed him in the chest and spilled him to the ground. The gunman had dropped downward at the edge of the rim for his next shots, but Blaine found him in his sights before the man could get another round off. Two more bullets from the SIG caught him in the head. McCracken snapped a fresh clip home.

Melissa was kneeling next to Kamir. His breathing sounded wet. Saliva slipped through his mouth, stained with blood.

"It is better this way," he managed.

"We'll carry you," Melissa insisted.

"No." He looked at Blaine. "The rifle, hand it to me." And, as McCracken placed the M-16 in his trembling grip with the final clip loaded, "I will cover you."

McCracken nodded and placed the ejected clip from Melissa's semiautomatic A-2 next to him. Melissa touched the dying man's shoulder.

"Thank you, Kamir."

"You are brave like your father, *Sayin* Hazelhurst. Go now. And may God be with you."

"Too much to ask for, I'm afraid."

Shapes darted about the rim, bullets fired wildly down into the pit. Kamir fired a token burst their way. McCracken eased Melissa ahead of him onto the ladder.

"The explosives," he said, gazing one last time at Kamir before he started down after her.

"I have the packs."

"We'll need them."

"For wh—" And then she realized his intention. "No, we can't!"

"We have to. If we don't blow the entrance after us, they'll follow us down. We'll be right back where we started, worse even."

"We'll be trapped!"

"One step at a time, Melly."

"Listen to me!"

Gunfire silenced her as she hit bottom with McCracken a second behind. The chamber's near-total darkness lasted only as long as it took Melissa to switch on the pair of powerful flashlights she had tucked in her vest.

"Give me the explosives!"

Melissa obliged reluctantly, her face a white oval in the utter darkness of the chamber.

The Dream Dragons, she thought. *That's what I'm going to find down here. That's what I'm finally going to have to face. . . .*

"God help us . . ."

"That was the same tone Kamir used," McCracken realized. "What gives? What is this place?"

"An entrance."

"An entrance to what?"

The flashlights parted the darkness enough for him to see the terror in Melissa Hazelhurst's expression.

"Hell," she said.

CHAPTER 13

"**D**ID you say *hell*?" McCracken asked, dumbstruck. Melissa tried to turn away and he grabbed her arm. "*That's* what all this secrecy is about? *That's* the great find your father spent all these years searching for?"

"You don't believe. I didn't, either. I . . . didn't want to."

Above them, Kamir's bullets continued to echo, certain not to last for much longer.

"We don't have much choice, in any event," Blaine said, unwrapping her packages of plastic explosives.

"You're still going to seal the entrance?"

"We let them come down here after us, we're dead. You wanna choose?"

"There's got to be *something*!"

"Right. I'm holding it."

McCracken had the first packet open now. The explosive looked like a chunk of khaki-colored clay. The detonator was wrapped in plastic alongside.

"Nice equipment. My compliments. Transistorized detonator would suit our needs better, though."

"Is that a problem?"

"Depends on how long it takes you to locate that secret passage out of here your father found."

112

Melissa's eyes swept the darkness around the chamber. "It must have closed after we pulled . . . him up. Damn!"

"How long?"

She thought fast. "A minute! I'll need a minute."

McCracken wedged the detonator into the first mound of *plastique* and set it to *1:00*. "That's all you're gonna get."

He repeated the process with the second mound and wedged both of them against the front wall, making sure the opening above was centered between the two packets of explosives. The blast would blow the walls outward in a way that would ensure that the entire ceiling would collapse, filling this chamber with tons of rubble.

Kamir's protective gunfire, meanwhile, had ceased. The enemy would be on its way down into the excavation above soon, if they weren't already. McCracken activated the first detonator and the second right after it.

:59, :58, :57 . . .

"Oh, Melly, the clock's ticking and we're gonna take quite a licking if you don't find that doorway."

She was feeling with her hands about the same area where her father had been standing right before he found the hidden door, fighting to recall what little the tape had shown her.

:40, :39, :38 . . .

McCracken was at her side now, pistol aimed upward, ready to fire at any shape that showed itself. At last she found something that felt like a handhold and pressed. With almost no effort at all, a large portion of the massive wall receded outward with a grinding sound. She aimed her flashlight down and saw the staircase her father had died on. She looked back at Blaine.

:26, :25, :24 . . .

He nodded, and she stepped through the threshold onto a small plateau at the top of the stairs. McCracken stopped just behind her and started to work the door closed again.

"Why bother?"

"So no unfriendly boulders follow us down here. Blast

percussion alone could shatter the foundation of these steps, if we leave an airway.''

It took almost no effort at all to ease the door back into the wall until the seal was tight.

:08, :07, :06 . . .

McCracken pressed Melissa against the wall and shielded her with his frame an instant before the explosion sounded.

Melissa had been around many blasts in her life from the time she was a child, but never anything like this. It felt as though she were on the inside instead of the outside, and the whole of her innards rumbled and shook with the debris caving inward in the chamber beyond. She pressed herself closer against McCracken. She couldn't catch her breath. The world was shaking around her. Then there was silence, utter and empty.

She felt Blaine McCracken ease her slowly away from him.

''Only one way to go now,'' he said.

And together they gazed down the steep steps into a black abyss.

''How many steps down was your father when . . .''

''Forty.''

''You're sure? It's important.''

''I counted from the tape.''

The stairs were just over four feet wide. The walls on either side of them stretched upward into the darkness; the effect created that of a tunnel funneling down. McCracken started to descend, flashlight carving a slim pathway of light from the darkness. The air was cold and . . . empty. Yes, he thought, that was it. Not damp or musty or dry—just empty.

Blaine took the steps carefully, testing what lay ahead of him the way a man on a tightrope might. His own silent count was approaching the thirty mark, when he heard Melissa gasp.

''Easy,'' he soothed, as his flashlight joined hers on the bottom of the staircase.

The beams captured the bloody residue of what might have been Benson Hazelhurst.

Melissa had drawn to within a single step of McCracken. "It happened ten more steps down. That's where my father was killed."

Blaine drew his flashlight slowly along the remaining twenty stairs lying between them and the bottom.

"Back up," he told Melissa.

She didn't question him this time. McCracken retreated upward a few steps, staying in front of her. His hand rubbed against either wall the whole time, feeling for any sort of change in their surfaces. He had retraced a dozen steps when he stopped and took his hand from the wall.

"We'll be safe now," he said without further explanation.

"What? What are you talking about? We can't get out this way. You said so yourself."

"That's not why we're climbing up."

"I don't understand."

Blaine leaned over and felt about the steps.

"What are you looking for?" Melissa asked him.

"A decent-sized chunk of stone or rock."

"What for?"

"I want to test something out."

"Let me see what I can do."

She pulled a hammer and chisel from her shoulder pack and chopped away at a section of the wall. A fragment the size and shape of a wide shoe came free in her hands, and she gave it to McCracken.

"You said your father took ten more steps," he said, gazing downward.

"Yes, from where you *were* standing. Not anymore."

Blaine aimed the flashlight that way. "Okay." He counted the steps out in his mind, then gave his flashlight to Melissa. "Aim both beams straight down," he said, adjusting her hands. "Right there."

He stood in the center of the step, the fragment of the wall held in both hands. He tested its weight and then measured

off an underhand toss. Melissa watched it float out of his
hands and impact on the same step Benson Hazelhurst had
reached when his screams began.

Suddenly huge segments of both walls slammed inward
toward each other, starting six steps down from them and
continuing all the way to the bottom of the staircase. It happened so fast that it took an extra second for Melissa to see
the gray steel spikes that had popped out in evenly spaced
rows along both walls.

The deadly steel teeth glimpsed in the recording, she realized. Once again the Dream Dragons had proven not to be
real. But the nightmare continued.

The walls closed together, with the length of the spikes
the only distance left between them. Then they began to churn
sideways, working against each other.

Melissa thought of her father trapped between them and
felt consciousness briefly sliding away.

The spikes had been fitted on each wall symmetrically to
create gaps that merged when the walls melded. The pressure
exerted was incredible. Anything caught between them . . .

"My father," she said over the ear-wrenching grinding
sounds beneath her, picturing him impaled by the spikes and
then torn apart. She shuddered. A lump rose into her throat
and choked her breath.

"You okay, Melly?"

"The others, too," she managed faintly.

"And not a monster in sight."

Suddenly the spikes receded into their hidden slots and the
movable walls slid back into place. Impossible to tell where
the deadly sections began and ended.

"You knew," she said suddenly.

"The walls felt different after a certain point. Chalkier,
not as cold." His expression softened. "And I had the advantage of viewing the tape of your father a lot less emotion-
ally."

"We're still trapped."

"I don't think so."

"You don't *what*?"

"Where are your archaeological eyes, Melly? Grooves were cut in those walls to match up with the steps. Accordingly, a gap was left on the bottom where there were no spikes."

"So?"

"So that's how we're going to get through. Like this," McCracken said, lowering himself onto his stomach. His body was suspended across four different steps like a snake's.

"The walls will crush us."

"No. Even if the trap springs, we can make it. It'll be a tight squeeze, but we can still make it. And if we avoid putting any pressure on the trigger points, the walls might not be activated at all."

She tried to smile. "You do this kind of thing every day?"

"Every other."

McCracken squeezed her shoulder and dropped once more to his stomach, single flashlight in hand. The flatter he made himself, the more evenly his weight would be distributed, thereby increasing his chances of not tripping the trap. He slid down to the last step reached on his original descent and gazed back at Melissa. She had lowered herself just as he had.

"Grab my ankles now and hold on. Let me pull you. Don't raise your head, and keep your eyes closed."

McCracken started on again, feeling her dead weight tugging behind him, thumping down the steps in his wake. He pulled himself across the last step Benson Hazelhurst had touched, especially wary now. If his assumptions were correct, pressure on any of the steps remaining to the bottom would activate the deadly spiked walls. The movable walls extended several steps higher to ensure that entire parties would be caught in the trap once the member most advanced had sprung it. That accounted for the bodies of Winchester's killers all lying at the bottom.

Blaine's torso crossed over the death-promising steps effortlessly, finding a rhythm.

It was working! It *would* work!

Blaine's hands probed ahead, easing his slithering descent. He could hear Melissa's soft moans behind him, could feel her hands latch around his ankles. The next moment he sensed her fingers had slipped off, and she lost her grip on one of his legs. She began flailing around, searching to regain her hold.

"No!" he started. *"No!"*

It was too late. In struggling to regain her grip, Melissa had dropped the entire weight of her shoulders on one of the deadly steps. The spikes snapped outward once more in the next instant, as the walls slammed toward each other. Blaine felt them stop with barely an inch to spare above him. Then the grinding began. *Back and forth, back and forth, back and forth . . .*

"Stay down!" he yelled up at Melissa, never sure if she heard him.

The spikes scraped at the top of his clothes. He could feel them flirting with his hair. Above him Melissa was screaming. Blaine tried to push himself backward toward her, probe out with his feet and hope that she retained enough reason to grab on to his ankles once more.

"Come on, Melly," he said, knowing she couldn't hear him. "You can do it. You can do it. . . ."

McCracken got one of his legs too high and a pair of spikes sliced through his flesh. He grimaced, but kept pushing his feet backward until he struck something.

"Grab hold, Melly!" he yelled above the awful grinding. "Do you hear me? Grab hold!"

It took another second, but she latched on even tighter than before. Then he started his downward motion again. Before him, his flashlight illuminated the spikes gnawing the air. He had the sensation he was trapped in the mouth of some great beast, fighting to avoid its teeth.

At last his hands touched a hard stone floor at the foot of the stairway. He dropped the flashlight and the beam swirled to one side, catching more mutilated remains in its spill.

McCracken continued to squirm along the floor and felt his hands swishing through the blood and gore the deadly trap had discarded down here yesterday. He steeled his mind against the stench and focused on Melissa's hands still locked on his ankles. He was safe, but she was anything but.

Blaine angled to the right and kept pulling. He was able to gaze back now and saw her stiff form thudding down the last of the steps, only her booted feet and ankles still beneath the grinding spikes. She cleared the final step too dazed to know she was safe. Her hands still held his ankles in a desperate grip. Her eyes were squeezed tightly shut. Blaine turned onto his back and sat up.

"It's over," he said, loosening her hold on his legs. "We made it."

She opened her eyes and looked up at him with a blank stare. He gently lifted her to a sitting position and cupped her chin in his hands.

"Are you okay?"

Still rigid, she pulled herself to her knees and then stood up. Behind them, the spikes snapped back into their slots and the walls receded.

"I . . . think so."

Blaine wrapped an arm around her shoulder and eased her away from the carnage. He stopped to retrieve the flashlight he had dropped and aimed the beam down the corridor to the left. The corridor sloped downward, but beyond that, the light showed nothing. It could have gone on forever or ended a hundred feet away.

"You're hurt," Melissa realized, seeing the blood seeping through his torn pants leg. "Let me have a look at that."

She leaned over and inspected the gash. "I'll need to dress and bandage this. Sit down."

Blaine did so gingerly, as Melissa pulled a first-aid kit from a large pouch in her vest. McCracken was astonished.

"What else do you keep up your sleeve, or should I say vest, Melly?"

She ignored his attempt at humor. "You don't believe it,

do you?'' she asked him, and started to clean the wound with
alcohol-soaked cotton. ''You don't believe we're standing
very near to the entrance to hell.''

''I've seen hell plenty of times, Melly, and it's got nothing
to do with secret underground passages.''

''Oh, but it does,'' she continued, starting on the bandage
and dressing now. ''You see, centuries before Christ was
even born, our ancestors had no knowledge of a fallen angel
named Lucifer. Instead they believed in the concept of two
equal gods, one good and the other evil. Ancient writings
tell of a vast underground temple where the evil god made
his headquarters. The concept of it is nothing new. Archaeological dig teams have been searching for centuries in the
valley between the Tigris and Euphrates rivers in Iraq.''

''But we're in Turkey now.''

''Yes. And that explains why it was never found until Hitler sent teams scouring the entire world for mythical artifacts.
Several of those teams were responsible for the maps that fell
into my father's possession. But only one of them found what
Hitler was most resolutely looking for.''

McCracken climbed back to his feet. ''Let's get going.''

Their flashlights chewed through the darkness to reveal a
well-finished corridor with a dirt floor and plenty of head-
room. But two hundred yards down from the foot of the
deadly stairs, a wall rose up before them to block their path.

''Maybe we took a wrong turn somewhere,'' McCracken
said.

''Wait a minute,'' Melissa said softly.

She moved to the wall on the corridor's right-hand side,
adjacent to its apparent finish. She felt about it with both
hands, searching for a switch or trigger similar to the one her
father had discovered in the entry chamber.

''Shine your flashlight over here.''

McCracken obliged and watched her rubbing and wiping
with a cloth grabbed from her pack. A brush came out next,
along with a small precision scraping tool. She gave Blaine
her flashlight to hold as well and went to work.

"What is it?" he asked, as the shape of something was being revealed beneath her work.

"Another doorway."

"Any knob there you plan on cleaning off?"

"There's writing on this door, instructions for how to open it."

Her work continued for several more minutes, Blaine powerless to do anything but hold the lights and aim them in the direction she pointed. He saw the shapes and outlines of ancient letters and symbols.

"I've got it!" she pronounced triumphantly.

"The missing key?"

"Just as good. The instructions on how to obtain entry are very explicit. See these up here?"

McCracken shone the light in the direction Melissa was pointing to just over her head. He could see *something*, though nothing that made any sense to him.

"I think so," he said anyway.

"According to what I'm reading, this is the first of five stages. There should be . . ." Melissa stretched her hand upward, probing about the bulges and finely chiseled shapes. "Yes! Here it is!"

Blaine watched her move what must have been some sort of lever down from the vertical to the horizontal position. It locked with a click. Melissa read on, tracing the ancient instructions with her fingers, wiping and blowing long-collected debris out of her way. This time she placed her palm against what looked like a fist-sized circle on the doorway's right side. The circle receded behind her push and disappeared into the door.

Melissa traced down and quite a bit to the left, where she needed both her hands to twist a pair of arrows so that their points were crossed. Again the click was distinctive. Another few feet lower she found purchase on the underside of a raised L-shaped fragment and removed it from the wall. Probing farther down the right, she located the slot tailored for it. It slid in as neatly as a key into a lock. Still following the instructions, Melissa turned it.

Click.

"One more to go," she said, crouching down now as she read on with her fingers and eyes. "This one's the most complicated. I've got to turn two of these symbols—here and here, I think—at the same time. Let's see . . ."

Blaine watched her hands feeling for the proper grip.

"That's got it. Okay, here we—"

McCracken tensed in that instant and threw himself into motion just before the dual clicks sounded together.

"—go."

He grabbed Melissa by the shoulders and yanked her sideways a millisecond before the huge door rocketed forward. It slammed into the wall directly before it. Fragments blew off and fell to the ground. The entire world seemed to shake. Then the door snapped backward into its slot as quickly as it had shot out.

Melissa clung to Blaine. "How—how did you know?"

"The five stages. There was no reason to be so specific about the amount, unless there was a sixth one only those who knew what to look for could find, after they skipped number five."

"Down here," she said, after crouching to better view the lowermost section of the door. "This must be the sixth instruction."

Melissa read on, tracing the outline of the characters with her fingers. A few times she whisked dust and debris away with her brush to clear the way for her flashlight.

"Simplest of all," she told Blaine, and twisted a square raised fragment on the door to the left. Instantly the door began to open toward them with a slight grating sound as its bottom rubbed against the ground.

Melissa rose to her feet. A flood of cold, dank air surged outward, enveloping both her and Blaine. She grasped his arm involuntarily. He had his flashlight on and aimed through the widening space.

At last the door stopped moving. McCracken handed Melissa back her flashlight and eased tentatively forward. Their beams swept before them, illuminating shapes in the darkness ahead. Blaine's eyes narrowed, squinted.

"My God," Melissa said.

CHAPTER 14

THE chamber was a massive cavern that seemed to stretch endlessly in every direction. A huge array of crates, wooden boxes of varying sizes, and steel drums lay directly before Blaine and Melissa. Beyond these were barrels that looked like beer kegs and black ten-gallon cans. Most of the containers were unmarked, but a few had faded writing on them in German. There were also symbols, one predominant, on some of the wooden crates: a swastika.

"The Third Reich," Blaine said, following Melissa's eyes to it.

She turned and looked at him. "What is this place?"

"A storage chamber, Melly. The Nazis must have made it farther than you thought and then proceeded to appropriate this chamber for their own use almost a half-century ago."

"Then all this . . ."

"Weapons, unless I miss my guess. And I don't plan on opening any box to find out."

He had heard all the stories about the undiscovered reserves of the Nazi war machine. Until now, though, he had totally discounted them as paranoid rhetoric. The Nazis had this, the Nazis had that. They were close to developing this, they were close to developing that . . . Then the war had ended and little of it had ever been found.

Because they had brought much of their stockpile here and left it for safekeeping.

The floor was arranged in the neat precision that any ordnance or records officer would be proud of. No wasted space. Everything had been neatly catalogued and arranged in this cavern to await the rebirth of another Reich.

"All this must have been stored in the war's waning days by the cadre of officers who had long given up on Hitler," McCracken explained. "It must have been his maps that directed them here, but they didn't come looking for hell: they came looking for a place to hide the best of their arsenal."

McCracken stopped when his flashlight beam illuminated a large vacant area of the floor, the only empty space of that scope in the entire chamber.

"And it looks like part of it is missing," he continued, as he moved in that direction.

The space in question was thirty feet square. He knelt down and examined the ground.

"Crates of some kind, it looks like. Can't tell how many or when they were moved."

Melissa approached him slowly. "You're saying somebody came down here and removed something the Nazis had stored for their own future use."

"And whatever it is, we've got to figure it's the pick of the litter," Blaine added, thinking of all the rumors surrounding the massive unfinished arsenal of the Nazi war machine.

Melissa walked about the perimeter of the vacant area. Several times she knelt to smooth the hard-packed dirt floor with her hand.

"There's something else," she said finally. "I think the crates that were stored here were removed in two separate shifts years, even decades, apart. Watch."

She placed her flashlight on the floor. Its beam cut through the darkness, hugging the ground.

"See," Melissa said, still kneeling.

"See what?"

Her finger guided his eyes. "Follow the beam and you can tell that the back section of where the crates were has a shallower depression than the front."

Blaine steadied his eyes. Melissa was right. The difference was slight enough to be almost nonexistent, but it was undeniably there, occupying perhaps a fifth of the total area.

"Shallower," Melissa continued, "because that set of crates didn't have nearly as much time to settle as the rest. The others remained here far longer."

"Until very recently, perhaps?"

"Almost certainly. Why?"

"It fits, that's all. Whoever dispatched that hit team in San Francisco wanted to make sure no one else found this place, because they must have found it first."

"We know they didn't get the missing crates out the way we got in," Melissa surmised, realizing that their discovery meant there had to be another way out, after all.

"For sure, Melly. But how did they?"

The helicopter hovered over the site of the find. The directions had been precise, and the pilot had had no trouble in locating it. The man in the front section of the American Bell JetRanger turned behind him to the lone passenger in the rear.

"We're too late," he said in German into his headset.

Beneath them, the chopper's floodlight illuminated a depression in the ground, like a sinkhole that had collapsed in on itself.

"Maybe not," the second man muttered, following his gaze downward.

"What do you mean?"

"The entrance was destroyed by a blast from the inside out."

"You're saying he could still be down there? You're saying he could still be alive?" The man in the rear stole another gaze downward. "Impossible!"

"We know who we are dealing with here. *Anything* is possible."

"For our sake, for our survival, we must hope so." He paused. "What do we do now?"

The man in the front twisted his shoulder so he was facing the JetRanger's rear. "The only thing we can do: keep looking."

"Blaine," Melissa called to him, after they had been searching for ten minutes.

"On my way," he said, the sweep of his flashlight advancing ahead of him.

She was standing not far from the area where the crates had been stored.

"Look at this," she said, holding something out to him.

"A notebook," McCracken realized, as he drew closer. "Handwritten in German."

"Think it has anything to do with our missing crates?"

"Maybe. I found it under some dirt in the same general area. Hasn't weathered the years well, I'm afraid. Paper's dried out and warped. Ink's gone. Not salvageable, least not all of it."

"What about some?"

"With the proper equipment, it's possible," she said, sliding the notebook into her pack. "That is, if we ever find the way out of here."

"I've got faith in you, Melly."

They moved off again in separate directions to check for hidden openings, doors, or hatchways. The chamber was so large that adequate inspection of the walls could be achieved only from very close up, especially given the limitations of their flashlights. They felt about and tapped the walls, hoping for the telltale hollow sound of a passageway beyond.

The minutes stretched on, with no results. Melissa had

abandoned her check of the walls and had moved back toward the area where the crates had been removed from. A pair of tarpaulins partially covered a neat stack of coffin-sized crates, and she pushed against one.

An entire row slid backward behind the pressure.

"Blaine!" she called. "These crates are empty," she continued when he rushed over. "A facade."

"To cover a passageway?"

"Let's find out."

Melissa joined McCracken in hoisting the empty crates aside. Beneath them the ground resembled the dirt floor covering the rest of the chamber. Melissa bent down and scooped away a portion with her trowel.

"There's something solid underneath this!" she reported excitedly. "Made of wood, I think!"

Fully exposed, the secret hatch was fifteen feet square, easily large enough to allow all the materials they had found to be raised or lowered through it. McCracken found handholds in all four corners. The hatch didn't seem to be hinged; it was simply set in place over the opening to be lifted off or pushed upward by a team of workers.

With only himself and Melissa to hoist the hatch, though, the weight of it seemed dead and immobile. They gave up trying to lift and attempted to drag it off instead. The hatch resisted, gave slowly at first, and then receded behind their determined pull. Leaning over the side, both shone their flashlights downward. Dull, dirt-encased steel shimmered slightly back at them from a drop of about twelve feet.

"Some kind of hydraulic platform," McCracken said to Melissa. "That's how the Nazis got everything up here."

"Through a passageway that must originate back at the surface," she followed hopefully.

McCracken used one of the discarded tarpaulins to lower Melissa down and then rested a steel keg atop the tarp's edge so he could lower himself after her. At the bottom he had the feeling he was looking upward from his own grave, waiting for the diggers to begin tossing the dirt upon him. The high-

ceilinged corridor that led away from the platform was wide
and curving.

"Let's go," Melissa said, taking the lead.

A hundred feet along, the floor suddenly grew uneven,
layered with mounds. The walls and ceiling were lined with
fissures and cracks. McCracken drew ahead of Melissa, while
she hung back to make a closer inspection.

"This looks like the result of an explosion. Normal wear
and tear could never—"

"Wait till you see this," Blaine interrupted, standing dead
still just around the next bank in the corridor.

Melissa drew up even and shone her flashlight ahead. Before them the corridor seemed to have collapsed on itself.
The passage was blocked.

"Oh, no," she muttered.

"And we've got company."

"What?"

"Over there on the right."

She turned her light that way and saw three long-dead
shapes with their backs resting against the remnants of the
wall. She moved toward them just behind Blaine. The dead,
dry air of this underground chamber had mummified the
corpses, which had a thick layer of flesh, like tanned leather,
hardened over them. Their clothes draped over their remains
in tatters. Bulging teeth and shrunken lips made it seem as
though they were smiling. Their eyes were dry-rotted
spheres. McCracken knelt down and inspected an old Mau-
ser pistol lying near one of the corpses. Something upon the
corpse's wrist caught his eye, and he shone his flashlight
directly against it.

"Then the Nazis blew up their own escape route," Melissa concluded in exasperation. "It makes no sense!"

"Even less than you think, Melly," Blaine said, looking
her way. "These aren't Nazis, they're Jews."

McCracken showed her the withered etchings that looked
as if they were embroidered onto the mummified wrists. The

numbers were no longer intelligible, but the size and location of the mark made for sufficient indication by themselves.

"Auschwitz," Melissa realized.

"Or a reasonable facsimile."

"Slave labor left here to die?"

"Not exactly. All three were killed with bullets to the head," Blaine said, after completing his inspection of the other two bodies.

"Killed by the one the pistol was next to, who then took his own life. Is that it?"

"Apparently. But not before they blew up the tunnel to make sure nobody else could ever retrace their steps."

"Except somebody did."

"How long would you say these corpses have been here?"

"Between forty and forty-five years."

"The end of World War II, then. And you said the crates in the cavern were removed in two shifts, *decades* apart."

"There's got to be another route!" Melissa finished, hope returning to her voice. "Let's start looking."

Melissa returned to the vast storage chamber and focused her mind on the construction of the cavern about her. The Nazis could not possibly have built this chamber. They simply made good use of something they had discovered, something that fit their needs perfectly. Melissa forced her mind to focus on her father's research, on some of his final words, spoken just in passing, deemed unimportant at the time . . .

What were they?

Egyptian! That was it! He had said that the construction reminded him of the pyramids, and the dating bore him out. Successive generations normally build new edifices squarely atop the previous foundations. Logically, there should be a chamber built above the exact center of this one. By pacing off the dimensions of the chamber she was able to pinpoint that spot.

"Up there," Melissa gestured.

Blaine shone his fast-fading flashlight upward to follow her hand. "I don't see anything."

"There's an exit up there, I'm sure of it, but it's been covered up. If not by the original builders, then by the Nazis." She stopped for a moment. "The trick right now is climbing up."

"Leave that to me."

Actually, they did the work together. Melissa dragged over a collection of the crates used to camouflage the large hatchway. Though empty, they were still plenty firm enough to support the weight of a person. McCracken stacked the crates to create a pyramidal stairway rising up to the ceiling forty feet up. Then, once atop the highest crates, he and Melissa were able to stretch their arms above their heads, searching for indications of a hatch or door.

"Got it!" Melissa told Blaine.

She clawed away at the dirt and debris affixed to the underside of a fold-down hatch. Blaine watched her locate the handhold and yank. The hatch popped downward.

Melissa first hoisted herself upward and then lent Blaine a hand. The chamber they had uncovered this time was circular in design, with a fifteen-foot ceiling. A single corridor led from the room, and Melissa took the lead into this passageway. It made sense that it would bring them back to the surface, since whoever had removed the second batch of the missing crates must have used this same passage. Their only fear, an unspoken one, was that this person or persons might have blown up that exit, too, after it had served its purpose.

When they were not far along the passageway, their last remaining flashlight flickered and died. The darkness around them became total.

"Melly," Blaine called softly.

"Take my hand."

"Keep talking. Where— Wait a minute, got it. At least I hope it's yours."

But he wasn't able to hold it for long. The height of the corridor dropped considerably, and they were forced to crouch their way along the slightly uphill grade. McCracken took this as a sign that they were heading back to the surface.

That hope made the darkness and claustrophobic feeling tolerable, and before long he fell into an uneasy rhythm.

"Can you smell it?" Melissa said all of a sudden. "Can you smell it, Blaine?"

At first he could smell nothing besides what the ancient earth gave up. Then a whiff of freshness entered his nostrils. Air! Wonderful, glorious air bled from the open sky! Air coming from not too far ahead.

"Greatest scent in the world," he told her.

The cramped passageway hit a steep grade at the last, and they emerged through a wide fissure camouflaged by underbrush into a dry riverbed.

"Any idea where we are?" Blaine asked Melissa, after she had helped him through.

"I think so."

"Good."

"Not really. We're twenty-five miles from civilization, and that means—"

Wop—wop—wop—wop . . .

Melissa's eyes followed the sound to the sky. A floodlight pierced the darkness, streaming toward them. The helicopter hovered for a brief moment, then continued on. Her first instinct was to rise up and signal it for help. But McCracken grabbed hold of her and took her down to the hard-packed earth of the dry riverbed's bank behind the meager cover of a nest of bushes.

"Stay low. Don't move," he told her.

The chopper sped closer. Its floodlight reached for them in the night.

"But who—"

"Don't speak!" McCracken ordered. The light came closer.

"Our fuel is low," the man in the JetRanger's front reported. "We should head back."

The passenger frowned. "We must fear the worst."

"No. Trust me."

"With our destiny? That is what it comes down to now, that and nothing else."

"It can still be salvaged."

"Not without help. Everything we have worked for hangs in the balance. Years, generations. We were so close. And now . . ."

"We will find it."

"How?"

"Leave it to me."

The guard at the gate, shotgun strapped to his shoulder, had been expecting Billy Griggs and waved him straight through. The black wrought-iron fence surrounding the estate was ten feet high. The individual bars were finished with arrowheadlike tops, and Billy had heard it said that the Twins sharpened one for every kill they successfully completed.

Probably not many left dull at this point.

The big house itself was hidden from sight beyond the gate, visible only once a visitor got fifty yards down the curved entry road. It was palatial in all respects, Victorian in design and color. The shade was a subtle mauve, the angles on the house gentle and curved. Billy parked his car and climbed the marble steps, where another pair of guards stood attentively.

"They're waiting for you," one said, "by the pool. Straight through the foyer to the house's rear."

Billy nodded and entered the mansion. The dozen guards on the property were not there to protect the Twins. No.

They were here to discourage them from leaving until their services were required.

The house was dark, and Billy proceeded through the foyer, which was like a luxury hotel's lobby, to the house's rear. There was a sunroom filled with plants beneath a roof of glass. Battling the plants for space was an incredible array of weightlifting equipment, everything shiny chrome. A bar loaded atop a bench press had been packed with just under four hundred pounds. The unused plates were stacked neatly, meticulously, upon steel-pegged weight trees. There were several more modern muscle-building machines as well, a few that Billy had never seen before. The entire rear wall was glass, and Billy could see the pool beyond it. One of the sunroom's set of sliding glass doors had been left open. Billy stepped through them.

The Twins were lying side by side on the baked asphalt surrounding the pool, no towels beneath them. The pool was crystal blue, and the water ruffled in the stiff breeze. Beyond them, at the far side of the pool, lay more weightlifting equipment, spillover from the cluttered sunroom. Billy advanced tentatively to within ten yards of the Twins and then stood there, waiting. In normal circumstances the sight of two men lying there with massive chests and arms, abdominals layered like washboards, would have aroused him. But these were the Twins.

Suddenly they rose to their feet together, motions easy and deliberate. They stood side by side, huge V-shaped upper bodies blocking the view of most of the weightlifting equipment behind them.

"Hello, Billy," they said in perfect unison, lips mirroring each other's.

"Did you know I was coming?"

"We were told to expect you," one said.

"What have you brought us?" the other followed immediately.

"A difficult assignment."

"No assignment is difficult," they said together, the harmony unnerving.

"Challenging, then."

"We'll be the judge of that."

"Blaine McCracken."

The Twins looked at each other. Their chest muscles rippled and danced. It was the most emotion Billy had ever heard of them showing.

"I have his file with me," Billy told them.

"We don't need it."

Again the Twins looked at each other. Then they smiled: together, as with everything else.

"Just tell us where we can find him."

PART THREE

Izmir

Israel: Thursday, nine A.M.

CHAPTER 15

ARNOLD Rothstein was happiest when he was in Israel. Though German by birth and American by choice, he considered the Jewish state his true homeland, a fact demonstrated by his donations of upward of a hundred million dollars to the various causes supporting her. Add to this the additional sums he had helped raise, and the total was much closer to one billion.

As one of the richest men in the world, no portion of it was untouched by his influence. He had made his original fortune in diamonds and later in oil, but now he owned a major Hollywood studio, a New York publishing house, a magazine distributorship, and a convenience-store chain, just to name a few. He had been likened to such tycoons as William Randolph Hearst, Rupert Murdoch, and the Rothschilds. At the age of sixty-five, life had never seemed more vital to him. There had never been more to do.

The only thing he truly hated about his success was the privacy it denied him. He could seldom go anywhere without being accompanied by an entourage or being accosted somewhere en route. Only in Israel could he come and go as he pleased. Only in Israel did he feel truly at home.

Especially at the kibbutz known as Nineteen.

Here he was treated like everyone else. Here people passed

by without taking special notice. The women greeted him respectfully and went about their chores. Occasionally the children would follow along for a while, growing tired at the lack of excitement. Most of the time they wouldn't. He passed the tank memorial inside the entrance and thought of similar vehicles he had driven in wars from different ages.

"She's been waiting for you," the female leader of Nineteen told him, as she led Rothstein toward the private home set apart from the rest. "She barely slept last night and won't tell us what's wrong."

Rothstein found the old woman seated behind her wrought-iron table. A shawl covered her shoulders to guard her from the early morning cold. The sight of her made Rothstein's heart sink. He wondered about himself, still fit and trim, thanks to making time for exercise. Sixty-five years old and he could still run three miles in a half hour. But would the mirror soon be betraying him as well?

How old she had gotten . . . How helpless she looked . . .

Had she been this bad the last time he had visited? Had her hands been so frail and bony, her wrists swollen with the disfigurement of arthritis? Even from this distance Rothstein could see how rapidly she was breathing. He steeled himself and approached her.

"You're late as always, Ari."

He had leaned over to kiss her lightly on the cheek but stopped at the mention of his real name.

"What's wrong?" she asked him.

"You know no one else calls me that except you. Everytime I hear it . . ."

"Do you wish to forget?"

"Of course not! You know I don't!"

"Then remember, Ari. You must remember, especially now."

"You think I forget, Tovah? Did I not build this place for you? Did I not have the best engineers in the world upgrade your water and irrigation system just six months ago?"

"I wasn't talking about that."

The old woman grasped a set of press clippings from her lap and raised them toward him. It was all she could do to hold them. And yet when Arnold Rothstein took them, the first thing he noticed was how carefully and perfectly the articles had been trimmed from their newspaper pages.

But his eyes scorned her. "You promised me you would stop."

"It's a good thing I didn't. Read them. You'll see."

Rothstein started the first one while standing. By the third he was slumped in the chair opposite the old woman.

"This . . . doesn't mean anything," he said, without looking at her.

"Doesn't it?"

"Just a few articles, Tovah . . ."

The old woman's face had flushed red. "They've come back, Ari. I can feel it in my heart. They've come back."

"Impossible! You know that's impossible!"

"I only know that's what you've always said. I always knew you were wrong. I knew what we unleashed would never retreat quietly; that kind of power never does." The old woman tried to steady her breathing and failed. "And now it has returned, *they* have returned, and one way or another it is our fault, our responsibility."

"That was forty years ago. My God, forty-five now . . ."

"And I'm supposed to believe such a responsibility fades over *any* time?"

Rothstein held the clippings before him as if they were burning his fingers. "Three incidents, Tovah . . ."

"There have already been others, and still more will follow, Ari, unless they are stopped."

"Stopped?"

"By you. You are the only one who can do it."

"How? The logistics would prove—"

"Enough!" She struggled to rise out of her wheelchair.

Arnold Rothstein saw that she could not straighten her spine. The sight made his eyes fill with tears. His throat felt heavy, and he unbuttoned his shirt collar.

"You and I, Ari, we remember the beginning." The old woman raised both her arms to the sides. "We made all this happen, so much good and worthy of every grace God ever gave." Her lips trembled. "You cannot let all our glorious work be marred by their return. You remember, we both remember . . ."

Rothstein came around the table to wrap an arm around the old woman's shoulder to support her. He felt the bones beneath the thin shawl and the meager flesh.

"Yes," he conceded, "yes . . ."

"You have power, Ari. You must do something. You *must*!"

"I will do . . . what I can, Tovah."

"So long as it is enough, Ari."

"For both our sakes." He nodded.

"And the world's."

CHAPTER 16

"T HAT'LL be seven dollars."

Wareagle handed the cabby a ten and climbed out of the back seat without saying a word. Joe Rainwater's two-story house in Chicago's Rogers Park on Touhy Avenue lay directly before him, and he found himself dreading every step that would bring him to it. It had a small yard and looked pretty much like every other house Johnny could see, except for a beautifully manicured front garden that was already starting to bloom.

Johnny would have known it was his friend's house, even without the number over the front door.

It was Thursday morning, and Joe Rainwater had not called him at the hotel at six A.M. as promised. Johnny had waited until six-thirty to call him, but there was no answer. He tried the precinct next and found Rainwater had not yet arrived. Johnny heard the soft murmurs of the spirits and knew there was trouble. Halfway up the walk, the murmurs had given way to a nagging in his gut that tried to choke off his breath. On the porch of Joe Rainwater's small house, Wareagle drew his knife.

The night before, Joe Rainwater and Johnny Wareagle were sitting in an empty office at the precinct when Sal Belamo called back. Rainwater answered the phone and handed the receiver to Wareagle.

"Who you got there with you, big fella?" Belamo asked him.

"A friend."

"He one of us?"

Wareagle looked at Injun Joe. "Close enough."

"Then put this on speaker so you both can hear."

Wareagle hit the appropriate button.

"You guys hear me okay? . . . Good, here's how it plays. You're onto something with this Oliveras killing, something big. Right down McCrackenballs's alley. Too bad he's otherwise involved."

"McCrackenballs?" Injun Joe wondered.

"Long story, Joe Rainwater."

"Let me give you what I got in a nutshell," Belamo continued. "Ruben Oliveras isn't the only bad guy to get snuffed as of late. Far fucking from it. List reads like a veritable rogue's gallery—and not just in the States, either. You guys hear about Javier Kelbonna?"

"It was on the news," Joe Rainwater replied. "Last night, I think."

"The man we couldn't get to with our smart bombs got toasted big-time. Holes himself up on an island after we force him out of his little dipshit country. I mean, this guy was really holed up. Like he expected us to mount Desert Storm Part Two to get him. We didn't, boys, but somebody else did. Twenty-seven guards and Kelbonna were all found torn apart. Sound familiar?"

"Oliveras," Rainwater muttered.

"That's not all. Sleazebag of a senator named Jim Duncan got whacked in a parking garage, five bodyguards along with him, earlier this very evening."

Wareagle and Rainwater looked at each other.

"And I got more, boys. Try the entire complement of guards for one Heydan Larroux, lady boss of New Orleans, wiped out. Miss Larroux hasn't been positively identified yet, but they're still fitting the pieces together, you get my drift. What the fuck you boys stumble onto here?"

"I don't know," Joe Rainwater told him.

"Well, here's the way it plays from my end. In all the killings, there are no leads, no firm suspects, no witnesses, and no evidence. Several of the sites look like war zones with kills registered only by the assailants. I figure we got maybe a thousand rounds of retaliatory fire here all told that didn't hit a *goddamn thing*. So come clean." And, after neither of them did, "Look, boys, I want in. Somebody's doing their best to clean up the world's scum. My kind of guys, let me tell you. You ask me, we should all join up instead of trying to catch them. You want, I can catch the next flight to Chi-town."

"Not yet," Wareagle said.

"I just wanna have a little fun, big fella."

"For now it must involve your computer, Sal Belamo. If there have been this many victims already, there will be more. I need you to generate a list of potential future targets."

"Gonna be a long one."

"A place to start, nothing more."

"Whatever you say, big fella."

Johnny broke the connection and found Joe Rainwater
staring at him intensely.

"I put queries over the wire, John Wareagle. Nothing came
back."

"Sal Belamo has better access."

Injun Joe stood up and stepped nearer to Wareagle. Though
Johnny remained sitting, they were not that far from being
eye to eye.

"Sounds like there's plenty you're not telling me, John
Wareagle."

"Only that which is not meaningful for you to know."

"You told me you were out. You told me the woods gave
you peace and you had no desire to leave them."

"Perhaps not desire, Joe Rainwater, but need. I didn't
realize it myself until another came looking for me some
years back."

"This McCrackenballs . . ."

"Yes."

"You knew him from the hellfire?"

"I never stopped knowing him, even after we parted."

"How often?"

"When the need is there."

Joe Rainwater moved away from the desk, spoke again
while facing the wall. "So you could not help me with the
cause of your people, but you could help the cause of this
whiteface."

"His causes are the causes of many."

Rainwater spun and aimed a finger at Wareagle. "The
cause of your people is the cause of many. You have abandoned them."

If Wareagle was hurt, he didn't show it. "I do what I must,
Joe Rainwater."

"Big battles, not little ones, in keeping with your style."

Johnny shrugged. "I'm here, aren't I?"

"Which scares me all the more, because I know now you
wouldn't be here if you didn't feel this was something right
in your ballpark. And it's turning out that way, isn't it? Jesus

Christ, *something's* killing criminals, something not from this world. It couldn't be in so many places at the same time if it was. Right or wrong, John Wareagle?''

''I don't know, Joe Rainwater.''

''I do.'' Injun Joe paced back to the front of the lieutenant's desk. ''Somebody out there who was fed up, somebody who knows of the old ways, conjured these things up. And now they're out there and they're gonna keep on killing until somebody else sends them back to . . .''

''Where, Joe Rainwater?''

''Back to wherever they came from.''

''And you think I can send them back.''

''I know you, John Wareagle.''

''Perhaps not as well as you think.'' Johnny stood up. ''I should leave now, Joe Rainwater.''

Injun Joe reached up to place a hand on Wareagle's shoulder. ''No, I'm sorry. Listen to me, I was inside the Oliveras mansion two minutes after it happened. I had put the hellfire and Shadow One behind me, John Wareagle. But what I saw there, what I felt . . .'' His eyes were pleading. ''It all came back and it hurt more than it ever hurt before. I could call no one else because no one else could grasp all of what I was feeling.'' Injun Joe swallowed hard. ''I need you, John Wareagle. Let me go home and grab some sleep. Then tomorrow morning we'll start over fresh.''

But now morning had come, with foreboding instead of hope.

The front door to Joe Rainwater's house was locked, the windows all closed. Johnny breathed a little easier. He stepped down from the porch and made his way around to the rear of the house. Not surprisingly, the shrubbery and grounds were immaculate. He could feel Joe Rainwater in every flower and hedge piece. Meticulous, detailed. Joe Rainwater would not have trusted any part of his home to anyone else.

He reached the backyard and saw nothing out of place. All seemed just as it should have been. There was a Florida room Rainwater had built himself, a jalousied door leading into it.

The door was open.

Wareagle held his knife higher as he approached. The latch had been shattered, the door shredded in the area of the knob. Johnny climbed the three steps and entered the Florida room. He glided soundlessly forward, as if weightless, and entered the house. Just outside the kitchen, he smelled it:

Gunsmoke.

He moved through the first floor and climbed the stairs toward the second.

Another smell alerted him even before the feel. Joe Rainwater's bedroom door was open. Blood trailed out into the hallway. Johnny Wareagle moved to the threshold and stopped.

Joe Rainwater's head looked up at him from the floor, its tongue protruding grotesquely outward, a puddle of blood still wet beneath it. The rest of his mangled corpse lay near the bed, left arm nearly severed and right hand missing. Johnny's feet grew heavy. The knife grasped in his hand felt suddenly ineffectual. He tried to feel from the room what had happened, *how* it had happened. There was nothing, as if the walls themselves had closed their eyes to the killing.

Resting against a wall, not far from Joe Rainwater's severed hand, was a .357 Magnum snub-nosed revolver. Johnny lowered his nose to it.

It had been fired recently. The empty cylinders told him at least six times.

But Joe Rainwater's weapon of choice these days was a Smith & Wesson 9mm. Johnny's eyes began to search anew. There it was, on the floor next to the rest of his corpse. Again he lowered his head, touched the steel of the barrel this time.

The clip was empty, all fourteen shots fired, the heat of the barrel told Johnny within the last hour and a half, just before dawn. Joe Rainwater had not gone without a fight. He had gotten off twenty shots.

Twenty shots and he had hit nothing.

Johnny gazed about the bedroom. Bullets had punctured a mirror and a pair of pictures, one showing Joe Rainwater in full police dress getting a commendation from the mayor. The other showed him receiving his Purple Heart after returning from the hellfire. The walls, too, had small chasms where bullets had ripped home. Wareagle stepped into the corridor and found similar chasms in the wall immediately opposite the door to the bedroom. Joe Rainwater had been ready for whatever was coming, then, and it hadn't mattered.

Johnny gazed at the phone still sitting on Joe's night table. Joe Rainwater could have called for help in the end, but he hadn't. He had been a warrior, and a warrior knows his time to fight. Johnny suddenly felt very empty. Joe Rainwater had been more like him than Rainwater had ever cared to admit.

Wareagle's eyes drifted to the wall once again. A photo that had been miraculously untouched by blood or bullets pictured Rainwater in the center of what Johnny assumed was a good portion of Shadow One. Arms around each other's shoulders. Happy. Confident. Johnny wondered if he belonged in that picture. He felt strangely calm now. His grip slackened on the knife in his hand. Whatever had killed Joe Rainwater was long gone.

But it had broken its own rules. Joe Rainwater wasn't a murderer, criminal, or drug lord. He had been killed simply because he had gotten too close, asked too many questions. Up till now Wareagle had felt a certain reluctance to interfere with a force that was ridding the world of its vermin. But all that had changed. Only a force as dark as those that it aspired to eradicate would have done this to a man like Joe Rainwater. Wareagle felt the familiar fires beginning to stoke deep within.

Another great battle loomed. He could feel the spirits around him, dressing his soul with a warbonnet. Johnny imagined he could smell the feathers.

He was halfway back to the stairway when the first of the policemen charged up the stairs.

"Freeze!" the man screamed his way, gun drawn and leveled with both hands. "Keep your hands where I can see them!"

A second policeman slid by the first and passed Wareagle en route to the second floor.

"Against the wall!" the first one ordered. "Move it! *Now!* I said—"

"Jesus Christ," the second officer said when he neared the doorway to Joe Rainwater's bedroom. "Oh, my sweet Jesus . . ."

Wareagle heard him retching. The other officer was fidgeting with his handcuffs. He had trouble fitting them around Johnny's wrists.

"You're under arrest," Wareagle heard.

"Look," the captain of Joe Rainwater's precinct was saying, "I'm sorry about the arrest. Nosy neighbor saw you enter the house and called 911. Since it was a cop's house, we . . . Well, you get the picture."

Johnny Wareagle looked at Captain Eberling from across the desk. "Yes."

"But I got this problem, see: one of my best men is dead. And I got you, who I never laid eyes on in my life before today, called in as some sort of consultant and you're the one who finds Injun Joe chewed up the same way Oliveras and his men were. You mind telling me how you two knew each other?"

"Vietnam."

"He was a hero over there."

"Yes."

"You serve together?"

"No."

Captain Eberling seemed to take a while to digest that. "Yeah, well, I got it on good information you read a report no one outside the department was supposed to see. I don't know how things are done back where you come from, but around here we like to keep things in the family."

"Injun Joe was part of my family."

"Just what is it that you do, Mr.—" Eberling had to look down to consult his notes. "—Wareagle."

Johnny said nothing.

"Injun Joe called you in 'cause he figured he was onto something that was over our heads. Now, you're a pretty tall guy, but not tall enough the rest of this department couldn't do anything you could do. Thing is, I got to figure Injun Joe told you things he didn't tell the rest of us. Things he left out of his reports."

"Perhaps because he knew you did not wish to read them."

Eberling's face reddened. "We want to read everything that might help us find his killers."

"They are things not important to you, Captain."

"Joe Rainwater was important to me, Mr. Wareagle, and that makes whatever might have gotten him killed important to me."

"Nothing I know can help you."

"Did you know he got off twenty shots in his bedroom before he died?" the captain asked.

"Yes."

"And did you know the slugs in his .357 were Glasers? Pellets suspended in liquid Teflon. Guaranteed one-shot stop. He fired six."

"Nothing was stopped."

"He was ready for whatever killed him."

"Perhaps."

"It didn't help."

"No, it didn't."

Johnny's seemingly curt responses seemed to further irritate the captain. "What was Injun Joe on to he couldn't share with the rest of us?"

"Nothing."

"But he called you."

"He thought I could help."

Eberling shrugged. "I told him to take some time off after the Oliveras thing. Eight months he'd been on the case and, boy, the way it ended . . . This doesn't happen today, I figure he's seeing things that aren't there. Now I know something was there, after all, and I feel like a goddamn idiot for putting a lid on this at the outset.''

Wareagle understood. ''He called me because he thought he was dealing with more than he could handle, more than you could handle.''

''Which makes you kinda special, doesn't it?''

''Joe Rainwater thought so.''

''Well, we're running your name through Washington, see what they think.''

''They won't think anything.''

''Excuse me?''

''There is no file on me.''

''What?''

As if on cue, Eberling's phone buzzed.

''Yeah,'' he said, answering it, and then accepted the news glumly. ''Apparently,'' he said to Wareagle, the receiver buried in its cradle again, ''you don't exist.''

Johnny looked at him in silence.

''Not even a military record, even though you told me you served in 'Nam.''

Wareagle just sat there.

''Man needs a lot of pull to work something like that out. Or he was involved in stuff maybe the government doesn't want anyone to know happened.'' Eberling waited for a reaction that didn't come. ''You that kind of man?''

''I have been that, and many other kinds of men, Captain.''

Eberling shot a finger his way and kept it there. ''You're starting to piss me off, you know that?''

''I'm sorry.''

''What killed Joe Rainwater, Mr. Wareagle?''

''I do not know.''

''Who did he think was behind this? Who did he suspect?''

''He did not know.''

"That's right; he called you."

"And I came. To help."

"You wanna tell me how exactly?"

"He wanted my opinion."

"On the Oliveras business. Who did he think was responsible? Did he mention names, someone in the department maybe?" Eberling leaned forward, as if he had finally gotten to the point.

"Nothing like that."

"Like what, then?"

Johnny said nothing and watched the captain lean back.

"You got a phone call, you wanna make it," Eberling told him.

"I thought I wasn't technically under arrest."

"Just extending a courtesy, Mr. Wareagle. Look, don't take this personal. Injun Joe was a good friend of mine, too. We both want to see whoever killed him put away. But you're a part of this now and I can't let you go till I get everything sorted out. See, I figure you're the kinda man might take things into his own hands, he gets the chance. I can't have that, Mr. Wareagle, no matter how close you and Injun Joe were."

Eberling leaned forward again. "Now let me tell you how we're gonna play this. We're gonna lock you up downstairs for your own protection until we can get your identity cleared up. I'm gonna know the last time you spit before you walk out of my precinct, and that won't happen until you come clean with everything Injun Joe told you. That clear to you, Tonto?"

Johnny told him that it was.

CHAPTER 17

THERE were six cells in the basement of the precinct building, and Wareagle was the only current occupant.

"I can't have that, Mr. Wareagle, no matter how close you and Injun Joe were."

Eberling's comment confronted Johnny with the reality that they hadn't been close at all. Johnny had known Joe Rainwater never stopped trying to reach him. He never missed a single message, but neither had he returned the few Rainwater had left for him in the past two years until the most recent one two nights before.

He used his one phone call to dial up Sal Belamo across the country at Gap headquarters.

"I got good news and bad news," Sal started. "The list of possible next victims for your mystery killers, given what you told me, has gotta be somewhere around the size of a city phone book. That's the bad news. Makes me think back to the ones they already hit. You remember me mentioning Heydan Larroux?"

"The woman in New Orleans."

"Yeah, lady crime boss. Get this: turns out her body wasn't with the others. Turns out she managed to get out of her house through an old tunnel that was part of the Underground Railroad. Police down there are just itching to get their hands

151

on her. The FBI, too. Figure maybe she can tell them something.''

"Then the killers of Joe Rainwater would know they missed her.''

"Bingo! And the way I figure it, that's something they're not about to take lightly. You find her first and . . .''

"I wait for those I seek to arrive,'' Johnny completed.

"You mean, *we* wait. I'm in, big fella. Got some heavy firepower being packed up to help us handle the job. I get away from this desk, I'll be on the first plane down to help.''

"Thank you, Sal Belamo, but—''

"Hey, I ain't finished yet. Got a line on one of Madame Larroux's lieutenants in the field. Guy by the name of Jack Watts, alias Jersey Jack. Apparently Mr. Watts is most eager to relocate but he's too hot to touch. What I hear, he was with Larroux minutes before the hit at her mansion. Got an address of a bar down in New Orleans where they might know where to find him. . . .''

Johnny memorized it.

"Where do you want me to meet you?'' Belamo finished.

"This is something I must do alone, Sal Belamo.''

"Excuse me?''

"Just me.''

Belamo was about to argue, then realized the futility of the effort. "You okay, big fella?''

"Yes.''

"You sound strange, different. You ask me . . .'' Belamo stopped. "Look, you need anything else, you know where I am. Stay in touch. Hey, I hear from McBalls you got a message?''

"Tell him the hellfire followed us home, after all.''

"Sure. Whatever you say.''

Sal's influence could probably have gotten him out of this cell in no time flat. But Johnny knew that accepting the favor would bring Belamo into this full-tilt, and this was his battle to fight. Alone. Besides, Johnny planned on being out of here long before morning. Then he'd be on his way to New Orleans and Jersey Jack Watts, on the trail of a victim who had escaped the clutches of the killers of Joe Rainwater.

Night fell, and Johnny felt it from deep in the bowels of the precinct building. He had accepted dinner gratefully and watched as the policeman carefully relocked his cell. He hadn't been stripped down and searched; as Eberling had indicated, he wasn't a prisoner, just a guest. Accordingly, Wareagle would wait a few hours and then set himself free.

The policeman returned for his picked-at tray one hour later, shrugging at how much Johnny had left.

"You want something different?"

"No, no thank you."

"You need anything, just holler." The man started to take his leave, then swung back around. "Injun Joe helped me out a lot when I was starting out. Everyone around here loved the guy. Word is he called you in 'cause you're something special. You catch this son of a bitch, there'll be a long line to get a piece of him."

The policeman stepped out of the cell and locked it behind him.

"Sorry, I got to do this."

"I understand."

"Yeah, well, give a yell you need something, okay?"

Johnny nodded. His eyes followed the policeman down the hall and then drifted up to the video camera mounted on the wall over the entry door. He knew his picture was being broadcast up to the desk sergeant, and this would prove the largest stumbling block to his escape. Disable the camera and attention would surely be drawn. Leave it operational and he ran the very real risk of having his entire escape witnessed.

A problem.

His best solution seemed to be to wait well into the night, as close to the six A.M. shift change as possible to maximize the desk officer's fatigue and boredom. Remain inactive and still through the whole of the evening to lull the man behind the monitor into not paying attention.

He even closed his eyes, but what he saw in his mind disturbed him. The enemy Joe Rainwater had uncovered had exposed itself to kill him. No, it hadn't been seen, but it revealed its very human vulnerability and fear of detection in the act of killing Rainwater.

And the only conclusion he could draw from this was that he was next on its list.

Wareagle's eyes snapped open. He was being hunted; he could feel it. And the best response for him was to return to the ways of the hunter himself.

His mind drifted, searching for the scent of his quarry, drifted back to the Oliveras mansion. In his mind Johnny could see the guards that night springing into action at the first sign of trouble outside. They had plenty of time to assume defensive positions. No one was taken by surprise. And yet, and yet . . .

Johnny thought of the plaster impression of the footprint that Joe Rainwater had told him about. Might it actually have belonged to some demon or monster? Had someone with the powers of the old ways conjured one or more of them up to quell the evil running rampant in the world? He could see why his friend had begun to accept that conclusion; there seemed to be no other conclusion to reach.

Except that Johnny knew of the old ways, too, and not once in all the teaching and training he had undergone had he ever seen evidence that such a thing was possible. The stories Joe Rainwater had referred to had been of warriors visited by spirits on the battlefield, of a ghost rider saving the lives of women and children when threatened by a massacre. But the conjuring of monsters? No, it was not part of even the most mystical Indian lore, not Sioux, anyway.

Still, something was doing all this killing. He had to get out of here now to find out what it was, to find it before it found him as it had found Joe Rainwater.

Johnny rose from his cot and slid toward the cell door. He was well ahead of his planned schedule, but there was no longer a choice. The spirits had taken that from him with their insistent warnings. He removed the bobby pin that helped contain his coal black hair and separated it into the two pieces that formed his picks. He stood there for a time, hands resting on the outside of the lock, the stance innocent enough not to draw any attention. Wareagle angled his body and tilted his head so as much of the task he was about to perform as possible would be lost to the camera.

He slid the L-shaped part of the former bobby pin into the lock to keep pressure on the tumblers. Then he worked the straight part into place after it to pop the tumblers. Wareagle had worked this kind of five-tumbler lock before and figured it would take fifteen seconds.

He was working on the second tumbler when the straight tool slid from his hand and dropped to the floor. Johnny didn't make any sudden moves to snatch at it; he just followed its roll, thankfully, back inside the cell.

As Johnny knelt to retrieve it, he heard a powerful blast, strong enough to shake the cellblock. The next sound was of exploding glass, followed by screaming, then gunfire. Individual pistol shots, by the sound of it, various calibers. More screaming ensued, horrible screaming.

The enemy was here!

Johnny began working the lock feverishly. Two more tumblers clicked into place, then a fourth. He went to work on the last one.

The enemy had come for him, here in the basement of a police station. Whatever was up there would let nothing stand in its way, not even fifteen or twenty policemen. They had killed Rainwater and now they would kill him.

Click.

The last tumbler fell into place and Johnny jammed the cell door outward. Automatic and shotgun fire were sounding from above now, the screams growing in intensity as more officers joined the battle and were wiped out.

The far end of the corridor contained an emergency exit and Johnny charged toward it. But the pushbar wouldn't give, the mechanism triggered only in the event of a fire. The door was steel. The lock was on the other side.

He was trapped!

On the floors above him, the sounds of the struggle had already started to abate, the screams less frequent and gunfire reduced as more of the policemen were downed. A part of Johnny wanted to turn round and confront whatever was up there now, but reason prevailed. If he confronted whatever was up there now, it would kill him, just as it had killed Joe Rainwater. There would be another time, another place, when he would understand what he was fighting before confronting it.

Johnny rushed back to the center of the corridor where a fire alarm was set into the wall. He reached a hand up and pulled it. The alarm began wailing immediately. The emergency exit door at the end of the hall would now be unlocked, and Wareagle bolted back toward it. Halfway there, he could hear the door leading down to the basement thrown open, a soft thud as someone or something began to descend.

The pushbar gave this time, and he was halfway through the exit when he heard the crash of the door leading into the cellblock opening. Something stopped him from turning back to look, a feeling he could not articulate or explain.

The spirits warning him, counseling him . . .

What did they know that he did not?

Another staircase lay before him, and Johnny charged up it toward the night.

Night fell over the bayou, moonless and black as tar. The crickets and night bugs sang incessantly in an eerie harmonic wail. The air was thick with humidity, and the old house was not blessed with air conditioning. Ceiling fans turned rapidly to slice through the heat. They kept the air moving, but could do nothing about the stifling humidity. Heydan Larroux was sweating as she gazed out over the black water that surrounded the house. Built on stilts in ten-foot-deep water, it was accessible only by a narrow, wobbly fifty-foot walkway running out from the shoreline.

Heydan Larroux had come here to hide after fleeing from her uptown mansion. The tunnel beneath it had once been part of the Underground Railroad, but the years had not been kind to it. Most of the city of New Orleans is below sea level. Accordingly, in her trek through the tunnel Heydan encountered a number of coffins washed from their graves by storms over the years. Many of the coffins lay shattered and ruined, their contents scattered alongside. After the first encounter, Heydan resolved to keep her flashlight pointed strictly forward and her eyes following the beam. At the close of the tunnel, on the opposite end of Chappatula, a car, its motor idling, was waiting for her up on the street.

The Old One was already inside.

In the house on the bayou, Heydan turned away from the window and faced the Old One, who sat cross-legged on the floor with a commercial-sized mixing bowl before her. Moving that way, Heydan saw that six stones had been placed on the floor on the opposite side of the bowl. She sat down across from the Old One and picked up the first one, ready to drop it into the water as soon as she completed her question.

"Will it still come for me?"

Plop.

Soft ripples churned through the bowl, slowing, then stopped.

"Yes," the old woman replied, seeming to read them through her sightless eyes.

Heydan took another stone. "When?"

Plop.

"You escaped its wrath, child. It seethes in anger. Failure is something it cannot accept. But it does not leave echoes the way most living things do. I cannot feel its approach, only its presence."

Heydan grasped a third stone, having to force herself to ask a question she dreaded the answer to. "What is it?"

Plop.

"Power, child. Raw and pure. It swallows. It absorbs."

"It does not kill for revenge."

"A question!"

"Does it kill for revenge or to eliminate those in its way?" And she dropped the fourth stone.

"It kills to kill, child. Its reasons are not comprehendible to me or you. Now that it has been unleashed, it will not be restrained again until all its work is done."

Heydan grasped a fifth stone. "Unleashed by who?"

The old woman squinted her dead eyes to follow the water's ripples. "I see the past. The present, too, but not as clear. They have melded, but the years and the ages are clashing. I see a force thought dead, but only dormant. The force reeks of frustration and impatience, of a vision it will not have sullied by anyone. Relentless. Unstoppable."

"Nothing is unstoppable."

"I can only respond to a question."

Heydan gathered up the final stone. "What must I do to survive?"

Plop.

The stone was larger this time, and the result was a louder noise and more ripples through the bowl. The Old One lowered her ear closer to the water. Then she looked up.

"There is a man, a warrior, who will come to know of this force. He alone can save you. Far away now, but soon he will be close."

"Who?" Heydan Larroux demanded.

"The stones are gone."

"Who?"

"We must let the waters recharge, revitalize. The streams of constant answers have grown still. We must wait, my child. Tomorrow. The day after."

Heydan gazed out the window into the night, praying for morning as if that might save her. She had rounded up her most formidable remaining guards and summoned them here, equipped them with explosives and armaments that could kill a small army. But it hadn't been enough in New Orleans and it wouldn't be in the bayou.

"You must wait," the Old One was saying.

"For tomorrow . . ."

"For as long as it takes for the warrior to find his way here."

CHAPTER 18

"**W**HERE to now?" Melissa asked when the bus had deposited them in the center of the Turkish city of Izmir just after ten o'clock Thursday morning. They had boarded it in Ephesus an hour after dawn, after walking fifteen miles through the night to a point where sightseers were dropped off and picked up later in the day.

"The Büyük Efes Hotel."

Melissa knew Izmir well enough to know it was the best in the city. "You're kidding."

"You travel with me, babe, you go first class."

"You know people there," she realized.

"Izmir still houses the headquarters for NATO's southeastern sector," Blaine explained, the wryness gone from his voice. "We get to the hotel, we can press all the buttons to keep our presence as secret as we can hope for."

She fingered the ragged notebook through the heavy canvas of her pack. "Izmir also houses one of the finest and

best-equipped archaeological museums in the entire Middle
East. And we need to find out what our notebook says.''

McCracken glanced at her pack. ''Too bad it can't tell us
who removed the more recent batch of those missing crates.''

''It might tell us what's inside them,'' Melissa responded,
''and that's the next best thing.''

At last a taxi pulled to a halt before them.

The man waited until the taxi's occupants were inside the
Büyük Efes and the taxi had driven off before entering the
lobby. Not surprisingly, his quarries had already vanished
from sight. But it didn't matter now. He moved to a row of
pay phones just past the front desk and dialed a number he
had memorized just hours before.

''Yes,'' a voice answered.

''Büyük Efes,'' was all he said.

The taxi driver pulled over at a restaurant just down the street
from the Büyük Efes. There was no pay phone inside, but he
knew the manager well enough to use the restaurant's own line.
The phone was located in the corner of the kitchen. The driver
knew he was being watched as he dialed the number.

''Ja?'' a voice greeted in German.

And the taxi driver whispered his message.

Inside the Büyük Efes, Blaine headed not for the front
desk, but the desk of the assistant manager. He introduced
himself on the pretext of having a problem and was ushered
into the privacy of a back office. Less than ten minutes later
he and Melissa were settled in a room on the hotel's seventh
floor with nothing signed and no evidence of their presence
recorded.

The Büyük Efes was indeed Izmir's finest hotel. Boasting
eight stories and nearly three hundred rooms, it featured three
restaurants, two bars, and an upscale nightclub that was a
main attraction in the city. The room given to Blaine and
Melissa looked out over the inlet which flowed in from the

Aegean Sea and the Ataturk Caddesi, the city's palm-lined seafront promenade.

Melissa took a long bath and then a shower, hoping the surge of water would revive and refresh her. While it could wash the grime and stink of the past two days from her, though, it could not swab clean the memories. The grief returned with stunning impact as her senses relaxed and uncoiled. Since McCracken's arrival at the dig site less than twenty-four hours before, there had been no time to feel it. Fighting to save her own life had spared her from dwelling on the loss of her father's. But now she had her thoughts for company again, and they behaved like unwelcome guests. She was exhausted and starving, and that heightened her depression all the more.

She stood with her back to the shower's jets. The grungy bathwater was still draining from the tub over her feet and now her tears began to drop into it. She cried herself out standing there, arms wrapped tight around her midsection and shaking no matter how hot she made the water. When she could cry no more, she stepped from the tub and wrapped herself in a thick white robe that had been hanging behind the door. She felt a wave of nausea overcome her and leaned over the toilet to vomit. But her stomach was empty and the heave was dry.

"Melly?"

McCracken's voice came from right next to her. He had entered the bathroom without her even knowing. She looked up at him with hands propped on either side of the sink, fighting to get her breath back.

"You should eat," he said softly. "The food came while you were in the shower."

"I . . . can't."

"You have to. Come on. . . ."

He slid an arm over her shoulder and eased her from the sink. She came away tentatively, wanting to cling to her perch there, and then pressed against him. She was trembling horribly, and Blaine held her tighter. He stroked her still-wet hair to comfort her. Outside the bathroom, near the table room service had wheeled in, she clung fast to him.

"My father used to do that," she said softly. "When I was a little girl."

"Ladies tell me all the time I remind them of their fathers."

Melissa eased herself away from him, the aroma of fresh coffee and hot food starting to revive her. "My father was in his late thirties when I was born. My mother was twenty-four, one of his graduate students. He always said he had meant to marry earlier, but there was always a dig, a project, some research to do. I guess the only person he could have married was one of his students."

"Your mother . . ."

"She died when I was four."

"I'm sorry."

"It hurts more now than it ever did. Does that make sense?"

"No one left to fill the gaps. It makes plenty. Not as much as eating a good meal, though."

McCracken had ordered generously, and the two of them attacked the covered plates of eggs, bacon, rolls, danish, and small steaks. The food made her feel better but couldn't fill the deeper hole in her stomach, the one that was hot and burning from the pain of loss.

"What now?" Melissa asked.

"You need rest."

"No, I'm . . . afraid."

"I'll be here," he soothed.

"That's not it. It hurts too much when I rest. I wouldn't be able to sleep."

"You're exhausted."

"Then eventually I'll pass out. But not now, not for a while." Her eyes fell on the tattered, nearly ruined notebook lying on the room's desk near the backpack that had held it. "And I've got work to do."

Blaine followed her gaze. "How much of it do you think is salvageable?"

"Impossible to tell until I've had a look at it under enhanced conditions. The Archaeological Museum's right in the center of Izmir, just a few miles from here. They know me there. Shouldn't be a problem to gain access to what I need."

"What time do they open?"

"Ten o'clock. What time is it now?"

"After eleven."

"I'm going to get dressed," Melissa insisted. "Then I'm going down to the museum straightaway."

"You need to rest," Blaine repeated.

"Nonsense."

"Be sensible."

She shrugged, relenting.

McCracken went into the shower after she was lying in bed, tucked under the covers still wearing her Büyük Efes bathrobe. He allowed himself to linger in the spray for far longer than usual, trying to plan his next step. The dig site had left him at a virtual dead end. He knew that something had been removed from the secret storage chamber on two separate occasions: first by Jews in the wake of World War II, and then by an unknown party far more recently. With such a vast array of deadly weapons before them, both parties had chosen the crates.

Why? Had the Jews made use of their contents? Did the unknown party intend to?

The only lead he had at present was the potentially useless notebook; he would rely on Melissa to make something out of it. He knew pain well enough to know that working through it was the best medicine.

He emerged from the bathroom in a second hotel bathrobe and found a ruffled space in the bed where she had been lying. The notebook was gone. So, too, was the change of clothes the assistant manager had sent up to the room. Blaine smiled. Melissa was truly an impressive woman, brave and

determined. He had sensed how close she was to her father,
how much she had come to depend on him for the direction
and meaning of her own life. Now she would have to find
those on her own, starting today, and Blaine knew he had to
let her.

He lay down on the ruffled bed and was asleep as soon as
his head hit the pillow.

The men came in five different vehicles, their arrivals separated by precise two-minute intervals. All sixteen slipped
into their assigned positions inside the Büyük Efes. All had
miniature microphones attached to the lapels of their suit
jackets. Thin wires snaked down and around to their backs
where their transmitting apparatuses were clipped. A tiny
antenna that looked like little more than a stray thread rose
up from each man's collar.

Among themselves the men had wondered briefly about
why so many of them were needed for so simple an operation. Questioning orders was something that was simply not
possible for them, not today or ever, so they accepted what
they were told. The man they were coming for must be very
important; that much was certain. And very dangerous; that
was certain, too. For this reason, the more-experienced
members of the team found the rather peculiar parameters of
this mission unnerving. If this man was dangerous enough
to require a team so large, their orders should have contained
considerably more latitude.

It would take eleven minutes for them all to reach their
positions. No one would make a move until everyone was
ready. The elevators and stairwells all had to be covered. So,
too, the hotel's service basement, rear area, and lobby. If the
initial strike team failed, the idea was to create a circle that
could be gradually tightened until the target was caught within
it. They had used the method before, but never with this
many men, and it had never taken long to close the circle
even on those occasions.

The operation began with nothing more than subtle nods. The men checked their watches and dispersed.

Billy Boy Griggs had the driver pull over a block from the Büyük Efes. Behind him he could hear the Twins stirring, whispering between themselves again. Jesus, these guys scared him. . . .

Billy knew all the stories, all the legends, about the pair. How they had killed their way through a hundred guards to slay the sultan of a small Arab country. How they had protected a charge who had hired them from attack by two dozen mercenaries armed with the best weapons available; killed them all, was the story. How they had already laid to rest an even dozen previously indestructible operatives who had finally crossed the line that required the Twins to be summoned.

The same line that Blaine McCracken had crossed.

Billy heard the back door open, but didn't turn around to watch the Twins exit.

''We won't be long,'' they said in unison.

The leader of the German team dispersing through the hotel was also its oldest member, twice as old as most of the rest. He had the same crew cut he had worn before his hair had turned white, and he had been fortunate enough to keep most of it. He had also kept the same rigid walk, arms swaying robotically by his side. None of the other team members had ever worked with him before and didn't even know his name. But he was the one who had assembled them and had eyed them stealthily when they entered the hotel.

The leader stepped through the lobby, studying the positions his men had taken up on this level. One glance was all they gave up to him. Good. They were excellent men, each and every one. The German ducked into an alcove and pulled back his sleeve. The watch revealed was scarred and scratched from constant usage, inconsistent with his finely tailored suit. It was a soldier's watch and had been since his father had given it to him as a boy.

The paradox was symbolic. It had been a long time since he had mounted an active mission. He had grown accustomed to the shadows, but now the light beckoned him once more. So much depended on his success tonight. Everything.

In three minutes his entire team would be in position. It would be time to move.

The German emerged from the alcove, too late to see the identical twins enter the hotel.

Independently of one another, the Twins picked out the presence of the men in the lobby instantly. It was a feeling that alerted them at first. Then their eyes swept the area, stopping at each of the well-dressed men at their posts.

The little man had said nothing about a force protecting McCracken. Could it be that these had come here for the same purpose they had? Fools. Did they really think that ordinary men, no matter how strong in number, could eliminate someone like McCracken? A hundred men posted in a hundred different places meant one man to kill a hundred times.

No matter what they were here for, these men would now inevitably prove an obstacle. They added not only complications, but also unpredictability to what was about to transpire. If four were posted in the lobby, three or four times that many would be scattered at strategic points throughout the hotel. In position already, they would move on McCracken before the Twins could possibly do the same. Alerted, he would be doubly dangerous and prepared. Their best hope was to eliminate these obstacles before they became an impediment. A change in plans, yes, but one that was clearly necessary.

The eyes of the German with the crew cut were glued to his old watch. Tucked back in the isolated lobby alcove, he lowered his mouth toward his lapel microphone.

"We move in one minute. All teams report."

"Team One in position. All clear."

"Team Two in position. All clear."

"Team Three in position. All clear."

"Team Four in position. All clear."

"Team Five in position. All clear."

The German waited. No reply filtered back through his earpiece.

"Team Six, come in."

Silence.

"Team Six, are you there? . . . Team Six, can you hear me?"

An equipment malfunction was probably to blame. He'd have to check on it.

"Team One," he said to the three men on the target's floor, the initial strike group. "Report status."

"No movement. Target inside."

Team Six was one of two posted in the lobby. The German recalled the layout in his mind. They were right out in the open, responsible for the elevators. He could send Team Five to check on them or he could simply let the plan go forward and check on them himself when time allowed.

"Thirty seconds," he told them all. "On my mark."

Inside his room, something snapped Blaine McCracken awake. He bolted upright in bed, shoulders board-stiff and neck hackles rising.

Had it been a dream?

No, there had been a sound, barely discernible to all but the long-trained mind.

He slid off the bed quietly and moved for his gun.

Team One approached the door slowly. Two of the three members took posts on either side and waited while the third angled straight for it. From beneath his coat he pulled a sawed-off shotgun loaded with a single antipersonnel round. Obtaining swift entry was of paramount importance here. Explosives took too long to plant and were too iffy to work with. The round was a much better choice, especially in this instance. Once they were inside, surprise on their side and their target too stunned to respond, the rest would take care of itself.

The third member of the team nodded and leveled his weapon. He waited until the other two had covered their ears before pulling the trigger.

The door exploded inward, the entire area around the latch reduced to splinters. The two members on either side of it crashed through the door's remnants with pistols drawn.

They had just registered the fact that the room was empty, and were turning toward the final team member, when a figure whirled toward them. The first man caught a glimpse of a dark beard before a rock-hard fist impacted on the bridge of his nose and plunged him into blackness. The second swung the figure's way and tried to right his weapon. Before he could fire it, though, something tore it from his hand and slammed him backward into the wall. His breath fled him in a rush that left him no air to scream with when the final blow smashed into his face.

McCracken watched the final man slump down the wall and backed out into the corridor. One of his own private security provisions in hotels like this was to insist on two rooms across from each other. Then he would purposely leave a trail of phone calls and even room service deliveries that his contact at the hotel would route through the dummy room. It was like setting a trap, Blaine right across the hall in case anyone took the bait. Better to have your enemies reveal themselves than remain obscured, had always been his thinking. And this time, once again, it had paid off.

Killing the assailants would have been excessive, unnecessary. Disabling them, albeit violently, was sufficient. McCracken stowed the unconscious frame of the third man, the one who had fired the round, inside the room before heading off.

He moved back into the corridor and stopped briefly at the fire alarm. The three men wouldn't be alone. Pulling the alarm would provide him with a reasonable cushion of chaos to aid his flight. But it would also render the elevators inoperative, and that would narrow his options.

Blaine continued on down the corridor. Since it was the middle of the day, few of the rooms along it were occupied, and the explosion had gone largely unnoticed. A maid was screaming in Turkish from behind the cover of her cart. A scant number of people were milling about. McCracken slid past them all and reached the elevator bank. The up arrow on one flashed, the down arrow on another a second after.

Blaine rushed for the stairs.

"Team Two, what's going on?" the German leader said into his lapel mike.

"Team One has been neutralized."

"*What?* Say again, please."

"Team One has been neutralized. We're in the room. No sign of target. All members of Team One are down. We must have just missed the target back at the elevator."

"Close from the top. All teams, please acknowledge. Close from the top!"

"Damn!" the leader muttered in exasperation, as the acknowledgments filled his ear.

What had gone wrong? The better question was what hadn't? He had reached the lobby to find that Team Six was missing from their posts, equipment failure not to blame at all for their failure to report. Where were they? His first thought was that McCracken had somehow crossed them up and was down there. But then, with the Go signal given, he had heard the blast, then the confused shrieks that followed. McCracken had crossed them up, all right, in a different and equally effective way.

"Team Two, where are—"

"Jesus," the leader heard in his earpiece, the voice recognized as that of one of the members of Team Two.

"What is—"

The staccato bursts of gunfire followed, then screams. Fi-

nally there was laughter, filling the microphone of one of his
men before drifting off into a dying echo.

CHAPTER 19

THE Twins were enjoying themselves. Eliminating the two
men they had initially seen posted in the lobby had been as
easy as brushing up against them. It looked totally innocent,
including the moment they jammed the blades deep into the
men's backs. The blades were custom-fitted with detachable
handles. Once pulled free and with the blade wedged deep,
a simple hand across the back covered all trace of the wound.
To anyone looking, the sight was that of a friend helping a
drunken companion. The Twins had mastered this method
to the point where they could even make it seem as if the
corpse were walking.

They deposited the bodies in the men's room down an
empty corridor; left them on the toilets with their pants down
to discourage anyone from checking. Then they bolted back
out toward the lobby. By this point, an agitated man with a
crew cut was nervously scanning the lobby. The leader, they
guessed, and they were moving toward him when one of the
Twins noticed him cock his head downward and speak into
his lapel. Whatever the rest of his men were here for was
well under way. They could take care of this man later. Right

now they had to reach McCracken. They walked casually to the elevator and boarded it.

They emerged on McCracken's floor seconds before two more members of the group led by the man with the crew cut appeared. By the time this pair turned, it was much too late. Without a word of coordination, each of the Twins chose a target and blasted away at it, keeping the bullets going well after the killshots. When it was over, they swung down opposite sides of the hallway firing at anything that moved. The lucky guests made it back into their rooms. The unlucky ones ended up sprawled on the hallway carpet, life pouring from them.

They exchanged glances when they reached McCracken's room, not at all surprised by what they saw. One of the Twins pushed the door open and saw the unconscious frames of three more well-dressed men resting against the wall. The Twins entered the room and cut their throats as they lay there.

Back in the corridor, they broke off in opposite directions. What little the element of surprise might have done for them was gone; the presence of the other party had seen to that. Their primary objective at this point was to locate McCracken before he could leave the building. One of the Twins headed left down the hall, the other right. They would descend on opposite sides of the building, certain that McCracken would be somewhere beneath one of them. Not exactly the way they had planned things, but close enough. And, of course, there was also the possibility that the team, now seven members smaller, might find McCracken for them.

Save time that way. Maybe even allow them to complete the kill together.

McCracken bolted down the stairwell from the seventh floor to the fifth, burst through the doors, and headed toward another exit sign. Since he had no idea of the enemy's number or position, the first order of business was to confuse them. His escape route through the hotel had to leave them thinking he was still inside, even that they might be closing in. It took longer but was infinitely more effective.

The one thing the hotel assistant manager had been unable to provide for him yet was a gun, so he had stripped a submachine gun from one of the men he had downed. Not his favorite weapon, under the circumstances. He'd much prefer a pistol, something he could conceal easily by his side. With no jacket to conceal the submachine gun, if he had to enter the lobby all eyes would be drawn to him.

By now, hotel officials would be converging on the site of the apparent explosion upstairs. It would be up to the assistant manager to square things once the investigation deepened. McCracken entered a second stairwell cautiously and began to thunder down the remaining floors.

His plan at this point was to bypass the lobby altogether. With any luck at all, these stairs would lead to the shopping and entertainment level contained beneath it. A garage was even possible, though his concern for Melissa's state of mind had distracted him from making a thorough reconnaissance of the Büyük Efes.

McCracken was swinging over the railing to the staircase leading down from the lobby level when he heard the heavy footsteps charging upward. A single voice spoke rapidly, stopped, and then spoke again. Whoever was approaching must have had a microphone pinned to his lapel, just as the men he had dropped in the room above had. And the language, the language was . . .

German!

But who were these men? And what had brought them to Izmir on Blaine's trail?

The man's shape came within reach. He had his finger on the trigger of a submachine gun and managed to squeeze it just as McCracken pushed off the railing and threw his legs up into the barrel. The bullets stitched a ricocheting barrage against the concrete. The noise stung Blaine's ears. He grabbed the German's head and the man responded by butting him just over the eyebrows.

Stars exploded in front of McCracken's face. The German had lost his grip on the submachine gun and flailed to get it back. That gave Blaine the time he needed to ram the palm heel of his right hand hard into the German's solar plexus. The man's mouth dropped to gasp silently for air. His eyes bulged and McCracken slammed him across the side of the head with both fists interlocked. His head whiplashed against the wall, face seeming to meld into it as he slid down hugging the asphalt. McCracken grabbed his weapon as well and continued on.

"I'm heading back up for the lobby now."

"Go back down!" the German leader ordered one of the members of Team Four.

"I did not hear that. I—"

The leader next heard the thud of impact, followed by a brief burst of gunfire. More thuds followed and then the echoing of escaping footsteps.

"Who is left? Do you hear me, *who is left*?"

Only four men reported in. He had lost a dozen, dammit, a dozen of the best the movement could provide. But not just to McCracken; that much was clear. Another force was at work here—one equally deadly, if not more so.

"All teams," the leader started, "converge on the lobby. Repeat, converge on the lobby. The target is coming this way."

Though several floors apart and on different sides of the hotel, the Twins' heads snapped up at the sound of gunfire in the exact same instant. It took only an instant more for them to pin down its origin. One was three floors away, the other four. Along the way each had been slowed by the necessary removal of another of the amateurish force. They hadn't used their guns this time, for fear of confusing the other and perhaps defeating their own purpose. Hands were more than sufficient, a neck broken in one case, a nose bone driven through the brain in another.

Still, the Twins felt the unfamiliar pangs of anxiety. The distance between either of them and McCracken was considerable. He could conceivably be out of the building before they closed the distance all the way. Separated by the length of several floors, the Twins smiled simultaneously. They had forgotten briefly that the remainder of the depleted force would have heard the gunfire, just as they had. Not that these men had any chance against McCracken, but they could slow him down—and that was all the Twins needed.

They rushed on.

McCracken took the stairwell to its absolute bottom, two levels below the lobby, and tried the door. It was locked. He hadn't anticipated this, knowing it reduced his enemy's options as well as his own. He had no choice but to retrace his steps and exit one floor up at the lower lobby. But his unfamiliarity with that level made it a poor choice under the circumstances. The lobby was a much better one specifically, because he knew the layout and could thus cut the fastest path possible through it. All his options were fraught with this risk. The trick was to choose the least of all evils and support himself with the forty-five shots remaining in the pair of submachine guns slung from either shoulder if necessary.

McCracken retraced his steps up the first flight and then started up the second leading to the lobby. He had the exit door in sight when a large figure lunged before him from the next staircase up, aiming a strange-looking square pistol Blaine's way. Blaine managed to get a hand on the bigger man's wrist and force it upward. A muffled spit rang out. The pistol's barrel seemed to cough.

Tranquilizers! Blaine realized.

The bigger man slammed him against the wall, still trying to bring his weapon down. McCracken smacked a knee into his groin. The big man fought the pain off and with brute strength began to succeed in angling the tip of his barrel back in Blaine's direction.

The force of the two men confronting each other resulted in a crunching pirouette, as they spun and slammed each other into the walls, which seemed almost ready to give. One of McCracken's submachine guns rattled to the floor when he tried to grasp it. The other dangled out of reach.

Suddenly Blaine heard the heavy rattle of footsteps, followed by a few words exchanged in German. Stationary against the big man for an instant, he was able to see another pair of men crouched in combat position on different steps of the staircase that wound toward the floor above the lobby.

"Halt!" one yelled, showing his machine gun just ahead of the other.

Before he had opportunity to use it, a barrage of automatic fire from above tore into both him and the man just above him on the steps. The two Germans crumpled down the stairs, while the giant tottered in utter confusion between McCracken and the staircase. He had taken an uncertain step forward when his huge body was pummeled by an unceasing cascade of bullets—two guns' worth, judging by the sound and angle. Somehow Blaine managed to keep his feet through the barrage, and the big man's frame provided enough cover for him to lunge for the door leading out of the stairwell.

The bullets of the new pair of killers traced him all the way through, and Blaine burst onto a short hallway that led to the center of the main lobby.

"Come in! *Anyone* respond!"

When no response came, the German leader knew the last burst of bullets he'd heard had wiped out the rest of his team. He alone was left to deal with McCracken, if the force that had killed his men hadn't killed McCracken as well.

He couldn't let that happen. There was too much at stake.

A fresh burst of gunfire reached his naked ear, followed by screams. The lobby seemed to still all at once.

He saw the only option he had left now and bolted for the lavish front desk across the lobby.

Blaine reached the lobby to find people starting to flood out in all directions, scattered by the sounds of gunfire. He let himself be swallowed by part of the mass and took cover within it.

The sound of terrified screams preceded the all-too-familiar clacking of automatic fire by barely a second. McCracken swung to see a wall of people behind him collapsing.

Innocent people! These animals were killing innocent people, goddammit!

Enraged by that reality, McCracken began shoving the panicked throngs around him aside, searching for a space in the chaos through which to fire the submachine gun still slung on his shoulder. He found a small gap and snapped off a single rapid burst through it toward a pair of figures that had at last emerged. The broad, curly-haired man took a lobby table over with him for cover, while the broad, curly-haired man—

Wait! They were *twins*!

Their firing resumed without any regard for the innocent bystanders between them and McCracken. Blaine pressed his trigger again.

Click.

The clip was exhausted. His only chance now was to flee. But he held fast to the Ingram to keep the twins guessing.

Blaine joined the surge of chaos in the main exit's direction, made all the worse by the arrival minutes before of three bus loads of tour patrons. He ducked low to remove himself from sight, but, again, the twin killers simply fired at anything that moved in an attempt to flush him out.

The crowd flooding from the lobby was jammed up at the doors, the wall of panicked desperation stationary and rigid. There was nowhere to go.

Suddenly a new surge of bullets erupted from the other side of the lobby, fired in the direction of the twins. Blaine caught a glimpse of a man with a crew cut ducking back behind the cover of the front desk to avoid the twins' return fire. Just as fast, the man bounced up again and opened fire with a fresh magazine, forcing the killers to scamper for cover of their own.

McCracken seized the opportunity to charge out of the

hotel with the rest of the crowd, the rush absorbing him. On the sidewalk, though, he stopped. Inside, a man had saved his life. The man was a professional, just like the Germans who had tried to take Blaine with tranquilizers. He could be part of that team. He could have *answers*!

McCracken had to save him.

He swung his eyes desperately about the circular drive fronting the hotel, searching for something to make use of, something—

Blaine's gaze locked on the lead tour bus in the procession of three. Its engine was still on, the driver having fled with the task of removing the luggage from the underneath compartment only half-completed. McCracken rushed to the open main door and up the steps and got the door closed before he had barely taken the driver's seat. Then he shoved the big bus into gear and drove it straight forward.

The screeching of the engine almost drowned out the sound of the hotel's glass front wall disintegrating upon impact. Glass was thrown everywhere as the bus roared right into the lobby, destroying everything in its path. The terrified bystanders managed to dive out of its way, as Blaine steered it for the front desk.

The twins' bullets began pounding its frame just before the bus got there.

"Get in!" he screamed out the open driver's vent. "If you want to live, get in!"

The man threw himself up over the counter and chanced a dash round the bus's front, firing all the way. He lunged up the steps and Blaine jammed the bus into reverse, as the doors hissed closed again. Bullets turned them into spiderwebs of flying glass, and the man with the crew cut returned the fire with his pistol.

The bus's tail end slammed through another section of the lobby's wraparound glass, taking a hefty portion of a wall with it this time. Its front hadn't made it all the way out when McCracken shifted into drive and tore off, turning the entire entryway into a ruined shell.

The windshield shattered under the force of the twins' gunfire, which peppered the frame as the bus started away. Ducking low beneath the dashboard, Blaine heard a pair of thumps as at least two of its outside tires were shot out. But that wasn't about to stop him from steering the bus straight onto the main road fronting the Büyük Efes.

"Who are they?" Blaine demanded of the man kneeling on the floor a yard away from him. "Who are *you*?"

"The man who's going to tell you what's going on," the man said breathlessly in German-laced English. "The man who has the answers you need."

CHAPTER 20

"I'M listening," McCracken said, watching the man's gun.

"Not here. Not yet. They'll be coming."

He bent the bus into a screeching turn and sped on.

"You're part of the team that came for me in the hotel."

The man nodded. "Its leader."

"One of your men was carrying a tranquilizer pistol."

"It was never our intention to kill you. We need you alive. We need your help."

"You could have asked for it."

"You wouldn't have given it."

"Why?"

"Because we are Nazis, Mr. McCracken."

The car's rear doors were yanked open simultaneously.

"Go!" one of the Twins screamed.

"After the bus!" the other added.

"Now!" they followed in unison. *"That way!"*

The driver sped off before Billy Griggs could catch his breath. He had seen the bus first crash through the hotel lobby and then screech away, but had thought the Twins were responsible, for who else would have—

"Take a right here!"

"Don't slow down!"

"A left now!"

"I see it!"

The Twins were out of the car again before it had come to a complete halt, rushing forward as if the traffic around them didn't exist. It moved in stops and starts. The snarl, they saw now, had been caused by the battered bus being abandoned by McCracken in the middle of the avenue. The Twins checked it cautiously, knowing this might be a ruse to get them to lower their guard. McCracken could be hiding or lurking anywhere, setting a trap, waiting to strike.

Just as they would have.

But he was long gone, and not alone, either. They hadn't killed the German team's leader when the chance was there and now McCracken had rescued him. That error seemed certain to compound their failure. The Twins looked at each other.

"Shit," they said together.

"At the dig, those were your men I found dead inside the find!" Blaine realized. "What was left of them anyway."

They had abandoned the bus nearly ten minutes earlier. The German was driving one of the four cars he had planted in all directions from the hotel, as an added and ultimately fortuitous precaution. McCracken sat in the passenger seat tensely.

"Not my men, Mr. McCracken. If they were my men, things would not have progressed to the unfortunate heights they did."

"They killed the head of the dig team."

"Their orders were to do nothing of the kind. And they never, under any circumstances, should have entered the chamber. They exceeded the parameters of their mission."

"And what about your mission?"

"My orders were to stabilize the situation in Ephesus and, once your involvement was uncovered, help you in any way possible." He looked McCracken's way. "I'm afraid I arrived too late to be of any service to you."

"The helicopter!"

"Yes."

"Who are you?" he demanded.

"Tessen. Hans Tessen. At least, that used to be my name."

"Until you were resettled after the war. Who by? ODESSA? The Comrades Organization?"

"We should not dwell on the past with the present in the peril it is."

"But you were a soldier."

Tessen's neck stiffened. "I *am* a soldier, Mr. McCracken, just as you are, and our enemy this time is a common one."

"Tweedledum and Tweedledee back at the hotel?"

"They killed my men, disrupted my orderly plan to establish contact with you."

"Orderly?" Blaine raised disbelievingly. "Your men blew up the door of the room they thought I was in."

"To take you by surprise, to give them a chance to explain."

"Hope they were going to do a better job than you are, Hans."

"Someone else sent those twins, Mr. McCracken. That someone is your true enemy."

Blaine thought of Billy Griggs and the battle that had spread onto the Golden Gate Bridge. "And just who is that?"

"I don't know, but if the past is any indication . . ."

"That's twice you've mentioned the past, Hans. Why don't we start there?"

Tessen pulled at his collar as if to stretch it. Clearly things were not proceeding in the order he had planned. His eyes drifted to the rearview mirror again, as if expecting the twins to appear at any moment.

"The beginning," he muttered.

"That would do just fine."

"A Catholic boys' school in France during World War II. I do not remember the name."

"Get on with it."

"Our division was assigned to ferret out the many Jews such places were known to be hiding," he continued, his voice soft and almost mechanical. "Our commanding officer was named Erich Stimmel. He was a proud man who felt that such toilsome work was beneath him. If he could not exercise his abilities on the front, then—" Tessen took a deep breath. "We pulled our trucks through the school's front gate. I remember the day well. It was raining, cold. I was shivering. The trucks stopped and we dispersed. The schoolboys were rounded up and placed in orderly lines, along with the teachers. The school's headmaster, a priest, stood not far from Stimmel in the front." Tessen's voice became harder, colder. "Edelstein, Sherman, and Grouche. . . ." He called them as if off a roll. Then his voice went flat again. "Those were the names of the boys we had come for. A local baker who delivered the school's bread had informed. We had not come to investigate. We had come simply to punish."

"Punish," Blaine repeated.

"The school would be closed, the three boys taken away and shipped elsewhere."

"Yeah."

"Let me finish, please. The priest would not turn the boys over. When their names were called, they did not come forward. Stimmel was enraged. He insisted that three other boys would be shot in their place if the Jews did not step out."

McCracken could see the bulge in his collar as Tessen swallowed hard.

"When they finally showed themselves, Stimmel had them shot. He lined them up against a brick wall and assigned six men to the firing squad. I didn't think he would really do it, not until the very last when he said *'Feuer!'* We had made our point. There was no reason to . . ."

"But you did."

"Yes." Tessen sighed. "First the boys, and then the priest. Only with him the firing squad was reduced to five. One still stood there but did not pull his trigger." His eyes sharpened and peered toward Blaine. "Me, Mr. McCracken."

"That wasn't all," Tessen continued. "Before the priest was shot, Stimmel let him speak." The Nazi's words seemed to be coming harder here, an undercurrent of fear rimming each and every syllable. "He placed a curse on us. He swore that he and the boys would be avenged for what we had done to them. He swore that his wrath would live beyond the grave, that we would pay horribly for the acts we had committed. Stimmel just smiled at him and gave the order to fire again. He died glaring at Stimmel. The colonel spit on his corpse and turned his back."

"A curse . . ."

"None of us paid it any heed. Only those nearest the wall could hear the words clearly anyway. By the time the war ended in shame, we had forgotten, all of us."

"But something made you remember, didn't it?"

Tessen nodded, and the car wavered slightly out of control. He tightened his grip on the steering wheel and pulled down a narrow side street. He parked in front of the closed storage bay of some sort of small factory or plant.

"Stimmel was the first," he replied. "It was two years after the war had ended. He was living in Vienna, also under a new identity. They found what was left of him in a hotel room. He had been torn apart. The other five members of the firing squad were killed in similar fashion. I was the lone

survivor, and I have tried to tell myself it was because I
refused to aim my bullets as ordered. I have tried to tell
myself that the powers that the priest's curse unleashed spared
me because they knew. But I always feared they would still
come for me another time.''

"Because Stimmel and the members of his firing squad
weren't the only ones to get what they had coming to them,
were they?''

Tessen nodded. "There were dozens of others, all with
new identities chiseled for them by those in the party who
wished to prepare the way for our rebirth. Some were protected, guarded. It didn't matter. Nothing could stop whatever force was unleashed that rainy day by the priest. And
now, now . . .''

"Now what?''

Tessen's face had turned ashen. "It has started again.''

"What?"

"All over the world, vengeance is being dispensed in the
same way it was in the years following the war. I have always
feared as much,'' Tessen said, terror underscoring his voice.
"And in more recent days I have expected it.''

"Why?''

"The dig site that the Hazelhurst team uncovered. We
were too late to stop them from opening the doorway. With
a path reopened to this world, whatever fulfilled the priest's
original curse was able to return.''

Tessen turned and stared at Blaine. McCracken's eyes returned the look skeptically without wavering.

"Refusing to believe was common among my fellows all
those years ago, Mr. McCracken. I suppose some of them
refused right up until the curse reached them. You see, the
stories you have heard about Hitler's obsession with the supernatural are underrated. I have spoken with members of
the teams that he dispatched all over the world. One of them
spent the last eighteen months of the war searching for the
entrance to hell. By the time I met him, a month before he
died, he was a raving drunk. But he claimed they found it in

the end, when it was too late to mount an effort to explor
and excavate it properly.''

"Oh, they explored it all right," Blaine muttered.

"What do you mean?"

"Never mind. What else did this man say?"

"They hid all traces of their work and made a detaile
map of how to find the site, a copy of which led both yo
and Hazelhurst to it. But the damage had already been done
The original discoverers had opened the same doorway Ha
zelhurst did, Mr. McCracken, and something emerged from
it to extract the justice the priest had called for in his curse.'
The Nazi took a deep breath. "The fact that it's happening
again proves the curse was real. We are talking about door
ways here, invitations. As soon as Hazelhurst's team re
opened the same doorway, the killings began again, because
whatever had laid dormant for all these years was free to
return to this world. Perhaps it was summoned to do anoth
er's bidding. Perhaps it is merely fulfilling its original man
date. But it is back." Tessen paused to search Blaine'
emotionless eyes. "You must believe me. You *must*!"

"You're close to the truth, Tessen, closer than you ca
possibly know."

The Nazi's lips quivered with his fear. His whole fac
paled and began twitching. "You went down there," he re
alized. "You *saw*!"

"I saw, all right, but not monsters or demons—a whol
cache of Nazi war machine remnants, stored in a secre
chamber for the next Reich to make use of."

"No, it can't—"

"And some of the remnants were missing, maybe hun
dreds of crates worth. . . ." Blaine detailed what he an
Melissa had uncovered. Tessen's eyes bulged when he reache
the part about finding the remains of the three Jews.

"So," Blaine concluded. "Let's say whatever was in thos
missing crates allowed the Jews to exact revenge on Stim
mel and dozens of others like him. Let's say when their worl
was done, they decided to destroy the crates and seal the

chamber forever. Only someone killed them before they could finish the job, someone who knew about another passageway.''

Tessen looked utterly befuddled. ''Then this person . . .''

''Very likely had something to do with the removal of the rest of the crates in the much more recent past.''

''Who? *Who?*''

Blaine looked the old Nazi in the eyes. ''Anyone with a desire to see this world rid of scum. Take your pick.''

Tessen stiffened. McCracken didn't give him a chance to respond.

''Just tell me how you knew I was here, how you knew I was at the site.''

''I didn't, not at first. I was reached when word filtered out of Turkey that one of Hazelhurst's teams had at last unearthed what many of us had lived in fear of since the end of the war. If the doorway was opened again, then perhaps none of us would be safe. Perhaps the forces summoned by the original curse would return to finish the job they started forty-five years ago. We dispatched a team to seal the newly found entrance. That was supposed to be the team's only mission, I swear it! Word that they had not reported in reached us at the same time we learned of your presence in Izmir. The reason for it seemed obvious.''

''The entrance is sealed again now.''

''I saw. Thanks to you and the woman.''

''Jesus,'' Blaine muttered, chilled suddenly. ''Turn this car around!''

''But—''

McCracken grabbed the old Nazi's arm. ''Listen to me, Tessen. Turn this car around. Back toward Bahribaba. The Archaeological Museum there.''

''I must—''

''Do it!''

CHAPTER 21

MELISSA did her best to deflect questions about her father at the Archaeological Museum in Bahribaba, the name given to Izmir's town center. Broaching the subject at all could only complicate matters further and cause her more hurt, so she simply smiled at the staff's pleasantries while tearing herself up inside. Her father was still alive, as far as the museum was concerned. He was well known here, one of the facility's largest benefactors. Favors were owed, and it was time to call at least one of them in.

She showed the tattered book to some of the research assistants, who frowned at the state of its decomposition.

"We can treat the ink to make it readable again," one explained. "But the problem lies with the condition of the paper. It's so brittle and parched, chances are the writing won't fluoresce even when treated."

"On the other hand," another said, "we could have a go at this with the electron microscope. Take about a week if—"

"No," Melissa said abruptly. "Today. It has to be today."

The two men looked at each other and shrugged.

"Let's have a go with the pages, then," the first said.

"Process takes about an hour," the second added.

* * *

186

And just that much later, Melissa found herself in a small closetlike cubicle with a single counter and chair. She was wearing special glasses that would allow her to see once the cubicle's black light was turned on. The pages of the book had been treated with a fluid that interacted with what remained of the ink and its lingering impressions to make the words readable again.

"We'll be right outside if you need anything," one of the research assistants offered.

"Thank you."

The door closed and Melissa locked it before sliding her chair beneath the counter and activating the black light attached to a swinging arm above her. She placed a pad of paper just to her right, so she could make notes on whatever she was able to decipher. Then she opened the book. There, on the inside cover page, the magic of technology revealed a name in bold, blue-tinted writing:

Gunthar Brandt.

Beneath the name was what must have been his home address. The street was indecipherable, but the hometown had fluoresced clearly: Arnsbcrg, Germany.

She slid the first page over so it was in direct line with the black light and began to read. The first six pages of Gunthar Brandt's notebook yielded a bit of inconsequential information. The handwriting resembled chicken scratches, and the German dialect used was filled with slang. It seemed to Melissa that this was actually some sort of diary or journal, penned by someone of average intelligence, at best.

Worse yet, this journal seemed to be a continuation of another, so it picked up in the middle: April 1944; the precise date was indistinguishable. It opened with complaints about the weather and the horrible food. Brandt wrote that he spent many nights crying. But his company was headed for the valley of Altaloon in the Austrian plains, where they had been chosen to fight a monumental battle. The mood in the camp was somber. Rumors of the war already being lost were running rampant. Desertion rates were increasing. The diehards, the most strident, feared that another company would be chosen for the battle of Altaloon.

To gauge that much, Melissa had to read between the lines and piece together fragments of sentences. The feeling in the pages remained, even if the words were gone. She had read war journals before. Her stomach panged with disappointment, for, unfortunately, this seemed no different from any of them. Perhaps it had been discarded within the secret chamber on purpose and had nothing at all to do with the mysterious missing crates. Still, she read on, progress slowed by the black light's inability to make a dramatic enough impact upon the book's poor state of preservation.

The further she got into the diary, the worse the deterioration became. The black light was able to reveal less and less with each flip of the page. She began skimming what little she could decipher, eager to find anything that might help her decipher the secret of the underground cache at Ephesus.

More than halfway in, a pair of words at the top of the page capitalized in bold print like a title grabbed her attention:

THE BATTLE

Melissa leaned closer to the journal and began to read. The early pages in this section were in decent condition, and she found her eyes glued to them. What she couldn't decipher, her mind filled in for her, and it read like a novel. Brandt's prose was clumsy and his use of German slang continued to make some of it incomprehensible. But he was able to relate his own fears and anxieties brilliantly. His description of their camp, of the fervor and agitation in the final hours leading up to the battle, were mesmerizing. She came to the bottom of a page and stopped, then reread a line that was actually whole to make sure she had gotten it right:

We are marching to our deaths. Only a hundred and fifty

in number, we must confront a force of two thousand. The logistics of the valley will help, but for how long? We are but an infantry unit. We have no artillery. Air support is questionable. We are lost. The war is lost. . . .

Melissa's hands were trembling when she shifted to turn the page. The condition of the next several pages frustrated her anew. It was like coming to the end of a mystery and finding the pages missing. She grasped what she could, which wasn't a whole lot.

The company had reached Altaloon and taken up positions looking down into the valley. Several deserters were shot. Men were crying, praying. Some of these were shot as well. The writer made his own final peace.

The Allied troops entered the valley. The writer could barely watch. Not only were they formidable in number, but they were accompanied by a number of tanks and armored personnel carriers. The Germans were going to be cut to shreds.

Two thousand against even less than a hundred and fifty now. . . .

Brandt repeated that phrase again and again. What was the purpose of this? Brandt wanted to know. Why was his company being sacrificed? Resigned to his own death, Brandt steadied his gun in trembling hands and waited for the order to fire.

As Melissa had feared, here in these final pages the writing became even more undecipherable. She could grasp his words only in fitful stops and starts.

The order to fire was delayed.

The enemy regiment entered the valley in a continuous stream, walking like men who knew their war was won. Suddenly an order was passed along the German lines. The words faded again here, but apparently Brandt's company was being ordered to put something on.

Melissa turned the page.

Out of nowhere . . . the sound . . . an airplane. I thought

. . . *theirs and . . . my pain would . . . quickly. The plane
. . . low. I looked . . . Ours? Ours? . . .*

The next four pages contained nothing but fragments of
words and phrases. All her attempts to fill in context failed.
Melissa felt the frustration gnaw at her. To have read this far
only to—

Wait. the last pages of Gunthar Brandt's diary grew
nearly legible again. Melissa made out the word *massacre*
and read on.

Her mouth dropped, eyes gaping. She read the legible
paragraphs over a second and then a third time. She drifted
back in her chair, certain she had it wrong.

She had to be reading this wrong! It was incredible, *impossible*!

Melissa found herself just staring at the pages now, going
over what she had already read three times. She had to be
missing something, getting the context wrong because so
much was indecipherable. Had to, because this couldn't be!

After a large gap of lost pages, Gunthar Brandt wrote of
the order to fire finally being given. Something important
must have been lost, because he kept referring to the "chaos
below" in the valley of Altaloon. But what did that mean?
More lost space was followed by descriptions of bodies falling without offering resistance, hopelessly outgunned and
overmatched, bodies falling everywhere.

The massacre . . .

But the members of Brandt's company weren't the victims;
they were the victors! A hundred and fifty against a regiment
of two thousand . . .

And the hundred and fifty had prevailed.

The knock on the room's door felt like a kick in the stomach to Melissa.

"Miss Hazelhurst," a voice called from beyond the door,
"are you all right?"

"Yes. Fine."

"Is there anything I can do?"

"No, no. I'm just finishing up."

Melissa wasn't reading anymore. The final page in the journal had been open on the counter before her for ten minutes now. The black light had saved its best magic for last. This final entry must have been made the day after the massacre, or perhaps even longer afterward. She was trying to understand the final words, at the very least believe what could not be.

Two thousand against a hundred and fifty at most . . . The hundred and fifty had dominated, had *slayed them like it was target practice.*

Melissa continued to reread the final entry.

. . . Not a single man left that valley alive. Only four of my comrades fell in the battle and all these, it was believed, to our own fire. A massacre . . . It had been so enjoyable, so fulfilling, that none of us realized then what had made it possible. But I realize now. The White Death . . . I didn't care then. I care now. This must be the last entry in my journal. What I had hoped could be shared with the world must never be shared with anyone. I am embarrassed. I am ashamed. I am terrified. . . .

That was as far as she could read. At the bottom of the last page, though, was an unreadable line that looked as though it was the name "Gunthar Brandt" again. His rank and company followed in readable form on the next lines. Here was an eyewitness to what had happened at Altaloon, and Melissa felt certain that event was directly related to the contents of the mysterious crates.

The White Death . . .

What was it? Might Brandt still be alive, and if so, could he tell her?

McCracken would find him. McCracken would know how.

Melissa gathered up all the notes containing her creative translation of the text and moved for the door.

The Büyük Efes Hotel was still buzzing with activity when Melissa returned at three o'clock. She didn't notice the con-

gestion of official vehicles and the terrible damage done to
the hotel's front until she was less than a block away. She
quickened her pace, heart racing. She was fearing the worst,
expecting it. The main entrance had been closed, two sets of
side doors replacing it. Melissa cautiously slid into the lobby
past Turkish police officers.

The level of destruction shocked her. There was still blood
all over the floor and the rugs. Glass and debris were being
swept up. Furniture and decorations lay in pieces. The win-
dowed walls had been reduced to splinters, and even now
boards were being nailed over where glass had been only a
few hours before.

Melissa felt a hand grasp her at the elbow.

"I did not mean to startle you," the assistant manager
said.

"What hap—"

"Please," he interrupted. "Walk with me. We must make
this fast."

"McCracken."

"He escaped. Plenty of others did not."

"How many?"

"Dozens. I don't even know myself. I don't want to
know."

Melissa looked at the bloodstains again, the randomness
of them. Many bodies had fallen, by all indications slain
indiscriminately.

"I have your passport and the money left in your deposit
box," the assistant manager said, producing a manila envelope from his pocket. "I'm sorry I can't do more."

Melissa's legs suddenly felt very heavy.

"Keep walking. Please."

It was hard, but she managed.

"McCracken knew where you were going, yes?"

"Yes, of course."

"Then, you must return there. That is where he will look
for you."

"No," she said, thoughts forming with her words. "Whoever did this might know that. They'd be waiting."

The assistant manager nodded in agreement. The nod gave way to a shrug.

"You must leave now. You are not safe here."

His voice was laced with dismay and disgust. He wanted her out of the hotel. Clearly he blamed her and McCracken for what had happened here today and, by connection, himself for assisting them.

"I will escort you to the service entrance," the assistant manager was saying.

All Melissa could do was nod, cold sweat beginning to soak into her clothes. Never had she felt more alone, more lost.

But she *wasn't* lost. There was a direction to go in, a beacon to follow.

Unraveling the mysteries of the journal, of the White Death, would go a long way toward unraveling the mysteries of the missing crates. If Gunthar Brandt was still alive, she would find him. The resources and friends of her father would be utilized. More favors would be called in.

Once she reached Germany.

"They're all assembled, sir," Arnold Rothstein's assistant informed him.

Rothstein maintained a residence in Herzliyya, a posh suburb of Tel Aviv, but for security reasons this meeting had been set up in a suite at the Tel Aviv Hilton. His assistant ushered him in through the service entrance and up to the eighth floor by private elevator. It hadn't been easy coming up with the men he needed for this mission; in fact, it had proven almost impossible on such short notice. Many favors had had to be called in, even more to keep people from asking questions. It was only last night that Rothstein had approved all the dossiers submitted to him.

Recalling their contents sent a chill through him. In his years of fighting for Israel, he had come to know men whose

ruthlessness and capacity for violence was unmatched.
But these ten men represented another level. The newer generations had proven even more militant and less yielding than
the older ones, a process Rothstein felt certain would continue. After all, while the men waiting for him in the suite
had grown up in the shadow of the Six Day War, the next
would grow up with the memories of gas masks donned from
fear of Scud missiles. Israeli history did not move in traditional cycles. It simply ascended on a constant diagonal, each
era building upon the one that preceded it.

"Good afternoon, gentlemen," Arnold Rothstein said after entering the living-room portion of the suite and taking a
seat.

The ten faces barely acknowledged him. If anyone was
surprised that it was Rothstein who had summoned them, he
didn't show it. All of them simply kept to their chairs as
caged predators do to their bars.

The group, meanwhile, was anything but homogeneous.
Several of those gathered were among the largest, most powerful men Rothstein had ever encountered. Several others
were quite small and might have even appeared frail at first
glance. What held them together had nothing to do with appearances.

It was the contents of their dossiers.

The ten individuals gathered before him were the most
efficient killers Israel had to offer. Their skills were expertly
refined and regularly practiced, first with the deadly and se-
cretive Sayaret, and then later on specially selected missions
that routinely went unlogged.

"Allow me to get right to the point," the old man continued. "You have been chosen for a mission of grave importance to the state of Israel and beyond."

"There is no beyond," one of them said.

"There is now," Rothstein said, and began to explain.

PART FOUR

White Death

The world: Friday, seven A.M.

CHAPTER 22

"*V*ERY *well, then. Let us move on to the subject you have all been waiting for.*"

Introductory remarks complete, the mechanically synthesized voice prepared to get to the business at hand. Across the world, men and women waited with receivers clutched to their ears for the final instructions that would forever change the face of civilization. Thanks to sophisticated translating equipment at the speaker's source, each heard the words in their own native language.

In Vienna, and Moscow, and Stockholm.

In London, and Dublin, and Prague.

In Tokyo, and Seoul, and New York.

In Los Angeles, and São Paulo, and Montreal.

In Cairo, and Tel Aviv, and Johannesburg.

Just to name a few. The time had come.

"*Our successes of the past seven days have set the stage for the achievement of a destiny so long in coming,*" the voice continued. "*The world begs for what we have to offer it on a scale grand enough to rid it at last of squalor and rot. We are justified in the task we are about to undertake. Our mission is a holy one. You are the messengers of a new order, dispensing wrath to those for whom civilization has exhausted all other options. Because of our work, evil will*

*cease to be, and we will maintain our vigil without pause to
make sure it never returns.''*

A brief staticlike sound filled the many lines as the network was rerouted once again to make tracing the caller's
origin impossible.

*"You all know what your roles are. You all know what you
must do. In four days' time, distribution will take place in
our western sector. Distribution will follow one day later in
our eastern sector. Then, one week from today, at your specified times, your work will begin in your designated areas. I
estimate it will take two weeks before saturation is achieved
in the primary sites, and we will then move on to the secondary ones.''*

The voice stopped this time for no reason at all. Nothing
filled the line in its place, not even static.

*"A glorious dawn is about to break, the dawn of a new
world purified of evil. Today, the evil grows and festers un-
checked, affecting everything and everyone, while the world
stands passively by, accepting. We will not accept. We will
stand and face it, as is our destiny. The tens of millions we
destroy will stretch perhaps into the hundreds of millions
before we are through. Let the number grow to whatever it
must. Our goal is clear, our resolve immutable. The world
cries out for us, begs for the tonic only we can supply. Survival—that is what this is about.''*

Static replaced the voice again, as the network automatically rerouted itself one final time.

*"Go now and brief your teams on the timetable I have
placed before you. There is no turning back. Say good-bye
to the world you have regarded with revulsion and disgust.
The new world begins in seven days' time.*

"Our world,'' the voice finished, and the connection was
broken.

"Well, lookee what we got here. . . .''

The bartender, a half-foot over six, leaned across the bar
toward Johnny Wareagle.

"What can I get for ya, Crazy Horse?" he asked, and the few inhabitants of Cooter Brown's, a bar on South Carrollton Avenue in the center of New Orleans, didn't bother to smother their laughter. According to Sal Belamo, this was the virtual second home of Jersey Joe Watts, the man who had been with Heydan Larroux just minutes before the attack she had managed to escape.

Johnny's expression remained unchanged. His eyes slid to a corner where a man was feeding change into a compact disc jukebox. Against the far wall the bar's oyster shucker had stopped slicing and was simply holding his knife.

"I have come for Jack Watts," Wareagle told the bartender.

The man grinned, and buried a chuckle. "Never mixed one of them before. How's about a beer? Indian lager."

Johnny heard more laughter, this time from behind him. "I wish to speak to Jack Watts. I have been told he comes here. Often."

"Never heard of him."

"He was here yesterday. And the day before." Wareagle's eyes roamed behind the counter. "His name is in the book where you keep track of bets."

The bartender leaned farther across the counter. His right hand disappeared beneath it.

"I lost plenty of ancestors to you injuns. Don't see much of your kind in these parts and don't miss 'em none neither."

Johnny saw the ax handle the instant it crossed the bar and snapped his right hand out against the bartender's to keep it from going any farther. At the same time, he heard the chair scratching backward against the floor behind him and whipped his knife out with his left hand. A quick glance that way was all that he needed to spot the pistol rising in the hand of one of Cooter Brown's patrons. The knife whirled out of Johnny's fingers and sliced into and through the man's wrist. The tip of the blade emerged on the other side. The gunman's hand jerked upward. A harmless shot rang out, the sound of it swallowed by his screaming. The rest of the patrons were still. They had guns; Johnny could feel that much. But no one else had any intention of drawing one.

"You fucking broke my arm, you crazy fucking In—"

"Not yet," Wareagle told the bartender, holding the arm straight out with no slack.

The bartender was heaving for breath, his face scarlet. "You want Jersey Jack, fine. Just let me go."

"After you have spoken."

"Jesus, it hurts. . . ."

"Tell me where he is."

"Rooming house on Ferrett Street. Twenty-seven, I think, or seventy-two. Yeah, seventy-two. Second floor, room five."

Wareagle let the bartender's arm drop. Numbed, it collapsed to his side. He slipped backward against the mirrored wall of liquor bottles.

"Hope he plugs your red ass full of lead. You hear me, you son of a bitch?"

Johnny did, but kept walking. The man his blade had found was whimpering now, seated on the floor and gazing in shock at his wrist.

"You can keep the knife," Johnny told him.

Ferrett Street was located in what the residents of New Orleans commonly refer to as "Slumville." Johnny walked to it from Cooter Brown's and felt uncomfortable every step of the way. This kind of work was far more up Blaine McCracken's alley than his. The presence of so many strangers unnerved him. He knew that he attracted their stares, but could do nothing but move on past them as quickly as possible. Venturing out on such a pursuit would have ordinarily been impossible for him; even responding to Joe Rainwater's call had been difficult. But now Joe Rainwater was dead, and the discomforting knowledge that his killers were still out there was worse than any unease he would feel on their trail.

The rooming house Jersey Jack Watts was holed up in on

Ferrett Street in Slumville was as shabby and decrepit as the neighborhood's name indicated. The sign advertising ROOMS was missing the top of the second "O" and the bottom half of the "S." Several of the windows had boards in place of glass panes. Several more were shattered or missing and hadn't been replaced with anything.

The lobby consisted of a single chair and couch. Johnny Wareagle walked right past a trio of black men sitting there drinking wine out of plastic cups. He mounted the stairs quickly to the second floor and moved to room five.

"Nobody fucking home," a tired, angry voice greeted his knock.

Wareagle rapped again.

"Get the fuck out of here!"

"I have come from Heydan Larroux."

Johnny heard the soft click and threw his body down. An instant later a huge chunk of the door's upper part was blown into splinters. They showered over Johnny as he shoved his body into what remained of the door and tore it clear off its hinges.

"Shit!" he heard a voice wail as he drove the door inward.

Impact smashed Watts up against the wall. His breath left him in a rush. His shotgun was pinned against his body. The air smelled of gunsmoke and ruined wood.

"Jesus, no!" Watts gasped. *"Please, no! . . ."*

"I need to find Heydan Larroux," Wareagle said simply. He tossed the ruined door aside and held Watts pinned against the wall with a single hand.

Watts's eyes sharpened at last, drinking in the sight of the huge Indian before him. The shotgun slipped out of his grasp and dropped to the floor.

"Who are you? Jesus, *what* are you?"

"You were the last one with Larroux before they came."

"She dead, man. They all dead."

"She got out."

"Fuck me, she did. I heard what went down in that house. I run away first 'cause somebody mighta figured was me that done it, and then 'cause I figured whatever really done it might wanna pay me a visit.''

"She's alive."

"No way, man. Nothin' go through what happened at the big house and live to tell." He looked the big Indian over again. " 'Cept maybe you."

A pair of men appeared in Jersey Jack's doorway. Wareagle turned enough for them to see his eyes. They rushed off, one muttering, "Fuck, let's call the cops."

"You worked for her," Wareagle said, his eyes back on Watts.

Jersey Jack shrugged. The wounds Larroux had inflicted on him with the cat-o'-nine-tails still had him grinding his teeth when he moved, but, shit, he'd deserved it.

"Bitch always treated me straight."

"You owe her."

"How you know that?"

"I do. You can pay her back."

"How's that?"

"Let me help her."

Jersey Jack tried to look the Indian in the eye. "Whatever showed up at the big house still after her?" he asked.

"Yes."

"And you can stop them?"

"I don't know."

"If anyone can, it's you."

"Where is she?"

"Only one place she could go to hide, place some of us call hell."

Johnny didn't seem surprised.

"Man, you don't know much, do ya? I'm talking about the bayou. Lady got a place down there. Been there myself. She in trouble, that's where she'd go."

"She's in trouble," said Wareagle.

The Old One held the stones before her out to Heydan Larroux.

"Take one, my child."

Larroux did so reluctantly. She held it in her hand but did not let it drop in the bowl of water. The afternoon air beyond her bayou hideaway was ripe with the sound of frogs and birds.

After the Old One's last admonitions, she had redistributed her guards around the bayou hideaway that rose on stilts over the muck and ooze. Some of the guards were perched within trees. Others used the mud itself for camouflage. Still more spent their shifts in steel-hulled rowboats in the black waters. A few hid themselves within the thick, rank foliage. No electronic signals, no sophisticated security devices. Just men who knew the bayou and could smell a stranger a mile away.

"The stone, my child," the Old One uttered in her ancient voice.

"Are they near?" Heydan asked.

Plop . . .

As always, the blind hag gazed down into the water as if she could see the ripples made by the stone. "They have learned where you are."

Larroux accepted another stone.

"Should I leave?"

Plop . . .

"You are safer here than anywhere else. Your chances of surviving are greater because . . ."

"Because why?"

"It is difficult . . . to see. Another stone. Quickly!"

"A warrior comes," the Old One resumed, after Heydan had let it fall into the water.

"You mentioned him before."

"This is not the one I recognize." The Old One's dead eyes gazed across at her. "He comes our way even now. He will be joined eventually by the first warrior I saw; but not here, not now."

Heydan Larroux got her fourth stone ready to fall.

"Who is he?"

Plop . . .

The Old One brought her face close enough to the water to drink. "I see a bird of prey dressed for war. An eagle, I think it is an eagle!"

Her head snapped upward with a start. She was breathing in rapid heaves.

"Another stone," she instructed. "Now!"

Heydan took the second-to-the-last and let it drop.

"Others come," the Old One said into the bowl.

"The enemy . . ."

"No. But not allies, either."

"Who?"

"The last stone. Quickly, before the vision fades."

Plop . . .

The Old One's head was bowed low once more. "So hazy . . . They, too, are warriors. They come in number. But they . . . wait."

"Wait?"

The Old One raised her head. "I can see no more."

"You must!"

"The vision is gone." Her dead eyes fixed themselves on Larroux. "But you will see for yourself soon, my child. That time is coming."

To underscore his fervent support for Israel, Arnold Rothstein was in the habit of making frequent public appearances throughout the country. Because of his stature, the government insisted on supplying him security in the form of agents from Shin Bet and Mossad for all public gatherings. The billionaire agreed, on the condition that the majority of them not be obtrusive. Today's appearance in Jerusalem was no exception. Minutes before his arrival, a dozen agents had blended into the crowd.

Uniformed security personnel, meanwhile, allowed a wheelchair-bound veteran of one of Israel's more recent wars to be pushed up to the front of the line. The man was missing both legs. It would make for good shots on television, a perfect backdrop when the American networks picked up the feed.

Because of their disguises, none of the security personnel, uniformed or otherwise, noticed that the cripple and the man pushing his wheelchair were twins.

Israel's greatest benefactor arrived right on schedule and stepped out of his car to a symphony of cheers and applause. He was waving and shaking hands with the first wave of supporters when the agents nearest the crowd's front noticed the empty wheelchair.

Witnesses nearby would later say that the commotion actually started *before* the explosion, as bodies seemed to lunge and leap through the air. The blast was shattering, the fireball swallowed almost immediately by a gray-black wave of smoke that coughed blood in all directions. The screams were the only sounds that remained when the echoes of the blast dissipated. The only sights were mangled, twisted bodies. When the screams died down, the sound of sirens replaced them and continued for the rest of the afternoon, seemingly without end.

CHAPTER 23

GERMANY maintains no official archive of World War II. The closest thing to it is called the Document Center, which had been administered by the Americans until reunification.

Located in Berlin, the center is a five-story building resembling a library. Melissa and her father had attended the ceremony when it was turned over to German control, because one of Benson Hazelhurst's oldest friends had been named administrator.

She did not call ahead that Friday morning to announce her intentions. Instead she simply showed up at the Document Center and asked to see the chief administrator, Wolfgang Bertlemass. The guard at the front desk held the receiver against his shoulder while he informed Melissa that Bertlemass was sending his secretary down to escort her up.

"Melissa, you're more lovely than I remembered," he greeted moments later inside his office, stepping out from behind his desk. Bertlemass was even heavier than he had been at the ceremony. His vest strained to reach the top of his pants. He seemed barely able to move.

Melissa accepted his hug and light kiss. "Thank you for seeing me."

"You are here no doubt on some adventurous research project for your father."

"Sit down, please, *Herr* Bertlemass."

"Wolfgang." His eyes grew uncertain. "Your tone of voice, Melissa, tells me you have bad news."

"The worst. My father . . . is dead."

Bertlemass's bulbous frame sank into his chair, mouth agape in shock. "*What*? I had not heard, did not know. Please forgive me. How did it happen? Where? Why wasn't I informed?"

"You are the first to be informed."

"I . . . don't understand."

"He died in the midst of his greatest discovery, *Herr* Bertlemass. But that discovery unearthed the promise of more death unless action is taken."

"What are you saying?"

"No more than I have to. I'm asking you to trust me."

"For your father I would do anything. You need keep no secrets from me."

"What I do, I do for your own good."

Wolfgang Bertlemass wiped the tears from his eyes. "I am so sorry, Melissa. . . ."

"You must help me."

"Of course. Anything."

"With no questions."

Bertlemass's nod came without hesitation. "Whatever you choose to tell me will be sufficient."

Melissa pulled Gunthar Brandt's journal from the shoulder bag she had purchased at the airport. "I found this in the excavation where my father died. It tells of a battle from near the Second World War's end but it is vague and much has been lost to the years. I need to learn everything about that battle. I need the holes filled in."

Wolfgang Bertlemass struggled to rise once again. "Come with me."

"We used to call these the stacks," he explained as they stepped off the elevator onto the fifth floor. "Now they are called the official archives of the war. Everything that was ever written or known of those years is here. And almost all of it has been transferred into our computer banks."

Around her everywhere, Melissa saw traditional library shelving packed with material of all shapes and sizes. There were maps, battle plans, discourses, first-hand accounts of various engagements, and accumulated interviews with tens of thousands of men and women. In essence, much of the Third Reich's legacy was contained here, what it had done and failed to do. Melissa was overwhelmed.

"As I said, we are computerized," Bertlemass said, and led her into one of the private cubicles. "It is really a simple matter. All the material you seek is cross-filed under a variety of headings."

He struggled into a chair but had to sit back from the keyboard, since his legs wouldn't squeeze under the table.

"Now," he said as the terminal whirled to life, "where should we start?"

"The battle in question was named in the journal."

"As good a place as any. What was it?"

"Altaloon," Melissa told him.

"Location?"

"Austrian plains."

Bertlemass called up the proper menu and activated the search procedure.

"It always takes a few seconds," he explained, and returned his gaze to the screen, just as the monitor beeped. "Oh," he said.

Over his shoulder, Melissa could see the results of the computer's search: NO REFERENCE FOUND.

"Not a problem," the administrator told her. "Many battles may have been named in private journals, but relatively few of those were ever recorded for posterity. We need another reference."

"What about the registration of the German company that participated in the battle?"

"Splendid. Our cross-referencing of all engagements is virtually complete. What was the registration?"

Melissa read it to him and Bertlemass typed it into the console. Again he waited with Melissa pressed over him until the response came seconds later: NO REFERENCE FOUND.

"Strange," the administrator said.

"What's it mean?"

"That this company never existed."

"No," Melissa insisted. "That's impossible. I've got the evidence right here."

"Show me."

Melissa produced her notes and Bertlemass's fingers worked the keyboard again, producing the same results.

"There is no record of such a company anywhere in our archives."

"I'm telling you it existed! It had to!"

Bertlemass was looking back at her. "Mistakes, omissions, are unlikely but possible. There is nothing to worry about. The journal's author, you said you knew his name."

"Yes. Gunthar Brandt."

"Spell it."

Melissa obliged. "And I have his rank and serial number as well."

"That should speed things along. . . ."

Bertlemass typed Gunthar Brandt's serial number into the machine as Melissa recited it. The computer whirled into action.

"No," she said in response to the results seconds later. "No. . . ." NO REFERENCE FOUND.

"Very strange indeed," Bertlemass said, clearly exasperated.

"What's it mean?"

"That the man who wrote this journal never existed either."

"There's got to be something more we can do," Melissa said.

The fat man shrugged. "We must face the fact that this journal can only be the result of fabrication, fiction instead of fact."

"No. I showed you my notes. I told you what I was feeling as I read it. It happened, I'm telling you, it happened!"

"The participating company doesn't exist. The man who wrote it doesn't exist."

"A ruse perpetrated by those behind the battle," Melissa insisted. "They were testing something that made it possible for them to kill a force more than ten times their size that had infinitely superior weapons. I showed you the reference. They only lost four men. Four men on one side, *two thousand* on the other! . . .

"The White Death," she finished after a pause that seemed longer than it was.

"Also no reference found."

"Which is hardly surprising."

Bertlemass sighed impatiently. "Melissa, I am a student of the Great War. I can tell you quite assuredly that I have never come across any mention of such an occurrence, or of a weapon that made it possible. And I ask you, if the Nazis possessed this . . . White Death . . . why didn't they employ it again? Whatever it is, clearly it could have won them the war.''

"I don't know.''

"I do: it never existed. Gunthar Brandt, the soldier, never existed.''

That gave her another idea, a recollection that had slipped her mind until now. "His hometown was mentioned in the journal. On the front inside page underneath his name. . . . Arnsberg!'' she remembered without consulting her notes.

"That will not help us find the reference we need.''

"Maybe not to the battle, but what about the man?''

"Melissa, I—''

"Please, *Herr* Bertlemass, for my father.''

The fat man shrugged. "I will see what I can do.''

Bertlemass was able to get the head of the local district post office in Arnsberg on the phone twenty minutes later. The conversation was brief. He made a few notes and hung up, returning his gaze to Melissa.

"Apparently there are two families named Brandt living in Arnsberg.''

"I told you!''

"Brandt is a popular name, Melissa,'' Bertlemass cautioned her. "You should not get your hopes up.''

"How long a drive is it?''

"Several hours, between six and eight anyway. If you leave tomorrow morning—''

"I must leave now!''

"Then let me call you a driver.''

"No. There isn't time. Just a car, *Herr* Bertlemass. If you could just get me a car.''

"This is that important to you?''

"It may be what my father died for,'' she said truthfully.

Bertlemass nodded and extracted a set of keys from his pocket. "Then you will take mine.''

* * *

"Any minute now," Tessen told Blaine again.

"It's been hours."

"Gaining access to the one we seek must go through channels."

"Channels, I gather, you're no longer accustomed to."

Tessen shrugged. "The diehards in our movement continue to hope for revival. Most of us merely wish to survive undetected."

"Which might be a problem if the latest possessor of those crates has you on their list, just as the original possessor did."

"Precisely why we have sought you out, Mr. McCracken, as I have already explained."

Tessen continued to maintain his vigil by the phone at this small inn located in the German countryside. McCracken paced about nervously, his thoughts locked on Melissa. He and Tessen had reached the Archaeological Museum in the center of Izmir to find that she had already departed. Against Tessen's strident objections, Blaine then insisted on returning to the Büyük Efes, where he found that they had missed her once again. His contact, the Büyük Efes assistant manager, had helped her in every manner he could before setting her on her way again. She had not told him of her destination, however, nor had he asked. To have done so might have placed both their lives in jeopardy.

Before they had even left Turkey, the old Nazi had begun the process of tracking down someone who could tell them what was in the missing crates the Third Reich had stored in Ephesus along with the rest of the supplies. He made phone calls every thirty minutes or so. One number led to another number, each contact to the next. They were waiting at this inn now for final instructions as to how to proceed. According to Tessen, his former comrades were being remarkably cooperative. There was strong reason for hope.

Blaine had tried to reach only one person since arriving at the inn. Sal Belamo had responded finally after thirty minutes.

"Where you been, boss?"

"I was about to ask you the same question, Sal."

"Putting a package together for the big fella. Some real goodies, you ask me. On their way to New Orleans as we speak."

"New Orleans? What in hell for?"

"Long story."

"I may need you, Sal."

"Big fella might need me more."

And Belamo proceeded to relate to Blaine the crux of what Johnny was involved in, and the crux was all it took.

"All of them torn apart," McCracken repeated, his mind numb.

"That's the way he described it to me, boss. Big fella ain't one to exaggerate, either." Sal paused. "They killed his friend, the injun police officer who called him in. Big fella didn't sound happy."

"How many?"

"I found a dozen already, all in the last week. Same M.O. Pretty weird shit, you ask me. . . . Hey, boss, you there?"

McCracken remained silent. His mind was swimming wildly. All over the world, evil was being exorcised. Justice was being extracted upon those who had managed to exist beyond it by a force even more ruthless and deadly than those it sought to destroy. But this force was not new. It had made its mark years before, as detailed by Tessen. Now it was back. While McCracken followed the trail of the pilfered crates, Johnny was following the trail of those who were surely making use once again of their contents.

"Did Johnny say anything about strange footprints?" Blaine asked finally.

"How the fuck you know that?"

"Because it's happened before."

"Huh?"

"He and I are after the same thing, Sal."

"You gotta be fuckin' kidding me. . . ."

"No. Different lines, different tracks, but it's the same thing. He calls in, I want to know about it."

"Where can I reach you?"

McCracken gave Belamo the number of the inn. But he hadn't called over the succeeding hours. And neither had any of Tessen's contacts.

"You were that certain I would help you?" Blaine continued, while their vigil before the phone continued.

"I was certain of nothing until our initial conversation. I knew—we knew—only that the chamber had been compromised. The fact that crates were what emerged from it instead of demons was meaningless. The threat was, in any case, the same as that we faced after World War II."

"You still haven't answered my question."

Tessen's expression was grim. "Whoever controls what was removed from that chamber, Mr. McCracken, has the power to do far more than extract vengeance. If my fears prove justified, the scope of that power is potentially unlimited."

"That's what the Arab said. That's what drew me over here in the first place. That kind of power in anyone's hands, no matter whose, is unacceptable, Tessen."

The phone rang.

"The man is many miles from here in Mönchengladbach," Tessen said when the brief conversation was over. "We have been granted access to him."

"Who is this man?"

"A member of Hitler's personal staff, some sort of liaison with the board of science. Apparently he was part of the team responsible for storing away our greatest munitions when it became obvious that the war was lost."

"While others salted away the billions of dollars necessary to found a Fourth Reich."

"A false rumor," Tessen insisted. "What moderate sums there were have now been squandered by those who believed another Reich was possible. They spent it toward the formation of groups all over the world that would someday join together as the first line. But the groups fizzled. No sooner would one start up than another would die. The world had changed, *has* changed. Most of the old guard failed to see that.''

''Not you.''

Tessen shrugged. ''I am merely a soldier. I see the battlefield for what it is. Come, we have a long ride ahead of us, many hours. We are expected just after nightfall.''

The elected head of the kibbutz known as Nineteen brought the news to the old woman herself. Tovah stiffened in her wheelchair behind the wrought-iron table at her approach. She looked down before the leader had a chance to speak.

''It is bad news.''

''Rothstein,'' Tovah muttered.

''An attempted assassination occurred earlier today.''

Tovah looked up with a glimmer of hope. ''Attempted . . .''

''It was an explosion. Apparently two security men saved him from the brunt of the blast. But, er . . .''

''Speak!''

''He was critically wounded. He is in surgery now. The prognosis is not good, even if he survives.''

The old woman's parched lips squeezed together determinedly. ''I warned him. The fool, he didn't take it seriously. He didn't realize . . .''

''I'm sorry. I didn't hear what you said.''

Tovah's hands clenched the sides of her wheelchair. She shoved herself backward from the table. The quickness of the action made the leader of Nineteen lurch away.

''No matter,'' the old woman spoke clearly now. ''Assemble the women in the cafeteria. I will address them in thirty minutes.'' And then, under her breath, too softly for the leader to hear, ''The time has come to go to war again.''

CHAPTER 24

JOHNNY Wareagle observed the house in the bayou from a distance of three hundred yards through the binoculars that Sal Belamo had included in his supplies. The rest of the supplies he'd picked up in New Orleans were either worn, pocketed, or slung from his back and shoulders. There was Kevlar body armor, a 9mm pistol, an Uzi, and a British Sterling SMG. There was a killing knife and two of the throwing variety.

"Hey," Belamo had said, "the only thing I left out was a bow and arrow."

The British Sterling SMG was fitted with explosive bullets called Splats that Johnny had worked with once before.

"Got a friend who makes 'em up special," Belamo had explained then. "Puts a glass capsule inside each with a mixture of ground glass and picric acid. Mixing the acid with the ground glass makes it less sensitive and allows it to be fired from a gun. When the bullet distorts on its way out of the barrel, the glass capsule breaks, which allows the acid to mix with lead, forming lead picric. Big boom when it hits its target. I call 'em Splats since that's what happens to whatever they hit. Only problem is the Sterling's your best bet to fire them."

Johnny had uttered a lengthy sigh upon hearing that.

"I know how you feel 'bout the Sterling, big fella, but Splats'll blow up in an M-16's barrel on account of the muzzle velocity. You'll get to love the Sterling, though. Trust me."

Johnny was holding it in hand now. He had parked a considerable distance back on the road, geared up under cover of woods, and trudged his way through the muck and ooze forming the shore of the bayou's water. He stood now within the shadowy cover of the mangroves and cypress trees with mud covering his boots up to his ankles. The feeling was nothing new to Johnny; he had lived it for the better part of five years in a place his memory called the hellfire. But here the jungle breathed with life, the night birds and bullfrogs haunting the sultry air with their peculiar chants. In the fetid stink of the hellfire there had been no sound and the silence had been agonizing, the silence of death itself. A branch on his right shuffled, and Wareagle gazed up to see a curious tree boa descending to inspect this new visitor to its world. Johnny smiled at it and the boa stopped, lapping at the air with its tongue.

A slight breeze disturbed the currents in the black pool beyond, pushing a shape through the night. Johnny waded out farther into the muck and made out a boat snailing along the murky waters. He moved in up to his knees and peered into the skiff as it slid by. Empty. A guard must have once been posted in it, but he was in it no more. Johnny retreated back into the cover of sweeping vines and branches and glided about the edge of the bayou.

He came upon the first body hidden in a hollow tree. Its positioning told him the man had squeezed himself in and had been killed at his post. A single bullet hole lay in the center of his forehead. His dead eyes seemed to be gazing up at it. Not the mark of the killers of Joe Rainwater, which could only mean . . .

Someone else was here! Besides the force he sought, besides Heydan Larroux's guards. . . .

Perplexed, Johnny slid back out into the swamp. The soft

bottom retreated beneath his step. Tangled weeds stroked his ankles, occasionally twisting themselves into a determined hold. A cottonmouth snake slithered past, ignoring him. He listened for the hiss of an alligator or the telltale thump its swinging tail made when it swiped against the water.

He found another pair of bodies hidden in the bushes they had used for camouflage. Again there were bullet wounds in the heads, the rear this time. The shots had been fired from in close, the killers obviously very sure of themselves.

Not Joe Rainwater's killers, though. This was the trademark of an entirely different, though very proficient, style. Whoever the killers were, it was clear to Johnny now that they had slain all of the Larroux woman's guards systematically, one or two at a time. The bodies in the bushes had been dead for at least thirty minutes, plenty of time for the killers to close in on the house and finish their work—if, in fact, that was what had brought them here.

To better investigate, Johnny risked moving across a narrow peninsula affording little cover to bring him closer to the woman's hiding place. He raised his binoculars and inspected the house for signs of intrusion or violence. The door was intact. The walkway leading to the small porch was unmarred.

He checked the windows. Also intact. The lights were on but the blinds were drawn. Johnny continued his patient scan. A shadow passed before one of the blinds. Thirty seconds later, it returned. A guard inside was making regular checks of the windows. The defensive perimeter erected had been primitive; the dead guards had not been in communication with each other or with those inside the house.

But those inside the house were still breathing. The mystery force that had isolated them had not made its move yet. Why? The apparent contradiction mystified Wareagle. He could not find the logic in what had occurred here.

The night breeze picked up. Gooseflesh prickled Johnny's flesh. He felt the presence of the spirits. They had never made themselves more known to him, had never been more insistent.

Something was coming, its movements dark, sleek, and one with the night. He waded back into the thick snarl of the shallow swamp waters to return to firmer land to await its arrival.

Melissa reached the town of Arnsberg in Bertlemass's Mercedes an hour before nightfall. At the first address for a "Brandt," the family had never heard of a Gunthar; at the second, the man who answered the door told her he had an uncle by that name. Melissa asked him if the uncle had fought in World War II. The man said he had indeed, after which he had taught science at a nearby high school. This Gunthar Brandt, he explained, had spent the last three months in a rest home operated by the Catholic church another hour away in Remscheid after suffering a stroke.

She felt certain this was the Gunther Brandt who had written the journal. Still, she had to realistically consider what condition the stroke might have left him in. He would be seventy-two now, hardly old age by modern standards. That gave her as much hope as anything.

Night had fallen by the time she reached Remscheid, an industrial town not far from Düsseldorf; provincial, Melissa thought as she drove through it toward the nursing home. The nursing home was located amidst a residential neighborhood on Hansastrasse. It was made up of two interconnected buildings, and Melissa followed the signs toward the visitor parking lot. From there she walked down a small stone stairway to a second driveway that led to the lobby. The huge glass double doors slid open automatically as she approached them, and she moved toward a reception booth formed by a long counter on the left.

The receptionist accepted her announcement that she was here to see Gunthar Brandt matter-of-factly.

"Oh," she said, after checking the log.

"Is something wrong?" Melissa wondered.

"You have not been here before?"

"No."

The receptionist seemed to be considering whether she should say more. "Ward Three," she directed. "Third floor. I will tell a floor nurse to expect you."

Melissa took the elevator to the third floor and stepped out into a large, open area. Before her, patients lingered in wheelchairs or walked about aimlessly. Some stood leaning against the wall. Others gazed vacantly out one of the large windows. Obviously this was the chronic-care ward, which did not bode well for her chances of obtaining any information from Brandt.

"You are here to see *Herr* Brandt?"

Melissa turned toward the speaker and found herself facing a kindly bull of a woman in a white uniform.

"I am *Herr* Brandt's night *Altenpfleger*."

"The word—I'm sorry, but my German is lacking."

"Nurse for the elderly, that's all." Her expression sombered. "The receptionist informed me you have not been to see *Herr* Brandt before."

"No, I haven't."

"I'm sorry to have to disappoint you, then."

Melissa's heart sank.

"You must be a long-lost niece or distant cousin of *Herr* Brandt's. You should have called ahead. We would have spared you the trouble."

"What are you talking about?"

"Let me show you."

The nurse led Melissa to the last room down an L-shaped corridor.

"Fortunately," she explained, "we've been able to keep him in one of the private rooms. It's quite smaller than the ambulatory apartments on the first floor, but I'm afraid he doesn't notice."

The door to the room was open. Melissa entered ahead of the nurse and froze.

The man in the bed lay in a state of virtual catatonia. The music of a radio by his beside droned on.

"He can eat. He can hear. We're almost certain he can see," the nurse explained. "But he's lost the ability to comprehend and communicate. I'm afraid he's completely lost."

"Can I have a few minutes alone with him?"

"Of course." The big nurse started toward the door, then swung back. "I am sorry."

"Thank you."

And she was gone.

Melissa moved to Gunthar Brandt's bedside. Her hope for an easy solution to the mystery of the missing crates fizzled and died.

"Mr. Brandt, can you hear me?"

No response.

"Mr. Brandt, can you hear me?"

His eyes didn't so much as flicker in her direction.

"Mr. Brandt, I need your help. If you can hear me, blink your eyes twice."

They didn't even blink once.

"Please try. I know you can try. I've come a very long way, and I think many, many lives may be at stake."

When Gunthar Brandt continued to just lie there, Melissa pulled the journal that he had penned almost a half century before from her shoulder bag. She held it forward in front of his glazed eyes.

"Do you know what this is? You wrote it. You described a battle you were a part of, a battle that for all practical purposes never happened. No record of it exists. Also, there is no record of your service or of your company's existence. It's all been wiped out, Mr. Brandt, and I think the lost contents of this journal are the reason why. Am I right? Please tell me."

His breathing remained steady and even. Melissa waited a few moments, pressed him again, and then gave up. It was useless. The man's mind was a sieve. He was lost to the world. Melissa turned away from him.

''Close the door,'' a voice whispered, and Melissa nearly jumped.

''What?'' Her eyes fell back on the bed.

The eyes of Gunthar Brandt flashed alive and looked in her direction. ''Close the door, *Fräulein*, and hurry.''

McCracken and Tessen waited in the car while their sanctioned access was confirmed within the large house on the Bokelberg. A residential area located fifteen minutes from downtown Mönchengladbach, the Bokelberg is actually a hill with several off-streets featuring mansions both large and small. The farther up the hill, the larger and more separated the residences become. Several of these, called *Villen*, had tall fences circling the property. The fence of the one they were parked in front of on Schwogenstrasse was rimmed with brick stretching ten feet up from the ground.

''I don't know the man's name,'' Tessen said. ''I'm not sure anyone does anymore.''

McCracken looked his way.

''I have heard that he had refused to share any of his secrets with anyone else. He believes to this day that this is the only thing keeping him alive.'' Tessen stopped and then started again. ''He has not been out of this house for fifteen years. The men you see around the grounds, he thinks, are his guards here to ensure his safety. Actually, they are his keepers.

''Your movement seems to have maintained plenty of resources, Tessen.''

The Nazi shrugged. ''Greatly depleted, I assure you. Most of our membership consists of the young, frustrated poor and unemployed—hardly people of means. Our funding these days comes from gifts to the party from abroad—America, most prominently.'' He smirked. ''I think those in your country believe even more strongly in the dogma than we do. The fools . . . None of them saw what it could do, what it *did* do in the war. They think hate is all they need. They think that is all we ever had.''

"Wasn't it?"

"For a time, perhaps, but not any longer." Tessen's eyes sought out Blaine's, in search of compassion, maybe, or understanding at the very least. "I don't think I was ever the same after that day in the schoolyard. I was just a boy myself at the time. What was the point? What were we proving? We drove others to hate as we hated, and that is what ultimately destroyed us. That is why there can be no more wars, no mythical rise from our own ashes. No Phoenix for this movement, McCracken, eh? We must be content to live our lives as we are."

Blaine turned to scrutinize the mansion beyond the gate. "So you wall up the man with the keys to your vast weapons storehouse in the name of peace, is that it?"

"The others are realizing slowly. Still more will come to their senses before long. They are old, frightened men, nothing more."

"A minute ago you were speaking of the frustrated young now making up the bulk of your movement. What would they do if they got their hands on what this old man can give them?"

Tessen's expression hardened. "The rest of us must ensure that never comes to pass. You have more influence in this regard than you realize. The chance that the curse might be unleashed again to complete its work was too much for the older members to bear. You became their greatest hope. They looked at your involvement as a godsend. They would have sacrificed anything to bring you to help us, to save themselves. Anything."

A pair of imposing-looking men gave them the okay to pass through the gate. Tessen drove on and parked the car along the circular drive fronting the mansion. Another Nazi was waiting just outside the front door.

"Was the old man told we were coming?" Tessen asked before entering.

"We informed him," the man replied. "Whether he heard us or not is anyone's guess."

Tessen signaled Blaine to enter ahead of him and closed the door behind them. McCracken froze. Around him everywhere were toys. Toys of all shapes and sizes. Dolls sat on a large mantel that ran the length of the foyer wall and they dangled from the ceiling like a town meeting of marionettes. The floor was littered with elegant shoebox-sized reproductions of classic trucks and cars. And there were games, dozens of games—none of which McCracken had ever seen before. Their boards were laid out on tables throughout the hall, complete with pieces, as if all were in the process of being played.

A guard posted at the foot of an ornate spiral staircase looked right past McCracken at Tessen.

"He's upstairs in his workshop," the guard said.

Tessen and Blaine chose their steps carefully to avoid the many scattered toys, and slid past the guard. The stairs were thankfully free of the clutter, so they climbed side by side. At the top Tessen seemed unsure of which way to go. A soft humming emanated from the right, and that was the direction they turned in. As they advanced closer, the humming took on a more raspy, choppy tone. Tessen entered the room that it was coming from through a set of open double doors. Blaine was just behind him.

"Professor . . . Professor?" Tessen called.

McCracken entered the room and froze once more. Again toys dominated the scene, but these toys were of a far different nature from the ones downstairs. They were exclusively devoted to war. Blaine could see a hunched figure toiling away with a paintbrush behind a workbench and realized that each and every toy in this house must have been made by this man over the years since World War II ended.

As he worked, the old man kept up his continuous, tuneless humming. Shelves lining every wall in the room were filled with toy soldiers of varying sizes, some miniature and some the size of small dolls. Many clutched at wounds that had been torn open and painted red. In several instances doll-sized figures were shown confronting each other, bayonets or knives rammed through plastic guts with gasps of agony frozen forever on their painted faces.

"Professor," Tessen called again.

"Almost finished," the old man said, still hunched over his work. He started to hum again, but stopped suddenly as if he had lost his place.

His workshop was a massive room lit with the tones of twilight, except for the old man's work area, which featured daylight-bright bulbs. McCracken continued to examine the room and noted that the vast bulk of its floor displays were battlefields, totally re-created in miniature and set atop tables. Somehow the old man had successfully captured the intensity and pain of war itself in these tiny stages. Tank treads were upraised over figures that were appropriately crushed and bloodied. Other figurines were shown shredded and torn by heavy-caliber machine-gun fire. Blaine could almost hear the sounds of machinery and men, of screams and orders. Each diligently re-created battle atop the various tabletops was different, and the old man had meticulously re-created the terrain as well. Where water was supposed to flow, the coloring looked real enough to drink.

Fascinated, McCracken ambled carefully about, treating the models with the same delicacy as expensive china. He moved toward several large tables arranged near the room's shelves on the far left side, their models covered by thin olive-colored sheets. Blaine reached a hand out toward one and felt Tessen grasp his shoulder.

"He would not want his work in progress glimpsed," Tessen advised softly. "And we do not want to upset him."

McCracken nodded his understanding and pulled his hand away.

"Professor," Tessen called one more time.

"That's got it!" the old man said, beaming.

He popped off his drafting stool with the bounciness of a child, a figure in his hand. He brought it to a battle scene being constructed atop a table to his right, lowered it lovingly into place, and stepped back to inspect his handiwork.

"Finished!" Then he looked up. "Polish hills, September 7, 1941," he said to his visitors. "I'm afraid it's not for sale. None of my work is for sale."

"We know," Tessen said.

The old man gazed around him. He was still wearing his thick-lensed work spectacles.

"Someday I will have the whole war in this room. Every major battle, every important engagement. I can't decide whether to organize them by year or geography. France there," he said, pointing. "Austria here. Poland not far from where you are standing." His eyes fell admiringly on McCracken and he continued, "Could I use you as a model? I need an American. Are you available?"

"Depends."

"On what?"

"On whether you're willing to help me."

"Something for your son, perhaps. Or is it a daughter?"

"Just me. And not a toy, information."

"So boring," the old man said, and started rearranging the figures on the model beneath him atop the re-created Polish hills. The smell of glue and paint intensified the longer they stayed in the room.

Blaine came a little closer. "Do your models include a certain chamber in Ephesus, Professor?"

The old man froze. His shoulders stiffened. He let the figure he was holding in his hand drop down randomly onto the model and turned. He looked at Tessen and then back toward Blaine.

"They let you in," he said softly. "They must know why you're here."

"They know," said Tessen.

"They are getting clever, I must admit, sending outsiders in to learn what they have been unable to. And an *American* yet." The old man came forward and shooed them forward as if they were unwanted pets. "Sorry you've wasted your time. Go now. There's the door. Close it behind you, if you don't mind."

"I know where the chamber is, Professor," McCracken told him. "I've been inside it."

The old man stopped in his tracks. "Impossible . . ."

"Is it?" And Blaine proceeded to provide a detailed description of the layout as he and Melissa had seen it. He elaborated on the placement of specific crates, canisters, containers, and drums. By the time he was finished, the old man had sunk stiffly into a leather armchair atop pieces of cut, discarded plastic.

"How did you find it?" he asked.

"Quite by accident. An archaeologist was looking for something else entirely."

"The traps . . ."

"Bypassed." And then Blaine realized. "They were installed by you. . . ."

The old man gazed up at him with a mixture of admiration and fear. "Who are you? *What* are you?"

"Someone who can share secrets you wish to keep," Blaine said, recalling something Tessen had said back in the car. "Someone who can eliminate the need for these men to keep you alive."

"No! You can't!"

"Only if you help me."

"Anything!"

McCracken crouched to face him. "Something was missing from the chamber, Professor. Something was hauled out."

"Someone *else* knows of the chamber, then?" the old man raised in shock.

"Through maps left by the first party to come upon the find. It doesn't matter. The latest to enter won't be coming back. They have what they need."

"Have *what*?"

"Crates, Professor. Crates that had been located just about in the center of the chamber between—"

"Stop!" The old man nearly jumped out of his chair and pushed McCracken out of his way. "I don't believe you!"

He was pacing nervously amidst his brilliant battle reproductions, gazing down at them as if to soothe himself.

"I'm not lying, Professor," Blaine said, close to the old man again. "Someone hauled them out, and they're going to use what's inside. In fact, I think they have already used it, just as it was used by Jews to gain revenge on certain Nazis at the end of the war."

"A trick! That's what this is, a trick!"

"People are dying horribly. Mutilated, ripped apart. Well-guarded men, men with armies protecting them. Whatever is in those crates is responsible, isn't it? That's what's making it possible."

"All the crates . . ."

"Every last one."

"My God . . ."

"Talk to us, Professor."

The old man walked dazedly toward what looked like a closet. Blaine and Tessen fell in behind him tentatively. The door came open with a squeak of disuse, and the old man turned toward them.

"It is better if I show you. You'll be the first to see this model." He flipped on the closet's light. "The battle of Altaloon."

CHAPTER 25

THE Israeli commando team assembled by Arnold Rothstein had arrived in the bayou just after the fall of night. Finding and dispatching the guards surrounding the house had not been a challenge for them. A far greater one would be to prepare for what would eventually be coming in their wake.

Locating the Larroux woman had proven surprisingly easy, thanks to the intelligence supplied by Rothstein himself. His logic in undertaking the pursuit was sound as always: he knew that the enemy would never leave one of its intended victims alive. That it would be returning for another go was not in question; the only issue was when.

The commandos settled back to wait.

They let themselves believe briefly that the time had come when their lookout spotted the large figure on the narrow stretch of land closest to Larroux's house. The commandos had not been expecting this. Another party had entered the scenario. He would have to be dispatched; no other option was viable.

"Wait," one of them said before the kill team moved out. He pressed the night-vision binoculars tighter over his eyes. "I know him."

"An Indian," another noted, after at last locking the large figure into focus.

"The Yom Kippur War," the first resumed. "I fought by his side. He was part of the team the Americans secretly dropped in." The commando lowered his binoculars. "He saved my life."

"What could he be doing here?" the leader wondered.

"The same thing we are, perhaps."

"He could not know."

"You didn't work with him," the grizzled veteran said to the younger man.

"What are you suggesting?"

"Any attempts to kill him, successful or not, will cost us several of our number."

The leader was looking through his own binoculars. "He's gone."

"I lost him, too."

"Damn . . ."

The grizzled veteran, a bear of a man, smiled. The leader turned his way once more.

"So what do we do?"

"Bring him into our fold. Let me handle it."

The force that had killed Joe Rainwater was approaching the area!

Johnny had spent the better part of his life preparing for battle, but this was a new feeling to him. Never had weapons felt so useless. Never had he felt so weak when measured against the potential of his opponents. He stood with his back against the widest of the cypress trees. Another tree boa, or perhaps the same one as before, ventured down and stuck its face into the air, as if to act as his sentry.

A sound like wind rustling through the low brush and mangroves reached him. The tree boa retreated back to its lair. Wareagle twisted away from the tree, Splat-loaded Sterling SMG aimed dead ahead, Uzi to the right. A pair of black-clad figures appeared from the thick tangle of vines behind him, weaponless with their hands in the air.

"Please don't shoot," the larger of the two said. "We have you surrounded."

Johnny Wareagle stood there looking at him, the moment frozen in time.

"Wareagle," the large figure said as it approached him.

"I know you," Johnny followed, relaxing slightly.

"October of '73. In the Negev."

"And now we meet here. . . ."

"Different times. Different enemies. Little changes."

Johnny lowered his guns. "Until now."

"We must hurry," Wareagle said to the commando leader minutes later, before they were even introduced. "I feel them approaching."

The leader looked at the big burly man who had recognized Johnny. The man nodded.

"You have any idea what you're dealing with here?" the leader asked him in a hushed voice.

"I am dealing with what killed my friend. I am dealing with some force that has ravaged untold numbers of people on its route here."

"Then you know pretty much the same thing we do. Since you were one of the Americans who helped us in 1973, I'm going to assume you've still got a G-5 security clearance. We're here on the orders of a rather powerful man who's had dealings with this force before. Apparently it's making what you Americans would call a comeback. He sent us here to pick up its trail and follow it to its source."

Wareagle gazed around him. He had no idea how many the commando team was in number, but six of them were huddled in the small muddy grove on the shore of the bayou now. He had seen their kind before; he had *lived* with their kind. If they weren't the best Israel had to offer, they were very close.

"Something from the past," Johnny muttered. "I should have felt that. . . ."

"How far away are they?" the burly man asked him.

"Those who advise me seem . . . confused. They are here, yet not here."

"We don't need riddles right now," the leader snapped, sliding away to find a clear view of the house.

"You will let the woman die," Johnny said in what had started out as a question.

"We wait for what comes for her to show itself and then we move. Her life is of no concern to us."

"She might be able to tell you something about what you face."

The leader turned and looked at him again. "We've already been told everything we need to know." He reached into a small pack hooked on his belt and came out with a pair of goggles like none Johnny had ever seen before. "Put these on. You're going to need them."

Gunthar Brandt had propped himself up in bed by the time Melissa made it back to his bedside. She had still not replied after the shock of hearing him speak, and now she struggled to steady her breathing.

"You never had a stroke," she said finally.

"Oh, but I did, *Fräulein*. I merely hid the truth of my rapid recovery from them. I needed to be at peace. I needed to be isolated."

"Because of Altaloon . . ."

"It has haunted me ever since that day of the battle." Brandt shivered. "And now you return and stick that blasted journal in my face. I destroyed it, threw it away! . . ." He stopped. "They must have been watching. Of course! They could have no trace. I should have burned it, assuming they would have let me." His eyes flashed with fresh alertness. "Where did you find it?"

"In an underground chamber full of stockpiled German weapons from the war. Near a collection of crates that were lifted out.'' She paused briefly. ''Crates containing what you called the White Death.''

Brandt's mouth dropped. ''That . . . can't be.''

''It is, believe me. I almost died because of it. Several others already have.''

''Several?'' Brandt tried to smirk and failed. ''I watched thousands die, *Fräulein*, and that day destroyed the rest of my life.''

''What happened?'' she asked softly, afraid in that instant of what the rest of the story of Altaloon might bring.

''You read my journal: a hundred and fifty men took on a regiment of nearly two thousand and wiped them out, massacred them.''

''I mean how? *How* could it have happened?''

''Simple, *Fräulein*: they couldn't see.''

''The White Death,'' the toymaker muttered to Mc-Cracken and Tessen, his sketchily drawn explanation complete. ''That's what they called it.''

The table containing the reconstructed model of the battle of Altaloon was the only content of the closet. It was wedged in the small space, lit by only a single dangling light bulb. There was scarcely enough room for the three of them to line up beside it. The bulb swung slightly above them, as if caught by a nonexistent breeze, the miniature panorama alive beneath it.

A hundred or so German troops were spread out on three papier-mâché hillsides that looked down into a large valley of green finished wood. The scene had been frozen well into the battle, perhaps even as it neared its end. The Germans had what looked like tight black goggles painted over their eyes. In the valley beneath them, plastic troops in red-smeared Allied uniforms lay in dying heaps. Some had discarded their weapons and seemed to be in the midst of searching for somewhere to hide. The carnage, even in the reconstruction, was horrifying. The old man was obviously a brilliant artist, able to re-create even agonizing pain on the faces of the tiny figures frozen near death. Not just pain, but confusion and terror as well.

"Blinded," Tessen said, echoing the toymaker's explanation, his gaze at the magnificent reproduction mirroring Blaine's. "They never had a chance."

"That was the idea, don't you see?" the old man followed. "I had nothing to do with the weapon's development, mind you. I was merely its caretaker once it was clear that the war was lost and we needed to salvage what we could. But I can tell you this: of all the weapons I stored in that underground chamber, this was the one I considered the most deadly and most effective."

The toymaker's eyes fell lovingly on the creation beneath him. He held out his arms the way a father might to a sleeping baby.

"Behold perfection. My greatest work, reconstructed with the help of a man from the board of science who traveled with the company pictured in the hillsides. Alas, it was the board of science's greatest accomplishment as well, the ultimate battlefield weapon. If discovered earlier and produced in sufficient quantities, it could—*would*—have changed the course of the war. But by the time of Altaloon, our production and transport capabilities had already been severely reduced. Then, before more of the White Death could be turned out, the plant producing it was destroyed by an Allied bombing run. We hoarded what had been salvaged. But instead of using up our precious reserves on a few more battles that wouldn't change the outcome of the war, we decided it would be better to save what we had for future generations to analyze and reproduce."

"It was delivered by air," McCracken theorized, looking over the old man's model as if expecting to see bombers dangling from the ceiling.

"Low-altitude drop. Our best pilots were used to lower the margin for error. Without any danger of antiaircraft fire, it was a simple matter."

"A gas, then."

"No, an aerosol containing an advanced neurotoxin. Do you know what a binary agent is?" the old man asked Mc-Cracken.

"A compound that must interact with another element in order to be activated."

"In a nutshell, yes. And the neurotoxin that formed the White Death was actually quite harmless until it came into contact with hyaluronic acid."

"Don't tell me," said Blaine. "This hyaluronic acid can be found in the eye."

"Precisely. Once the aerosol and the acid joined, the neurotoxin was activated, passing through the cornea and paralyzing the rods and cones of the retina in a matter of seconds."

"Permanently blinding all victims," McCracken added.

"It was brilliant, perfect," the toymaker said. "When the canisters containing the aerosol ruptured over Altaloon, a fine mist was sprayed outward and down, the effect that of an open umbrella trapping everything beneath it as it dropped." His gaze fell fondly once again on his model. "It was to have been just the beginning. The White Death was to be utilized as an equalizer on the battlefield as well as off, and what an equalizer it could have been! Imagine the possibilities! What parts of the world we didn't overrun, we could have held hostage. Civilization would have cowered before us."

"That sickens me," Tessen scoffed.

"Are you not one of us?" the old man shot back.

"One of *what*? I am a soldier, a warrior. I fight with honor and dignity. I could not kill that which was unable to fight back."

"Now, perhaps, but what about then, when we were all gripped with the fervor of the times? It was our destiny. Nothing else mattered. *Nothing!*" The old man again turned his gaze lovingly on the model before him. "And here it is, frozen in time for all to behold, frozen as an example of what someday will be a—" He stopped suddenly, face suddenly pained and unsure. "But it's gone," he said sadly, as he turned toward McCracken. "You say it's gone."

"How was it stored?" Blaine asked him. "In the crates, I mean."

"In small tanks. From them the aerosol could be easily channeled into virtually any explosive. Missiles, rockets, grenades—why limit ourselves?"

It all made sense, McCracken reflected to himself. The Jews who were behind the killings of vengeance in the war's wake, as well as whatever force had pulled the rest of the crates from the secret chamber more recently, had discovered a way to release the White Death within a confined area. It wouldn't be hard. The explosive shell would have to be composed of some material that vaporized upon detonation so that no trace would be left. Then, since the microdroplets would dissipate rapidly into the air, no evidence of what had really transpired would remain. To the authorities first on the scene, even as quickly as minutes later, it would seem as though men armed and able to defend themselves had been slain by something that was impervious to their weapons.

Because they couldn't *see* what they were firing at.

The wild, random shooting that struck nothing . . . The fact that none of the victims had tried to run . . . The way that access through impenetrable lines of defense had been gained . . . This was what Johnny Wareagle was up against halfway around the world.

An invincible army . . . Blaine felt chilled by the prospects.

"How many crates were stored in the underground chamber?" he asked the old man, almost reluctantly.

"The exact number escapes me now. In the area of a hundred, I think."

"How many tanks in each?"

"It varied with the size of the tanks. Between eight and twelve. A few more in some cases."

"But more could be produced."

"Not easily. All traces of the original formula were lost

before we could retrieve them. All attempts to re-create the White Death since have failed.''

Blaine swung intensely toward Tessen. "Which implies someone's been trying, doesn't it?''

"And failing,'' Tessen reminded. "Leave it there.''

"I can't, Tessen, not by a long shot. Don't you get it? Whoever's got the White Death has known about its presence in that chamber for a long time. So why pick now to bring it up? Answer: because they've figured out a way to reproduce the formula.''

"Of course!'' The toymaker beamed. "Our plan exactly. Massive quantities to do the job, to perform the true task the White Death was created for.''

"What task?'' Blaine and Tessen asked almost together.

"To unleash it on entire cities of our enemy, of course.'' The old man's gaze turned distant, yet bright. "Imagine the model of a city captured in the grip of the White Death. The fires, the looting, the desperation. All order gone. No possible way to return it. I would have pictures, even videos now!'' His eyes rotated feverishly between Tessen and McCracken. "I will have to obtain them. It shouldn't be hard, shouldn't be—''

His words were cut off when gunfire erupted outside on the grounds enclosing the house. The screams were hideous, the cries desperate.

"Mein Gott," muttered the old man.

"They're here,'' McCracken said.

CHAPTER 26

"*B*LINDED," was all Melissa could say after Gunthar Brandt had finished the story of the battle of Altaloon that his journal had started. "But not you."

"No. We had been issued protective goggles. We donned them just before the White Death was dropped."

"Yes!" she remembered. "I read in your journal that you were ordered to put something on. But that section was too badly damaged to make sense of. What happened afterwards?"

"Our company was broken up. We were all reassigned, mostly to the front lines where the kill rates were the highest. The reason was obvious: they didn't want us to survive the war. I got lucky." He chuckled humorlessly. "Or maybe I didn't."

"And when the war was over?"

"The few of us that were left kept our mouths shut, but I for one never got over Altaloon. I never will."

"Then the White Death was never used again."

"Why don't you tell me? I mean, that is why you're here, isn't it? If the crates are gone, it means that someone must have the intention of unleashing it once more." Brandt sat up farther in his bed. "Now it's my turn to ask the questions, *Fräulein*. Who are you working with?"

"No one. I told you."

"How did you find me?"

"I told you that, too."

"And no one else knows you're here?"

"Only the administrator of the Document Center in Berlin."

"Leave me, *Fräulein*," Brandt said coldly. "Leave me and never come back. Altaloon has chased me all my life. I do not wish for it to finally catch up."

"Good-bye," Melissa said, and turned.

"I'm . . . sorry," Gunthar Brandt's voice called after her.

Before she had reached the door, it crashed open and the big nurse, Brandt's *Altenpfleger*, lunged in, holding a pistol in her hand aimed straight at Melissa.

"No!" Melissa shrieked.

The pistol spit once, twice. Melissa felt her breath freeze up. She gasped and would have screamed had not the nurse clamped a hand tight over her mouth.

"Look!" the nurse ordered.

Melissa turned to see blood seeping from a pair of bullet holes in Gunthar Brandt's face.

"Under the sheet!" the nurse directed. "His right hand! Quickly!"

Melissa moved to the bed and lifted up the sheet on that side. A silenced pistol was still gripped in Brandt's hand.

"He would have killed you," the nurse said.

"Why? Who are you?"

"Later."

"But—"

"There could be others. We leave now."

Melissa stood there suspended between actions, between thoughts. The nurse grabbed her arm and yanked.

"I said *now*!"

And together they plunged into the corridor. The big nurse held her pistol hidden by her side the whole time that she and Melissa advanced down the hallway. Her other arm rested distressingly against Melissa's back, and Melissa couldn't tell whether she was being taken hostage or rescued. The confused succession of events had numbed her, and, having no choice, she simply went along.

She could feel the big nurse's tension through the course of the walk to the third-floor elevator.

There could be others.

The nurse was taking her own words seriously. Melissa followed the woman's eyes as they darted across those of everyone they passed, half expecting her gun to begin spitting fire again any moment.

Gunthar Brandt had had a gun, was seconds away from killing her, when the nurse had burst in. What did it all mean? As incomprehensible as things already were, they had gotten worse.

After an interminable descent in the elevator, the nurse led her outside into the cool early-evening air. Melissa felt the woman decrease the pressure against her back. The nurse guided her toward a car parked in the staff area, an old Volkswagen. Melissa resisted briefly.

"You must come with me," the nurse told her. "It is your only chance to live."

"Who are you?"

"Get in."

"Who are—"

"Do as I say!"

Melissa climbed into the passenger seat, and the woman slammed the door behind her. She then got behind the wheel and started the engine.

"Now tell me who you are," Melissa demanded.

"We will drive through the night to an airfield and a plane," the nurse said instead of responding. "By midmorning it will all be clear."

"You knew I would be coming here," Melissa assumed. "You knew I'd be coming to Brandt."

The nurse pulled the car onto the road from the rest home, eyes maintaining a vigil in the rearview mirror.

"No," she corrected.

"Then what . . . Wait a minute! You were watching *Brandt*! That's it, isn't it?"

The woman stripped off a wig to reveal hair of an entirely different color and texture. She smoothed it as best she could while she kept driving.

"I took the place of the real nurse only today. The time had come."

"Time had come for *what*?"

"Mobilization. Brandt's name was on a list of those who could be valuable to us. . . ."

"Us," Melissa repeated.

"He was a link, one of the few left. We knew there was a chance that someone would be coming to see him, though not to talk."

And then Melissa realized. "You thought I came to kill him."

"And we thought you'd then lead us to those you represented. Listening to your conversation with Brandt told me otherwise. I knew Brandt would have to kill you to protect the secrets he had held for so long. But, based on your questions, I also knew you could help us in ways you could not possibly be aware of."

"And just who is *us*?"

"When we get there," was all the woman would say.

"Get *where*?"

"Israel. A place known as Nineteen. . . ."

The panic in Tessen's eyes, Blaine knew, mirrored his own. They had only seconds, a minute at most, before they would be under siege to the killers now on the grounds. Killers who never lost a single member of their number to whatever counterattacks their victims were able to mount.

The screams beyond dissipated as quickly as they had come. Somewhere downstairs glass shattered. The White Death had entered the house. McCracken's eyes had wandered to a model of an especially grisly battle scene where

Nazi soldiers were launching a chemical warfare attack, pro-
jecting themselves with—

"Gas masks!" Blaine blared over the screams mixing with
futile gunfire on the first floor. He recalled the toymaker's
insistence on the accuracy of his work. "You have them,
Professor, you must!"

"Of course! In the closet!"

"What closet?"

The old man led Blaine to it. McCracken grasped his elbow to make him go faster and threw back the double doors
for him. The neatly arranged shelves and hooks featured a
wide assortment of weapons and equipment. In addition,
there were five fully clothed mannequins in different Nazi
uniforms. One of the mannequins wore a gas mask. Another
had a similar mask clipped to his belt.

Blaine reached inside and tore the one off the plastic face
it concealed. Tessen reached for the other. Downstairs, the
gunfire had stopped. Tessen was already tightening his mask
over his face. McCracken started to follow suit.

"What about me?" the old man wondered.

"Hide in the closet and keep your eyes closed."

"They're my masks! This is all mine!"

"And we're your best chance of keeping it," Blaine said,
and started to reach inside the closet for the rifles.

"They're not loaded," the old man told him.

"Where are the bullets?"

"I . . . have none."

Tessen and McCracken exchanged glances, Tessen through
the plastic lenses covering his eyes. The two of them drew
their pistols.

"They won't be expecting a fight," Blaine said hopefully,
pulling his mask over his head.

"If they know you're here, they will."

The door to the workshop fragmented inward. A small
grenadelike thing fluttered through the air and shattered on
impact with the floor.

Sssssssssssss . . .

It sounded like a snake to Blaine. The deadly droplets of the White Death were filling the room. Screaming, the old man staggered toward the closet with one arm covering his closed eyes. He banged into a pair of display tables en route, and their fragile contents tumbled to the floor. A third table nearest the closet pitched over entirely on impact. McCracken spun toward the door, Tessen hanging back.

The first of two figures whirled into the room, as the hissing wound down and the White Death filled the air. Blaine instantly noticed the shiny black steel extremities that they had for hands. Some sort of razor-sharp prostheses, he realized. *So that's how they had pulled it off, not just now but forty-five years ago as well*. . . .

Tessen opened fire an instant ahead of McCracken.

"Head shots!" Blaine screamed his way as the Nazi's first three shots plunked into the bulletproof vests that the invaders wore.

Blaine had no sooner shouted the words than he got off a trio of bullets into the lagging figure's face. The third bullet snapped his head back, and then he went limp. Tessen's misjudgment had cost him the luxury of space and surprise; the killer was almost upon him when he at last put a bullet dead center in his forehead.

Blaine and the Nazi met halfway across the floor and slid toward the doorway. McCracken reached it first. The house beyond had grown deadly quiet. How many more of them might there be in the house? Whatever the number, they would have heard the gunshots and might be approaching even now.

"Scream!" Blaine said loudly through his gas mask back to Tessen.

"What?"

"You heard me. Scream. Like they were killing us now." His eyes fell on one of the corpses, at the deadly black weapons that had been pulled over their hands. *"Scream!"*

Tessen lifted his mask up to expose his mouth and screamed. Blaine followed, joining him. When they finished, deathly quiet returned to the house. The overpowering scent of gunpowder had made its way to the second floor. Mc-Cracken peered outside into the hallway.

"Empty," he whispered.

"Not for long," Tessen warned. "They'll be coming."

"I think if we—"

"Not 'we,' McCracken. I don't matter anymore. It is only you." He pointed to the opposite end of the hallway. "You can get out through that window. Climb down and escape while their forces are still concentrated in the front."

"While you . . ."

"Hold them off for as long as I can."

"Might not be long enough, Tessen."

"You will make it long enough. Once you are over the wall, you will be safe."

"Unless they see me."

"The mask will still protect you. Go! *Now!* Before it is too late!"

Blaine handed his gun to Tessen. "Thank you," he said, and started off.

"It is I who must thank you, for what you are doing for us. Get out. Hurry. Stop them. *Destroy* them."

McCracken charged off. He had to swing right at the end of the corridor to find the window that held his route of escape. He had it up and was halfway outside when the horrible screams reached him from well back down the hall, real screams this time.

Tessen . . .

From the window, Blaine dropped onto a branch and then climbed down the tree adjacent to the window as quickly as he could. He hit the ground running. Footsteps thumped behind him, closing the gap. He didn't bother looking back. A pair, a trio perhaps, of the killers were giving pursuit, and more were sure to join them.

Blaine could see the brick wall enclosing the grounds just ahead. Ten feet high and nearly impossible to scale, unless he could grasp one of the vines wrapped upon it and pull himself up. He hit the wall climbing, razor-sharp death about to swipe at his heels. He grasped a vine and propelled himself upward, not stopping when he reached the top. He let himself tumble over and dropped onto a thick bush that cushioned his drop, but tore off his gas mask in the process. Impact on the ground was soft enough to let him have his feet back instantly.

McCracken was dazed, though, and the utter blackness of the night added to his disorientation. He could hear the pursuers behind him scaling the wall. More dark figures poured out from the mansion's gate and charged toward him like a storm in the night.

A car was speeding down Schwogenstrasse. McCracken bolted into the street directly into the spill of its headlights. He intended to make the vehicle stop so that he might commandeer it. The car skidded to a halt just in front of him.

"Get in!" a woman's voice ordered through the driver's window, rear door thrown open.

Blaine stood there for a long moment.

"For God's sake, do as I say. *Now!*"

McCracken lunged into the back seat, struggling to get the door closed as the car tore away.

CHAPTER 27

"I UNDERSTAND now," said Wareagle after the Israeli commando leader had completed his explanation of what they were facing.

He tightened the strap of the goggles that had been handed to him behind his head. They had been fitted with infrared lenses, but donning them had reduced even further a view that was already restricted thanks to the black bayou night. He was alone now in the shielded clearing with the leader and the burly man named Joseph. The others had silently retaken their positions, eight commandos in all.

"And these will protect us?" he asked.

"They should," the leader told him. "They haven't been tested."

Johnny's mind strayed briefly to Joe Rainwater. He had died horribly, unable to even see his killers, much less fight them. The dishonor of it sickened him. The soul and spirit of his warrior friend had been done a terrible disservice. Johnny tightened his grip on the Splat-loaded Sterling SMG.

"You don't know who those in possession of this weapon are," he said, feeling his own warrior blood heating up against his flesh.

"Only that this is a return engagement for them. We knock

out what we can here and hope for clues that lead us back to the nest.''

Wareagle tensed suddenly, the spirits alive in his ears. The night had turned rancid, ranker than even the hellfire's. He moved forward until he was dangerously close to being visible.

''What are you doing?'' the leader barked, as the man named Joseph started after Wareagle.

Johnny stood there motionless, his spine arched and whole body rigid. Joseph touched his shoulder and pulled his hand away instantly, a feeling like heat and an electric shock surging through it.

''What is it?'' the Israeli asked.

''Pull your men back,'' Wareagle told the leader.

''What?''

''Get your men out of here, Commander, get them out now!''

Inside the house Heydan Larroux sat in a chair facing a window with drawn blinds. Beyond them the night sounds spoke to her, and she tried to listen for their message. She heard the Old One ruffling stones through her aged hands, the sound curiously like that of a shooter at a craps table. The thought had her almost smiling until the familiar sound of a stone hitting water came, louder and flatter than normal.

She swung round to see the Old One's hands empty and her wrinkled face wet with the splash that had resulted. Her hands were trembling.

''They have come,'' she said.

''What are you talking about?'' the commando leader demanded, storming toward Johnny.

''Act before it is too late!''

''My men would have signaled, I tell you. We're prepared. If I pull them out now . . .''

The leader stopped when a soft splash split the other sounds of the night. A few seconds passed, then a single gunshot rang out.

"My God," Joseph muttered.

"How?" the leader wondered, as he tried in vain to make his men respond to his contact signal.

"The water," Wareagle had just finished saying when a black figure that was one with the night sprang out of the thick ooze and underbrush rimming the shore of the bayou. There was a dull flash of metal, and the commando leader gasped.

Johnny recorded the action in slow motion within his mind's eye. But even that was barely sufficient to show him that the killer's hands weren't wielding the weapon; they *were* the weapon. The killer had driven them straight through the Israeli leader's torso. Johnny saw them emerge through the man's back like spikes as his ears recorded the tearing, wrenching sounds. The leader started to fall.

Johnny fired his rifle.

The Splat bullet struck the dark killer squarely in the chest and blew him backward into the water. A shower of gore sprayed in all directions. Johnny spun in time to see Joseph firing a burst into a second figure as a third took the big Israeli from behind with its hands closing on his throat. Before Wareagle could aim, the dark hands had torn Joseph's head clean off. A fountain of blood shot upward, and Joseph's body spasmed horribly before crumpling. Johnny fired a Splat into the killer's head, and it ruptured with a fiery *poof*.

Whatever they were, they could be killed. . . .

Wareagle took some comfort in that, although not a lot. He leaned over and checked the headless body of the second figure he had shot. It was a man, all right, everywhere except . . .

Johnny checked his hands. They weren't hands at all, but molded gloves formed of steel that was honed razor-sharp all the way down the fingers. The method of Joe Rainwater's and all the other deaths was clear to him now. The victims had been blinded first and then killed in awful fashion up close, unable to see and thus unable to defend themselves. The killers were out to achieve more than effectiveness. There was a ritual element to this, almost like the fanaticism of a cult. Johnny's eyes shifted quickly to the house. The sounds he had heard prior to the appearance of these now-dead killers confirmed that there were more of them out there. They would now be heading toward the woman they had come for.

Wareagle waded into the muck of the swamp. His feet again sunk into the soft bottom, and the dense undergrowth tried in vain to hold him. He was waist-deep when the bottom firmed out. The water glistened instead of oozed. Johnny pushed himself in and began swimming the last stretch to the house that rose out of the bayou.

At the sound of the explosions, Heydan Larroux lunged from her chair and moved for the front room, where a pair of guards stood as her final line of defense. She knew already that all the other men she had posted were dead. The explosions she had just heard might have been a last-ditch effort by the few that had managed to take action.

"He is out there," the Old One rasped from her unyielding perch over the water bowl.

"I haven't got time for—"

"The warrior!" the Old One continued. "He is out there!"

Heydan was already into the living room, and the words barely reached her. Her last two guards held their machine guns at the ready, poised before either window. Heydan moved to the one that provided the clearest view of the walkway leading out from the shore, the only way to reach the house from land. In her hand was a detonator. Not hesitating at all, she pressed it.

Instantly a pair of blasts sounded, and the walkway collapsed into the swamp, sinking slowly. She discarded the detonator and pulled a 9mm Beretta pistol from the belt of her jeans. Whoever was out there would have to approach by water now. And it was deep this far out, ten feet where the house's supports had been planted.

Heydan left her two guards at their vigil and returned to the first floor's back room. She closed and locked the door behind her. An attack from beyond via the rear was much less likely, given the logistics of the house's construction. The windows were seven feet above the water here, instead of four in the front, an impossible lunge for anyone. As for the upstairs, well, that seemed an unlikely route of entry at best.

Heydan Larroux steadied herself by one window and then shifted to the other. The Old One remained in the floor's center, seeing without eyes. The longest two minutes of Heydan's life had passed when a blast rang out in the front room. She heard her men yelling at each other, followed by the distinctive clacking of automatic-rifle fire. They continued shouting as they fired, but their words were indecipherable to her.

"My God," Heydan muttered, staring at the door before her. "My God . . ."

Her men were shrieking now, ear-piercing screams that grabbed her gut and twisted. The pistol trembled in her hand. Heavy footsteps thumped toward the door leading into the back room. Heydan backpedaled and tried to steady her pistol.

Something cold grasped her arm.

"The warrior is coming," the Old One said, suddenly by her side.

"What?"

The Old One looked at the door as if she could see through it. "No. He is here."

The Old One moved away from Heydan just before an explosion sounded that blew the door inward. Something crashed into Larroux and flung her backward. Impact against the wall stole all of her wind and a measure of her consciousness. She was pinned down by something as black and heavy as the night, as death itself.

* * *

Johnny Wareagle had made the night his ally in swimming his way through the bayou's black water toward the house. The water would not give him up to his enemies, because it, too, was part of nature. Existing in harmony with its heavy currents made for the best camouflage of all.

He swam like a great fish just below the surface, stealing only what little air he needed to make his way forward in the night. He was a hundred yards from Heydan Larroux's bayou house when the explosion disturbed the smooth flow of the thick water. The ripple effect disrupted his stroke, and his head cleared the surface to see the last of the smoldering walkway disappearing into the bayou.

The woman inside the house was better than he had thought. Johnny turned that way and stopped dead in the water.

A trio of the blackened figures were climbing up from the black water directly under the house. Ropes dangled down from its front to the water's surface, affixed to pylons that must have been shot into place by the same kind of pistollike device that Johnny had used plenty of times himself.

The need for subtlety was finished. Wareagle pulled himself through the currents in quick bursts of incredible power. He had covered more than half the distance when he saw the figures reach the door. They jammed something on its center and it blew inward, half-torn from its hinges.

The water hid the screams that followed from Johnny's ears, but he heard them clearly enough in his mind and imagined that they were Joe Rainwater's. He shot through the final stretch of water without slowing for air. The killers had left their ropes dangling, and he grasped one to pull himself upward.

Special goggles donned, Wareagle threw himself over the threshold and brought his Sterling SMG upward. One of the black figures was laying another explosive charge against an inner door when Johnny pulled the trigger. The Splat blew out his midsection and rocketed him against the door just as his charge detonated. Airborne, he crashed through the door's remnants and into a woman who seemed to be poised to make a defense.

Another pair of black figures spun away from the blown door toward Johnny. One had a dark, egg-shaped object clutched in his hand. In the instant it took him to aim the Sterling, Wareagle realized that the blindness-inducing aerosol would be released as soon as the egg-shaped housing shattered. He fired his next bullet at the figure wielding it.

The Splat lifted the figure into the air and slammed him against the wall, his blood spewing in all directions. The egg-shaped housing shattered with a *poof!* within the outer room.

The third and final figure turned away from the blown door and lunged at Wareagle. Johnny got his barrel righted and went for the trigger.

Clang!

The thud of something smashing down hard on the rifle's barrel weakened his grasp. In the next instant what felt like a vise grasped the weapon and tore it away. Johnny wavered, and before he could fully recover his balance, the figure had rammed the rifle's butt under his chin. Johnny staggered backward through what remained of the door into the inner room.

One woman lay dazed on the floor, partially pinned by the first of the figures Wareagle had killed. A second woman, ancient, sat cross-legged in a corner, undaunted by what was happening.

The dark figure stormed forward and lashed at Johnny with one of its black steel hands. Johnny lurched from the hand's path, and the steel sliced through his Kevlar vest and nipped at his flesh. The burst of pain made his back arch. He saw the next strike surging toward him like a spear. He twisted sideways and blocked it downward, but the move left him open for the figure's second hand, which sliced upward.

Johnny turned again, and the blow scratched against the left lens of his protective goggles. He backpedaled and faced off against his adversary, thinking that Joe Rainwater had not been granted such a chance. The black figure lashed at him with his right hand and followed up quickly with a swipe from his left. Johnny deflected both blows, then ducked under a sweeping side-mounted double strike and dropped into a roll. He snapped quickly to his feet, shaking the wall he came to rest against. Above him something that had been hanging there dropped onto a nearby dresser. Wareagle stole a glance at it.

It was a cat-o'-nine-tails.

Johnny grasped the ancient whiplike weapon and sent it swirling outward, just as the figure spun into another attack. Enough of the cat's tails raked across his face to draw blood and a gasp. Wareagle swung his weapon in again and the figure, on the defensive now, blocked it with one of his steel hands.

He tried to grab it with the other, which opened up his midsection for Johnny's feet. A kick landed squarely in his groin, and he bent into an agonized hunch. Johnny drew the cat back and around, the tails catching his assailant in the right shoulder and spinning him into the wall.

The dark figure retaliated by surging forward again, Johnny's throat his target. Johnny let him think he had it and whipped the cat-o'-nine-tails out with a snap at the last possible instant. Air surged by Wareagle's throat as the cat tore down across the figure's face.

And eyes.

The man's scream was bloodcurdling. It was barely a breath in length, but a breath was too long. His hands whipped down from his ravaged eyes. By then, though, Johnny had come in fast and to the side, the cat whistling through the air ahead of him. The tails swirled together and sliced into the black figure's exposed throat. Wareagle felt warm blood splatter him, as the figure's breathless scream gave way to a wet gurgle. The figure collapsed, writhing and twitching. Johnny backed away, and his eyes fell on the old woman who had remained seated calmly through it all.

"I was waiting for you, warrior," she told him, her mouth

squeezed between thick layers of wrinkled flesh. "What are you called?"

"Wareagle," Johnny replied, breathing hard.

"Yes," the Old One said, showing a glimpse of a smile. "Yes."

Across the room, Heydan Larroux moaned and stirred.

"My lady," from the Old One.

Johnny lifted the corpse off the woman he sought. She was still groggy, but had recovered her senses in time to hear the Indian-looking figure call himself "Wareagle," and recalled the Old One's vision of a bird of prey painted with the colors of battle.

An eagle.

"Jesus Christ," she muttered, accepting the giant's help in getting to her feet.

Johnny then crouched alongside the figure he had killed with the cat-o'-nine-tails. After removing the goggles the Israelis had given him, he pulled the corpse's strange-looking headpiece off and regarded the face curiously. He knew the face of a killer when he saw one; death could not take that look away.

Wareagle's eyes scanned the man's upper body where the cat had shredded his body armor and shirt. There was a mark on his left shoulder, partially covered by blood that Johnny wiped away.

The mark was a tattoo, a swirly line stretched across the top of a slanted one.

It was the Greek letter tau.

"His boot," the old woman said from the corner, pointing. Wareagle realized that she was blind. "What you seek can be found in his right boot, warrior."

Johnny crouched down next to it and ran his hand along the boot. He squeezed the thick heel and felt it move a little. A harder pull snapped it off and revealed a secret compartment containing a state-of-the-art pager complete with miniature LED screen. Johnny switched it on. The screen remained blank.

"Nothing," he told the old woman.

"Its secrets remain within."

"Told and gone."

"No, warrior. Not for one who knows the box's ways."

Johnny almost handed it out toward her. "You?"

He watched the old blind woman smile. "No. Another we will meet soon."

"Where?"

"Where we are going, warrior."

"There could be more of them," Johnny Wareagle told her, as he slid the sleek pager into his pocket. "We'd better be fast."

The old woman turned Heydan Larroux's way. "Tell him of the boat, child."

Heydan couldn't take her eyes off the giant Indian. "There's a raised platform built onto the underside of this house. A boat is stored upon it. Not much, just a small outboard . . ."

"It will do," said Johnny.

"You will make it do, warrior," the blind woman said quite assuredly.

Heydan instructed Wareagle to pull up the throw carpet from the center of the floor. When he did so, a small hatchway was revealed. He yanked it open, and the black water of the bayou glistened beneath him. He could see the rigging holding the boat to the platform. A hand crank resting just to his right would lower it onto the water ten feet below.

It took a full minute of turning before the outboard's bottom kissed the surface. The boat wobbled under Wareagle's bulk when he dropped down into it. Steadying himself as best he could, he stood up and raised his hands toward the hatchway.

"Let me help you," he said to Heydan.

She slid her feet over the edge and felt a pair of powerful hands lock on to her ankles and accept her weight. Then she watched as the warrior named Wareagle lowered the Old One into the swaying boat as well.

''The engine,'' Heydan said, shifting toward it.

Wareagle had a guide pole already in hand. ''We won't be using it.''

''We're miles from anywhere,'' she protested. ''Without the engine, it'll take us hours, even—'' She stopped when a feeling of incredible stupidity swept over her. ''I'm sorry. If we use the engine, of course, they'll know where we are.''

''They already know where we are,'' Wareagle told her. ''I want to hear them if they come.''

Johnny pushed off with the guide pole and eased the boat out from beneath the house and whatever security it provided. A sea of still, black glass, blistered by the overgrowth from the shore and draped by the overhanging foliage, welcomed them. Johnny's motions were smooth, and the boat rode the currents easily, his rhythm broken only when his guide pole lodged in the soft bottom.

Heydan was transfixed by the subtle power of his motions. She tried to speak several times but didn't until the big Indian's eyes at last met hers.

''You came down here for me.''

''Because I knew they would be returning.'' Wareagle paused. ''Because they must be stopped.''

''*Who* are they?''

''I do not know.''

''Yes, you do, warrior,'' the Old One said suddenly. ''Back in the house you saw something that told you.''

''On the arm of one of the killers,'' Johnny acknowledged. ''A letter.''

''What letter?''

''Tau, from the Greek alphabet.''

The Old One squeezed her face up tight in consternation. ''These men represent a cause, the true scope of which is not yet clear to me. But there are many, many more of them. And what they seek stretches far beyond these dark waters. That much, warrior, is clear.''

Wareagle stiffened his grip on the guide pole. ''And what of our route to them?''

"Where we head now is the right direction, warrior. Partly over land. Known by few. My home long ago." She turned her dead eyes on Johnny. "The first stop in a journey that will reveal to you the answers you seek."

PART FIVE

The Tau

Nineteen: Saturday, eleven A.M.

CHAPTER 28

MELISSA fought for sleep during the long journey through Friday night and into Saturday morning. It came in fits and starts, brief moments of repose inevitably broken by the need to switch to another mode of transportation. Both speed and security were taken into consideration by the woman who had gone from savior to escort.

The woman had said virtually nothing through the trip's duration. Her few words were mechanical, instructions given and warnings handed down without benefit of explanation. That would come later, she assured, once they reached Israel and this place called Nineteen.

The last leg of the journey was made in the back of a truck that had picked them up at a small military airfield in Israel. Melissa had not thought that civilian air traffic was permitted to use such fields under any circumstances, which made her wonder exactly who it was she was being taken to see.

Rich in archaeological treasures, Israel was a country Melissa knew well. Not only had she accompanied her father on a number of digs here over the years, but part of her own schooling had been an internship with some of the team that had unearthed Jerusalem's Christian relics.

Their truck's rear flap had been tied down, yet her escort did not seem to mind Melissa peering out through what chinks she could fashion for herself. A half hour into the ride she knew exactly where they were:

The Golan Heights.

She could see numerous guard stations and missile batteries dotting the landscape as they made their way through. There was no sign announcing their arrival at the place called Nineteen. The truck simply rumbled through a guarded gate and into what Melissa recognized as a kibbutz. The truck came to a halt, and the back flap was thrown open. Her escort helped Melissa climb down.

The scene around her in the bright sunlight was much as she would have expected it to be in the late morning. People went about their chores, limited on this day, the Jewish Sabbath. Most others she saw were out strolling or lounging. Children ran and played in a nearby field. The scene spelled normalcy, except for one thing:

Melissa could not find a single man in the kibbutz's population.

"She wants to see her immediately," an armed, uniformed woman said to Melissa's escort tersely. "I will take her."

The armed woman grasped Melissa's arm.

"Thank you," Melissa called to the big woman who had saved her life back at the nursing home when they started off.

The woman didn't so much as turn to acknowledge her, and her armed replacement led Melissa through the large expanse of the kibbutz in silence. Structurally it was comparable to any of the many others she had visited over the years. But she continued to be dumbstruck by the total lack of males other than among the children.

A clearing appeared, in which a small cabin stood by itself in the shade. Before it, beneath a vast leafed tree, an old woman in a wheelchair sat behind a wrought-iron table. She turned slightly as Melissa approached, but did not acknowledge her. Not far into the clearing, her armed escort stopped.

"Go on," she instructed, after Melissa had also come to a halt.

Melissa moved toward the old woman slowly. The pounding of her heart had slowed, anxiety giving way to exasperation. She had been hoping, expecting, an audience with someone who could explain everything she did not understand about Ephesus, about her father's death. Could it be this woman? Had she been the one responsible for having her life saved?

Melissa stopped just to the side of the wheelchair.

"Sit down," the old woman instructed. "You'll excuse me if I don't stand up to greet you."

Melissa sat in the chair opposite her and pulled it farther under the table. She noticed that a second chair rested against the table between hers and the old woman's.

"Are we expecting someone else?" Melissa wondered.

"Yes, we are. Any minute now, I trust." She leaned forward. "Are you hungry? Thirsty?"

"Yes. Thirsty."

"I have orange juice inside. Squeezed from our own oranges here."

"Thank you."

The old woman waved a hand back toward the small house. The wind blew, and patches of her scalp appeared when her hair parted. It settled so that the patches remained bare. Her skin was creased and wrinkled. Her legs were little more than withered sticks beneath her dress. Her hands trembled slightly on the sides of her wheelchair.

"Do you approve?" she asked. "Of this place, I mean."

"I don't understand."

"Yes, you do. You have a scholar's eyes. You couldn't possibly have missed the fact that our community is composed solely of women and children. War veterans or war widows. Women who are beaten and frustrated and want to withdraw. We let them withdraw here, where their lives can still be worth something, where they are never forced to prove anything to anyone, where they can rebuild themselves. Some leave after a time.'' She looked down at her trembling, liver-spotted hands. ''Some never leave.''

A young woman came with a tray containing a pitcher full of pulp-rich fresh-squeezed orange juice, a pair of tall glasses, and napkins. She left without saying a single word. Melissa poured herself a glass and then poured one for the old woman, which she placed within easy reach of her.

''You saved my life,'' Melissa said after gulping some of the delicious juice.

The old woman nodded. ''Yes, from Brandt. Wily devil he was. Doesn't surprise me at all. We've been watching him for some time. We've been watching all those who bear any connection to the White Death.''

The now-empty glass nearly dropped from Melissa's hand at the old woman's mention of the deadly contents of the crates from Ephesus.

''You discovered it was missing,'' she continued. ''You discovered what I have feared would come to pass for forty-five years now, since we tried to bury it from the world forever.''

Melissa felt a chill slide up her spine, thinking back to the mummified remains of the three Jews inside the cavern. ''My God, the first time the White Death was removed, you were part of it!''

The old woman did not bother to deny it. ''So many years ago,'' she said softly. ''So much has changed since, and yet so little.'' Her eyes sharpened, and she continued before Melissa could start up again. ''I founded this place, you know. I founded it because I needed it for myself. I could never have children of my own.'' A veil of sadness swept over her face. ''The Nazis at Auschwitz took care of that. Auschwitz was where it all began for me. For others it started in different places, but the pain was always the same.''

''Who?'' Melissa asked in exasperation. *''What?''*

''This is a tale I do not wish to tell twice. We must wait.''

''Wait for—''

"The wait is over," the old woman said, casting her gaze beyond Melissa's shoulder. "He is here."

Melissa turned around, and the sight sent a joyous shock wave pounding against her. She couldn't believe her eyes no matter how much she wanted to.

Blaine McCracken had stepped into the clearing.

As Blaine's eyes met Melissa's, he froze in his tracks. The next instant she was out of the chair, running his way. She leapt into his arms and hugged him with all her strength.

"The hotel, all the killings," she muttered.

"I know," he tried to soothe.

"I didn't think I'd ever see you again." She eased herself to arm's length, still holding tight to him. "God, that sounds ridiculous."

"Not to me."

She dropped her arms away now. "The journal! I've got to tell you what I found in that journal!"

"The White Death . . ."

"You know," she said, dumbfounded. "How could you know?"

"Same destination. Different route."

And the last of that route had been traveled with the woman who had rescued him outside the old toymaker's house. They had journeyed through the night—two planes, several cars, and even a bus—to reach here. The second plane had landed on a military airfield in Israel, and twenty minutes into the drive that followed he recognized the Golan Heights. The woman had told him the name of the kibbutz and nothing more when they approached it. Whatever else Blaine needed to know about Nineteen, he had learned from the flower-encased M-60 tank placed two hundred yards inside the gates. The symbolism was striking: where war had once reigned, a new life and world had bloomed over it.

"Come here, both of you," the old woman called in as loud a voice as she could manage. "Since you are both present, the tale can be told."

"She had me brought here," Melissa explained.

"Me, too, it would seem. Saved my life, maybe."

"No maybe in my case."

They turned toward the old woman and, almost in unison, said, "Why?"

"Sit," she told them after they had made their way back to the table. Then, as Blaine took the chair between her and Melissa, "You know what this place is?"

"That tank near the front makes things pretty clear in my mind."

"It was one of the tanks used in the battle to take the Golan Heights. We had it restored, and then the children designed the monument it now has become. It was they who insisted that we leave it fully armed and functional. Every week when Friday brings the Sabbath, a different one of them starts it up at sundown. To make sure we remember . . ."

"And what do you remember about World War II, about a certain secret chamber in Ephesus, Turkey?"

The old woman looked at Blaine closely. "Plenty. And you need to hear it all. Everything."

Melissa had retaken her seat. McCracken pulled his further away from the table so he could squeeze his legs beneath it.

"We have little time," the old woman started. "Perhaps none at all."

"Because of the White Death," McCracken followed.

"Yes."

"She was involved with the first shipment of crates that was removed from the chamber," Melissa elaborated, eyeing the old woman.

"And now the time has come to finish something that should have been done with forty-five years ago. That task falls upon you."

"Us," McCracken echoed.

"I brought you here to aid you in this quest. To help you save the world from them."

"From who?"

"The Tau."

* * *

"We will begin the day they were born," the old woman continued after introducing herself as Tovah. "A late winter day in 1942 at a Catholic boys' school in France, a school where three Jewish boys were being sheltered from the Nazis."

"Tessen," Blaine muttered, speaking while his eyes shifted between Tovah and Melissa. "A Nazi who may have saved my life in the hotel. He was at the school that day, a member of the firing squad."

The old woman flinched and shuddered. "Then you know what happened."

"Three boys were shot, and then the priest."

"The three Jewish boys."

"Yes."

"Edelstein, Sherman, and Grouche," the old woman added as if she were calling the roll.

"How could you know?"

"Because my brother was one of them, except he didn't die."

"*What?*" Melissa raised.

"Another boy took his place. A friend he had made who had helped shelter him from the very beginning." Tovah's voice tailed off. "A friend who was dying of cancer. It was a pact they had made long before. The friend asked only that my brother take care of his family, make sure they were watched over when the cursed war was over. And my brother did as he was asked. To this day he continues to do just that."

"Your brother's still *alive*?"

Tovah nodded almost imperceptibly. "We found each other again after the war. I had survived Auschwitz. After the school was closed down, he became a youthful member of the French Resistance. The experience served him well in later years with the Haganah and the Irgun."

"The founding of Israel . . ."

"He was one of its best soldiers. No one served this country better.'' The old woman's eyes filled with tears. Her lips trembled. ''And he will serve it again, once he recovers.''

''Recovers?'' asked Melissa.

''They tried to assassinate him three days ago. My brother is Arnold Rothstein.''

CHAPTER 29

"HE helped build this place,'' the old woman continued, as Blaine and Melissa exchanged shocked glances. ''And he has helped maintain it, providing us with a brand-new irrigation system for our fields six months ago.''

''And what about fifty-one years ago?''

''If you know of that last day at the school, you must know of the priest's final words.''

''A curse aimed at his killers, if not unleashed by holy powers, then by unholy ones.''

''My brother was standing in the back of the assembly. He could barely hear the words, but he never forgot them. When we found each other after the war, they were among the first things he told me. I looked in his eyes and knew he was not the boy, even the person I had known. He had become a killer.''

She looked at Blaine knowingly, and Blaine looked back, meeting her stare.

''He was a survivor,'' McCracken added, ''just like you.''

"And both of us burned for vengeance in our hearts. We were filled with a hate so vast, even the joy of finding each other again could not overcome it. My brother swore he could not rest until the men in that firing squad and their leader were brought to justice. We met others in those first months. All of them had similar stories to tell. They had been forced to watch their children killed, their wives raped—my God, just thinking of it now brings the old vile taste back."

"It never goes away," Blaine told her. "It's too strong."

"You understand."

"I've been there, Tovah."

"Which is why God brought you into this. While the plans of men are fraught with the random, His are not."

"And what about the plans of the others you and your brother met up with after the war?"

"You draw ahead of me."

"The direction's clear."

The old woman shrugged. Melissa poured her a fresh glass of orange juice and set it down where she could easily grasp it.

"The lives of so many had been ruined," she continued. "How could they go on? How could any of us go on? Where could we find the strength? We were afraid to love, so we lived on hate. There would come a day, we promised ourselves, there would come a day . . ."

"When did it come, Tovah?"

"When a Jew who had survived by betraying his faith and accepting the Nazi cross reached one of our members. Guilt was eating him away, just as hate was doing likewise to us. He worked for Hitler's board of science. He worked on the White Death."

Melissa and Blaine looked at each other, then back at Tovah.

"He told us what it was, what it could do and had done. At Altaloon." She glanced at Melissa. "He gave us a map that pointed the way to a secret underground chamber where it had been stored. The way in was clearly laid out. If you could have seen how jubilant we were! Imagine! We had the means to gain the vengeance we so desperately sought. My brother and I summoned the others to a meeting, just those who had seemed as driven and as fanatical as we were. There were twenty-nine in all, but after we had announced our plans the number dwindled to nineteen.''

"The name you gave to this kibbutz," Melissa realized.

"The symbolism is important to me. Nineteen is one more than the Hebrew number representing luck. We took this as a good omen, prophetic even. Ours was a holy mission. We convinced ourselves that God had blessed our actions.''

Tovah pulled up her sleeve and held her wrist out. The numbers stitched into her arm at Auschwitz had shrunk together with the withering of her skin. Less clear, they remained just as chilling, just as meaningful.

"I carried a second tattoo in addition to this one, on my right shoulder, until I had it removed. There were nineteen of us and we took that as our symbol." She stopped long enough to stretch her left hand across to where the tattoo had been. "The Tau . . . We all carried its mark on our flesh and its imprint on our souls. We divided ourselves into teams to begin the holy task before us. One team went to Ephesus to retrieve a supply of the White Death for us to begin our work. Another, led by my brother, went about tracking down potential targets. A third, led by me, began to recruit others, others like ourselves whose lives had been destroyed by the Nazis. Our selection process was discreet. Out of every hundred we considered, only five or six were actually chosen. An indoctrination process followed, along with training, of course. But we still needed a strategy, a plan of attack. The White Death gave us power, yet we had to make that power work for us." She paused to catch her breath. "The priest's last words were ingrained in all our hearts and minds by then. What if we stayed true to them? What if we made it seem that our work was the fulfillment of his curse?''

"Word would spread," Blaine picked up. "The resettled Nazis you couldn't get to, and you couldn't get to them all, would have their lives turned upside down by fear. What lives you couldn't take, then, you'd disrupt, perhaps irrevocably.''

"They would live forever in fear of potential violent death,'' the old woman acknowledged. ''They would live forever under the threat of some unworldly monster coming to call on them in the dead of night.''

"Which left behind the footprint of an unidentifiable creature that tore its victims to shreds.''

The glass of orange juice slipped from Tovah's grasp. She managed to regain control of it before it smashed, but the pulpy contents splashed her. She seemed not to notice.

"How could you know that?'' she demanded fitfully.

"Two sources actually. From that Nazi named Tessen who seemed desperately afraid that the monsters had come back to finish their job. And from someone I know back in the U.S. who's investigating the Tau's rebirth.''

"Someone like you?''

Blaine shrugged. "Pretty much, yeah,'' he said, not sure of how to explain Johnny Wareagle to someone who had never seen the big Indian operate. ''They made the mistake of killing a friend of his. He doesn't take kindly to that.''

The old woman's bony hands clenched into fists. "None of us do. My brother lies near death, because he dispatched a team to your country to ferret them out.''

"And this team?''

"Contact has been lost with it. I expected as much. I warned him to take this threat seriously. He wouldn't listen.'' Her voice trailed off. ''Just as he didn't want to listen all those years ago. . . .''

"About what?''

Tovah's face became almost pleading. "You've got to understand that ours was, in truth, a holy mission. We were doing something that God Himself would have approved of.''

"But something made you stop, didn't it? When the Tau came here to fight the battle of the founding of Israel, they didn't bring the White Death along.''

"No, we didn't.''

"Thanks to you?"

She smiled slightly between trembling lips. "You are very perceptive, Mr. McCracken. Even my brother wouldn't believe me at first, but the White Death brought with it too much power, the power of life and death itself. We started to believe ourselves invincible. We started to believe we were above the mission we were performing." She took a deep breath. "Mistakes were made, terrible mistakes. Innocent people died senselessly, horribly. The White Death did not discriminate between good and evil, and eventually neither did we. We were driven. We were obsessed."

"And eventually you went back to Ephesus and sealed the entrance to the storage chamber."

She nodded. "Or so we thought. The original nineteen of us had miraculously survived through the entire duration of our mission. We drew marbles out of a box for the task of destroying the White Death and sealing the remnants in the tomb forever."

Melissa and Blaine looked at each other. "The corpses!" she said before he had a chance to.

Tovah sighed. "When they never returned, we knew something had gone wrong."

"Something big," McCracken told her. "They were murdered."

The old woman's mouth dropped, the surprise on her face replaced quickly by resignation.

"There must have been a fourth person down there with them," Blaine continued. "They got the entrance sealed all right, but the White Death was never destroyed."

Tovah raked a withered hand across the iron tabletop. "I suppose I have always known it would come back. I always feared that someday someone else would revive what we had sought to hide from the world forever. I *felt* it. I read newspapers from all over the world every day, waiting, keeping my vigil." She paused. "The items first began to appear not even a week ago. They had come back, bringing with them the same thirst for vengeance.

"The vengeance of the Tau," Tovah said, almost too hushed to hear.

"You called your brother."

"And implored him to take action. Now he lies near death, a victim of the very force he helped to create."

"A victim of another member of the Tau, Tovah."

"No," she protested. "No! That can't be. It just can't!"

"Who else could have preserved your legacy for all these years? Who else could have known about the intricate details of your methods, the training procedures? Who else could have known the exact location of the chamber where the White Death could be found?" Blaine stopped and stared deeply into her eyes. "The fourth person who ventured down into that cavern and killed the other three, Tovah. That's who's responsible for reviving the vengeance of the Tau."

The old woman's face became eerily calm. "But they can be stopped. *You* can stop them."

"How did you find me?" McCracken asked her.

"The manner was rather indirect." Tovah eyed first Blaine, then Melissa. "The trails the two of you followed led to individuals we have been watching for some time. When my brother was nearly killed, I knew the time had come to intensify our surveillance. Women of Nineteen were dispatched to watch over our subjects. The woman at the toymaker's alerted us of your presence. I ordered her to assist you, if it became necessary."

"Lucky for me," said Blaine.

"But why watch Gunthar Brandt?" raised Melissa. "He was simply a soldier at Altaloon. I found him through his journal. Why would you bother watching him?"

"Shouldn't you be asking instead why he wanted to kill you? The answer to both questions is the same. Gunthar Brandt did not write that journal; he merely supplied the notebook that already bore his name to a young soldier."

Melissa recalled that the name "Gunthar Brandt" and his hometown had been penned on the inside page of the journal.

A name at the end she had assumed to be Brandt's must have been that of the journal's true author.

"Gunthar Brandt was the board of science's representative at Altaloon to oversee the operation and report on it," Tovah continued. "Until his purported stroke, he remained militantly active in the rising neo-Nazi movement within Germany today."

"But why would he try to kill me?" Melissa raised.

"He must have thought you were getting close to the truth. When he had learned what you knew and who you had seen, killing you was the soundest strategy to keep himself safe."

"From you?"

"Very perceptive, young lady. I would imagine that he initially feared that we had sent you. He spoke only after being satisfied there was no connection, at least not yet."

"And in spite of all this you let Brandt and the toymaker live," Blaine challenged.

"Because it was equally important for us to know who our true enemies were. I preferred to watch who might come for an audience with either one of them."

"Quite a risk."

"The stakes were worth the risk. I don't have to tell you about the dangerous state the world lies in today." The old woman's stare grew distant. "In Germany, the marches and parades have begun again. The persecution of foreigners has begun again. Outlawed Nazi anthems are sung in public with the police standing passively by; sympathizing, even supporting the madness." Her eyes sharpened again. "You see, the Tau is not the only thing that has returned. Imagine for a moment the White Death in the hands of a new generation of madmen!"

"Something that never could have happened if not for the return of one of the Tau's original members to Ephesus to remove the rest of the crates containing it. We've got to track down the surviving members, Tovah. It's the only way to—"

McCracken broke off speaking and stiffened, as a pair of armed women rushed into the area and headed straight for the table. One of them leaned over and whispered a message into the old woman's ear. She nodded and sent the two of them on their way.

"It seems," she told McCracken, "that we have company."

CHAPTER 30

"**W**HO?" Blaine asked, rising deliberately to his feet.

"Terrorists, or some pretending to be terrorists."

"The Tau," Melissa said, eyes meeting McCracken's.

"Whoever they are, how'd they get through the IDF security lines?"

"Such things have been known to happen before," Tovah explained. "There is no need to worry. We are prepared for this. Our early warning system makes use of its own security lines."

McCracken was suddenly fidgety, agitated, like a Doberman straining at its leash. "If it's all the same to you, I'd like to check that out for myself."

"I have no problem with that, Mr. McCracken, so long as you take me with you."

* * *

They came in a single wave attack from the west: eight
gunmen dressed in camouflage gear with Arab headdresses
and masks covering their faces. Judging by the figures they
saw at the kibbutz, bent to their accustomed tasks, the gunmen's presence had gone undetected. Once within range,
they would kill everyone they came across en route to their
primary target.

The men fanned out as planned and easily bypassed the
trip wires in entering the grounds of the kibbutz. Each one
headed toward his assigned sector. In the fields and within
the kibbutz itself, the figures they had glimpsed continued to
go about their business, unknowing, unseeing. Thirty seconds later, the leader gave the signal.

The men lunged into the open, their bullets slicing the air
in constant fire. The victims who had the misfortune to be
exposed took the brunt of the initial barrages, slammed again
and again by bullets.

The leader screamed hoarsely as he opened fire on another
victim from in close. At once his mouth dropped. The victim's guts had been spilled into the air. There was no blood,
though, just raggedy straw stuffing.

"What . . ."

"Take them!" a voice screamed in Hebrew.

The leader had barely had a chance to move before the
bullets found him. He crumpled to the ground, just managing to press the single red button on his communicator.

"Take them!"

The order had been given just after McCracken had stowed
Tovah's wheelchair in a position that afforded a clear view of
the kibbutz's western side. He had begun to advance himself
when the next wave of gunfire froze him.

"As I said," Tovah reminded, "everything is under control."

"Dummies," Blaine realized.

"Inevitably effective against the overanxious attacker."

"So it seems."

With the signal given, the armed commandos of Nineteen had appeared from dozens of concealed positions. Before the terrorists could respond, they were cut down in incessant hails of fire that spared nothing. Not a single one was left standing after mere seconds.

"A pity we didn't have a chance to witness your skills," Tovah called forward to McCracken.

Blaine had remained rigid, immobile. "When was the last time you faced an attack?"

"Two years ago. But why—"

The sound of revving engines stopped Tovah in midsentence. Her face crinkled with fear, mouth trembling and gaze swinging in search of the sound's origin.

"Because I don't believe in coincidence," Blaine said.

Heavy-caliber automatic fire begin to ring out. Before them the armed women of Nineteen had begun rushing toward the front of the kibbutz. In the narrowing distance, Blaine could see eight six-wheeled, armored enemy jeeps storming the area, each heavily armed.

"Help me!" Tovah implored, starting to wheel herself forward over the uneven ground.

Melissa grasped the handles of her wheelchair to hold her in place. McCracken took up position directly in front of the old woman.

"I think you'd better sit this one out."

"This is my *home*!"

"Then let me save it for you," McCracken said. He had been studying the flower-encased tank at the entrance to the kibbutz and now turned to face Melissa. "Come on, we've got work to do."

He shielded her with his body, as they drew closer to the center of the battle.

"What are we going to—"

"Just stay close to me! Move when I move!"

"For the *tank*?"

"For the tank."

First glance when he came within view of the kibbutz's open front showed the eight large jeeps tearing forward onto the grounds in spread fashion. Each boasted either a 50 caliber machine gun or a 7.62mm Vulcan minigun pedestaled in its rear hold. The machine gunners fired on the run, while the Vulcan-equipped vehicles needed to come to a halt or at least slow considerably before firing with reasonable accuracy.

A trio of the buildings closest to Nineteen's entrance were torn apart by minigun bursts. Those scampering away from the cover the buildings had provided were traced by machine-gun fire and hopelessly pinned down. More of the kibbutz's female commandos charged forward with rifles blasting, but they were no match for the enemy's superior weaponry.

But who was the enemy? McCracken could accept a small team of terrorists sliding through the Israeli Defense Forces beyond, but eight heavily armed vehicles? It was unthinkable!

The vehicles streamed farther into Nineteen, crisscrossing each other as they fired. The unarmed residents of the kibbutz were fleeing toward the rear with the aged and children in tow. Vulcan fire blocked their path on several occasions and had many hugging the ground, the adults shielding the bodies of the youngsters.

Blaine and Melissa darted behind the cover provided by the huge dirt-encrusted structure of the tank.

"What do you need me for?" she asked him, heaving for breath.

"One person can't operate a tank like this alone, never mind fire it."

"Operate? *Fire?*"

"On the money, Melly."

McCracken lunged atop the tank ahead of Melissa and yanked open the top. He beckoned her to follow and eased her down into the M-60's innards ahead of him. His eyes began studying the interior layout of its cab, even as he was closing the hatch behind him.

"I haven't had much experience with tanks," Melly reminded.

"That's okay; I have."

In truth, he only had experience with the M-60A1 and A2, more complex generations of this version. But the control panel on this one was virtually identical—an easy transition, so long as his memory cooperated. Blaine flipped a switch, and the tank's interior filled with a dull glow. The weapons rack was a full five feet behind him, a dozen shells accounted for in its slots. With the gunfire continuing to rage outside, he moved to the tank's control console and pressed its starter button.

The engine grumbled, growled, then shook to life as it did every Sabbath evening. McCracken slid to his right toward the gun sight, then turned fast toward Melissa.

"Back against the wall, do you see that stack of shells?"

"Yes."

"Bring me one."

After a momentary twinge of fear that the shells might be dummies, he was reassured by the weight of the first one Melissa handed him. He chambered it and sighted forward again.

"Take the chair in front of the control console on my left," Blaine instructed. "Red control arm there controls the turret. Take it in both hands and move it the way I tell you."

Through his sights, Blaine could see that one of the vehicles bearing a minigun had come to a halt twenty degrees to the right.

"Move the control lever clockwise. Slowly, Melly, that's it."

The turret rotated with a rough grinding sound.

"Stop!" Blaine ordered when the Vulcan-wielding jeep was dead center in his crosshairs.

At the very last, he thought he could see the occupants of the vehicle turn his way.

Then he fired.

The old tank kicked backward slightly as the shell burst outward. Melissa was jostled out of her chair.

Come on, he urged. *Come—*

The first Vulcan-wielding jeep exploded in a shower of flames, metal fragmenting in all directions.

"We did it!" Melissa beamed.

The percussion of the blast forced an enemy vehicle equipped with a machine gun fifteen yards from the blown jeep to waver out of control and cross the path of another. As Blaine watched through his sights, they collided in a rolling cloud of twisted, shrieking metal that slammed finally into the remains of one of the blasted outbuildings. McCracken checked the area through the open view plate and found a second of the Vulcan-wielding jeeps bearing down on the M-60.

"Another shell!" he called to Melissa.

The tank shook from the impact of the minigun's powerful 7.62mm ammo. Blaine steadied himself and sighted forward again, while Melissa pulled herself across the floor for a second shell. The jeep holding the Vulcan was already charging away.

"Hurry!"

An instant later, Melissa eased another shell into his hands and resumed her position in the pilot's seat farther forward. McCracken slammed the shell home and returned to his sight.

"Counterclockwise, fifteen degrees," he instructed. "Easy, easy . . . That's got it!"

He aimed slightly ahead before firing. The shell thumped out behind the gun's recoil. Blaine kept his eyes glued to the viewer and saw instantly that his aim this time looked slightly off. Fortunately, though, the jeep struck a ridge that slowed it enough for the shell to impact upon its rear. No flames this time, just a rolling carcass spilling its occupants into the air along the way.

Four down, Blaine thought, *and four to go* . . .

"Got him!" Melissa beamed.

"Still got plenty of company."

The sight through the view plate confirmed his warning. The three remaining jeeps equipped with machine guns were speeding along toward the larger congestion of buildings and kibbutz residents. The final one with a Vulcan dragged a bit behind them.

"Change seats with me!" McCracken ordered Melissa, and shifted into the pilot's chair, while she slid past him.

The moment he was seated, he began working the controls of the old warhorse to get it moving. The tank refused to cooperate at first, and it took several seconds of coaxing with the floor pedals as well before it lurched forward with a jolt. The top layer of plantings and ornaments were thrown off. A pile of dirt built up before the view plate, and Blaine jammed on the brake suddenly to force the debris aside.

A severe list to the right told him that only one of the tank's treads was functioning properly, and McCracken compensated with the T-bar steering control as best he could. The gears screeched and whined in protest; the tank was a sleeping bear stirred from its hibernation ahead of the seasons. He figured he could fire without sacrificing significant pace or control, so long as Melly could take his place as driver.

"Watch what I do," he told her. "Get ready to switch places again."

The tank continued to shake the ornamental plantings off itself, as he shoved it on. Before him a determined charge by Nineteen's commandos had neutralized one of the jeeps equipped with a machine gun. He searched the area for the final Vulcan-wielding vehicle and found it measuring off shots toward the kibbutz's largest buildings, where most of the inhabitants were likely to have gathered.

"Okay," he called to Melissa again. "Switch!"

They swapped seats without missing a beat, and Melissa took over the controls. Determined to succeed, she frowned in concentration and bit into her bottom lip with her front teeth, struggling to mimic McCracken's moves. Her hands squeezed into the T-bar, but it took all her strength to keep it steady. Her arms began to throb, then shake. She bit her lip harder.

The jeep's driver noticed the oncoming tank and shot forward before the gunner was ready. The man was nearly thrown from the jeep and was actually the first to notice the tank wavering out of control toward a small storage shed.

"Watch out!" Blaine screamed, raising the shell he had pulled from the rack to the loader.

Melissa tried with all her strength to force the T-bar to the left. It barely budged, and the tank began to list even more severely to the right. Nonetheless, Blaine had managed to work the turret control himself and then waited for the rushing jeep to enter his crosshairs. He fired on timing this time.

The tank's rightward heave threw him off a bit, and impact came several yards in front of the target vehicle. The percussion of the blast, though, was enough to strip the driver's control away, and the jeep slammed into a tree, its occupants left to Nineteen's commandos.

"Uh-oh," Blaine muttered.

The right side of the tank tore the side of the storage shed away, and McCracken managed to close his hands over Melissa's on the T-bar before the rest of the structure perished as well. There were just two jeeps left now, both toting machine guns. The open view plate provided no sight of them, but the sounds of gunfire crackling in the wind gave him the bearing he needed.

"They're behind a row of low buildings over there to our right." Blaine gestured, replacing Melissa in the pilot's seat. "Heading toward the fields."

"Where the residents would have fled to . . ."

"Let's get this thing turned around."

The grinding of the tank's engine almost drowned out his words, as McCracken worked the controls hard. It responded sluggishly. McCracken spun it to the left and demanded of it all the power it would give.

"Come on," he urged. Then to Melissa, "Grab another shell!"

The tank jolted forward as the gears finally caught. The engine was screaming, and the smell of oil was thick in the air. Blaine didn't ease back, the speedometer nearing thirty and the engine warning gauge well into the red. The only way to reach the fields and cut off the jeeps' attack angle in time was straight ahead.

Through the buildings.

"Hold on to something."

But Melissa chambered the shell she was toting first, just as she had watched McCracken do.

Blaine never hesitated. The old tank crashed through a small dormitorylike building, chewing up wood and plaster en route and rolling over the debris it created. The last of the building's remains were still being spit from its treads when one of the jeeps passed fifty yards before it. The jeep's machine gun hammered away at those kibbutz residents who had abandoned the precarious cover provided by buildings for a dangerous dash through the fields. McCracken looked to his right and saw Melissa's eyes pressed against the targeting sight.

"Turret, twenty degrees right—I mean left!" she called to him.

There was no time for Blaine to argue, nor was there time for them to switch places. She realized it and so did he. He worked the controls as she had instructed.

"Got it!" she said, feeling for the firing button.

She pressed it. The shell thumped out.

"Yes," Melissa said softly. *"Yes!"*

The explosion rocked them. Before him, Blaine could see that the jeep was gone, in its place flaming charred metal with no real shape, scraps of bloodied clothing lifting off it in the breeze. Then black, rank smoke filled the inside of the tank's cabin.

"We've lost the main gun," Blaine realized, swiping the smoke away from his eyes.

"Still one more jeep to go."

"Where? Can you see—"

"There! A hundred feet dead ahead." She looked his way. "Running away."

McCracken smiled and pushed the tank's engine till the smell of oil was added to the other noxious vapors already filling the cab.

The jeep's driver saw the onrushing tank and turned quickly to the right. The suddenness of the move caught the jeep's tires in the mud, and the tank gained the last bit of ground it needed. The jeep's occupants managed to lunge free to be rounded up by Nineteen's commandos, just before the tank rolled up its side and compressed it to half its former size. Tires blew out in blasts as loud as the shell explosions had been.

The tank sputtered and died. Black oil smoke belched into the cab, then followed McCracken upward as he threw open the hatch and helped Melissa out ahead of himself.

Arms over each other's shoulders, they approached Tovah, whose wheelchair was being pushed through the soft dirt to meet them. Her face was deathly pale. She was still trembling.

"Such a concerted attack," the old woman muttered. "Never before, I tell you, never before . . ." She stopped, then started again. "The Tau . . ."

"A safe assumption," Blaine acknowledged.

The old woman's eyes sharpened with realization. "They came for you! They must have!"

"No, Tovah," Blaine said, with an icy stare fixed upon her.

"Then who— *Me?* No, it can't be, I tell you. It can't!"

"This operation didn't come up overnight. It's been planned for some time, days at the very least. They couldn't have known I would be here."

"Why?" the old woman posed desperately.

"Because you're the only one who can identify all the members of the original Tau, and one of them is behind the return. Now we've got to find him."

"How?"

"Get me to a phone."

CHAPTER 31

"**W**ELCOME to my home, warrior," the Old One said proudly, as morning rose over the place she called No Town. "No phone, no electricity, no running water. This place has been unchanged since I grew up here when people thought the Civil War could never happen. Got us some generators now and propane tanks. That's about it."

Wareagle nodded knowingly. The woods to which he had retreated for a dozen years were equally infused with solitude and a sense of timelessness. Once situated in such places, it was difficult to leave.

No Town stood close enough to the shores of the bayou for its sounds and smells to linger forever in the air. They had walked over land the last eight miles of the way after the waterway they were traveling on became too shallow for their boat. After abandoning it at around one A.M., they had found shelter in a nearby abandoned barn. Heydan had made beds out of straw for herself and the Old One. Johnny rejected her offer to make one up for him and maintained a vigil long into the night. Whether he slept or not, she could not say; come morning he was the same stoic, tireless figure he had been the night before.

Catching first glimpse of No Town two hours after dawn was like taking a giant step back in time. Homes and small farms dotted the town's outer perimeter. Drying laundry flapped in the breeze on clotheslines strung up behind the houses. Even at this early hour, plenty of people were out doing chores. Johnny could see a number of larger farms occupying the outlying land and figured, as the Old One had suggested, that almost all of No Town's food supply was grown right here.

The buildings in the town center itself were formed of unfinished wood and clapboard. The signs above the few businesses were hand-painted or, in a few instances, simply scrawled. There was a general store, an outdoor produce market, a bakery that was already pumping the scent of fresh bread into the air, and a combination restaurant-bar-roominghouse that didn't bother hanging a No Vacancy sign. Johnny could find no trace of a post office, but a small sign drawn in scratchy letters did advertise BANK. A sign carved in wood with a star above and below it revealed the sheriff's office.

People on bikes or in horse-drawn carriages gave him a long look when they passed. When they noticed the Old One, however, they stopped and seemed to bow their heads in reverence, not taking their eyes off her until they were out of sight. In several instances she greeted them by name before they'd had a chance to announce themselves. Most times she simply bid them good day.

"I haven't been back here in a dozen years," Wareagle heard her mutter to Heydan. "Too long to remember the feel of everyone's aura."

Wareagle slowed, and the two women drew up even with him. He was conscious now of the fact that the two or three dozen residents about them had come to a dead stop and were watching their every move.

"Folks here don't see white people very often, warrior. They see even less of Indians. Nice place to grow up, let me tell you, though." The Old One turned to Heydan Larroux.

"Maybe show you the house where I was born later, introduce you to my mammy."

Heydan's eyes bulged at the suggestion.

"Well, I'll be gawdamned . . ."

Johnny turned toward the voice's origin and saw a rail-thin black man emerge from the sheriff's office. He wore a badge pinned to his shirt but had no gun. He stepped down from the curb and headed their way.

"Tyrell Loon, that you?" the Old One called in his direction.

"It be," the sheriff returned happily.

He reached the Old One and kissed her hand, paying Heydan and Johnny no heed at all.

"I missed you," she told him.

"We *all* missed you."

"There was a need for my services elsewhere."

"You fixin' to stay?"

The Old One looked at him as if she were considering the prospects for the first time. "I just might at that. Years be ready to cash me in, Tyrell Loon. Person got to end things where she started them."

Loon's eyes scorned her. "You been sayin' that since 'fore I had hair on my privates." He stole a quick gaze at Heydan and then a longer one at Johnny. "What brings you back here?"

The Old One fixed her sightless gaze on Wareagle. "The warrior here saved my life. I come back to repay my debt."

Tyrell Loon stuck out his hand and Johnny took it. "In that case, you done come to the right place."

"And this here," the Old One continued, "is my lady."

"So you the one," Tyrell said, taking one of Heydan Larroux's hands in both of his and squeezing tenderly. "Was your donations built us the new school," he said, and pointed to a small building at the very edge of town. He turned his finger toward an old church diagonally across the street from it. "Helped us rebuild the church, too. Gonna get us our own permanent preacher, soon as we can build him a house."

"I never took much to men of that kind," the Old One said. "Never saw the need."

"Always figured that's why No Town never had one." Tyrell Loon looked the three of them over again. "We best go inside my office 'fore the town stands totally still a lookin'."

He took the Old One's hand and guided her toward the building with two stars marked SHERIFF. She stepped up onto the curb ahead of him. Johnny and Heydan walked behind them. Loon swung the door open, and bells affixed to the other side jingled. He led the Old One inside and then held the door for Johnny and Heydan.

Inside the room were a simple pair of desks, a dust-coated filing cabinet, and twin jail cells that were both presently unoccupied. The beds inside the cells were freshly made. The floors shone. A trio of stuffed game birds sat respectively atop the front counter, Loon's desk, and the filing cabinet.

"Let me grab some chairs for ya."

He set two rickety wood ones in front of his desk and then looked back at Wareagle.

"Don't think I got one that'd fit ya."

"I'll stand," Johnny said.

Loon helped the Old One into one of the chairs and then slid back behind the desk to take his own. "Now, what is it I can do for ya?"

"You up to some tinkering, Tyrell?" she asked him.

"Not much 'round these parts to tinker with."

"There is today."

Johnny handed over the miniature pager to the sheriff.

"I was in the Signal Corps over in 'Nam," he explained, inspecting it. "Army done give me a great technical education. Guess you could say I haven't done much with it."

"We need to know the contents of the last message, Tyrell Loon," the Old One told him. "Can your tinkering bring it up for us?"

"Don't know. It's possible, if this thing has the kind of memory chip I think it does. Let's take a gander."

He used a small screwdriver to pry the back off, and then a pair of thin explorers to work through the pager's insides.

"I love tinkering," he said without looking up. "Just like I figured. Chip keeps the last message received stored until one comes in to replace it. Yup, here we go. . . ."

With a few more seconds of manipulations with his tools, he turned the pager over and gazed at its miniature screen.

"There it is."

He slid the pager toward Johnny, who leaned over the desk to study the message that was scrawled across two tiny lines:

*Livermore Air Force Base. Hanover, Kansas.
The final phase begins.*

It must have been a signal to come in, a recall. The team of killers in the bayou would have gone straight there upon completion of their mission. Johnny had his next destination.

"Not alone, warrior," the Old One shot at him, seeming to read his thoughts. "You can't beat them alone." She turned toward Loon and continued before Wareagle had a chance to object. "My warrior here has got hisself a problem, Tyrell. Got an enemy been doing plenty of harm and plans to do lots more. Got to be stopped."

"Uh-huh," Loon acknowledged.

"Big in number the enemy be now, though. Too much for one man to best, even my warrior. You hear?"

"Uh-huh."

"How many men can you round up, Tyrell?"

Johnny spoke before the sheriff had a chance to. "I can't let you do that," he said to the Old One.

"I don't remember asking your permission," she shot back at him.

"You know what we're dealing with."

"But you don't know the kind of man lives down here."

"She's right," Tyrell said. "I'm not the only man here

who paid his dues elsewhere 'fore he come home. Some of the older men was in Korea. More of the younger ones been to the 'Nam. You was there." A statement.

"Yes, I was."

"I can always tell. Never could figure out how. Anyways, most of the men here knows what it be like to fight for your life. And not just abroad, neither. No way. Some been fighting all their lives till they came here."

Johnny looked down at the Old One. "We can't fight this with just experience."

"How about with the best weapons money can buy?" Heydan Larroux suggested. "I've got plenty stockpiled for emergencies. I'd bet they'd impress even you," she said to Wareagle.

"Where are they?"

"New Orleans. In storage."

"How many men you figure we need?" Sheriff Tyrell Loon asked the Old One.

"Twenty-five."

"Make it twenty-four. Sorry, forgot the Indian. Make that twenty-three."

"Why?"

"Got my reasons."

A boy who cleaned up around the jail building came by seconds later. Tyrell whispered something in his ear and sent him on his way.

"Hurry up now!" he called after the boy, as the bells jingled again. Then he looked back toward his guests. "Problem we got is some of the men I got in mind ain't hardly ever left No Town since they got here and won't take kindly to flying, even if we had us a plane. We gonna use them, we gotta make them feel at home, if you know what I mean."

"I'm not sure I want to use them at all," Wareagle said.

"You can't win this by yourself, warrior," the Old One told him. "And you can't afford to lose. Fact that this enemy is holing itself up at an air force base can only mean one thing."

"Kansas is up north quite a ways," Sheriff Loon followed somberly. "Quite a ways. Don't know if the Blue Thunder can make it."

"The blue what?" raised Heydan.

Loon had started to answer when a cluttering, clanking sound outside made him stop. A series of backfires like a machine-gun spray followed, and the sheriff's face lit up with a smile.

"Here she comes now," he said, and stood up.

Johnny and Heydan followed him to the door. The Old One stayed back in her chair.

"Yup," Leon continued, "here she be."

Johnny fixed his eyes on a twenty-four-passenger bus painted in what had once been a royal shade of blue. Much of it had worn down to the dull gray primer now, and there were rust patches and even gaps where the rust had eaten its way through the metal. The tires were different makes and sizes. The windshield was cracked, and plenty of the side windows were covered by boards. Rust had eaten away most of the wheel wells, as well as a hefty portion of the metal over the bus's rear bumper. As Johnny looked on, the door jerked open with a grinding rasp that had once been an easy hiss. A toothless driver gazed down from behind the wheel and grinned with his gums.

Blue Thunder had arrived.

Blue Thunder sputtered and shook, but held fast to the road like it was afraid to let go. Hours before, while Sheriff Tyrell Loon had gathered up the men to pack it for the journey, the Old One had made the rounds of No Town with Heydan by her side to gather up a select group of women. Several looked as old as she was. Others were young enough to cart babies with them to the center of town. All of them brought beads and rattles and other implements Johnny knew were used to evoke blessings or curses depending on the manner in which they were used.

"Must be the water," the Old One advised him. "See, I wasn't the only one to be born in No Town with special powers. These women all born here, too, and they all got their special ways."

Led by the Old One, the women surrounded Blue Thunder in a circle and went about their individual ceremonies. One threw stones against the old bus's few still-whole windows. Another blew dirt down its rusted tailpipe. A third spit repeatedly on its engine, chanting between each expectoration. A few sang. Others took more accepted positions of prayer. The Old One oversaw it all, feeling her way amidst them without participating in the ritual directly.

Johnny watched from a distance. As the ritual drew to its close, he turned suddenly to his right. The Old One was standing right next to him.

"You will travel safe now, warrior. You will be delivered. And you will not fight alone. Another comes to join you."

Wareagle's lips quivered ever so slightly. "Blainey," he muttered.

"I have not seen his name," she told him. "But his pursuits now mirror yours."

Johnny had spent part of the ride to New Orleans in the back of Blue Thunder wondering what Blaine McCracken had uncovered in Turkey that had led him to the Tau. He'd had plenty of time to study the rest of the men crowded in the old bus with him. Under the circumstances, Johnny found them to be most impressive. These were indeed men who had fought many fights in their time and would never shy from another. There was a monster of a man, called Bijou because he was as big as a movie house. There was a man who looked to be formed all of knobby bone called Pole, so thin he had to cut a new hole in his belt a foot from the last one in the row. There was a former military demolitions expert, called Smoke because he knew how to blow things up.

Some had fought for their lives just because they were black. Others had served in whatever branch of the service would have them. Married or single, young or old, their status mattered not at all. Each one had not hesitated in the slightest after being selected. For the Old One, apparently, their duty knew no bounds. And the fact that she had blessed them filled each with a certainty that they would be returning unharmed when all this was done.

Wareagle wished he could have shared their optimism.

The weapons would be waiting for them at a warehouse in New Orleans, and Tyrell Loon had already chosen a crew to do the loading. The street leading to the warehouse was narrow. Toothless Jim Jackson was forced to back up several times to manage the turn. Blue Thunder's gears creaked and clunked but somehow held. There was a pay phone down the street, and Johnny stepped off to use it.

He called Sal Belamo's private line. A series of clicks followed, indicating that the line was being rerouted. Johnny was ready to hang up as soon as the phone was answered if Belamo's voice was not on the other end.

"That you again, McBalls?"

Johnny didn't hang up.

"It's me, Sal Belamo."

"Hey, big fella! Your friend and mine's been hoping you would check in. You're not gonna believe this, but the two of you are chasing the same son-of-a-bitching thing."

Silence.

"Hey, you surprised or what?"

"Nothing about this surprises me, Sal Belamo. Tell Blainey I'm on my way to an air force base in Kansas. Tell him what we both seek can be found on this base."

Johnny's gaze slid back to the shuddering shape of Blue Thunder. The last crates were being loaded. The old bus's frame had dipped closer to the ground.

"Tell him he'd better meet me there."

the vengeance of the tau 291

McMasters looked back at Teruh. "I'll open at nine one."

CHAPTER 32

"LIVERMORE Air Force Base?" Blaine raised. He had been calling Sal Belamo every half hour or so since the end of the battle here at Nineteen to see if Wareagle had called in, knowing the big Indian was his only hope of finding where to take his search for the White Death next. Though Tovah had supplied him with the names of the rest of the original Tau, she didn't know where they could be found or how to contact them. And at the speed things were progressing, there was no way he could rely on traditional intelligence methods to track them down.

"Straight from the big fella's mouth, boss. Want me to call in the cavalry?"

"No, Sal. We're keeping this private."

"That a good idea, given what you've told me?"

"That's the point. Any official types who help are gonna want to know what it is we uncovered. You can figure out the next step."

"They'll want it for themselves. . . ."

"You're learning, Sal. The White Death has to end here."

"You mean in Kansas."

"Yes."

"Gonna need help from somebody, boss. And, you ask me, plenty of it."

McCracken looked back at Tovah. "I'll think of something."

McCracken explained the specifics to her as soon as he was off the phone, and Tovah was all too happy to comply with his request. First, he let her choose the best commandos Nineteen had to offer to accompany him back to America for the final battle against the Tau; after the attack on the kibbutz, it wasn't hard to find volunteers.

From there, the old woman called on her many contacts both inside and outside Israel to arrange the logistics of their journey. From Nineteen the small army would be driven to the same airstrip Melissa and McCracken had been flown into earlier in the day. A jet would be waiting with a flight plan filed for New York's Kennedy Airport. To avoid scrutiny, it would fly under diplomatic markings.

"Thank you," Melissa told Blaine when they were finally airborne. The jet was a twenty-four-seater, and all but two of the seats were taken. Weapons gathered from Nineteen's stash had been stowed in the cramped baggage compartment.

"For what?"

"For not trying to tell me I couldn't come along."

"You've got it coming to you." He eyed her warmly. "Your father died for what we uncovered, Melly. You deserve to be there for the finish. I never really considered otherwise."

She turned to the window and then back at McCracken. "Do you ever get used to it?"

"Used to what?"

"Loss. Fear. Anxiety."

"No. To all of the above."

Melissa took his hand and they sat in silence.

Sal Belamo was waiting as planned at the diplomatic terminal at Kennedy Airport when the jet landed. McCracken climbed down out of the plane and met him on the tarmac.

"You bring the specs on Livermore, Sal?"

Belamo frowned. "You ask me, maybe you forgot who it

was you were dealing with here. Mothballed SAC base located on the outskirts of a little town called Hanover. I got us a flight plan to an airport forty miles away in Hastings, Nebraska.'' Sal was smirking now. "What'd you bring, boss?"

Blaine turned back toward the women of Nineteen who were stretching their legs on the tarmac.

"Oh," Belamo said.

"So what's eating you, boss?" he asked before Blaine could start back for the jet.

"It shows that much?"

"Does to me."

"It's just that things aren't clear-cut this time, not black and white. It's tough to argue with what the Tau is attempting. Every name comes off their list makes this a safer world to live in." Blaine's expression grew reflective. "I don't know, it seems to me that what the Tau are doing—what their predecessors did forty-five years ago—isn't much different from what I've been doing for the last decade or so."

"Bad comparison."

"Is it?"

"Yeah. Maybe you're forgetting 'bout the big fella's cop friend or the fact that they went after the big fella himself. You never killed anyone who wasn't in a position to do likewise to you. The Tau don't fit your style in the slightest."

"I've been trying to tell myself that. I keep thinking that the key to this is what happened all those years ago in that chamber Melissa and I uncovered. One of the original Tau's been waiting a long time to make a comeback. He could have done it at any time, but he chose now. Why? Only thing I can figure is it took this long for the technology to become available to reproduce the White Death in the quantities he needed for multiple dispersals. Livermore Air Force Base must be his primary distribution point."

"And you just solved your own problem, boss."

"How?"

"This White Death shit, maybe it'd be okay in the Tau's

hands if we left things alone. Maybe. But somebody else gets their hands on it might have a different agenda. You told me yourself that's why you wanted to keep our trip to Livermore in the family. So it ain't really the Tau we're after, it's the White Death.''

The way Belamo put it made Blaine feel instantly lighter and more relaxed. "So let's go find it."

"Can you fix it?" Sheriff Tyrell Loon asked Toothless Jim Jackson, as Johnny Wareagle looked on.

"Engine block's got a crack in it wider than the Liberty Bell's and the fuel line looks like she's been chewed by a gator," Jackson replied. "I'll fetch me my toolbox and give it my best shot."

"How long?"

"Anywheres between an hour and never, Tyrell."

The stink of something burning had Toothless Jim easing Blue Thunder over even before the first of the black smoke began to show itself from under the hood. Of course, the signs had been there two states back. Blue Thunder had covered the second half of its journey grudgingly, in fits and starts, each corner and road bringing a new adventure. By northern Texas the clanking and clamoring had given way to a constant rattle that the passengers from Tyrell Loon on back felt down to the pits of their stomachs. Through Oklahoma the old bus was drinking a quart of oil every hundred miles and belching black smoke from its tailpipe. And halfway into Kansas Blue Thunder's shocks had given up, so every uneven patch of road sent the occupants lurching upward in their seats. Four of its tires were losing air as fast as the engine was bleeding oil. A bit farther north, the rear emergency exit had sprung permanently open, causing an ear-wrenching buzz that had the makeshift army covering their ears to stifle the noise. It wasn't until Toothless Jim Jackson figured out the right wire to cut that they could relax again.

As he watched Toothless Jim emerge from Blue Thunder carrying his toolbox, Johnny Wareagle found himself still surprisingly calm. He knew no matter how bad things got for Blue Thunder that the old bus would get them to their destination. Mechanically it should never have made it out of No Town, much less Louisiana. But the ceremony the Old One had supervised was better than any tune-up or engine replacement. The magic of No Town passed like glue through Blue Thunder's gas line and stuck tight to those parts of it that had long since lost their seals. In one of the towns they had stopped in, the mechanic feeding Blue Thunder oil had looked at its engine the way he would if his dead uncle drove up to the pump and said "Fill her up."

Such stops had served as the only breaks in their constant journey through Saturday night and into Sunday morning. Toothless Jim stopped not far from Johnny and threw open his toolbox. Wareagle knew tools fairly well and engines a little better, well enough anyway to tell him that nothing in this box was even remotely related to repairing the kind of problem Blue Thunder had come down with.

Toothless Jim grabbed some duct tape and a small plastic container. He held these items in one hand, while he rummaged with the other through the box's contents and finally came up with what he was looking for: a thin, dried-out paintbrush.

"Here we go," he said, flashing his gums.

Wareagle watched as he moved to the cooling engine and wedged a hand in deep.

"Bigger than I thought," he said, as he fingered the crack. "I best clean it first. Sheriff, bring me that bottle I got tucked under my seat."

Loon came back seconds later with a bottle of homemade whiskey corked at the top and half-empty. Johnny hadn't seen Toothless Jim take a single swig on the journey, but he was certain all the same that the bottle had been full when they'd left No Town. Toothless Jim poured a hefty portion on an old rag and felt for the crack again.

"That oughta do her," he said, sliding his hand back out. "Time for some black magic now."

In this case the ''black magic'' referred to a thick tarlike epoxy substance that Toothless Jim spooned out of the plastic container and smoothed out in one of his hands. The other hand pushed the brush down into the flattened lump and forced as much black magic on as the bristles would hold. Then his right hand disappeared back into the engine, toward the crack.

''Where are you?'' Toothless Jim muttered, as he probed about. ''Come out, come out wherever you are. . . .''

He smiled again at Loon and Wareagle. They could see his forearm flexing, the crack being found, and the home-made epoxy filler being worked home.

''Be an hour, if I can seal the fuel line,'' he said, grimacing from the exertion. ''Never, if I can't.''

CHAPTER 33

Pop Keller sat in the only bar Hanover, Kansas, had to offer, sipping club soda and doing the best he could to shell the peanuts before him. Not so long ago, his drink would have been considerably stronger than club soda, and the peanuts would have been long gone. But the increasing severity of his arthritis had sworn him off booze and made cracking shells an act that he could perform only with gaps in between to let the pain go way.

If this didn't beat the fuck out of life . . .

After all he had been through, all he had survived, to be done in by something the doctors said was out of his control. It had gotten bad in a hurry and worse even faster. Shit-rotten timing, with his road show hitting peak season and attendance records shattered everywhere he had been. While Pop sipped club soda, his people were setting up for next weekend's show in the five-hundred-acre remains of a leveled amusement park.

Not that Pop was one to shy away from work—far from it. It was just since the arthritis had gotten really bad, he wasn't much good helping out anymore. And Pop had always been one to figure that if you couldn't pull your weight, it was best to stay away. Besides, the setup had always been his favorite part of the gig, full of anticipation, trying to guess the crowd and sniffing the air to smell for the weather. Now all the setup did was serve as a reminder that his body had turned against him. Be better once Friday rolled along, though, with a three-day weekend gig expected to draw upwards of two hundred thousand people. Christ, during the last stretch of the Flying Devils in his former life he hadn't seen that many people in a year. Hell, probably closer to two or three.

Still, there had been some grand times back then, with no arthritis to mar them. What the fuck good was money when it hurt like a bastard to count it? It just wasn't fair, as plenty hadn't been in his life, so far as Pop Keller was concerned.

His former life in the World War II air-show business had begun early, before the full-blown warbird craze caught on. He bought most of his fighters for the Flying Devils in the fifties and sixties at rock-bottom prices. Through the seventies, the Devils had been the best in the business. They had barnstormed the country with their Piper L-4s, T-6 Texas trainers, P-51 Mustangs, and P-40 Warhawks, just to name a few. Their specialty was mock air battles that flat-out thrilled their audiences. No jet-powered engines, no gymnastic circles in the air. Just plain old gutsy flying in reconditioned fighters.

The planes carried live ammunition in their front-mounted

machine guns. The highlight of the exhibition had often been Pop himself putting on an amazing display of target practice from a thousand feet. He'd been able to shoot the horns off a bull, until his eyes went, that is, and that was long before his joints had gone south.

He should have gotten glasses, but the truth was they looked lousy under his leather flying goggles. A dozen years ago now he had been squinting to focus when his fighter had taken a sudden dip and scraped the wing of another. The collision had torn the wing off his buddy's plane, and a moderate crowd of 1,200 had watched the man crash to his death in a nearby field.

That hadn't been what ended Pop Keller's former life, but it came close. He had escaped jail but not scandal. The insurance company had laid into him heavy, and there were so many lawsuits, he had figured he might as well move a cot into Superior Court. Then his best fliers, the young ones, had fled the Devils for the Confederate Air Force or the Valiant Air Command and had taken their planes with them, leaving him with a ragtag unit of both men and machines.

Pop had stuck it out as much for them as for himself, even when pranksters regularly changed the first "e" in his name to an "i" on the billboards, proclaiming him Pop "Killer." In the end he had been down to thirty-seven fighters, and there had seldom been a day when more than twenty of them were able to take the air. Pop had hired mechanics to patch his fleet together with Scotch tape, Elmer's glue, whatever it took.

Truth was, he'd been ready to pack it in even before that day his former life had ended eight years before when a stranger had walked into the Texas bar he'd been drinking in. Turned out the man was fighting a war to save the whole goddamn country. By enlisting the aid of Pop and the Flying Devils, who won a battle in the skies over Keysar Flats, the man had succeeded in saving the good ole U.S. of A. But the remainder of the Devils' fleet was lost in the process. A grateful government wanted to make amends, but they couldn't replace the only thing Pop cared about: his glorious warbirds. Think of something else, they told him.

Pop thought about it and told them he wanted to establish the nation's first artillery show. He saw it all in his head, and the sight had him excited. Artillery pieces from past and present blowing the shit out of targets for ninety minutes. Call it something like the National Artillery Brigade. Yeah, the NAB. Government went for it. Set Pop up with the equipment for free and agreed to supply ammo on request.

His present life had begun.

Right now his truck was parked outside in the lot with the National Artillery Brigade's smoke-and-barrel logo stenciled across both its sides.

And the people loved it. The NAB performed to packed crowds at every stop for its first four years, and things went off generally without a hitch. Then the war in the Gulf had given the nation new pride and a fresh fascination with the weapons of war. After seeing it on television, live seemed even better. Capacity crowds had become jam-packed ones. A few times Pop had *turned away* more folks for one performance than the Flying Devils had performed before in a month. Extra shows were added. Pop had to hire drivers just to keep him supplied with ammo. He figured he should take a trip to Iraq and buy Saddam Hussein a beer. Shake his hand right before he stuck a Patriot missile up his ass and fired.

Patriot missile . . .

The thought had given Pop an idea, and he'd called his friends in Washington one more time. Any chance he could add a Patriot missile battery to his show for just a little while? The answer had been no, and it had stayed no until quite recently, when the Patriot ran into some unwelcome publicity. The good PR certainly couldn't hurt, and three months later the NAB had its Patriots—for a while, anyway.

The battery, complete with its own heavy security, had joined up with the NAB for this Kansas performance, assuring attendance records that might never be broken. Of course, the battery wasn't really going to do anything except sit there on display, and patrons who wanted a view would only be able to get one from a hundred feet away. Pop was charging ten bucks a head, and that meant two million dollars for a weekend's work, the NAB well on its way to becoming the hottest attraction in the country.

Move over, Ice Capades.

Give it up, Ringling Brothers.

Pop would have enjoyed it a lot more if his hands didn't ache so much. A few drinks would briefly drown the pain, but he'd pay for it tomorrow, and tomorrow was getting too close to opening day. So he nursed his club soda and cracked peanuts as best he could to kill the time that it took for the NAB to set up shop. He had the bar to himself, except for a nervous-looking woman sitting in one of its three booths. She'd been staring into a cup of coffee that had long lost its steam, and Pop had looked toward her a few times to see if what she needed was a friend. He always looked away, though, before she had a chance to return his stare. Pop had gotten burned enough times helping out strangers; boy, had he ever. Nope, he was gonna sit this one out. Spend the rest of his downtime doing what he used to do best and remembering what it felt like.

"Give me another, Jimmy."

But Pop Keller couldn't resist staring the woman's way, turning on his stool so he was facing in her direction. The bartender set the club soda down on the bar, and Pop reached back for it. He'd give himself as much time as it took to finish it and then, what the hell, he'd join the woman in her booth.

"Livermore Air Force Base," Blaine said, and he handed the binoculars to Sal Belamo.

Sal pressed them against his eyes and spun the focusing wheels. From their position atop a hill, they had a clear vantage point of the base across a double-laned highway. They had taken off from Kennedy six hours earlier, half of that time spent getting here from the small airport in Hastings, Nebraska. This time Blaine had insisted that Melissa not accompany them. In spite of her determined protests, she was waiting things out in nearby Hanover, Kansas.

"They got the right uniforms, guns, jeeps, the whole works," Sal Belamo was saying. "Shit, place doesn't look like it was ever even closed down."

"That way no questions are raised," Blaine told him. "Military might have left a small transition staff in place, so people see a little added activity, it doesn't stand out."

Belamo swept the binoculars across the base's length. "I count a dozen guards on the perimeter. 'Bout what I figured."

Livermore Air Force Base was one of the first of nearly a hundred such bases to be closed down in the latest round of military cost cutting. In its heyday it had had upwards of 3,700 servicemen in its population and been home to a wing of B-52 SAC bombers. Blaine gazed down and imagined the roar of engines shaking nearby walls and spirits at all hours of the day and night. Neighbors must have learned to bolt down their china.

The living quarters, apartments, and small homes rimmed the fenced-in base's perimeter. Centered between them were ten runways, at least that many hangars, a control tower, and a three-story building that served as the base's headquarters. But what had commanded most of McCracken's attention from the time they scaled the hill were the eight small transport planes laid out in neat rows across the edge of the tarmac.

"This what you were expecting?" Belamo asked him, as he lowered the binoculars.

"Pretty much. Some sort of massive distribution's about to get under way, by the look of things. What Johnny latched on to with those killings was just the preliminaries."

Belamo fingered his binoculars. "Wish we could find the big fella with these."

"He'll be here, Sal."

"Yeah, but meanwhile . . ."

"Meanwhile, we get started without him."

* * *

Blaine waved the first team of commandos into position. They worked their way forward toward the fence enclosing the entire base complex, making sure they were well out of line of the nearest guard's vision. The weapons they had brought along had been part of Nineteen's stockpile. Accordingly, the bulk of their inventory was composed of M-16s, Galil machine guns, Uzis, and sidearms, along with limited supplies of grenades and a small complement of Stinger missiles. The element of surprise was the best thing they had going for them, and if that broke down, the battle might be over in a hurry.

The women pulled themselves along through a stretch of high grass the last bit of the way. The grass covered not only their approach, but also their slicing through the chain-link fence that was rimmed with barbed wire. Livermore had been closed for nearly two years now, and the grass had been cut only sporadically since then.

"You read me, Sal?" Blaine said into his hand-held walkie-talkie.

"Loud and clear, boss," Belamo returned from the opposite side of the base. "All team members in position and cutting through."

"Almost showtime."

"Rock and roll. Hey, McBalls."

"I'm here, Sal."

"I was born for this shit. When this is over, no way I go back to a desk."

McCracken watched through his binoculars from a position of high cover across the highway, as the women of his team began to slither through the holes they had snipped in the fencing. There were eight in all, eight in Sal's team as well. That left four with him to cover phase two of the plan.

Sufficient communications gear for all of the women had not been present in the Nineteen stockpile, so once inside the base they were on their own. Each had a patrol area. Each knew the rules. The kills had to be silent and quick.

Once these were completed, they would take up positions around the airfield perimeter and wait for Blaine's fiery signal to move in.

He swept his binoculars across the fence once more.

"My team's in, Sal."

"Boy," Belamo's voice returned, "these babes are good."

"Nothing they haven't done before."

"Us either."

McCracken pulled the van off the main road at the sign reading RESTRICTED AREA. OFFICIAL PERSONNEL ONLY. He drove down a narrow chopped-up roadbed where two guards waited at the base's main gate. He stepped down out of the van, and the camera looped around his neck bobbed a little. Two of the female commandos, scantily dressed in the clothes of tourists in the midst of a long drive, fell in behind him.

"Hey," he said, as he neared the gate, "we get a look inside?"

One of the guards shook his head. The other hung back, hand not far from his M-16.

"Sorry, sir," the closer one said. "No visitors."

"But they been letting people in ever since it closed up. I lived here ten years and never saw the inside. I'm just back for—"

"Sir," the other guard said, coming forward now, "I'm afraid I'm going to have to ask you to leave."

"Come on. How 'bout a break?"

The guards were almost close enough to touch through the gate now.

"Sir, this is still a restricted area. You are trespassing on—"

The guard's head snapped back before he could say another word, his eyes turning upward toward the crimson hole in his forehead. The second guard hadn't even had time to register what had happened when a similar shot dropped him. A third bullet from the markswoman perched behind the van took out the video camera that hovered over the gate.

"Cutters!" Blaine called.

Instantly one of the women came forward and sliced through the latch that affixed the gate into place. The other two shoved it open just before a rented 4×4 pickup with covered cargo bay pulled down the road, driven by the final commando. The pickup came to a halt just outside the gate at the same time as the two largest women finished pulling the dead guards' uniforms over their clothes. They moved quickly toward a jeep parked alongside the guardhouse and made sure that their helmets covered as much of their faces as possible.

The plan now was for the jeep, apparently driven by the gate guards, to lead the 4×4 onto the base. McCracken would ride in the pickup's enclosed rear. The two other commandos would ride up front. The precision of all the women, especially considering there had been no opportunity for rehearsal, was incredible. He realized that these particular women, at least, had come to Nineteen not to forget, but merely to wait for the time when they were needed again.

In all, the time lapse between the downing of the gate guards and the point when McCracken climbed into the back of the pickup was barely thirty seconds. Excellent under any conditions.

"Go!" he called.

The driver of his pickup hit the horn lightly. The signal given, the woman in the driver's seat of the jeep drove off toward the center of the base with the 4×4 right behind.

"Sal, you read me?"

"Loud and clear, boss."

"I'm in."

"No more signs of guards. I'm following now. These women are beautiful, ain't they?"

"No question about it."

"See ya in a few."

"Showtime, Sal."

* * *

The most important weapon in Blaine's arsenal remaine
confusion. He had to hope that the fact that the jeep wa
leading the pickup in would assure him of getting clos
enough to the tarmac to accomplish what he had come for.

The two-vehicle procession cleared the last rows of resi
dential buildings. The runways and official base structure
came clearly into view now. The transport planes looked lik
big fat birds lined up to await feeding. Well, Blaine had jus
the meal for them. In the covered rear of the 4×4, he brough
the first Stinger missile into his lap.

A number of armed guards patrolled the open area, man
of them concentrated around the transports. Still more hun
back by the hangars, and a half-dozen were posted in th
area of the three-story building that had served as Liver
more's headquarters. McCracken could just make them ot
through the small window that looked into the 4×4's cat
The firing of his first Stinger would serve as the signal fo
the rest of the commandos of Nineteen to move in. His pri
mary objective was to prevent the White Death from bein
evacuated during the battle. Take out the transports, and th
rest would fall into place accordingly. Blaine was readyin
the Stinger when he felt the 4×4's brakes being applied.

"Company," one of the women called back to him.

He gazed through the glass again and saw that the jee
with the women inside had stopped when another jeep bein
driven by three armed men approached it. The width of tw
runways still separated him from the transports, but that dis
tance would be simple to cover for the Stingers. He knev
what was coming next and readied for it.

The approaching jeep came to a halt and its passenger
climbed out. The guards still had their guns shouldered whe
the women dressed in the uniforms of the dead men spran
outward. The pair of staccato bursts were brief but deadly
The three guards were dropped where they stood.

At that point, Blaine threw himself out through the truck
rear with the first Stinger already at shoulder level. He sighte
and pulled back on the trigger in the same motion, even as

hefty complement of the guards closer to the transports opened fire on the Israeli women.

The missile slammed into the first transport in the line just above its wing. The blast lifted the plane up onto its side and then toppled it over to be consumed by a flurry of flames.

Blaine's ears rang from the Stinger's percussion. Around him the four women had taken cover behind the nearest vehicles. Then, as he reached into the 4×4's cab for another Stinger, he could make out the steady bursts of gunfire that began streaming into the main area from all directions at once.

Nineteen's commandos were working their magic!

Bringing the second Stinger up to steady his aim, he could see a number of the enemy falling to the barrage of the sixteen additional members of his party. Still more of the Tau faithful, dressed as soldiers, lunged desperately for cover. McCracken fired his second Stinger.

He heard a heavy thump as the second missile shot outward. A second transport was turned into a corpse of flaming metal before his eyes. It slammed into another one, shredding it, and leaving Blaine with one less target to worry about in the process. He pulled a third Stinger from the 4×4, and this time the explosion blew his target straight into a nearby hangar, the front portion of which collapsed on impact. Numbers four and five were on target as well, but he had only one Stinger left to deal with both of the two remaining transports. No matter. With the women moving in to secure the strategic center of the base, blowing the final transport with traditional explosives would be a simple task.

As it turned out, his concern was needless. The transport that his final Stinger struck spun madly with the explosion, and its wing cut straight through the fuselage of the final plane. The fire's fingers reached high and spread fast, as the loosed gas fueled them. Secondary explosions coughed huge shards of metal into the air.

Blaine charged into motion across the tarmac, holding an M-16 in place of a Stinger now. His priorities had changed.

With the transports destroyed, his next objective was to find
the leader of the Tau and, short of that, secure the reserves
of the White Death. He was nearing the center of the battle
when powerful automatic fire began raining down from the
twin control towers at either end of the complex.

Vulcans! Blaine realized, recognizing the distinctive me-
tallic clacking of a minigun.

The 7.62mm shells chewed up three of the commandos
who were trapped in the open, and threatened to turn the tide
of the battle all by themselves.

"Sal!" he screamed into his walkie-talkie, throwing himself into a dive.

"Ripe and ready, boss."

He saw Belamo emerge from between a pair of hangars.
Blaine realized he had never seen Sal in battle dress before,
much less holding a belt-fed MK-19 grenade launcher. He
pumped three rounds into the right-hand tower and snapped
the remaining three into the left. The explosions, separated
ever so briefly, tore the tops of the towers clean off and sent
them to the ground in showers of rubble and debris.

McCracken rolled onto his stomach and fired a burst at an
enemy stronghold in a second-floor window that the commandos of Nineteen hadn't yet been able to penetrate. The
angle required to hit the window meant firing in the open
with no cover nearby, an easy target for the opposition. To
minimize his chances of getting hit, Blaine spun into a roll
before draining the rest of his first clip, as asphalt was
coughed all around him by enemy bullets. He knew that
Nineteen's commandos would seize the opportunity his move
had opened up for them, and true to form, they launched an
all-out attack that caught the remainder of the base guards in
a crossfire.

Some of the women fell back into positions of cover. Others advanced cautiously toward the headquarters, from which
no return fire was coming any longer. Directly before him,
Sal was poised against one of the hangars, slamming home
another grenade belt into his MK-19. He bounced away from

the hangar suddenly, as if jolted by a surge of electricity. He went for his walkie-talkie, but it was too late.

The hangar doors burst open behind the savage thrust of a pair of armored personnel carriers. The APCs rolled over the chewed metal in their path, the heavy-caliber machine guns mounted atop them firing incessantly. The commandos of Nineteen were caught totally by surprise. A flood of troops poured out from the hangar in the vehicles' wake and opened fire on the fleeing women. Sal Belamo managed to knock out one of the steel killing machines with a fresh grenade from his MK-19 before a barrage slammed him against the hangar. He slumped down clutching his shoulder.

McCracken closed into the very center of the battle, hurling a pair of grenades into the oncoming troops. Bodies were tossed airborne in great plumes of smoke, which provided him limited cover to open up on the troops that were still emerging from that damned hangar.

He had fallen into a trap, goddammit! Somehow they had been expecting him!

Blaine tossed another grenade as he darted for cover behind a sturdily built maintenance shed. He snapped a fresh clip into his M-16 and gritted his teeth against the apparent certainty of defeat. What screams he heard now between the lessening gunfire were clearly those of the women of Nineteen being slaughtered.

"Alive!" a voice chimed through a loudspeaker somewhere. *"I want him alive!"*

McCracken spun out from the shed directly into the line of fire of two dozen guns, all leveled his way. Dead before him was one of the APCs, its centrally mounted machine gun angled for his head. The command over the loudspeaker fresh in their ears, none of the enemy fired. But Blaine had no doubt they would if he squeezed his own trigger. That was senseless. His only hope for success now was to play along with the owner of the voice that had spared his life, a man who could only be the member of the original Tau behind the group's return.

Blaine tossed his M-16 away and eased his hands into the air. A dozen gunmen charged him and forced him against the asphalt, pinning his arms and legs. Cuffs were slapped on his wrists and, after a brief pause, irons strapped tight around his ankles. He managed to keep his eyes righted long enough to see a half-dozen of the female commandos, some wounded, being led off as prisoners. He noticed that the wounded Sal Belamo was nowhere to be seen before a heavy boot squashed against his skull and forced his eyes down. His view of what was happening to the rest of his team was cut off. All he could see were a pair of small feet encased in boots shuffling slowly forward. Flanking them were two pairs of far larger boots worn outside identical pairs of precisely creased khaki trousers.

"Let him up," the voice he recognized from the loud-speaker said.

He was yanked to his feet, and the first thing he saw were the empty expressions on the twins that had barely missed killing him at the hotel in Izmir. Between them stood a much smaller, older man who faced Blaine from ten feet away.

"*Shalom*, Mr. McCracken," said Arnold Rothstein.

CHAPTER 34

JOHNNY Wareagle watched the end of the battle from the same hill that Blaine McCracken and Sal Belamo had made their final plans on. The sight turned his stomach. His breathing stopped altogether when a figure he knew was Blaine's emerged into the killing range of two dozen guns. He took a shallow breath when McCracken dropped his gun and surrendered.

The fact that McCracken was still alive was reason for hope. The Old One had told him that they would be finishing this battle together, and had hinted that they would win. Besides, now that Blue Thunder had gotten him here, the rest seemed simple by comparison. Toothless Jim Jackson's toolbox had turned out to contain just enough magic to do the job. It took three additional stops along the route north, but somehow he kept the bus sputtering on its way, top speed reduced successively and the grinding of the engine reaching an ear-splitting pitch.

"Looks to me like we be in a heap of trouble," Tyrell Loon said from Wareagle's side on the top of the hill. Blue Thunder was parked not far from the bottom, its occupants waiting outside it in nervous expectation. "We goin' in against *that*?"

It took a while before Johnny responded. "Not we, Sheriff."

"We got us a job to do, 'case you're forgettin'."

"Not anymore."

"What chance you figure you got alone?"

Johnny didn't say a word.

"Well, whatever it is, it be a hell of a lot better with us along. You can't argue with that."

Wareagle nodded reluctantly. "We'll need more firepower than what we have with us."

"Find it in town, you think?"

Maybe, Johnny reflected, in the unlikely event that the stores in downtown Hanover contained the kinds of supplies he required to add substantially to their firepower.

"You forgettin' we're still blessed," Sheriff Loon reminded when Johnny remained silent. "Old One ain't here, but she blessed me 'fore I left. Made me a kind of luck charm

for ya. I got to stay around, got to stay close for her magic
to work, she say. We go into town, we find what we need.
You can rest assured of that.''

"Then we must go," Johnny said. He had moved past the
sheriff when something on the ground grabbed his attention
again.

"What's wrong?" Loon asked him.

Johnny seemed not to hear him. His eyes traced a path up
the last bit of the hill to the position they had been occupying
until seconds ago.

"Someone else was up here," Wareagle said finally.

"Your friend, probably."

"Besides him, I mean. Here between Blainey and us. Left
in another direction just before we arrived. Left in the midst
of the battle after he had seen what he needed to."

"Who?"

Wareagle's response was to brush past Sheriff Loon and
pick up his pace down the hill.

"You don't seem surprised to see me," Rothstein said
after McCracken had been hoisted to his feet. His leg irons
clanged together.

"I'm not. Not totally, anyway."

Rothstein nodded knowingly. "Ah, my ill-fated attack on
the kibbutz, no doubt."

"Seemed a difficult trick, slipping forty men and eight
armed vehicles by the IDF lines. Takes a man who knows
the territory—and the weaknesses of its security. You were
trying to kill your sister."

Rothstein didn't bother denying it. "Besides you and that
troublesome Indian friend of yours, she's the only one left
who can hurt me." He eyed the Twins. "Bring him," he
ordered.

The Twins moved to either side of McCracken and beckoned him forward with their eyes, while a hefty complement
of guards kept a safe distance. Blaine walked toward the
entrance to the base headquarters between the Twins. The

deterrent they presented would have been enough, even if his hands hadn't been cuffed.

"Ah, Tovah," Arnold Rothstein said softly, from just behind Blaine now. "So brave and persistent, and yet such an annoyance to my work. I should have killed her years ago, of course, but what kind of man would that make me?"

"Not much worse than the kind of man you are now."

"You have hard feelings because you have been defeated. But you were up against powers you couldn't possibly comprehend. You never had a chance."

McCracken's mind flashed back to what he had seen in the secret chamber and had learned later from Tovah. "You killed the other three members of the original Tau in the cavern. You stopped them from destroying the White Death."

"Because even then I saw how much it would be needed another time. Now."

"What exactly are you planning to do?"

"Join me inside, Mr. McCracken, and I'll share the future with you."

"Might be a whole lot better, if you went ahead and told me what was troublin' you."

Melissa looked at the old, leathery-faced man who had slid into her booth without invitation. She mustered up a slight smile for him, more ironic than anything else.

"You wouldn't believe me if I told you."

"You'd be surprised." Pop slid a little closer. "You know, we don't get too many talk like that in these parts. You a Brit?"

"Yes."

"Then just what is it that brings you here?"

Before Melissa could respond, the door to the bar creaked open, and Pop swung around to see an Indian whose head barely cleared the doorway when he entered. He might have been a giant of a man, but he walked like a jungle cat.

"Is that your truck outside?" the Indian asked him.

Pop gave him a *Who, me?* look and then shrugged. "You hit it or something?"

"Something," the Indian said.

"Huh?" from Pop, as confused as he was relieved.

"I need your help."

Pop slid out of the booth and gazed up into the big Indian's eyes. He'd only seen that look once before, but he remembered it well.

"You're shittin' me, right? This is some kind of joke."

"No joke," the Indian told him.

"Not again," Pop followed. He almost laughed because it was the only thing he could think to do. "Not fucking again. . . ."

Then he realized that the nervous woman had stood up and was staring hard at the big Indian as well.

"Johnny . . . Wareagle," he heard her mutter and watched the Indian's back tense as he turned his gaze upon her.

"Blainey," the Indian said in what had seemed to have started as a question.

"I know where he is," the woman followed.

"So do I."

"Jesus Christ," Pop said. "Jesus H. fucking Christ. . . ."

Billy Griggs had seen the Indian enter the bar. Man, was he big! Didn't even have to look twice to make that fucker.

Wouldn't have been so bad if there wasn't a truck outside marked NAB. Must have belonged to some big cheese who had something to do with the artillery show he'd seen being set up in the remnants of an amusement park, as he cruised the nearby area in search of his quarry. After the hit team had failed to return from the bayou, the old guy seemed pretty certain that the Indian would be arriving in the area before too very long. Billy's assignment was to watch for him and report in. That was it. Don't even think of approaching. Guy was so big and, well, scary, that Billy was glad for the order.

What he'd do now was wait and see what happened when the injun came outside. Anything other than alone just wouldn't do. So when he emerged between an old man for whom walking was a chore, and a woman Billy recognized as the one McCracken had been with back in Turkey, he knew what he had to do next.

"Help Mr. McCracken to a seat on the couch," Arnold Rothstein ordered the Twins.

The Twins each grasped an arm and led Blaine toward the rear of the office that Rothstein had appropriated. Not surprisingly, they carried no weapons, nothing McCracken could make use of, on the chance that he got lucky and managed to overpower them. Fat chance. He had witnessed the Twins' work in Germany. Two minds that thought and acted as one; conceivable to eliminate one all by himself, impossible to take out both.

"You faked your own attempted assassination," Blaine said to Rothstein, still standing between his captors.

"With the help of the Twins here, it went exceptionally well."

"You used a stand-in."

Rothstein shrugged. "Regrettably, of course, my death will be announced in just a day or so. Or should I say *his* death."

"Effectively closing the book on the man you really are."

"No." The old man shot out a finger to punctuate his words. "I have hidden the man I really am for a generation: the man who was born that day in a schoolyard when a classmate took his place before the firing squad. I learned to hate that day. I learned how powerful a motivator it can be."

"And you haven't stopped hating since," Blaine said sharply. He was pushed into the sofa by the Twins, both pairs of eyes staring fixedly at him.

Rothstein shrugged in concession. "I suppose you are correct, but I had no choice. I couldn't let the Tau die, because we were meant to serve as the world's policemen, and that is what we will do. The White Death gives us the means to stop evil, to stamp it out before it has a chance to spread its venom.''

"How?"

"You must understand the background first. My sister was conservative. She and the others did not wish to acknowledge the awesome power the White Death gave us. They refused to even consider using it during the early years of our struggle to found the state of Israel, if you can imagine that.''

"Yes," Blaine told him, "I can.''

The old man looked disappointed. "I had expected more from you. Right from the time I learned of your involvement, I thought if I could explain it to you, reason it out . . .''

"What kind of man do you think I am?"

"One who pursues justice, just as I do.''

"Not as you do.''

Rothstein smiled condescendingly. "All I have read and heard about you indicates otherwise. What we did to the Nazis in the years following the war was not enough. Nothing could have been enough.''

"On that much, we agree.''

"Then you're saying vengeance on the Nazis who had escaped war-crimes trials was justified?''

"Yes,'' Blaine responded without hesitation.

"And you see a difference between that and what we have risen again to destroy today?''

"I'm not sure what exactly that is.''

Arnold Rothstein's breathing had picked up. His eyes glistened with determination and resolve.

"We struck fear into the hearts of the Nazis we did not kill, Mr. McCracken. Those that eluded us knew we would always be out there, waiting, watching. But why stop at the Nazis? There were other battles to be fought, other enemies to put down; there always would be.''

"Obviously your sister and other original members of the Tau did not share your feelings,'' Blaine said, feeling the eyes of the Twins locked upon him.

"What choice did I have? I took matters into my own

hands. There were enough who felt as I did to begin building the kind of army we needed: a Tau presence in every nation watching, waiting. Ready to be mobilized when the time was right.''

''The killings . . .''

''Here in the United States and all over the world, justice is being served. The slime is being swept away, dead skin of the world peeled back. As a prelude.''

''For what?''

''The world has seen enough ugliness. The time has come to vanquish it.''

Slowly McCracken realized what Rothstein was intimating. ''Large quantities of the White Death distributed all over the world to be released as you deem fit.''

''Not just me, the entire Tau. The time was right.''

''Only because you had finally figured out a way to duplicate the original formula,'' Blaine advanced. ''But you still went back into the chamber to remove the remainder of the crates. Why?''

''Because the process required to produce the White Death remains painfully slow. To accomplish all that we must, we needed the considerable reserves stored in Ephesus as well.''

''And what exactly is that, Mr. Rothstein.''

''Can't you figure it out?'' Rothstein raised, half challenging, half scorning Blaine. ''In centers of the world where crime festers, where evil rears itself on hate, in the breeding grounds for violence that will destroy innocent lives without compunction, the White Death will be released. Look at me, Mr. McCracken, and tell me you don't approve. Tell me you would not take these very same steps if given the opportunity.''

''Not if it means destroying the lives of others who are just as innocent as those you're trying to protect.''

''A regrettable, but necessary, sacrifice. Our point will be made before too very long. Just as the original Tau made the Nazis cower and withdraw, our legacy will do the same to the evil that has followed in their wake.'' Rothstein shook his head in disappointment. "I thought of all people, you who have seen so much senseless death and suffering would understand. You who have seen the world come to the brink of destruction on so many occasions only to be pulled back by your hand at the last instant. The Tau can at last control these madmen who seek to rule others. That is where I differ from the others you have faced. I do not seek control or power. My work justifies itself, a means *and* an end. Tell me it isn't tempting. Tell me it doesn't appeal to you."

"I won't lie to you, Mr. Rothstein. I've lain awake plenty of nights trying to come up with the kind of plan you're putting into operation. I think of terrorists who kill school-children and madmen who terrorize entire nations. . . ."

"Yes! Yes!"

"But I always come up short of committing to something like the Tau because of what pursuing this kind of vengeance ultimately boils down to: to destroy your enemy, you must become as he is. The disregard for innocent life, the willing-ness to accept sacrifices, putting your dogma above every-thing else—all those things are part and parcel of what you're suggesting. Your sister was right: the power the White Death brings with it is terrifying. It allows you to define standards of existence. Sure, it all sounds good now, but what happens when you've wiped out all those you consider evil? You'll have to come up with new standards to justify your own existence, and others will have to pay. Others will *always* have to pay."

Rothstein looked at him for what seemed like a very long time. "You disappoint me, Mr. McCracken. I have heard of your work on behalf of Israel in 1973. I felt that I, that Israel, has always owed you something for that, so I ordered your life to be spared today."

McCracken looked up from the couch. The Twins tensed slightly and followed his line of vision. He could never hope to overcome both of them, even if he could improvise some sort of weapon without them realizing.

"Can't you see the world needs what we bring to it?"

Arnold Rothstein challenged. "Can't you see it is begging for it?"

"What I see," Blaine replied, "is someone who has become what he set out to destroy forty-five years ago. Deciding who's fit to live or die."

"We're merely trying to rid the world of those determined to make that very same decision without any regard for conscience."

"Listen to yourself, Rothstein. My God, in seeking vengeance the Tau is becoming the Nazis all over again."

The old man's eyes flared with anger. "How could you suggest such a thing? How could you say such a thing?"

"To show you what you sound like to me. This isn't the first time I've had a discussion like this, and the thing all of them have in common is that the speaker is always convinced he's right. That he alone can chart the proper course for human existence. Sorry. You can't save the world; it has to do that all by itself."

The door opened suddenly and Billy Griggs strode inside.

"You want me to *what*?"

Johnny's request made Pop Keller jam down on the brake. They were squeezed into the cab of his truck, still three miles from the former amusement-park grounds where the NAB was setting up for their coming series of performances. Blue Thunder fought to keep up the pace behind them.

Johnny had explained about the Tau and the White Death as best he could in rapid fashion, ending his tale with what he had seen at Livermore Air Force Base prior to finding Pop in town.

"I want you to bomb the base," Wareagle said again. "I can give you the coordinates."

"Hold on a sec. You can't expect me to just open up my guns on a government installation."

"It belongs to the Tau now. And if they manage to get their White Death distributed in the quantities they must surely possess . . ."

"Yeah, yeah. I get the picture. Could be worse than the last time," he finished in a mutter.

"Last time?" Melissa raised.

"Never mind. Suffice it to say I've been through this kind of thing before. Just wanted you folks to know that. Otherwise there wouldn't be a chance in hell I'd even be listening to ya now. But I still can't up and start blowing the crap out of Livermore Air Force Base."

"Because you lack equipment capable of doing it?"

Pop seemed to take offense at that. "Listen, fella, I got it all. Eight-inch guns, 155mm howitzers, 105s. But, hey, I ain't about to start firing on a U.S. military installation just on your say-so. I'll help you seal it off until we can get real help here. That's the best I can do."

The National Artillery Brigade was well along in its process for setting up by the time Pop Keller drove his truck into the parking lot and through the dilapidated fence that would be shored up by week's end. Johnny's eyes gaped at the sight of the artillery pieces being slid into place in the field beyond. Keller had not exaggerated at all. There was a towed 155mm howitzer and a self-propelled gun of the same power, in addition to a smaller 105mm and a monstrous eight-inch cannon with a range of over twelve miles. The smaller artillery pieces had not been unloaded yet and neither had the older, more fragile ones which were mostly for show anyway.

But the NAB's roster of main battle tanks was already lined up in a row across the field's center. There were five of them, dating back to the Sherman of World War II, the Pershing of Korea, and the M-47 Patton. In a relative sense, these three were dwarfed by their massive offspring, the original M-60 and its cousin the M-60A1. Wareagle was truly impressed.

For his part, Pop was more interested in checking on his people. A number of them were busy erecting wooden targets that the tanks and smaller artillery pieces would shoot at. Still more were towing the steel carcasses of other vehi-

cles and heavy equipment that would make grand fodder for
the big guns. Basically this was just target practice on a massive scale, especially when a member of the audience who
was holding the lucky ticket got to fire a howitzer.

All of his people who weren't working, and plenty of those
who should have been, were surrounding the Patriot missile
battery off in the corner of the field by itself. It was a lot
bigger and more menacing than the image of the gentle de-
fender of the Gulf War, the missile battery itself set apart
from the enclosed, cubicle-sized control console. The team
members manning the console were explaining their wares
to the marveling group, while the six-man security team
looked on, unsure of what to do. While it was true that none
of the weekend crowd would be permitted within a hundred
feet of the battery, the participants in the show felt it was
their right to examine it closely. Accordingly, there was even
a cluster of onlookers gawking at the battery's quartet of
missile launchers, under the watchful eyes of the security
team.

"You boys mind getting back to work?" Pop scolded those
crowded near the open door of the control console. And
when the men turned back to their chores, he caught a glimpse
of the most complicated radar screen he had ever laid eyes
on, a yellow arrow sweeping across a green grid.

"This thing on?" Pop called up to the two men seated
behind the controls, much to the chagrin of the security personnel.

The two men's eyes gestured toward the truck behind them.
"Once it's out of the box, we got no choice. Kill the batteries
and blow the circuit board otherwise."

"Just watch you don't lean on the fire button. I ain't got a
spare mill lying around."

"Will do, sir."

"You're quite certain of this, of course, Mr. Griggs."
Billy Boy looked McCracken's way. "I know I saw his
injun friend you told me to watch for and the owner of some

artillery show powwowing in town. Injun gets his way, they
could do us some damage.''

"Then I suppose we will have to do them some damage,
won't we? Where are they, Mr. Griggs?''

"Field about six miles from here.''

"You have more specific coordinates?''

"Come up with them in a few seconds for you.''

The old man had already picked up his walkie-talkie.
"Wheel out the FROG missile batteries,'' he ordered into
it. "Prepare to fire on the following coordinates. . . .''

Jed Long and Teddy Worth had shipped out to Germany
with the first-generation Patriot batteries. They'd been transferred to Israel during the Gulf War and spent the rest of their
tour there trying to teach their headstrong Israeli replace-
ments how the system really worked, then update them when
the new and improved software arrived. Long and Worth had
been made to feel like heroes in that country, and they missed
not only that but also the constant edge they had lived on
during those months. They'd shot down all four Scuds they
had locked onto, and if there was a greater rush than the
roughly forty seconds between detection and impact, neither
of them had ever felt it.

They returned Stateside just in time for the success of the
Patriot to be challenged on all quarters. Some asshole from
MIT had turned against the system, and the Senate Appro-
priations Committee was quick to follow suit. Even segments
of the military had jumped on the bandwagon. Jed Long and
Terry Worth fumed. Why don't they ask the people who
really know? they wondered. They offered to testify in front
of anyone who would listen.

No one was interested.

Someday, Long and North told themselves frequently,
someday we'll show them. . . .

But not today. Long was seated in front of the radar screen
with legs streched before him and hands clasped behind his
head. Worth was checking the final connections, thinking

maybe it would be better if they packed everything back up and brought it out again come next weekend. Truth was, somebody at the Pentagon had told them opening day was yesterday, so they'd scrambled to get here a day late only to find out they were five days early.

A sudden rapid chirping sound had Long lunging forward in his chair, almost toppling it behind him.

"What the fuck . . ."

Worth had leapt up behind him. "Shit," he said disbelievingly, "we got incoming."

"This some kind of joke? . . ."

"Thirty seconds to impact," Long said.

"Four incoming," Worth followed. "I got four incoming."

"Positive ID obtained. FROGS!" Long shouted, referring to the computer's identification of the missiles hurtling their way. "*Four* fucking FROGS!"

"Jesus Christ . . ."

Worth knew that even under the best of conditions, the Patriot's strike rate was .72. With four Patriots to fire at four incomings, that meant the odds of successful intercept were not good at all. Still, this updated version of the Patriot contained a stronger explosive designed to detonate the enemy warhead on impact, instead of just destroying the missile. But it hadn't been tested in battle yet.

"System is enabled." Long glanced back at Worth. "What the fuck do we do?"

"Time to impact?"

"Fifteen seconds . . ."

"Fire!" Worth exclaimed. In that instant he was back in Israel. The feeling was the same, everything was the same, including the devastation four FROG (free rocket over ground) missiles would cause if they impacted.

Long hit the auto button three seconds later when the screen flashed red, signaling that the Patriot computer had locked on. The auto button swung the battery into intercept mode. The launcher had already turned to face the incomings, and the four Patriots shot out at millisecond intervals with deafening roars that split the air over the field. Some of the NAB's workers figured there'd been an accidental explosion and hit the ground for safety. Others just stood there dumbstruck as the red and white missiles rocketed upward toward nothing.

"Oh fuck," said Pop, who like the others could not yet see the FROG missiles the Patriots were speeding to intercept.

At the very last, several NAB members briefly glimpsed the streaking Patriots converging on shiny spots in the sky. In the next instant, four explosions sounded over the field, great thunderclaps in the sky that showered sprays of what looked like fireworks down toward the ground.

Instinct had forced Pop Keller into a crouch. He couldn't believe what had just happened. The bastards at the air force base had goddamn *fired* on him! The son-of-a-bitch Indian was right! Pop stood up painfully, still half squinting, and pulled the hands from his ears.

"Now I'm mad," he said. "Now I'm fucking pissed." He looked toward Wareagle. "Let me have those coordinates, Injun. This is gonna be like the Little Big Horn all over again."

CHAPTER 35

ARNOLD Rothstein smiled at the muffled sound of the distant explosions. He stayed by the window for several moments before turning back toward McCracken.

"It would seem the threat your friend posed to us has been eliminated."

Blaine gritted his teeth. In that instant he wanted more than anything to lunge at the old man, but he knew he'd never get past the Twins.

"We are the world's only chance," Rothstein insisted. "I must ask you to reconsider or join your friend in futility."

Blaine shook his head. "Sorry."

"Such a waste . . ." The old man's eyes moved from McCracken to the Twins, then back again. "They will be quick in their work. It is the least I can do for you. Of course, it would have been easier still if you had just let them dispatch you quietly in that hotel in Turkey. Losing you after that became a real concern of mine."

"Until the toymaker's, of course."

Arnold Rothstein looked at him with a mixture of confusion and disinterest.

"You don't know what I'm talking about. . . ."

"Nor do I care. Good-bye, Mr. McCracken."

"But if it wasn't you, then who . . ."

Arnold Rothstein was gazing at the Twins once more. "You understand how I want it done?"

"Yes," they replied in unison.

"Lock him in one of the basement storage rooms, while you sweep the grounds one last time." Rothstein's eyes fell on Blaine. "Make sure he has no more surprises waiting for us before we bring out the remaining transports. Then kill him."

"You're making a mistake, Rothstein," McCracken said, as the Twins hoisted him to his feet and started to lead him to the door. "Listen to me. You've missed something here— we both have."

Rothstein waved Blaine off and turned his back so that he was facing the window. Before McCracken could speak again, the Twins brought him into the corridor and yanked him forward to the stairs. There was no sense in resisting. His mind, in any case, was elsewhere.

Rothstein hadn't been behind the attack at the toymaker's in Germany!

Someone else was involved. Another party, another force . . .

Who? Why?

Four flights of stairs later, they reached the basement. A door to one of the supply rooms was already open. The Twins pushed him through. One of them turned on a light.

The manacles were waiting for him, fastened into the far wall of a room that was utterly empty. The Twins were grinning. One led him forward. The other hung back slightly. The closer one removed his leg chains and handcuffs, then locked his feet and hands into the manacles. He was spread-eagled, face against the wall, with no room for maneuvering.

"We'll be back for you," they said together, and McCracken heard the door close behind them.

"Soon as you get there," Pop Keller had instructed just before Johnny set off for Livermore Air Force Base, "call me up on the radio and I'll start the barrage." After the big

Indian had nodded, Pop's gaze drifted over his shoulder.
"You really fixin' on bringing these boys with you?"

Johnny turned to look at the men of No Town who were
packed again in Blue Thunder. In the driver's seat, Toothless
Jim Jackson was giving the old engine gas to keep it from
stalling out.

"I don't believe I have a choice," Wareagle replied.

"Yes, you do, friend. Yes, you do," Pop Keller had said,
the last of his words nearly drowned out by the approach of
a tank column led by the Sherman and backed up by the
M-60A1 with the three others in between. "Figure you could
use some close support."

Johnny had flashed one of his rare smiles.

He drove Pop's truck at the head of the procession that had
Blue Thunder bringing up the rear. The artillery barrage
courtesy of NAB's two 155mm, 105mm, and eight-inch guns
would begin as soon as Johnny and his tanks reached the
perimeter of the base. His small column was able to maintain
a respectable clip of just over fifteen miles per hour straight
over land, cutting across roads only when necessary. The
Pershing slipped a tread just past the halfway point, and the
Patton's engine overheated with just a quarter-mile to go,
leaving the crusty Sherman and the far feistier M-60 proto-
types to aid in the assault.

A hundred yards from the main gate of the base, Johnny
lifted Pop's CB to his lips.

"Come in, Pop."

"Right here, son."

"I'm ready."

"So am I."

McCracken was still trying to figure out a way to slip out
of the chains fastening him tight to the wall when the first
explosion rocked the building. A second one followed almost
immediately, and loosened plaster from the walls showered
him. Three more blasts came in rapid succession, and fragments of the ceiling caved in.

Johnny! It had to be Johnny! Not dead at all and outdoing even himself!

The next explosions shook the floor and opened wide fissures in the walls. His manacles, only crudely driven home, showed signs of weakening. Blaine began pulling with all his strength, feeling them begin to give. His right hand came free first, followed by his left. From there, it was a simple matter to pull the manacles binding his legs from the crumbling wall.

It was impossible to open the manacles. While they would be uncomfortable, they would hardly prove a hindrance. With the explosions sounding even more regularly now, Blaine rushed for the door. It had been locked from the outside, but the mechanism was simple and already weakened by the blasts. A quick series of kicks shattered the latch, and Mc-Cracken burst into the corridor.

Not all the initial explosions were on the mark, and Johnny called back to Pop to adjust the coordinates slightly. He stepped out of the truck to find Tyrell Loon coming his way, while the rest of Blue Thunder's passengers distributed Heydan Larroux's weapons amongst themselves, each searching for the one that best suited his fancy.

"We be ready," Loon announced.

"Not yet, Sheriff."

"When?"

"First I have work to do by myself inside."

Loon wasn't arguing. "Fine with me. Think even the Old One would understand. Shit, I'm still close enough to bring ya luck, don't ya think?"

"I do," Johnny said, turning away.

"How will we know when to follow?"

Johnny looked back at him. "You'll know."

Wareagle left the sheriff and his men there outside the fence and gave the tanks the signal to roll straight on. He walked alongside the old Sherman, as the M-60 and M-60A1 plowed right through the base's security fence.

The explosions in the central area were coming every three or four seconds now. Huge plumes of smoke and debris coughed into the air with each blast. The tanks continued on, crashing through what they could not easily avoid. The Sherman hung back long enough for a path to be cleared for it, but had pulled up even by the time its offspring rolled onto the tarmac. A few of the hundred or so troops rushing about caught sight of the trio of tanks and pointed their way frantically. The tanks stopped and began to fire.

One by one their gun turrets snapped backward as shells were expelled. The explosions caught the enemy where they stood. The M-60A1 made a trio of armored personnel carriers its primary targets and blew them apart before any could start into motion. The Sherman and the M-60 focused their fire in any direction where congestions of the enemy could be found. All return volleys were token. The opposition was being blasted from all angles at once, and fear had replaced confidence in their motions.

The gunner in the M-60A1, who had performed the same service in Vietnam for considerably less money, saw the big Indian dart suddenly before his view plate toward the enemy forces. The gunner closed his eyes for an instant, as another shell was expelled. When he gazed back outward, the Indian was gone.

Arnold Rothstein grasped Billy Griggs by the lapels.

"The White Death, you've got to save it! Do you hear me? You've got to save it!"

Griggs looked at the old man in bewilderment.

"Drive it out of here! Wait until the battle recedes and drive it out of here. The tanker's armored. You can make it. Get to the backup rendezvous point! I'll meet you there!"

Billy Boy knew that the old dude was crackers, had known it for some time, but playing along at this point could be his ticket to bigger and better things. Besides, maybe he'd just up and drive that supertanker, three times the capacity of a normal oil truck, full of the White Death wherever he damn well pleased. Use it for his own gains before the old guy was any the wiser, his own plan in shambles.

Griggs headed for the basement and the underground passage that led to the hangar where the tanker was stored.

McCracken knew the White Death would be hidden out of plain sight and well protected. That made one of the hangars the most logical choice, but which one?

Blaine burst out of the base headquarters into the chaos that the explosions had caused. The huge artillery shells continued to carve craters everywhere they hit. The Tau rushed about in all directions. In the confusion, Blaine decided he could safely bypass the hangar the army of the Tau had poured from to catch his commando team in an ambush. Instead, he headed for the one next to it first, worked open the door, and slid inside.

Windows shattered by the numerous explosions provided the only light, but it was enough for Blaine to see dozens of crates spread out everywhere. Weathered and browned, they were obviously the ones that had been pulled from the Nazi storage chamber at the dig site in Ephesus. Closer inspection revealed that the crates were empty. The tanks that had held the White Death were gone.

Glass shattered, and McCracken blamed it first on another explosion until he heard the faint flutter of footsteps. He froze, turned left and then right.

The Twins were approaching him from either side of the hangar. They were bare-chested, massive muscles rippling with each step. Neither showed a weapon. Both were smiling.

"Ahhhhhhhhhhhhh!"

The one in the hangar's rear rushed at him with a throaty rasp. The burst of speed he managed was incredible, so fast that he never noticed Blaine grasp the lid off one of the worthless crates and slash it forward. The rushing Twin managed to get his hands up, and the lid shattered into splinters over them, catching just enough of his head to daze him. He wob-

ɔled on his feet and started to list. Blaine drew his arm over-
nead for the kill and felt his still-manacled hand jerk
ɔackward as it was twisted. The force of the move pitched
nim through the air, and he collided with yet more of the
abandoned crates.

Stunned, Blaine nonetheless regained his feet without even
ɔausing for breath. The smiling Twin who had tossed him
effortlessly aside stalked toward him, hands held leisurely
near his waist. The wounded Twin was just regaining his
senses and joined the approach. Blood dripped from his scalp
and soaked his hair.

McCracken backpedaled, feeling his way with his feet.
The Twins closed on him from angles that made escape between them impossible. Blaine continued to back up until
nis shoulders came to rest against the hangar wall, with one
ɔf the blast-shattered windows just to his right.

The unbloodied Twin threw himself into a lunge, as
Blaine's hand darted up and to the side. He snapped off a
thick shard of glass from the window and thrust it toward the
midsection of the lunging Twin. In his mind McCracken pictured the shard slicing through flesh and shredding everything in its path. He was surprised to see the Twin still smiling
at him and gazed down.

The Twin had caught the shard and closed his hand around
it. Blood oozed from it to the asphalt surface below. Blaine
lashed out with his free hand, steel manacle employed as a
weapon, but the Twin parried the blow and grabbed hold of
the chain dangling from McCracken's wrist to tie him up.
They struggled across the floor, while the other Twin moved
warily, choosing his spot, waiting.

The Twin McCracken was locked up with succeeded in
driving the glass shard backward. Now it was Blaine's hand
that began to spill blood. Before he could reroute the motion,
the Twin had somehow twisted the shard from his grasp and
sent it slashing upward behind his own momentum. Blaine
tried to deflect it with the manacle that the Twin still held,
but the shard sliced a thin gash diagonally across his stomach

and chest. The Twin followed with a downward swipe that McCracken managed to block with his other manacle. He fixed his arm on that side into an elbow strike and slammed it into the Twin's face.

Blaine felt teeth crunch on impact. The Twin recoiled, and McCracken realized that he had lost track of the other just in time to spin to the side. As a result, the second Twin's blow caught him in the hard part of the skull instead of the temple. The blow stunned him and it was all he could do to deflect the blinding flurry of blows that followed.

His motions brought him right back into the range of the Twin whose front teeth were now missing. A fist slammed into Blaine's kidney, and then his knee was kicked out. Mc-Cracken never hit the floor, though, because the Twin who still had his teeth caught him and drove him headfirst into the wall. Stars exploded before Blaine's eyes, and he flailed out wildly. He managed to rake the Twin's face with his manacle, but the bastard caught his next blow at its weakest, and McCracken felt his own momentum joined and used against him.

Blaine had time to actually record the fact that he was airborne and flying toward the hangar's entrance. It was like diving off the high board, but the surface he was heading for was not nearly as hospitable. He managed to get his hands out, and the manacles clanged against the floor on impact. His chin took the brunt of the rest. He could feel it split and the blood stream outward. He tried to push off with his hands, but his arms were numb and wouldn't support him. He realized that he was looking at a pair of brown boots that had somehow materialized before him. He feared that one of the Twins had circled round for the kill.

Except that he recalled that the boots the Twins were wearing had been black. McCracken turned his gaze higher.

And Johnny Wareagle looked down at him.

The most glorious, wonderful, perfect sight McCracken had ever seen!

Johnny smiled at Blaine and stepped past him, placing his frame between McCracken and the Twins.

The Twins hesitated briefly before coming at Wareagle. When they attacked, closing from opposite sides, their moves were perfect reflections of each other.

At the last possible instant, in a motion that defied the eye, Johnny twisted from their path. The Twins' blows slammed into each other. Wareagle grabbed hold of the one with ruined teeth, and this Twin made the mistake of trying to match strength with him. The Indian didn't give at all. A fist pushed into the muscles layered over the Twin's solar plexus. His gasp sounded like air pouring out of a spiked tire. The Indian slammed a second blow into his face, and blood exploded from the remnants of his nose.

The second Twin spun toward Johnny and actually leapt over the body of his crumpling brother. Wareagle stretched out his arms and pushed him farther through the air. He landed near McCracken and dropped his hand toward a pistol stowed in a leather ankle holster.

Blaine grabbed the hand before he could reach it.

"Not today," he said, and twisted the hand sharply to the right, snapping the wrist.

The Twin grasped for the gun with his other hand, and McCracken slammed a blow up under his chin and then rammed his knuckles into the Twin's strung-out throat. Cartilage crackled. His Adam's apple snapped free on impact. The Twin keeled over, heaving for air as he fell dying.

The other Twin had gone for his gun as well, managing to free it with an enraged scream as he saw his brother die. Wareagle stopped its progress before the final Twin could aim. A harmless shot flew skyward as the Indian clamped a knee against the man's elbow and jerked his wrist.

The snap sounded like a door slamming. Johnny looped his free hand around the Twin's head and twisted it violently. The body stiffened, then crumpled to the floor.

"Blainey," Wareagle said, turning.

" 'Bout time you showed up, Indian."

* * *

The monstrous tanker truck had been armored from front to back. Billy Boy Griggs pulled himself into the cab and realized that his biggest problem might be the fact that he could barely see over the dashboard. He placed his pistol on the seat right next to him and propped himself up as high as he could. The tanker was facing the hangar's front, but there was enough room inside for him to turn it all the way around and slam his way out through the back. Outside the battle was receding, the explosions far less numerous now. The invaders had come with tanks, and there was no way one of those was going to catch up with this baby. If he played his cards right, they might not even notice his departure through the rear of the base until it was too late. The cover of buildings would shield him well enough to ensure his escape.

Billy jammed his key into the ignition and turned it. A click followed, but it came from behind him rather than from the steering column. He felt the cold steel of a gun barrel touch the back of his head. His right hand was already going for his pistol, and he had closed on the handle when a voice found his ear.

"Fuck you," said Sal Belamo.

And Sal pulled the trigger.

Outside, the tanks had ceased firing. Before them, the remaining members of the Tau had begun scampering out from their positions of cover with flight on their minds. Some searched for still-functional vehicles. Others sought still-workable weapons. Still more simply tried to run.

None of them succeeded.

On cue, the men of No Town swept onto the ravaged, charred air base led by Sheriff Tyrell Loon. There was no real plan to their approach, no complicated pattern to adhere to. But there were enough of them to cover a spread sufficient to prevent the flood of armed and unarmed men from escaping. Loon held his M-16 to the sky and fired off a burst.

"Good idea if all you just stay as you be!" he yelled out

to them. When they had obliged, he turned to share a smile with Toothless Jim Jackson.

And the Old One smiled back.

Tyrell Loon rubbed his eyes and held them closed, then opened them slowly.

She was gone. Jackson was standing a yard past where Tyrell thought he had seen her, grinning at him toothlessly, obviously not having seen a thing.

"Let's round 'em up," said Sheriff Loon.

Sal Belamo was watching the roundup in amazement, when Blaine and Johnny emerged from the hangar.

"Looks like we missed all the fun, boss."

"My guess is you had plenty of your own," Blaine said.

Johnny had helped him wrap some cloth around the neat slice in his palm from the glass shard. It had stopped the blood from dripping, but could do nothing about the throbbing. Sal's shoulder, meanwhile, was a mess, bloody and shredded, a makeshift tourniquet doing the best it could to stem the flow.

"You find the White Death, Sal?"

"In a tanker big as a house. No sign of Rothstein, though."

"I didn't think there would be."

"You don't sound too worried about it."

"Let's see if I'm right first."

CHAPTER 36

THE figure that descended under cover of darkness through
the hatchway into Nineteen's new irrigation works did so
using his flashlight only sporadically; he knew this land well
enough not to require its use any more than that. The hose
he needed to perform his task was stored in a cabinet within.
When all was ready, he would call for his trucks to make
their way onto the property in the guise of the propane vehicles that provided the residents with most of their energy
needs.

He slid by the massive tanks and was almost to the cabinet
holding the hose when the thick fluorescent lighting snapped
on. Arnold Rothstein stiffened and turned slowly.

"They're empty," Blaine McCracken said as he stepped
out of the shadows.

"You were expecting me," was all Rothstein could think
to say.

"I also found your boxes containing the White Death already loaded into those explosive activators you've been using around the world. Excellent design. My compliments."

"How could you have known to come here?" he asked
McCracken, exasperated. *"How?"*

Just to McCracken's rear stood Johnny Wareagle, Melissa
Hazelhurst, and Sal Belamo with his arm held firmly in a

ling. His free hand held a gun low by his hip. Blaine's in-
ured hand was bandaged as well, and his chin showed a
gauze strip taped across it.

"I remembered Tovah saying that you had recently arranged for a system upgrade," he said. "I figured you had
your own plans for it."

Their eyes wandered to the tanks simultaneously.

"How long since they've held water?" Blaine asked the
old man.

"Since they were installed six months ago."

"Backup system?"

Rothstein nodded. "Built at the same time."

"With the groundwork laid well before that. I'd say dating
back to the original construction of this kibbutz, because you
planned to someday make use of it even then."

"Apparently, Mr. McCracken, I underestimated you."

"No, you just made it easy for me. The White Death we
found at Livermore came exclusively from the empty crates
you returned to Ephesus for. That meant the stockpile you
were able to manufacture after you finally re-created the original formula was somewhere else. Here." Blaine hesitated
and took a single step forward. "At least was."

Rothstein regarded him quizzically. "What do you mean
'was'? What have you done with the White Death, Mc-
Cracken?"

"Nothing."

"But you said it was gone."

"It is, Rothstein, but not thanks to me. You were too late.
And so were we."

McCracken had returned to Israel in the same jet that had
brought him and the commandos of Nineteen to America,
arriving a few hours before dawn on Monday. Accompanying
him along with the survivors who were well enough to travel
had been Johnny, Sal Belamo, and Melissa. Blaine's numerous wounds had made for a very uncomfortable journey.
Though none was serious, they all ached nonetheless, and

the bandages and dressings had him feeling confined an
restricted.

"Something's wrong," one of the commandos had sai
as they came within range of the front gate. "I don't se
the—"

She had stopped because suddenly she had seen, seen th
security gate flapping slightly in the wind. Blaine ha
emerged from the lead car ahead of her. They had notice
the first of the bodies at the same moment. One of the guard
had been dragged into the low underbrush rimming the en
trance. Only her boots protruded. McCracken had swun
round to find Johnny Wareagle inspecting the ground be
tween their lead car and the gate.

"The killers are gone, Blainey."

"How long, Indian?"

"Less than an hour. Three trucks, two of them heavy."

"Tankers?"

"Possibly."

Beyond the gate Nineteen had become a killing ground
McCracken had walked slowly with Johnny by his side, see
ing things as they had unfolded. Women would have emerge
from their houses at the first sign of trouble. But whoeve
had come in the trucks were well prepared. Bodies lay o
porches or near them. Some of the rifles had been fired
Some hadn't.

"You expected this," Rothstein said before Blaine ha
finished his story. They were still standing in the cellar tha
held the works for Nineteen's irrigation system.

"I feared it, thanks to you."

"Me?"

"You tipped me off without even realizing it yourself. Yo
said you lost me after the shootout with the Twins at the hote
in Izmir. That meant somebody else had to be behind th
attack in Germany."

"What attack? I don't know what you're talking about!"

"That's the problem, Rothstein. Someone else was shad

owing you all along, mirroring your moves. Waiting. And you played right into their hands.''

"And you're saying they have the White Death? Impossible! A lie!''

McCracken slid forward and froze Rothstein with his stare. "The killings were no lie. Would you like to take a stroll with me and count the bodies? Eleven women were killed here tonight. It's your fault, Mr. Rothstein. You used these women, and it cost those eleven of them their lives.''

"I didn't know. How could I?''

"You didn't bother to. Fanatics like you are convinced your vision is so pure that nothing can stop it from being attained. But it never happens. Sometimes you stop yourselves. Sometimes you get stopped.''

Rothstein tried to look strong. "And you are going to stop me, of course.''

"No, I think I'll leave the rest of that task to someone else. . . .''

Blaine and Johnny moved to the side to allow Tovah to wheel her chair forward. It was all her bony hands could do to manage the effort. A shawl covered her legs. A 9mm pistol rested atop it.

"Tovah!" Arnold Rothstein gasped.

"You lied to me, Ari," the old woman accused.

"Only to spare you.''

She shook her head. "No. Again, to spare yourself. You began planning this forty-five years ago. Everything else was just a stepping-stone. And what you have sown the seeds for, what you have done to us—to our people—without realizing. . . .''

"What?" Rothstein raised, dumbfounded.

"You really don't get it, do you?" Blaine asked him. "It's right here before your eyes and you can't see it.''

"Help me. Let me make amends. *Tell me!*''

As Blaine told his story, Arnold Rothstein sank to his knees and began to sob.

* * *

"Leave us," the old woman told those around her sternly ten minutes later.

Blaine led the way toward the stairs.

"Tovah," her brother pleaded, "part of what I did was for our own good, the good of Israel. I know you cannot see that now, but you will. I could have fashioned a world without fear for us. I could have ensured the safety and sanctity of our borders until the end of time."

"And which end is that now, Ari? We have shared many, seen many. Tonight must come another," the old woman said, and raised the pistol.

Blaine and the others were halfway up the steps by then and none of them looked back.

"Tovah, you *must* listen to me!"

"Ari," Tovah muttered. "My poor Ari . . ."

Sal Belamo was the last one out of the underground structure, and Blaine lowered the doors after him.

"Listen to me, Tovah. Please lis—"

Rothstein's words vanished behind the sealed door. The next sounds reached their ears as dull thuds.

A gunshot, followed by one more, and then another.

"Let's go, Johnny," Blaine said. "We've got a long day ahead of us."

The mansion high up on the Bokelberg where McCracken had met the toymaker and encountered the Tau was situated off by itself, with the nearest other *Villen* only vaguely in sight. There would be at least two dozen guards patrolling the grounds tonight, two or three times as many as the night Blaine had come here before. He was certain of that much, just as he knew that a frontal approach to the house was out of the question. How to get inside, then?

The idea had come from Sal Belamo, the necessary equipment obtained after a single phone call Tovah had suggested they make. The helicopter that was now closing on the house was part of that equipment. It was equipped with silent-running capability and infrared sighting that allowed the pilot to fly without lights. Because "silent" was a relative term in this case, it was arranged that an emergency repair crew would be jackhammering away at the road just down the street.

From a hundred and fifty feet above the house, McCracken could see little of the grounds below. He kept his focus on the roof as the chopper circled and tested the wind. To prevent being spotted from ground level, he had donned black clothes, gloves, and boots, and had smeared blackout cream all over his face.

McCracken checked his watch. Right on cue, Sal Belamo's construction crew went to work. It was time.

Blaine dropped the black nylon line from the belly of the chopper. It uncoiled swiftly like a snake and dangled a few feet from the roof's surface, swaying in the night. McCracken took one last deep breath and hoisted himself out onto it.

The slide came easily, except for the stinging pain it brought back to his bandaged hand. He covered the distance in less than four seconds and hit the roof with a *thump*.

The sloping roof was formed of slate. McCracken eased himself to its rear, where the congestion of guards below was somewhat lighter than the front. He removed his pack from his shoulders and took from it pylons and black nylon cord. Then he knelt down and set about the task of wedging the pylons into the roof with a small hammer.

When this task was completed, he slid the nylon cord into the pylons and then ran it through the proper slots in his vest. He was now ready to rappel the short six-foot drop to the window through which he planned on gaining entry. McCracken stuck the handle of his glass-cutting knife in his mouth and eased himself off the roof. Popping the lock would have been simpler, but Blaine suspected that an elaborate alarm system would be triggered should any latch be opened.

He dropped off the roof and dangled briefly in front of the window before sliding over to the left of it. Pressed against the house, he held himself steady with his left hand and worked the blade along the frame with his bandaged right hand, gritting his teeth against the pain as he sliced through the putty holding the glass into place. He managed to do a little more than half the window before switching to the right side, and he used his left hand to complete the job. After a few more seconds of work, the lines of cuts were on the verge of joining up with each other.

Afraid of what would happen if the glass popped inward and shattered, McCracken maneuvered so that he was directly in front of the window. He affixed a pair of handle-equipped suction cups to the glass, and only then did he finish cutting through the window. He tugged slightly on the suction cups, and the glass came back with them. He lowered the large pane cautiously in through the now-vacant space. He set it to the side of the frame and then climbed into the room.

Blaine moved straight for the door of the darkened room and pressed his ear against it. Footsteps were approaching, a patrolling guard not in any particular rush. Blaine turned and pressed his back against the door. Gazing into the deep part of the room now, something about the far wall grabbed his eye. He slid away from the door and reached back for his flashlight. Its narrow beam found the wall and began tracing its length.

The wall was taken up completely by a map of the world that stretched from floor to ceiling. McCracken had never seen a more complete one. Major cities and their populations the world over were highlighted. Then, as he gazed at it closer, he realized it wasn't a map at all.

It was a battle plan.

The cities highlighted were the centers of the world's commerce and government. The White Death released randomly within them would cause chaos and panic on an unthinkable level as millions of innocent people were blinded. It would be done simultaneously, every part of the world thrown into total disarray at the same time. The chaos would feed off itself.

Until someone stepped in to restore order.

McCracken moved closer to the map again. It did not reflect the vast changes in the old Soviet Union, or even the reunification of Germany. The city populations were significantly off as well, the figures more consistent with a decade ago, or even longer ago than that. Those who had drawn it had been waiting a very long time for what seemed at last to be within their reach.

He scanned the room further. Flat wooden tables were arranged haphazardly, apparently at random. Other maps, more focused and detailed, were spread upon them. On some the folds were still present. This room was evidently a planning or command center, and it had recently been the center of much activity.

Blaine glided back to the door and pressed his ear against it. Nothing. The guard must have been at the other end of the hall. McCracken moved his hand to the knob and turned it. The door gave, and he cracked it open enough to make sure the guard would notice when he came by on his rounds. Then he stepped back and pressed himself against the near wall.

The footsteps returned down the corridor seconds later, a shadow sliding through the crack in the door when the guard stopped before it. Blaine watched a hand push the door slowly open, and then a figure entered wearing a black uniform with the insignia of the Nazi SS upon its shoulder.

McCracken sprang before the guard was all the way inside. He clamped a hand over the man's mouth and slammed his head backward against the wall. When the guard continued to struggle, he smashed it again until he felt the skull give. The guard's eyes glazed over. He slumped downward, dragging a trail of blood behind him.

Blaine closed the door and pulled the body into the center of the room. It took under three minutes to replace his own clothes with the SS uniform. The fit was tight, but good enough. McCracken had no illusions that the guise would hold up to close scrutiny; he was merely looking for any edge that would lead to more freedom of movement. He finished tightening the belt and wiped the blackout cream from his face before stepping into the corridor.

He was on the mansion's third floor; the toymaker's workshop was on the second. He headed down the main stairwell, crossing paths with no one. On the second floor, the door to the toymaker's workshop was open. A radio was badly tuned to a station that played old German music. He recognized the pungent scents of model glue and molded plastic from his previous visit here. The toymaker's head was resting on his worktable next to the radio on the other side of the room. McCracken's first thought was that he might be dead. Approaching closer, though, he heard the old man snoring, lost in a deep sleep. Blaine continued on toward the far-right-hand portion of the room, toward the sheet-covered collection of models that Tessen had steered him away from in his last visit here. McCracken pulled one of the sheets back and instantly understood why.

The models, still in progress and reeking of strong glue, were of a number of cities. They weren't marked yet, but Blaine easily recognized London, Washington, and Tel Aviv from their distinctive skylines. These were by far the toymaker's largest and most intricate creations, each taking up the size of a Ping-Pong table. Removing the rest of the sheets would undoubtedly reveal more cities from all across the world, not re-creations this time, but predictions of things to come. Years of work had gone into them and, ironically, they seemed at last on the verge of completion. All that was missing from London and New York were the bodies, the depictions of chaos and bloodshed in the streets below. But they would be added soon enough, once the White Death was released to wreak havoc throughout the world. The old man would have his pictures, his videos. And he would be busy for years to come, because these cities marked only the beginning.

McCracken came to the models of Washington and Tel Aviv and froze. Apparently, in these two cases the toymaker hadn't been able to wait, and the resulting sight was bone-chilling. The old man had outdone himself. Even in miniature, the panic, the utter desperation of cities caught in the merciless grip of the White Death, was clear. Cars had smashed into each other. Small figures writhed and clawed at the air. Blaine could almost hear the screams.

"You look quite good in that uniform, Mr. McCracken," a voice called from behind him.

Blaine turned around slowly.

"You didn't go for your gun. I'm disappointed," said Hans Tessen. "Take the pistol out slowly with two fingers and toss it toward me, please."

McCracken did as he was told. The pistol clanged against the floor and slid the Nazi's way.

"Congratulations on a brilliant acting job," Blaine told him.

Tessen kept his gun steady, a smile brewing on his lips. "I was quite good, wasn't I?"

"I should have killed you myself."

"But we were allies, were we not? Don't forget that I saved your life in Izmir. From the Tau, of all forces."

"To further your own interests, of course."

Tessen nodded, beaming. "And why not, Mr. McCracken? So strange life is, so theatrical."

"Correct me if I'm wrong: you're one of the leaders of this bunch. Yes?"

"If by 'bunch' you are referring to a Nazi movement that now spans all corners of the globe, yes, I am." He stiffened his chin. His crew cut gleamed in the naked light of the room. "Ever since the end of the war, I have worked toward the day that is almost upon us. A day, I regret to tell you, you will not live to see."

"Not a sight I would cherish."

"Oh, but it will be one to behold. Our destiny achieved at long last. We were not wrong in our aims in World War II; we were merely ahead of our time. Time has finally caught up with us."

"You're dreaming."

"Apparently so is a very large segment of the population of your country. That is where our literature has been shipped from, where our swastikas have been sewn and molded, and where a huge portion of the funds that helped sustain our dreams has originated." Tessen came a little closer, one of his hands sliding affectionately over one of the toymaker's World War II models. "Look around you, Mr. McCracken. Look at the world. The economic structure is on the verge of collapsing. The middle class has been lumped into the lower class. People are poor. People are angry. They crave order, anything that can give them back what they feel right-fully belongs to them. In every country, not just the U.S., support for our movements has been overwhelming, because order is what we offer. The anger and frustration that has allowed our movement to flourish again here in Germany is being mirrored all over the world. Our people are out there and they are ready, they are committed. They go by different names in different corners of the world—the Ku Klux Klan, the German People's Union, the African Resistance Move-ment—but they stand for the same thing, and they are waiting for the chance we can give them. We will rise back to power because the world will want us, need us."

Blaine fixed his gaze briefly on the nearly completed mod-els. "Not all the world, apparently."

"We know where our enemies are, Mr. McCracken. This time they will be neutralized before they can lead the resis-tance against us."

"Neutralized with the White Death you now have in your possession."

Tessen's smile continued to glow. "I prefer to say *back* in our possession, and that is precisely why we so desperately required your services. Not to disappoint, you performed wonderfully. You brought us to the White Death. We never could have done it without you, so you see that, more than anyone, you deserve to wear that uniform."

"The maps that fell into my hands and Hazelhurst's . . ."

"Copies made from documents opened up with the reunification of the two Germanys. A terrible oversight on our part, but eventually a blessed one."

Blaine was nodding. "Because Rothstein's revived Tau had already removed the White Death from your chamber, and only because of Hazelhurst's dig did you become aware of that fact."

"Thanks to your participation, of course."

"You were in Kansas, at the air force base."

"Not me, one of my men. We followed you from the time you 'escaped' from this house the first time. Unfortunately, the man who trailed you to the United States left the area of that air force base before you turned the tables on your captors. But he had found what I had sent him for, and with the identity of the Tau leader shockingly clear, it was an easy guess as to where the White Death was stored. Of course I don't have to tell you this; you came to the same conclusion yourself."

"You never were able to come up with the formula yourselves, were you?"

"But Rothstein was all too happy to fill the void. What we found at that kibbutz was five times the contents of the crates. *Five times!*" Tessen gloated. "Strange, isn't it, that we could not act to achieve our destiny until vast reserves of the White Death were available to us? Thanks to Rothstein, that came to pass. And thanks to you, we found Rothstein."

"So in pursuing its vengeance, the Tau ends up aiding the rise of the Fourth Reich."

"And why not? The symbol of the Jews helped give birth to the Third. It's only fitting that the work of the Jews gives rise to the Fourth."

Again Blaine looked back at the toymaker's latest models. "Except it's not going to be only the Jews this time, is it?"

"We have learned from our mistakes, Mr. McCracken. Far more than ethnicity will determine who our enemies are and whom we destroy."

"The thing that doesn't figure here is that when your com-

rades were dying horribly after the war, you must have known
the White Death was to blame.''

"We were scattered, running for our lives. By the time we
had reorganized sufficiently, the killing had stopped and the
entrance to the chamber the Jews had found had been sealed
again.''

"Yes, by them.''

"Only we didn't know about Rothstein. We assumed that
our greatest secret was safe again, waiting for us to come
and retrieve the reserves to join a new and vast supply.''

"Which might never have happened . . .''

"If not for the Tau's return,'' Tessen completed. "And
then you brought us to them.''

"And now you have the White Death.''

Tessen nodded. "Right here, stored in tanks concealed in
a secret subbasement. The tanks have been waiting for it for
years. Too bad your mission to destroy it has failed.''

Blaine shook his head. "That wasn't my mission at all.''

"Please, McCracken,'' Tessen scoffed, "spare me.''

"Sorry. Not part of my mission, either. My mission was
to find out where you stashed the White Death to make sure
it doesn't live beyond you.''

Tessen was about to respond when gunshots rang out on
the grounds of the estate. Rapid fire intermixed with horrible, twisted screams.

"No,'' the Nazi muttered, moving toward the window but
keeping his eyes fixed on McCracken. "No . . .''

Blaine held his ground. "You didn't get all the White
Death, Tessen. I found two boxes of explosive devices loaded
with it, ready for use. Don't worry, I've already destroyed
all of them, except for the ones I thought I might need.''

The screams outside continued, joined by fresh ones from
the mansion's first floor. Glass shattered. The sounds of
pounding, desperate footsteps shook the walls. Louder
screams followed, lessened, and then became sporadic along
with the gunfire. Tessen's face was a frozen mask of agony.
He swung from the window.

"This can't be!"

"You underestimated your enemies yet again, Tessen. Must be a Nazi trademark."

"But I can still kill you!" he ranted, fighting to steady his gun Blaine's way.

"Maybe. Still leaves you just a frightened old man, though. The future of *any* Reich ends here, no matter what happens to me."

"Then take that to your grave!"

Tessen's hand started back on the trigger.

A shot rang out.

The pistol flew out of the Nazi's hand and shattered the window. He crumpled to his knees, holding his wrist.

"Took you long enough, Indian," Blaine said to Johnny Wareagle, who stood in the room's doorway.

"It was more difficult slipping past the exterior guards than I expected, Blainey."

Blood sliding down his chin from where he had bitten his tongue, Tessen gazed beyond the big Indian at the tight pack of men gathering around him. All of them had thick goggles dangling around their throats, removed from their eyes because there was no longer a need for them. Downstairs and on the grounds beyond, all sounds of resistance had ceased. Tessen knew that even if he yelled out, there was no one left to hear him. He fixed his eyes on a fat, balding man who had advanced ahead of the Indian.

"Who?" he half muttered, half mouthed.

"This is Wolfgang Bertlemass, Tessen," McCracken explained, "chief administrator of the Document Center and watchdog committed to making sure his country does not fall into the hands of animals like you again."

"We have had enough of your kind," Bertlemass accused Tessen, leading the others past Wareagle into the room. "All of us Germans have. And look, Nazi, not all of us are Jews."

But Wolfgang Bertlemass was a Jew. And back at Nineteen, Tovah had explained the reason behind his role as permanent watchdog, along with his lifelong commitment to the

Document Center: Bertlemass was one of the original members of the Tau! Accordingly, he had been all too happy to help them in their efforts following Tessen's raid on the kibbutz. Bertlemass had supplied the helicopter and equipment, but only on the condition that he and the group he had founded could have a hand in the end. Blaine had agreed without hesitation. The final demise of the Nazi movement deserved to be at the hands of Germans. History had come full circle. The past had at last been atoned for.

Bertlemass and his people, few of them young, most of them carrying at least distant memories of World War II, enveloped Tessen and lifted him to his feet.

"You will watch us set the explosives, Nazi," Bertlemass spat out. "You will watch your dream die before you do. And I have a message from someone who knows much about death at your hand from a day long ago."

Tessen looked up at him.

"She says that the priest's curse is finally complete."

Bertlemass nodded, and the others led Tessen out of the room. Blaine and Johnny took their time in following. They had just started from the room when a sudden stirring behind them made both turn around fast.

The toymaker stretched his arms behind a yawn and looked their way.

"Did I miss something?" he wondered in a sleepy voice.

"No," Blaine told him. "It's over."

EPILOGUE

"**W**HEN does it end, Indian?" McCracken asked Wareagle outside the mansion, when all the explosives had at last been planted.

"With those who began it, Blainey, as we saw tonight."

"We got lucky tonight."

"Did we? Or is this merely the way of all things? My people have a legend that tells of a demon who rises to wage war on an entire tribe. The tribe fights bravely with its most valiant warriors, but to no avail. The demon's evil cannot be overcome. It is fueled by the killings as it consumes the warriors' spirits with their flesh. When all is over, and the demon has consumed all of the tribe, his lust is still not satisfied. His hunger insatiable, he consumes himself."

"Evil doesn't always destroy itself, Indian."

"But it inevitably leaves us a means to help it on its way."

Blaine's stare had turned reflective. "It left Rothstein a means, too, and I can't help thinking that he had things more right than we ever did. I can't help thinking that maybe I just should have left him and his Tau alone to finish what they started."

"Then why didn't you?"

"I don't know. Maybe because I was afraid it would leave me—us—with nothing to do."

351

Wareagle smiled ever so slightly. "Each battle we face leads us to the next one. My people have a ghost dance, Blainey, in which the spirits recognize them and inscribe their names on the totem of our ways. There is a similar totem for our ways in the hellfire, a black granite slab incised with those whose journeys ended in the jungle. But the names of the ones we lost, the ones who traveled the jungle with us, are not there. I wonder if they can rest or if they are lost, as my people would be if the spirits bid them no regard."

"They knew the rules, Indian. What we did over there never happened, no accounts made in Uncle Sam's daily log. The steps of our ghost dance were different."

"Except I never performed it with my people, Blainey. With you and the others, yes, but never with those Joe Rainwater wanted me to stand up for. And since our work in the hellfire can never be acknowledged, perhaps my name remains inscribed nowhere."

"Better nowhere than that black granite slab."

"True enough. But I must stand up for my people now. In my own way, my own time. I must be faithful to all that remains a part of me."

Blaine frowned. "Maybe that's my problem. Somehow I feel I wasn't true to myself in destroying Rothstein."

"It wasn't Rothstein you destroyed so much as the White Death. You came to understand that true essence lies not in proposed ends, but in prescribed means. The White Death was wrong, Blainey, it was evil. Anyone who reached out to grasp it, then, could only be the same."

"But more people are grasping, Indian, if not for the White Death, then something else."

Wareagle smiled ever so slightly. "In the hellfire, we entered the dark world and survived it. When we returned, the world above lacked many things but at least it always had light. Somewhere."

"The trick sometimes is finding it, and it seems to be getting harder. Less of it out there, if you know what I mean."

"Not less light, Blainey, just more clouds we must part to find it. And this time, perhaps, we have a chance to part the greatest one of all."

McCracken nodded. "Just maybe we do."

"You don't know what you're doing!" Melissa protested. She stood before the narrow opening on the bank of the dry riverbed that she and Blaine had climbed out of ten days before, stood before it as if to block the way down. She had been mounting arguments ever since McCracken had informed her of his intentions. But this last-ditch attempt seemed to be her most determined.

Blaine and Johnny looked at each other before McCracken spoke. "I think we do, Melly."

"Please," she begged, "not until I have an opportunity to explore what lies beneath the chamber we found. Let me figure out when it was built and by whom. The Nazis didn't choose this site randomly. They came here because the chamber was already in place! They came here because they suspected what this site truly holds!"

"All the more reason to bury it forever."

"The Nazis didn't have time to explore what else might lie down there. If they had, if we could . . ."

McCracken shook his head.

Melissa turned her impassioned gaze on Wareagle. "Talk to him. *Please!*"

"He is right," Johnny said softly. "All that can ever be allowed to emerge from here is what we have seen already. We must prevent any further evil from escaping. Further discoveries can only serve to release more secrets the world is not yet ready to bear."

Melissa's eyes bulged in response to the Indian's last words. "You believe it, then. You believe my father was right. You can feel it. You *know* it. This really is hell."

"There are many hells," Johnny explained after exchanging a quick glance with McCracken. "This is one of them."

"And I suppose the two of you plan to blow all of them up?" she said cynically.

Blaine looked at Johnny, thinking back to the conversation they'd had before the mansion and the White Death had been destroyed. "The world will never run out of its hells," he told Melissa.

"Please! You don't know what you're doing, I tell you!"

"No, Melly. I think we do."

They entered the tunnel that led into the storage chamber minutes later, weighted down slightly by the necessary supplies. A work crew hired by McCracken and supervised by Sal Belamo waited back near the find itself to level the land soon to be ruptured and pitted by the explosion. Otherwise, the invitation would always be there for future parties to try to find and explore what Blaine had come to feel quite certain was better left alone. The crew would not only level the land, they would also disguise it so that it would blend in with the rest of the surroundings. Virtually no trace whatsoever of the discovery would be left behind, even to aerial photography.

Melissa insisted on leading the way, for her own good as well as theirs. With the proper equipment and lighting, the trek should have been much easier, but her legs were lead-heavy and her mouth dry beyond water's ability to help. She waited for them while they set the explosives within and around the chamber, feeling in her heart that far more than its contents would be lost to the world when they were set off. Blaine and Johnny were careful to plant the charges to ensure that the contents of the cavern would be entombed, not exploded, even though samples taken from containers bearing stockpiled nerve and chemical agents had revealed that the years had stripped them of their potency.

The three of them emerged into the light of the dry riverbed with plenty of time to spare, and waited. Remote detonation wouldn't work, given the logistics involved, so they had set the timers to the one-hour mark. The blast at that moment came as a mere rumble that barely shook the ground about them. It was enough, though, to tell Blaine and Johnny that they had been successful, that the final remnants of the Third Reich had been sealed from the world at last.

And that all doorways leading to what might have lain beneath them had been closed forever.

JON LAND

Published by Fawcett Books.

Don't miss the thrilling adventures of Blaine McCracken, rogue secret agent.

THE ALPHA DECEPTION

An Oregon town is wiped out by a laserlike beam, leaving nothing behind but a whirling cloud of smoke. Another town in remote Colorado is taken over by a mysterious army. The war is on for an ancient gemstone whose possession could shatter the world balance of power. Blaine McCracken, the exiled secret agent with fourteen ways to kill a man in under two seconds, joins forces with beautiful Natalya Tomachenko, the KGB's number-one assassin. They must gain control of this deadly gem on a mission that takes them from New York to Bangkok to a mysterious island shrouded in legend.

JON LAND

THE GAMMA OPTION

In the Middle East, a very rational madman is pursuing a plan to resolve the area's long-standing conflict through the quiet death of twenty million people. The most destructive weapon ever created has rested for forty years beneath the sea until now. Only one man can stop a crazed conspiracy out for world domination. And Blaine McCracken has a very personal motive—for they have kidnapped his son.

THE OMEGA COMMAND

Why was a top secret agent brutally slain in a New York City pleasure parlor? Who is reclusive billionare Randall Krayman? What is the meaning of the bizarre information a desperate man gives to TV reporter Sandy Lister moments before he dies? Rogue agent Blaine McCracken is brought out of exile to find the answers to these deadly questions and to prevent the loss of millions of lives, including his own.

THE OMICRON LEGION

In the United States, the world's most highly skilled killers have been assembled. No one can believe that a vast serial assassination is under way, except for agent Blaine McCracken. A conspiracy of death has been conceived in the East, nurtured in the Brazilian jungle, and is now primed to strike in the United States. McCracken must confront the most horrifying threat mankind has ever faced, and he must not lose.

JON LAND

More fiendishly exciting novels of
action and suspense by

JON LAND

THE COUNCIL OF TEN

In Miami, four seemingly harmless grandmoth-
ers are professionally terminated. Then it is
revealed that the victims are key links in a
global cocaine operation. And this is only the
beginning of the horror. Journalist Drew Jordan
is drawn into this mystery and must enlist the
aid of an ex-assassin and an Israeli secret
agent. This desperate army of three must battle
to the death with tremendous forces of evil to
save the day.

THE NINTH DOMINION

At a maximum-security sanitarium for the
criminally insane, eighty-four of the most dangerous psychopaths alive have vanished from
their cells without a trace. Leading their ranks
is the Candy Man, the most ruthlessly brilliant
serial killer in captivity. The only way to catch
a crazed killer is to think like one, and agent
Jared Kimberlain is the only man driven
enough to get the job done. Or die trying.

JON LAND

THE EIGHTH TRUMPET
Billionaire Jordan Lime is savagely killed by a weapon that tears him apart limb from limb. An army fortified by an arsenal against which there is no defense has fired its first shot. The battle lines are drawn, and Jared Kimberlain finds himself face to face with an army of superkillers who may prove unstoppable.

LABYRINTH
In strategic locations around the globe, it begins in only two weeks. "The Committee" has masterminded a malignant conspiracy rooted in the highest corridors of power. Christopher Locke, an unsuccessful college professor, is the only person who can expose a trail that begins with the brutal execution of every person in an obscure South American town. Everywhere Locke turns someone is trying to kill him, and the only way to stay alive is to expose the Committee's sinister plan.

THE VALHALLA TESTAMENT
Jamie Skylar finds himself in the midst of a devious conspiracy that is gathering its forces. A beautiful secret agent called Chimera receives a warning from a dying man that sends her around the globe in search of a force that can destroy half a continent. Together Jamie and Chimera must race against the clock to unearth the secret of the Valhalla Testament.